LEVIATHANS OF JUPITER

TOR BOOKS BY BEN BOVA

LEVIATHANS
OF JUPITER

BEN BOVA

TOR®

A TOM DOHERTY ASSOCIATES BOOK
NEW YORK

This is a work of fiction. All of the characters, organizations, and events portrayed in this novel are either products of the author's imagination or are used fictitiously.

LEVIATHANS OF JUPITER

A Tor Book
Published by Tom Doherty Associates, LLC
175 Fifth Avenue
New York, NY 10010

www.tor-forge.com

Tor® is a registered trademark of Tom Doherty Associates, LLC.

Library of Congress Cataloging-in-Publication Data

Bova, Ben, 1932–
    Leviathans of Jupiter / Ben Bova. — 1st ed.
        p.   cm.
    "A Tom Doherty Associates book."
    ISBN 978-0-7653-1788-9
    1. Jupiter (Planet)—Exploration—Fiction.   2. Life on other planets—Fiction.
I. Title.
    PS3552.O84L48 2011
    813'.54—dc22

                                                            2010036115

First Edition: February 2011

Printed in the United States of America

0   9   8   7   6   5   4   3   2   1

To Barbara and Peter Brusco, with love

But ignorance more frequently begets confidence
than does knowledge: it is those who know little, and
not those who know much, who so positively assert
that this or that problem will never be solved
by science.

—CHARLES DARWIN

LEVIATHANS
OF JUPITER

THE BOUNDLESS SEA

t is an endless ocean, more than ten times wider than the entire planet Earth. Beneath the swirling clouds that cover Jupiter from pole to pole, that ocean has never seen sunlight, nor has it ever felt the rough confining contours of land. Its waves have never crashed against a craggy shore, never thundered upon a sloping beach, for there is no land anywhere across Jupiter's enormous girth: not even an island or a reef. The ocean's billows sweep across the face of the deeps without hindrance, eternally.

Heated from below by the planet's seething core, swirled into frenzy by Jupiter's hyperkinetic spin rate, ferocious currents race through this endless sea, liquid jet streams howling madly, long powerful wave trains surging uninterrupted all the way around the world, circling the globe over and over again. Gigantic storms rack the ocean, too, typhoons bigger than whole planets, hurricanes that have roared their fury for century after century.

Jupiter is the largest of all the solar system's planets, more than ten times bigger and three hundred times as massive as Earth. Jupiter is so immense it could swallow all the other planets easily. Its Great Red Spot, a storm that has raged for centuries, is itself wider than Earth. And the Spot is merely one feature visible among the innumerable vortexes and streams of Jupiter's frenetically racing cloud tops.

Yet Jupiter is composed mainly of the lightest elements, hydrogen and helium, more like a star than a planet. All that size and mass, yet Jupiter spins on its axis in less than ten hours, so fast that the planet is clearly not spherical. Its poles are noticeably flattened. Jupiter looks like a big, colorfully striped beach ball that's squashed down as if some gigantic invisible child were sitting upon it.

Spinning that fast, Jupiter's deep, cloud-topped atmosphere is swirled into bands and ribbons of multihued clouds: pale yellow, saffron orange, white, tawny yellow-brown, dark brown, bluish, pink and red. Titanic winds push the clouds across the face of Jupiter at hundreds of kilometers per hour. What lies beneath them? For a century planetary astronomers had cautiously sent probes into the Jovian atmosphere. They barely penetrated the cloud tops before being crushed by overwhelming pressure.

But the inquisitive scientists from Earth persisted and gradually learned that some fifty thousand kilometers beneath those clouds—nearly four times Earth's diameter—lies that boundless ocean, an ocean almost eleven times wider than Earth and some five thousand kilometers deep. Heavily laced with ammonia and sulfur compounds, highly acidic, it is still an ocean of water. Everywhere in the solar system, where there is liquid water, life exists.

They also found that organic compounds form naturally in the clouds and precipitate down into the sea: particles constantly wafting into the restless ocean, like manna falling from heaven.

Eventually the scientists found that life exists in Jupiter's boundless ocean, as well. Enormous creatures, as big as cities, cruise through those raging currents as easily as a lad poling a raft along a quiet stream on Earth, feeding themselves on the organics constantly drifting down from above. Lords of their world, these creatures exist where humans and their most inventive technology can barely penetrate.

The humans called them leviathans. And they wondered: Could these beasts be intelligent?

I
FUSION TORCH SHIP
AUSTRALIA

To follow knowledge like a sinking star,
Beyond the utmost bound of human thought.

—Alfred, Lord Tennyson
Ulysses

Big George Ambrose was far from happy.

"I still don't see why they need a fookin' microbiologist," he grumbled. "Bloody beasts on Jupiter are big as mountains, aren't they?"

His daughter Deirdre nodded in agreement. The two of them were waiting in *Chrysalis II*'s departure lounge for the torch ship from the Earth/Moon system to dock at the habitat. No one else was in the departure lounge; no one else from the habitat was heading for Jupiter.

They did not look much like father and daughter. George was a huge bushy mountain of a man, with a tangled mop of brick red hair and a thick unruly beard to match, both bearing the first tell-tale streaks of silver. Deirdre was almost as tall as he, but seemed dwarfed next to him. She was strikingly beautiful, though, with wide innocent almond eyes that had a slight oriental cast to them and high cheekbones, thanks to her mother. She had her father's strong jaw and auburn hair that glowed like molten copper as it streamed down past her shoulders. She was wearing a simple pull-over blouse and comfortable slacks, but they couldn't hide the supple curves of her ample figure.

"You'll miss my retirement party," George growled.

"I'm sorry about that," Deirdre said. "But they promised me a full scholarship to the Sorbonne if I'd put in a year at the research station in Jupiter orbit. A full scholarship, Daddy!"

"On Earth."

"Yes! On Earth!"

George shook his shaggy head. "Earth's a dangerous place. Too many people. All sorts of diseases and maniacs runnin' around."

"Daddy, it's *Earth*!" Deirdre exclaimed. "It's civilization. It's culture. I don't want to spend my whole life cooped up in this habitat. I know you love it, but I want to see the real world!"

George muttered something too low for his daughter to catch.

George Ambrose had been director of the rock rats' habitat orbiting the asteroid Ceres for the past quarter century. He had helped build the original *Chrysalis* for the miners and prospectors who combed the Asteroid Belt in search of the metals and minerals that fed the human race's expansion through the solar system. He had directed the building of *Chrysalis II* when the rock rats' first habitat had been destroyed in the Asteroid Wars.

And he had presided over the trial of the mercenary killer who had wiped out the original habitat.

Now he stood with his only daughter scowling at the display screen that spread across one entire bulkhead of the departure lounge. It showed the long, sleek torch ship from Earth making the final delicate maneuvers of its rendezvous with the slowly revolving wheel of the habitat. George saw tiny puffs of cold gas squirting from the ship's maneuvering rockets: thruster farts, he said to himself.

Like most of the habitat, the departure lounge was strictly utilitarian: a row of hard benches ran along its facing gray bulkheads, the scuffed, dull heavy steel hatch of the airlock between them. No windows; the only outside view was from the wide display screen that stretched above one of the benches.

Across from the wall screen, though, was a mural that Deirdre had painted as a teenager, a seascape she had copied from memory after studying a docudrama about Earth's oceans. Deirdre's murals decorated many of the otherwise drab sections of the habitat: Even the crude, gaudy daubings she had done as a child still remained on the otherwise colorless bulkheads of *Chrysalis II*. They were little better than graffiti, but her father would not permit anyone to remove them. He was proud of his daughter's artistry, which had grown deeper and richer as she herself blossomed into adulthood.

But George was not admiring his daughter's artwork now. Still staring at the display screen, he impatiently called out, "Screen, show Ceres."

The display obediently shifted from the approaching torch ship to show the cratered, dusty rock of the asteroid around which the habitat orbited. Largest of the 'roids in the Belt, Ceres was barely a thousand kilometers across, an oversized boulder, dusty, pitted, dead. Beyond its curving limb there was nothing but the dark emptiness of infinity, laced with hard pinpoints of stars bright enough to shine through the camera's protective filters.

Big George clasped his hands behind his back as he stared at the unblinking stars.

"I only came out here to get rich quick and then go back to Earth," he muttered. "Never thought I'd spend the rest of my fookin' life in the Belt."

Deirdre gave her father a sympathetic smile. "You can go back Earthside any time you want to."

He shook his shaggy head. "Nah. Been away too long. I'd be a stranger there. Leastways, I got some friends here. . . ."

"Tons of friends," Deirdre said.

"And your mother's ashes."

Deirdre nodded. Mom's been dead for nearly five years, she thought, but he still mourns her.

"You can visit me on Earth," she said brightly. "You won't be a total stranger."

"Yeah," he said, without enthusiasm. "Maybe."

"I really have to go on this ship, Daddy. I've got to get to Jupiter; otherwise I won't get the scholarship."

"I could send you to school on Earth, if that's what you want. I can afford it."

"That's what I want," she said gently. "And now I can get it without putting the burden on you."

"That ship'll be burning out to Jupiter at one full g, y'know," George said. "Six times heavier than here."

"I've put in tons of hours in the centrifuge, Daddy. I can

handle it. The station orbiting Jupiter is one-sixth gravity, just like here."

George nodded absently. Deirdre thought he had run out of objections.

They felt the slightest of tremors and the speaker built into the overhead announced, "DOCKING COMPLETED."

George looked almost startled. "I guess I never thought about you leavin'."

"I'd have to go, sooner or later."

"Yeah, I know, but . . ."

"If you don't want me to go . . ."

"Nah." He shook his head fiercely. "You don't want to get stuck here the rest o' your life, like me."

"I'll come back, Dad."

George shrugged. "It's a big world out there. Lots of things to see and do. Lots of places for a bright young woman to make a life for herself."

Deirdre didn't know what to say.

His scowl returning, George said, "Just don't let any of those sweet-talkin' blokes take advantage of you. Hear?"

She broke into a giggle. "Oh, Daddy, I know how to take care of myself."

"Yeah. Maybe. But I won't be there to protect you, y'know."

Deirdre grabbed him by his unkempt beard with both hands, the way she had since she'd been a baby, and pecked at his cheek.

"I love you, Daddy."

George blushed. But he clasped his daughter by both shoulders and kissed her solidly on the forehead. "I love you, Dee Dee."

The airlock hatch swung open with a sighing puff of overly warm air. A short, sour-faced Asian man in a deep blue uniform trimmed with an officer's gold braid stepped through and snapped, "Deirdre Ambrose?"

"That's me."

"This way," the Asian said, gesturing curtly toward the passage-way beyond the airlock hatch.

George Ambrose watched his only child disappear into the passageway, the first step on her journey to Jupiter. And then to Earth. I'll never see her again, he thought. Never.

Then he muttered, "I still don't see why they need a fookin' microbiologist."

FUSION TORCH SHIP *AUSTRALIA*

Suppressing an impulse to look back over her shoulder for one last glimpse of her father, Deirdre stepped carefully along the curving tube that connected the *Chrysalis II* habitat to the fusion ship. She could feel her pulse thumping along her veins. *Chrysalis II* was all the home she had ever known. She was heading into the new, the unknown. It was exciting—and a little scary.

The tube felt warmer than she was accustomed to. Its walls glowed softly white, as if fluorescent, with a spiral motif threading along its length. The flooring felt slightly spongy to her tread, not hard and solid like the decks of the habitat. She knew it was her imagination, but somehow she felt slightly heavier, as if the docked torch ship had a stronger gravity field than the habitat she was leaving.

She heard the airlock hatch clang shut behind her and a moment later the crabby-looking little ship's officer scurried past her without speaking a word and disappeared around the curve of the tube. He's not very friendly, Deirdre thought.

When she got to the end of the tube he was standing there, by the ship's gleaming metal airlock, glaring at her with obvious impatience.

"Embarkation desk," he said, jabbing a thumb past the hatch.

Deirdre stepped through the open hatch into a compartment of bare metal bulkheads, not much bigger than a closet. There were three ordinary-looking doors set into the bulkhead opposite her. She hesitated, not sure of which door she was meant to take.

"Right-hand side," the officer snapped from the other side of the hatch, pointing again.

Deirdre opened the door and immediately saw that the torch ship's interior was colorfully decorated. The compartment's walls were covered with brightly patterned fabric. The overhead glowed with glareless lighting. The deck was thickly carpeted in rich earth tones of green and brown. Carpets! she thought. Incredible luxury, compared to *Chrysalis II*'s utilitarian décor. And this is just an anteroom, she realized.

In front of her there was another door, marked EMBARKATION RECEPTION. Deirdre tapped on it, and when no one answered, she cautiously slid it open.

A man in a white uniform was sitting behind a metal desk in the middle of the compartment. The bulkheads on both sides glowed pearl gray: smart screens, Deirdre recognized. Behind the seated officer another wall screen displayed a scene of golden-leafed trees, a forest of Earth, heartbreakingly beautiful.

The man got slowly to his feet. He, too, was Asian, and no taller than Deirdre's chin. He smiled and made a courtly little bow, fists clenched at his sides.

"Welcome to *Australia*," he said. Gesturing to the gracefully curved chair of leather and chrome in front of the desk, he invited, "Please, Ms. Ambrose, be seated and allow me to introduce myself: I am Dr. Lin Pohan, ship's medical officer."

Dr. Pohan was as small as the surly officer who had ushered Deirdre aboard the *Australia*. He was almost totally bald, except for a fringe of dull gray hair, but a luxuriant mustache of silver gray curled across his face. His skin was spiderwebbed with creases, and as he smiled at Deirdre his eyes crinkled with good humor. He looked like a wrinkled old gnome to Deirdre. She realized this man had never taken rejuvenation treatments. She had learned in her history classes that some people on Earth shunned rejuv on religious grounds. Could he be one of them?

"I'm pleased to meet you," she said, a little hesitantly.

Dr. Pohan bobbed his head up and down, then replied, "We must go through the formalities of checking your boarding file and medical record."

"That should all be in your computer," Deirdre said.

"Yes, of course. But then I'm afraid I must subject you to a complete physical examination."

"But my medical records—"

"Not good enough," said Dr. Pohan, almost jovially. "You see, we have had a death aboard ship on our way out here from Earth. It is my duty to make certain we don't have any others."

"A death? Someone died?"

"One of the passengers. Most unusual. And most puzzling. If I can't track down the reason for it, we will not be allowed to disembark our passengers. We will have made the long voyage to Jupiter for nothing."

CAPTAIN'S QUARTERS

Australia was a passenger vessel, designed to carry paying customers swiftly from the Earth/Moon system out to the rock rats' habitat in orbit around the asteroid Ceres. It was built like a slim tower, with a dozen decks between the bridge in the ship's nose and the fusion propulsion plant at its tail. Unlike the cumbersome ore ships that plodded across the inner solar system, *Australia* drove through space under constant acceleration, usually at one Earth-normal gravity or close to it, accelerating half the distance, then flipping over and decelerating the rest of the way. Except for the brief periods of docking or turn-around, the passengers would feel a comfortable one *g* environment for the entire voyage. Comfortable, that is, for those who were accustomed to Earth-normal gravity.

This trip was special, though. Instead of terminating at Ceres and then heading back Earthward, *Australia* was going on to the research station in orbit around the giant planet Jupiter, a journey that would take an additional two weeks from Ceres.

Captain Tomas Guerra's quarters were up at the top of the stack, within a few steps of the bridge. The rooms were comfortable without being overly sumptuous. Guerra did not believe in showy displays of privilege: He kept the décor of his quarters quite simple, almost minimalist. Bulkheads covered in brushed aluminum. A few silk screen paintings of misty mountains and terraced rice paddies on the display screens. Spare, graceful Scandinavian furniture. His one obvious display of luxury was his set of solid gold cups in which he served sherry to special guests.

Katherine Westfall was indeed a very special guest. Reputedly the wealthiest woman in the solar system, she was a member of the powerful governing council of the International Astronautical Authority, the agency that controlled all spaceflight and much of the scientific research done off-Earth. Rumor had it that she was being considered for the chairmanship of the council.

"It's very good of you to invite me to dinner," said Katherine Westfall, in a hushed, little-girl voice.

Captain Guerra dipped his gray-bearded chin once. "It is very good of you to take the time to join me."

Katherine Westfall was as slender and petite as a ballerina, and like a dancer she calculated virtually every move she made far in advance—as well as every word she spoke. She should have been at ease in the comfortably upholstered recliner in the captain's sitting room, but as she smiled demurely at the man he got the impression from her steel gray eyes that she was wary, on guard.

"I hope you weren't inconvenienced by the lower gravity while we were docked with *Chrysalis*," the captain said politely. "The rock rats keep their habitat at lunar *g*."

Katherine Westfall thought a moment, then replied, "It was rather exhilarating, actually."

"Low *g* can be stimulating, can't it?" the captain said. "But we make better time under a full gravity. Once I had to make an emergency high-thrust run to the research station in Venus orbit: two *g*." He shook his head. "Not comfortable at all. Good thing it was only for a few days."

Captain Guerra had lived on his ship since receiving his commission from the IAA many years earlier. The ship was home, his life, his reason for existence. Rarely did he go down dirtside at the Moon or Earth. He had never deigned to set foot on the *Chrysalis II* habitat orbiting Ceres in the Asteroid Belt or the *Thomas Gold* research station at Jupiter. Nor the scientific bases on Mars, or orbiting Venus. To say nothing of the massive habitat in orbit around Saturn, which he regarded as little more than a penal colony. Mercury he had visited once, briefly, because he had to oversee the unloading of a cargo of construction materials there. But most of his time he spent aboard his ship, his mistress, the love of his life.

Of course, he did not lead a completely celibate life. Sometimes very attractive women booked passage on *Australia,* and rank has its privileges. He wondered if Katherine Westfall would succumb to the romance of interplanetary flight. She hadn't given a hint of such interest over the weeks since they'd left the Earth/Moon system, but still it was a pleasant possibility.

He had once been lean and sinewy, but the years of easy living as he ran *Australia* across the solar system had plumped his wiry frame. Now, as he sat facing the IAA councilwoman, he looked as well padded as the seat he reclined in.

Guerra poured two heavy gold cups of sherry, handed one to Mrs. Westfall, then touched the rim of his cup to hers.

"To a pleasant journey," he said.

"It's been quite pleasant so far," Katherine Westfall said, with a smile. She sipped delicately.

"I am curious," said the captain, "as to the reason for your traveling all the way out to Jupiter."

For a moment she did not reply, simply gazed at the captain with her gray eyes half closed, obviously thinking about what her answer should be. Her face was long and narrow, with a pointed chin and nose so perfect it could only be the product of cosmetic surgery. Her hair was the color of golden brown honey, stylishly cut to frame her face like a tawny helmet. She wore a pale blue business suit, simple and unadorned, except for an egg-sized sapphire brooch on its lapel.

"As a member of the International Astronautical Authority governing council," she said at last, so softly that the captain had to lean toward her to hear her words, "I feel it's my duty to personally review each major research facility the IAA is supporting throughout the solar system."

Captain Guerra nodded. "Starting with Jupiter?"

"Starting with the *Gold* station," Katherine Westfall concurred. Then a slightly impish smile curved her lips. "I feel one should always go for the gold."

She had been born Kate Solo, named thus by the mother who'd been abandoned by the man she had thought loved her. Growing up in the underground warrens of Coober Pedy, in the heart of Australia's forbidding outback, little Kate swiftly learned that determination and courage could make up for lack of money and social position. While her mother slaved away in restaurant kitchens, Kate strove to be the best student in the region's far-flung electronic school system, consistently at the head of her digital classes, even if she had to cheat a bit now and then. She won a university scholarship by the time she was fifteen and moved to Sydney. With her mother.

It was at a party on campus that she met Farrell Westfall, twenty-seven years her senior, quite wealthy from old family money. He was a university regent, she an economics major in her second year of study. "Go for the gold," her mother advised her.

Kate married Westfall before she graduated, and lived in a fine house hanging over the rocks on a rugged beach north of Sydney. With her mother.

Kate Solo became Mrs. Katherine Westfall. He was more interested in polo than the business world; she was determined to make certain that the family fortune she had married into was not dissipated in the ups and downs of the global economy—or by the importunings of her husband's lazy and whining relatives. She guided her feckless husband through the booms and busts of the next quarter century, and by the time he died of an unexpected massive coronary she was one of the wealthiest women in Australia. By the time her mother died, a decade later, Katherine Westfall was one of the wealthiest women on Earth.

She shared her wealth ostentatiously and was ultimately rewarded with a membership on the International Astronautical Authority's governing council. The directors of the IAA expected their new member to be flattered and malleable. They planned to use her as a public relations figurehead: a handsome, philanthropic woman who could speak the usual platitudes about the importance of scientific research before government councils and influential donors.

They did not realize that Katherine Westfall had her own agenda in mind. "Get to the top," her mother had often told her. "Whatever you do, get to the top. You're not safe until you're on top."

So Katherine Westfall initiated a subtle yet relentless campaign to be elected chairman of the IAA's governing council. From that position no one could challenge her, she would never have to worry about falling back into obscurity.

There were others who coveted the chairmanship, of course, but Katherine realized that her most dangerous rival was a man who claimed he had no interest in the position whatsoever: Grant Archer, director of the research station out at Jupiter. Archer was a danger to her, Katherine knew, despite his protestations of modest disinterest. He had to be stopped.

Halfway through dinner in the captain's quarters, Guerra asked her, "But why Jupiter, if I may ask? Why don't you start with the research bases on Mars? After all, that's where the most interesting work—"

She didn't wait for him to finish. "The leviathans," she said, her voice still muted but quite firm. "The leviathans are on Jupiter. Nothing else in the entire solar system is so interesting, so . . . challenging."

Captain Guerra's shaggy brows knit. "Those big whales? What makes them so interesting to you?"

Katherine Westfall smiled sweetly, thinking that if Archer could prove that those Jovian creatures were intelligent, the IAA would offer him their chairmanship on a silver platter.

To Guerra, however, she said merely, "The scientists want an enormous increase in their budget so they can study those creatures. I've got to pay them the courtesy of visiting their facility in person to see what they're doing."

To herself she added, I've got to stop them. Cut them off. Bring Archer down. Otherwise I won't be safe.

Leviathan glided among the Kin along the warm upwelling current that carried them almost effortlessly through the endless sea. But the food that had always sifted down from the cold abyss above was nowhere in sight. All through Leviathan's existence, the food had been present in abundance. But now it was gone. The Elders flashed fears that the Symmetry had been disrupted.

At least there was no sign of darters, Leviathan's sensor parts reported. They watched faithfully for the predators. As a younger member of the Kin, Leviathan was placed on the outer perimeter of the vast school of the creatures, constantly alert for the faintest trace of the dangerous killers.

Even so, a deeper part of its brain puzzled over the strangeness. Could the Symmetry truly be broken?

More than that, something new and different was imposing on the Kin. Something alien. Strange, cold, insensitive creatures had appeared in the world. Tiny and solitary, they came from the cold abyss above, cruised off at a distance from the Kin, then disappeared up into the cold again. Uncommunicative creatures, smaller than one of Leviathan's flagella members. When Leviathan and others of the Kin had flashed a welcome to them, the aliens blinked in gibberish and then fled.

Troubling. It disturbed the Symmetry, even though the Elders maintained that such pitifully small creatures could pose no danger to the Kin. They do not eat of our food, the Elders pictured, and they do not attack us. They can be safely ignored.

But then the flow of food from the cold abyss above had faltered and finally stopped. Leviathan wondered. Could the aliens be the cause of the break in the Symmetry?

Leviathan remembered back to the time when one of those aliens had seemingly helped Leviathan itself when it had wandered far from the Kin and was attacked by a pack of darters. The predators were tearing at Leviathan when this tiny, dark, hard-shelled alien had come to its aid. By the time the Kin reached Leviathan and drove off the darters, the alien was dying, sinking toward the hot abyss below.

Leviathan had tried to communicate with the alien, to thank it, but all the pictures Leviathan displayed on its flank went unanswered. Fearing that the alien would dissociate itself as it sank into the hot depths, Leviathan nosed beneath the pathetically tiny creature and lifted it on its back toward the cold abyss from which it had come.

Leviathan's reward for this kindness was a spray of painful heat as the alien apparently gathered its last strength and flew upward, never to be seen again.

That was more than two buddings ago, Leviathan remembered. In that time, other aliens had invaded the Symmetry. Invaded. That was how Leviathan thought of them. Strange, cold, hard-shelled creatures that flashed colored images that made no sense at all. They came down from the cold abyss, loitered near the Kin for brief periods, then returned whence they came.

Aliens, Leviathan thought. Not darters or the filmy tentacled creatures that dwelled on the edges of the cold abyss. Creatures the like of which none of the Kin had ever seen before. Not even the hoariest of the Elders had any idea of what they might be.

Aliens. The thought troubled Leviathan. Perhaps the Elders were correct and these aliens could be safely ignored. But why were they here, disrupting the Symmetry? What did they want of Leviathan and its Kin?

Were they responsible for the interruption of the food flow, for the disruption to the Symmetry?

A s Deirdre slowly undressed in the tiny privacy cubicle of the ship's infirmary she heard her father's warning in her mind. The gnomish little ship's doctor certainly didn't look like a smooth-talking bloke, but Deirdre wondered if this medical examination was nothing more than an excuse to see her naked. Peering at the cubicle's overhead panel of lights, she could not see any obvious signs of a camera. But still . . .

She piled her clothes and underwear neatly on the little stool beside her and slipped into the shapeless green medical gown that was hanging from a peg on the bulkhead. It barely reached down to her thighs. Then she hesitated. If he's watching me, she thought, he'll know that I'm finished undressing.

Nothing. Not a sound from beyond the flimsy partition. Deirdre stood there for as long as she could stand it, then cautiously slid the partition aside and stepped back into Dr. Pohan's office.

He wasn't even there. Surprised, she didn't know what to do. She felt slightly ridiculous in the flimsy medical gown. It was a dull olive green, not good for her complexion, she thought.

"DEPARTURE IN FIVE MINUTES," announced the speaker set into the overhead.

The corridor door slid back and Dr. Pohan came in again, his wrinkled bald face quite serious. "The scanner was off-line," he said, apologetically. "I had to get a technician to reboot it."

Deirdre nodded and unconsciously tugged at the hem of her absurdly short garment.

The doctor led her down the corridor past three closed and unmarked doors, then pulled open a fourth. It was another small compartment with a glass booth standing in its middle. White medical cabinets lined the walls.

Dr. Pohan gestured to the booth. "Kindly step inside. This will only take a moment."

Wordlessly, Deirdre entered the booth. The doctor shut its transparent door, then went to one of the cabinets. When he opened it, Deirdre saw that a control panel was inside, rows of switches and dials surmounted by a circular display screen.

"Please stand still and hold your breath," the doctor called, his back to Deirdre.

She heard a faint buzzing, then a single pinging note.

"Very good," said Dr. Pohan, turning back to her. "You can come out now."

"That's it?" she asked as she stepped out of the booth. "That's the test?"

"Complete three-dimensional body scan," the doctor said, bobbing his head. "Now all we need is a blood sample."

He went to another cabinet, rummaged in a drawer, and pulled out a medical syringe. "This won't hurt a bit," he said.

Deirdre thought otherwise, but she held out her bare arm for him to puncture.

"DEPARTURE IN SIXTY SECONDS," said the overhead speaker.

"MAIN DRIVE IGNITION."

Australia's departure from Ceres was barely noticeable. Fully dressed once again, Deirdre felt a slight jar, nothing more. But then she realized that she was beginning to feel heavy, almost sluggish. The ship's building up to one *g*, she told herself as she followed Dr. Pohan back to his office. It's going to be like this all the way out to Jupiter.

Deirdre sank gratefully into the chair in front of the doctor's desk. Dr. Pohan was smiling pleasantly at her as he tilted slightly back in his chair. The tips of his curling mustache almost reached the crinkled corners of his eyes, she saw.

"You have been a good patient, Ms. Ambrose."

"What happens now?" she asked.

With a slight shrug, the doctor replied, "Now we wait for the computer to analyze your scan and blood test. That might take a few hours. You are free to go."

"Go? Go where?"

Dr. Pohan glanced at his wrist, then answered, "It's almost the dinner hour. Go to the ship's lounge. Meet your fellow Jupiter-bound passengers. Your luggage has been delivered to your stateroom, of course."

Deirdre felt puzzled. "But I don't know where the lounge is. I don't even know where my stateroom is. I've just come aboard—"

"Of course," said the doctor. "This is all new to you, isn't it?"

With a preening brush of his curly mustache, the doctor rose from his desk and took Deirdre by the hand. She got to her feet, towering over the diminutive Asian, and let him lead her to the corridor door.

"That way," said Dr. Pohan, pointing down the passageway to the right. With his other hand he fished a remote control box from his tunic pocket.

"Main lounge," he said to the palm-sized remote.

A series of yellow arrows began flickering along the deck tiles.

"Follow the arrows," Dr. Pohan said. "They will lead you to the lounge."

"But my stateroom?" Deirdre asked.

"Oh, just ask any of the map displays in the passageways. They'll show you. It's simple."

Deirdre nodded, but she felt more confused than reassured.

F eeling disconcertingly heavy, Deirdre followed the blinking arrows along the passageway, then turned down a shorter segment that ended at the double doors of an elevator. The doors slid open as she approached them. Without her saying a word or touching a button, the doors closed silently and Deirdre felt the elevator dropping. Before she could catch her breath the cab stopped so abruptly that her knees buckled slightly. The doors slid open again.

Another corridor, with more yellow arrows beckoning her onward. There were other colored arrows, too, she saw: red, blue, green. They must lead to other parts of the ship, she thought. Maybe one set of them will guide me to my quarters.

Like the passageway upstairs, this corridor curved noticeably. The corridors run along the outer perimeter of each level, Deirdre figured. The offices and other compartments are built around the core. Wishing she'd spent more time in the centrifuge back home, Deirdre plodded along the passageway.

She hadn't gone more than a dozen steps when she saw a tall, lanky fellow standing up ahead of her, all arms and legs, scratching his thick strawberry red thatch of hair and looking very puzzled.

He was peering at the various blinking arrows on the deck, Deirdre saw.

"Are you lost?" she asked.

He twitched with surprise. "Oh! Hi!" he said, in a squeaky, high-pitched voice.

"Are you lost?" Deirdre repeated.

With another scratch of his bushy red mop he said, "I'm trying to find the main lounge."

"Oh, that's easy," said Deirdre. "Just follow the yellow arrows."

"That's just it," said the lanky fellow. "Which ones are the yellows? I'm color blind."

"Color blind?" Deirdre had never heard of such a thing.

"I can't make out any colors at all," said the young man. "The world's all black and white to me. With a lot of gray."

"That's awful!"

"It's genetic. I was born with it."

"You mean you can't see any colors at all?"

"Not a one. I can tell that your hair is darker than the skin of your face. And your clothes are sort of pale gray."

Deirdre felt terribly sad for him.

"My name's Andy Corvus," he said, sticking out his right hand.

"Deirdre Ambrose," she replied, taking his hand in hers.

Andy Corvus was a centimeter or so taller than she, which somehow pleased Deirdre: she was almost always the tallest one in any group. He was thin as a reed, though, lanky and loose-jointed. His unruly thatch of red hair reminded Deirdre of her father. He's what Dad must have looked like when he was young. A lot skinnier, though. His eyes were pale blue and his face was kind of cute, she thought, with a little button of a nose and a sprinkling of tiny freckles across it. There was something a little odd about his face, she realized, something slightly out of kilter. The two sides didn't exactly match up, as if they were separate pieces that were pasted together a little unevenly. Deirdre decided it made him look more interesting than he would have otherwise.

He was wearing a bright red short-sleeved shirt over garish orange slacks. Terribly mismatched, Deirdre thought. Then she remembered that colors meant nothing to him.

"Deirdre's a beautiful name," he said. "A poetic name."

Smiling shyly as she disengaged her hand, Deirdre said, "My friends call me Dee."

He broke into a wide, toothy grin. "I'd like to be your friend, Dee."

"Good." She slipped her arm into his. "Now let's go find the main lounge."

The yellow arrows ended at the open double doors of the main lounge. With Andy Corvus beside her, Deirdre stood indecisively at the doorway.

The lounge was luxuriously decorated with colorful sweeping draperies along the bulkheads and wide flat screens that displayed scenes from space: the beautiful swirling clouds of Jupiter, Saturn with its gaudy rings, the stark grandeur of the battered, pockmarked Moon, even the breathtakingly deep blue ocean world of Earth, flecked with brilliant white cloud formations.

Every table was occupied, she saw. More than two dozen men and women sat in small clusters at the little round tables scattered across the lounge. Most of them seemed intent on private conversations, heads nodding, expressions serious. But there was one group of a half-dozen men off in a corner, talking animatedly and suddenly roaring with laughter.

"Somebody told a joke, I betcha," said Andy, needlessly.

"I didn't realize there were so many going to Jupiter," Deirdre said. "I thought it was only four replacements for the scientific staff."

Corvus nodded vigorously. "Well, there's a whole crew of scoopship people. But just four of us scooters. Plus a couple of dozen bean counters and paper shufflers."

"Scooters?" Deirdre felt puzzled. "Bean counters?"

With a slightly lopsided grin, Corvus explained, "Scooters is a name for scientists. Don't ask me where it comes from; that's just what they call scientists at the research station. Bean counters are accountants, the people who handle the budgets and try to keep the scooters from spending too much."

"And paper stuffers?"

"Paper *shufflers,*" Corvus corrected. "Administrators. Department chiefs and such. Back a long time ago they actually kept records on paper, y'know."

"I've heard," said Deirdre.

"Well, let's find a table. I'm hungry."

"They all seem to be filled."

Pointing, Corvus said, "There's one over by the wall with only one guy sitting at it. Maybe he won't mind some company."

Deirdre followed Corvus as he threaded through the occupied tables toward the lone passenger sitting by the bulkhead, beneath the screen displaying the sad, cratered face of the Moon, half in harsh sunshine, half in cold shadow.

As the two of them made their way across the lounge, heads turned. Men and women alike stared openly at Deirdre. She was accustomed to being stared at and gave no sign of noticing their attention, keeping her face perfectly serious as she walked beside the gangling, grinning Corvus toward the table by the bulkhead.

As they approached, Deirdre saw why the man was sitting alone. Half of his head was metal. His left arm was a prosthetic; through the open collar of his short-sleeved shirt she could see that the left side of his chest was metal, as well.

A cyborg. She shuddered inwardly. How could anyone allow himself to have half his body turned into a machine? Then she remembered: The mercenary soldier who had destroyed the original *Chrysalis* habitat had turned himself into a cyborg. He had murdered more than a thousand rock rats, innocent men, women, and children. Her father had put the man on trial years later, once he'd been captured. Dad wanted to execute him, she knew. But the rock rats decided to exile him permanently, instead.

Could this be the same person? Deirdre wondered. It has to be, she told herself. A cyborg, half man, half machine. Even his face was half sculpted metal, etched with fine looping swirls, like those tattooed tribesmen from some primitive tropical island on Earth.

The cyborg noticed them approaching and got to his feet.

Gracefully, Deirdre noticed. Not ponderous at all. Like an athlete or a dancer.

Andy didn't seem bothered at all by the half-man's appearance. "Okay if we sit here with you?" he asked.

"Yes, of course," the cyborg answered in a deep baritone voice. "I welcome your company."

A simmering suspicion pulsing along her veins, Deirdre sat beside Corvus, facing the cyborg. He remained standing until she was seated, then resumed his chair.

Before any of them could say anything a squat little robot waiter trundled up to the table, its flat top glowing with the bar menu. Andy tapped the image of a beer, then selected the brand he wanted from the list that instantly appeared on the screen. Deirdre chose a glass of Earthside chardonnay: expensive, but she figured it would be the last of her luxuries for a long while.

The cyborg already had a tall glass of something dark in front of him. Machine oil? Deirdre wondered, realizing it was a nonsensical thought, a stupid bit of prejudice.

"My name is Dorn," the cyborg said. His right eye was gray and somehow mournful-looking, Deirdre thought. His left was a red-glowing camera lens.

Dorn. That wasn't the name of the man who'd destroyed the old *Chrysalis*, she knew. His name was . . . she rummaged in her memory. Dorik Harbin. That was it.

Corvus, meanwhile, had stuck his hand across the table. "Andy Corvus," he said amiably. Dorn grasped the offered hand in his human one.

Then the cyborg looked at her. Trying not to stare at the prosthetic arm, Deirdre mumbled, "Deirdre. My friends call me Dee."

"Dee," repeated the cyborg, almost solemnly.

The robot rolled back to their table with drinks on its flat top. Andy picked up the stemmed wineglass and handed it to Deirdre, then took his own tall, tapered pilsner glass of beer.

"What should we drink to?" Deirdre asked.

Dorn immediately replied, "To a pleasant trip to Jupiter."

"To the leviathans," Andy said.

Both men turned toward Deirdre. She gave them a tentative smile, then suggested, "To understanding."

"Yes," said Dorn. "To understanding."

They clinked glasses. Then Andy asked, "Understanding what?"

"Ourselves," said Dorn, in his slow, heavy voice. "I believe it was Socrates who said, 'Know thyself.'"

"And Goethe," Deirdre countered, "who said, 'Know myself? If I knew myself I'd run away!'"

Dorn made a sound that might have been a chuckle, deep down in his half-metal chest. Andy looked puzzled.

"What're you?" Corvus asked her, "some kind of a philosopher?"

Deirdre lowered her eyes and replied, "No, not at all. I just have an eidetic memory."

"A photographic memory? Wow!" Corvus was obviously impressed.

"What is your technical specialty?" Dorn asked.

"Actually," she answered, "I'm a microbiologist."

"Microbiologist?" The human half of Dorn's face looked incredulous.

She made an almost apologetic smile. "I know. It sounds strange, a microbiologist living at the habitat orbiting Ceres. But our health and safety people are very concerned with biofilms and other microbial threats. *Chrysalis II* is a pretty small community, and we live in a completely sealed environment. We have to be very careful about the microbes we carry around with us."

Deirdre thought that Dorn's human eye flickered momentarily when she mentioned *Chrysalis II*, but it was so brief that she couldn't be sure.

"Don't you have disinfectants?" Corvus asked. "Ultraviolet bug killers?"

Dierdre's smile turned almost condescending. "Andy, our bodies are habitats for whole ecologies of microbes. If you took an ultrascan of your body, and removed all your own cells from the image, you'd still see your body and all your organs outlined in microbes. They're everywhere."

Dorn said, "It's not *Chrysalis II* that surprised me. I'm wondering why a microbiologist is needed at *Gold*."

"Yeah," Corvus said. "Those whales are big, not little."

With a slight shake of her head, Deirdre replied, "All I know is that the request for a microbiologist came from Grant Archer himself, the head of the whole Jupiter team."

"He specifically asked for a microbiologist?" Dorn sounded incredulous.

"I suppose they want me for the same kind of thing I do at *Chrysalis II*: health protection."

"It still sounds strange," Dorn insisted. "*Gold* must have its own medical staff."

With a shrug, Deirdre said, "I suppose we'll just have to wait until we arrive there to see why they asked for me." Then she added, "But it doesn't matter what they expect me to do there. They've promised me a scholarship to the Sorbonne. I'll be going to Earth! I'll be going to our home world."

JUPITER ORBIT: RESEARCH STATION
THOMAS GOLD

Grant Archer slid wearily into bed next to his wife. Marjorie smiled at him and murmured, "Two more weeks."

Grant tried to smile back, but failed. All these years, he thought. All these years and it's going to end in failure. Abject failure.

Grant Armstrong Archer III had originally come to research station *Gold* as a graduate student, doing his mandatory four years of public service. He had dreams of becoming an astrophysicist, of studying collapsed stars and black holes, of perhaps learning how to create space-time warps that could allow humans to span the mind-numbing distances between the stars. But once he saw the leviathans he forgot all that. He never left the Jupiter region again, brought his wife to the *Thomas Gold* station and had two children with her, eventually became director of the station.

He was a quiet type, his demeanor usually serious, his actions studied and methodical. No blazing genius, Grant Archer was a fine administrator, smart enough to allow the younger men and women who showed flashes of brilliance to do their work without being overly bothered by the bureaucracies that dogged every research program. He had kept his youthful slimness, thanks to a metabolism that seemed unable to produce fat. After a quarter century of marriage he was still the earnest, broad-shouldered, good-looking man that Marjorie had fallen in love with back in their college days on Earth.

His one obvious physical change over those years was that his sandy brown hair had turned silver. Grant kept it cropped militarily short, almost down to a skullcap. And once he had been named director of the station he had grown a trim little beard; it made him look more mature, he believed, more impressive. His wife thought it gave him an air of authority, but it evaporated whenever he smiled.

"Is she really coming out here?" Marjorie asked drowsily.

Staring up at the shadowed ceiling of their bedroom, Grant nodded. Then, realizing his wife couldn't see him in the darkness, he said, "She's on the passenger list. Her, and a half-dozen of her personal staff."

"Don't let it worry you," Marjorie advised sleepily. "She's probably coming out here to give you some kind of award. You deserve it."

Grant knew better. Marjorie turned over and went to sleep, but Grant could not close his eyes. Katherine Westfall is coming here. Herself. With her hatchet men. That's what they are, Grant knew. He'd looked them up in the nets. Since being named to the IAA's governing council, Westfall and her flunkies had ruthlessly slashed the organization's research budget. The teams exploring Mars depended now entirely on private money; they were even allowing tourists to visit the Martian village that they had excavated. The work on Venus was down to almost nothing, as well.

And now she's coming here.

Turning on his side, Grant told himself, They can't close us down! They can't! Those creatures are intelligent. I'm sure of it.

His mind kept returning to the mission, the journey into that immense alien sea. Twenty years ago, almost, yet he remembered every agonized moment of it. The surgical implants, the pain, the cold dread of being immersed in the high-pressure perfluorocarbon. Living in that slimy gunk, breathing it into his lungs instead of air.

The rapture of being linked to the submersible's systems, feeling the power of the fusion drive as your own heartbeat, seeing through the dark forbidding sea with eyes that went far beyond puny human capability. What was it Lane had said about being linked? Better than sex. It was, in a way. Beyond human. Godlike.

It was dangerous, feeling all that power. The sin of pride. Hubris. They had nearly died in that deep, dark sea.

But meeting the leviathans had been worth all the pain, all the danger to body and soul. Seeing those incredible creatures, bigger than mountains, huge, immense, living deep in the Jovian ocean, lords of their world.

The mission had nearly killed them all. Lane O'Hara had been seriously hurt. Zeb Muzorewa, kind, thoughtful, gifted Zeb had almost died. Zeb had been Grant's mentor, his guide. Grant had been lucky to survive the mission, lucky to return to the world of humans.

Not luck, he reminded himself. It wasn't luck. That Jovian creature helped us. It saw we were sinking and it carried us on its back, like a dolphin carrying a drowning man, up to where we could get our propulsion systems working again and get out of the ocean, back into orbit and to the station.

They're intelligent. Those immense creatures are intelligent. Grant believed it with all his soul. The Leviathans are intelligent. They have to be.

Grant glanced at his wife, lying beside him. For several moments he listened to her breathing: deep and regular. Sound asleep. I wish I could sleep, too.

The memory of that mission haunted him. No humans had tried to penetrate Jupiter's ocean since then. The cost in human lives was too high. People had been killed, people had been permanently disabled. Grant himself still limped from the electronic implants that had been dug into his legs. Stem cell treatments, years of physical therapy and psychological counseling, yet still he limped. Psychosomatic, the medics told him. Yes, of course. But his legs still ached.

Lane O'Hara had returned to Earth for recuperation. She never came back to Jupiter. Muzorewa spent months in recovery and once he'd returned to *Gold* he was named director of the research station. He immediately started planning a new mission into the ocean of Jupiter, but this time it would be robotic. Zeb would not send fragile humans into that alien environment. Not willingly.

When Zeb retired and Grant succeeded him as station head, he continued that policy. Uncrewed vessels of increasing sophistication went into the Jovian ocean. To study the Leviathans they had to go so deep that communication with the orbiting station was cut off.

The scientists had to wait impatiently until the probes returned to find out what they had learned. Many probes never returned, and the scientists never learned why.

Grant knew that there was only one way to save the work he directed, one way to continue studying the leviathans. He had to prove beyond a doubt that the Jovian creatures were intelligent. And to do that, he had to send a human crew back into that cold, deep, alien sea. For years he had quietly, secretly, diverted funding from the research station's normal programs into a furtive effort to build a new submersible capable of carrying a human crew down to the depths where the leviathans dwelled.

Now Katherine Westfall was on her way to Jupiter to slash the funding jugular of the research station. Once she found out about the new submersible she would have Grant's head on a platter. Maybe she already knows, he thought, and she's coming out here to preside at my execution personally.

He lay on his back and stared sleeplessly into the shadows of his bedroom. I can't send people back down there, Grant told himself. It's too dangerous; I can't send people to risk their lives like that. How can I ask them to go where I can't go myself?

But there's no other option. We've learned as much as we can from the automated probes. We've got to get a team of scientists down into that ocean, with equipment that will allow us to make meaningful contact with the leviathans. Or forget about them altogether. Give up trying to make contact with an intelligent alien race.

He closed his eyes and muttered a prayer for guidance. No answer came to him, but Grant accepted God's seeming silence. He hears, Grant told himself. He'll send the answer. One way or another.

FUSION TORCH SHIP *AUSTRALIA*

W hat's so great about Earth?" Corvus asked, looking puzzled. "I've lived there most of my life. It's no big thrill."

Before Deirdre could think of a reply, Dorn said gravely, "I can see where Dee would be excited about it. If you've never been there before, well . . . it *is* big, and lots of it is still quite beautiful. The tropical rain forests—"

"What's left of them," Corvus grumbled.

"The open plains, the mountains, the oceans. They truly are beautiful, more beautiful than any space habitat, certainly."

Corvus shrugged impatiently. "And the cities, with the crowds and crooks, the noise, the dirt, the diseases."

"Don't you like Earth, Andy?" Deirdre asked.

His expression softened. "Oh, I guess so. But it's not paradise, believe me."

"I still want to see it, experience it," she said.

"It's worth seeing," said Dorn, almost wistfully.

"Why are you going to Jupiter, Andy?" Deirdre asked.

Corvus made a half-embarrassed grin, glanced at the cyborg, then looked back at her. "I'm going to make contact with those big critters in the ocean there."

"Make contact with the leviathans?" Dorn said.

Bobbing his head up and down, Corvus said, "Yep. The leviathans."

"Make contact?" Deirdre prodded. "What do you mean?"

Both hands fidgeting with his tall beer glass, Corvus replied, "You know what DBS is?"

"It's a sort of brain probe, isn't it?" she said.

"Sort of. But it's more than that. A lot more. Deep brain stimulation. It's a whole new field."

"Didn't they try treating cases of depression that way?" Deirdre asked.

Corvus waved a hand in the air. "It didn't really treat depression. It just tranquilized the patient so he didn't show any symptoms anymore."

"The zombie machine," Dorn muttered.

"That's what some people call it," Corvus said, looking slightly nettled. "They used it on convicts in jail. Kept them pacified, cut down on prison violence. A lot."

"But the suicide rate tripled."

Deirdre said, "You seem to know a lot about it, Dorn."

The human half of his face twitched into what might have been a grimace. "I've received an accelerated education on the subject."

"How come?" Corvus asked.

Flexing his prosthetic hand, Dorn replied, "I have been hired by the scientific directors of station *Gold* as a sort of experimental animal. They want to see how my body might be advantageous when it comes to probing Jupiter's ocean. For the past year I've been a prime research specimen at Selene University, on the Moon."

"Ooh." Corvus's face lit up with understanding. "Being half mechanical, you might be able to take the pressures of a deep dive better, is that it?"

"Something like that."

"Humans haven't gone down into the Jovian ocean in twenty years," Deirdre said. "They tried two crewed dives and both were disasters."

"Still," said Dorn, "the scientists would like to go deep enough into the ocean to observe the leviathans."

"They send automated probes down deep," Corvus said.

Dorn nodded. "Now they want to send people."

"But why?" asked Deirdre. "It's so dangerous! And the robot probes can do anything people can do, can't they?"

Corvus shook his head. "They can do everything except react to the unexpected, Dee. The robots can only answer the questions that we knew how to ask before they go into the water. You can't program a computer to handle unexpected situations."

"You can link human controllers," she pointed out. "Have them in charge in real time so that—"

Dorn interrupted her. "As I understand it, the probes must go so deep into the ocean that they can't maintain contact with the orbiting station. Electronic signals can't penetrate the depth of water. Not even laser beams can get through."

"Couldn't they put relay stations into the ocean?" Deirdre asked. "They could pass the signals—"

"It's too deep," Corvus interrupted. "And the relays would have to stay more or less fixed in position."

"Impossible in the currents of that ocean," added Dorn.

Deirdre said, "Oh. So that's why they want to send humans again."

Both men nodded.

"But it's so dangerous!" Deirdre exclaimed again. "Who would want to go down there?"

"I would," Corvus answered, without a microsecond's hesitation.

Deirdre looked aghast at the idea. "Why would you—"

"To make contact with the leviathans," Corvus said before she could finish her question.

"Using DBS?" Dorn asked.

Bobbing his head again, Corvus said, "It's a variation of the deep brain stimulation concept. You can link your brain to the brain of another person. It was originally developed for the intelligence services, and police. You know, you can probe a person's brain, pull out everything he knows, whether he likes it or not."

"Is that legal?" Deirdre wondered.

Ignoring her question, Corvus went on, fairly trembling with growing enthusiasm, "Well, back at the University of Rome, our professor got the idea of linking with nonhuman animals. Great for biological studies. Ecological, too. You can experience what an antelope or a lion experiences, see the world the way they see it. We started out with elephants, then chimpanzees. The anthropologists went crazy over it!"

"I can imagine," Dorn muttered.

"No, seriously," Corvus said eagerly. "I was one of Professor Carbo's best students. I could link more easily than any of the others. I was an elephant out in the Serengeti for a solid week!"

Deirdre giggled. "I hope it wasn't mating season."

Looking almost hurt, Corvus said, "This is the only way we're going to make any meaningful contact with the leviathans. Using neuro-optronic probes to link our brains with theirs."

"Assuming the leviathans have brains," Dorn said.

"They've got to! Critters that big? They've got to have a central nervous system with a brain to direct those enormous bodies."

Dorn shook his head slightly. "You're assuming that Jovian biology works on the same principles as our own. We have no way of knowing that's true."

"Wrong!" Corvus snapped. "We've studied those living balloons that float through the Jovian atmosphere, and some of the other airborne creatures. They all have brains."

"Do you intend to try to link with them before you try to reach the leviathans?"

"I sure do."

Deirdre put a hand on Corvus's arm. "Andy, does that mean you'll have the linking equipment implanted in your own brain?"

"Doesn't have to be implanted," Corvus said. Tapping his temple, he explained, "You just fit the sensors on your head, like a crown."

"But how will you fit the sensors on the leviathans?" she asked.

Corvus's enthusiasm wavered the slightest bit. "Well, we'll have to get close enough to one of 'em so we can attach a sensor rig to its hide."

"Like harpooning a whale?"

"Sort of."

"Shades of Moby Dick," Dorn muttered.

"And you intend to go down into the ocean and do this yourself?" Deirdre asked.

Corvus nodded. "Yep. Sure do."

The three of them looked at each other, none of them knowing what to say next.

"DINNER IS SERVED IN THE MAIN DINING ROOM," announced the ship's intercom through the speakers set into the lounge's overhead.

D inner!" Corvus fairly leaped to his feet. "Let's go. I'm starving."

Deirdre felt relieved as she pushed her chair away from the cocktail table. She felt uncomfortable about Andy's blithe willingness to immerse himself in the dark depths of the Jovian ocean and connect his brain to an optronic stimulator system. And my other companion is a cyborg, she said to herself. I sure can pick 'em.

Dorn got to his feet too and the three of them joined the others heading for the dining room.

Before they went a dozen steps, though, a burly, shaggy man in a tan one-piece coverall strode up to them and took Deirdre's wrist in his thick-fingered hand.

"You've got to be the most beautiful woman aboard this ship," he said, staring at her with unabashed admiration. "No, I take it back. You're the most beautiful woman this side of Earth."

"Thank you," Deirdre said, deftly removing his hand from her wrist.

"I'm G. Maxwell Yeager. Don't ask what the G stands for. I'm your dinner partner."

G. Maxwell Yeager was almost as tall as the lanky Corvus and almost as wide across the shoulders as the cyborg Dorn. His face was stubbled with the beginnings of a dirty-brown beard and his hair, also sandy-colored, was a smoothly brushed mane that fell past his shoulders. He wore a rumpled khaki jumpsuit and an incongruous pair of shiny black cowboy boots, into which he had stuffed the legs of his coveralls.

He appraised Deirdre with a look that was halfway between sheer admiration and a blatant leer.

Reaching for her wrist again, he said, "Come on, let's go to dinner."

Deirdre backed away a step and Dorn moved between them, grasping Yeager's extended arm with his prosthetic hand. "The lady is with us," he said.

Yeager stared at the cyborg for a moment, then shrugged nonchalantly and said, "Okay, okay. In that case, I'll join you."

With Dorn on one side of her and Andy Corvus on the other, Deirdre left the lounge and entered the adjacent dining room. Shaggy-haired Yeager kept in step with them, on Dorn's other side.

"Hey, Max," a younger coverall-clad man called to him. "I thought you were gonna eat with us."

Yeager waved at him dismissively. "I found somebody better-looking than you ugly mugs."

Deirdre saw that the younger man was part of the raucous group that had been sitting together in the lounge.

"Scoopship team," Yeager explained to her. "Engineers. You know what they say about engineers: so narrow-minded they can look through a keyhole with both eyes."

Andy giggled. Dorn remained impassive. Deirdre wondered why Yeager made fun of engineers.

"I've heard about you," Yeager said to the cyborg. "You're a priest or something, aren't you?"

"Or something," Dorn muttered.

Deirdre felt Dorn's reticence like a palpable force. She said to Yeager, "And what's your reason for going to Jupiter, Mr. Yeager?"

"It's *Doctor* Yeager," he replied, drawing himself up haughtily. "Doctor of engineering physics, University of Arizona." Then he grinned at her. "But you can call me Max."

"Hi, Max," Corvus said good-naturedly from Deirdre's other side. "I'm Andy."

Yeager hadn't taken his eyes off Deirdre. "And pray tell, fair one, what might your name be?"

With some reluctance, she told him, "Deirdre. Deirdre Ambrose."

"Deirdre," Yeager echoed. "That's an Irish name. It means 'passionate,' doesn't it?"

"I don't know," Deirdre lied.

The dining room was just as sumptuously decorated as the lounge, and it was filling up rapidly. Yeager spotted a table for six halfway across the big chamber and led the others to it. He moved around the table to sit beside Deirdre, then tipped the chair on his other side to lean against the table.

"Put up the chair beside you, Andy," he said to Corvus as they all sat down.

Blinking in puzzlement, Corvus asked, "Why?"

"They'll think we're saving the seats for another couple of people," Yeager explained. "That way we can just be the four of us without any strangers butting in."

"But we're all strangers," Corvus blurted. "I mean, we just met a few minutes ago."

Yeager waved him down. "Nah, we're old buddies. Shipmates."

He dominated their conversation all through dinner, talking almost exclusively about himself.

"So I tackled the challenge. Me and my grad students. That's three of them over at the table across the room, with the scoopship team. We designed a submersible vehicle that can carry a maximum of six human crew a thousand kilometers deep into the Jovian ocean and allow them to cruise down there for at least five days."

"A considerable engineering challenge," Dorn admitted, as he carefully brought a forkful of hydroponic greens to the human side of his mouth.

Yeager agreed cheerfully. "There've been two human missions into that ocean and both ended in disaster. Casualties. People got killed."

"The pressure down that deep must be incredible," Corvus mused.

"It is, and then some," Yeager said. "Some of the uncrewed probes have been crushed. I mean, it's *tough* down there."

Deirdre listened with half an ear as Yeager nattered on. She wondered about Dorn. He was a priest? That was weird. He wasn't wearing anything that looked clerical: just plain gray coveralls. The left side of his face was etched metal, as was the top of his head. His left arm was prosthetic. A priest? she wondered. He said the scientists wanted to see if he could handle the pressures of a deep dive better than a normal human. That means they're planning a crewed mission into the ocean. After nearly twenty years. After killing people both times they tried it before.

"So I completed the design and my people have built the dingus out at Jupiter orbit," Yeager was saying. "Now I'm heading out to the *Gold* station to supervise the final checkout before we start testing the beast."

Andy Corvus looked impressed. "A submersible that can carry humans safely deep down into that ocean."

Yeager mopped up the sauce on his plate with a crust of soybread. "It was a tough design challenge, let me tell you."

No one responded to that, so he went on, holding the dripping crust in two fingers, "The secret is, you've got to make the beast big. I mean *big*. Big as the research station, almost. The problem with those earlier birds is they made 'em too small."

"As big as *Gold* itself?" Dorn asked, intrigued despite himself.

Yeager nodded as he popped the bread in his mouth and chewed vigorously.

"That big, just to hold six people?" Corvus asked.

Gulping down the crust, Yeager said, "You need the size to handle the pressures. Compression. The vehicle's built like a series of nested shells, one within the other. Like those Russian dolls, you know."

"Babushka dolls," Corvus said.

"Matryoshka," Deirdre corrected.

Yeager grinned at her. "You know, for an incredibly beautiful woman, you're pretty smart."

Dorn bristled visibly, but Deirdre simply gave the engineer an icy glare.

Yeager took it all without malice. "Freedom of speech," he said, almost wistfully. "It can get you into a lot of trouble. Ah well. What's for dessert?"

"Tell us more about this ship you've designed," Corvus said. "I'm going to be one of your passengers."

"You?" Yeager looked surprised.

"Me," Andy said. For once, he looked totally serious.

D orn accompanied Deirdre to her stateroom once dinner was finished. As Dr. Pohan had told her, the map screens placed strategically along the passageway bulkheads showed where her quarters were and how to get there. All she had to do was ask.

Despite her assurances to her father, the higher g force of the ship's acceleration was making Deirdre feel weary, slow.

"Thank you," she said as they walked slowly along the passageway. "I appreciate your protecting me from Dr. Yeager."

"I learned courtesy from a very noble woman," Dorn said, his voice low, heavy.

With a tired smile, Deirdre added, "I've fended off showoffs like Yeager most of my life, but I'm glad I didn't have to do it alone, tonight."

"*De nada,*" he said.

"You speak Spanish?"

"She did."

"You must have loved her very much."

Dorn shook his head slowly. "It's not that simple."

"Oh."

Following the maps displayed upon the wall screens, they at last found Deirdre's stateroom. Its door was like all the others that lined the passageway except that the oblong electronic screen on it bore her name. Another couple came up the passageway from the other side, deep in whispered conversation. They stared at Dorn as they squeezed by.

"I should be jealous of you," Deirdre said, once they had passed.

"Jealous?"

"Usually I'm the one people stare at."

Dorn said nothing.

"Since I was twelve," she went on.

It was impossible to read the expression on the human side of his face. For long moments they simply stood there in the passageway, silent. For the first time in many years, Deirdre wasn't sure what she should say, how she should handle this . . . cyborg.

"Thank you," Dorn said at last.

She blinked at him. "For what?"

"For not asking about my past. For not probing into my life story."

"It's painful to you."

"Painful. Yes."

Very softly, she said, "Everybody has pain in their lives, Dorn."

"I suppose that's true," he said, without much conviction.

Even more unsure of herself, Deirdre said, "Well, if you ever want to talk about it, I'll listen."

"That's very kind of you."

"Good night, then."

"Good night."

This was the moment when guys made their move, Deirdre knew, but the cyborg merely bowed stiffly a few centimeters, then turned and started walking up the passageway.

But after a few steps he stopped and said over his shoulder, "My dossier is on file at Ceres. Look under the name 'Dorik Harbin.'"

Then he proceeded up the passageway, the overhead lights glinting off the etched metal of his skullcap. Deirdre watched him for several moments, then touched the fingerprint-coded lock that opened her door.

Dorik Harbin, she thought. He *is* the man who wiped out the original *Chrysalis*, slaughtered all those people! He's the man Dad wanted to execute. Yet he doesn't seem like a murderer now.

He's . . . She searched for a word, decided at last to give it up. Then she remembered that Yeager said Dorn was a priest of some sort.

A priest?

It's been a strange first night, Deirdre thought as she stepped into her stateroom. And we have two more weeks to go.

She closed the door behind her and leaned against it. She felt that it would be good to get into bed and stop fighting this heavy gravity that was pulling on her.

Then she looked around the spacious compartment for the first time. Deirdre's stateroom was considerably more splendid than the quarters she was accustomed to at home. All this space for one person! she marveled. Of course, she realized, it's designed for a couple. Eying the wide, low bed, she giggled at the thought that it was big enough for a team of acrobats.

Her one travel bag was sitting on a luggage rack at the foot of the bed. She unpacked, then undressed, did her ablutions in the handsomely appointed lavatory, and avoided the temptation to try out the deep tub of the spa. Pulling on a shapeless old pullover shirt that reached to her hips, Deirdre sat on the bed and tried not to look at the blank wall screen.

Go to sleep, she told herself. Don't pry into the man's past.

Yet it was Dorn himself who told her that the rock rats' settlement at Ceres held a dossier on him, under the name Dorik Harbin. She wondered why he no longer called himself that.

Yeager seemed to know something about him, Deirdre thought. All through dinner the engineer behaved as if he knew all about Dorn's past. But then Yeager acted as if he knew everything about everything, she told herself.

Forget about it, she told herself. Let sleeping cyborgs lie. She stretched out on the bed and pulled the thin sheet up to her chin. But in her mind's eye she kept seeing Dorn, half human, half machine. Why? How?

She remembered a line she'd read at school about a famous financier who had faced an ethical problem of some importance. "Bernard Baruch sat on his favorite park bench, struggling with his conscience," the author had written. Then he added, "He won."

Smiling to herself, Deirdre decided that she would override her conscience, too.

She sat up and called, "Computer, what's the time lag between here and Ceres?"

The wall screen glowed softly and the computer's synthesized voice answered, "Four seconds, one way."

I can get the information in less than eight seconds, Deirdre realized.

"Computer, query the *Chrysalis II* habitat for the personnel dossier of Dorik Harbin."

"Acknowledged."

Deirdre lay back on the bed again and commanded the lights to switch off. I'll read his file in the morning, she said to herself. After a good night's sleep.

But she found that she could not sleep. Tired from the heavy gravity though she was, she was too curious to fall asleep. She got up and went to the tiny swivel chair at the compartment's built-in desk and switched on the computer again.

And there it was: Dossier, Dorik Harbin. Born in Montenegro, Earth. Parents, two sisters killed in ethnic cleansing. Joined local militia at age twelve. Recruited by International Peacekeeping Force. Quit IPF to join Humphries Space Systems as mercenary soldier. Convicted of destroying original *Chrysalis* habitat, killing one thousand seventeen men, women, and children. Sentenced to permanent exile from *Chrysalis II* and all other Asteroid Belt communities.

Deirdre stared at the words on the wall screen. Her blood ran cold. He's been involved in death and murder since he was a child!

She watched the video of Dorik Harbin's trial. He offered no defense. He seemed to expect to be executed, seemed to *want* to be killed. But then an elderly woman in a powerchair rolled herself up to the cyborg and pled for mercy, saying that he had completely changed his personality, begging the inhabitants of *Chrysalis II* to exile Dorik Harbin, not kill him.

The dossier stopped with the rock rats' decision to exile Dorik Harbin. They had no further interest in Dorik Harbin. But Deirdre did. She was riding out to Jupiter with a mass murderer. He may say he's a priest now but he has blood on his hands. She wanted to know a lot more about this Dorik Harbin, or Dorn, as he now called himself. A lot more.

KATHERINE WESTFALL'S SUITE

Katherine Westfall's three-room suite was up near the top of *Australia*'s long, slim body, one level down from the captain's quarters. The staff people she had brought with her were ensconced two levels lower, separated from Mrs. Westfall by "officer's territory," the compartments where the ship's officers were quartered. Still, even her staff's accommodations were much more spacious and sumptuously decorated than the compartments for ordinary passengers and the ship's crew.

Katherine was reclining against a mound of pillows on her bed, gazing out through the glassteel port set into the bulkhead of her bedroom. Countless stars hung out there, brilliant jewels against the eternal darkness, steady and unblinking. Earth and its bleak, sad-faced Moon were far behind the ship as it hurtled through space toward distant Jupiter.

Her personal communicator lay on the bed beside her, its palm-sized screen displaying a star chart. Katherine was teaching herself astronomy, or trying to. The chart didn't seem to match what she was seeing outside, though.

Her slim brows knitting in frustration, she thought she understood where the problem was. The stupid tutorial on the screen was displaying how the stars would look from the surface of Earth. The ship was in space, and many, many more stars were visible. Thousands of stars too dim to be seen through Earth's thick atmosphere now glowed at Katherine, blanketing the outlines of the constellations that she should be finding.

Her frustration gave way to understanding. Too many stars, she told herself. God's overwhelming me with more information than

I need. It was a trick she had used herself, from time to time. Drown an investigator in data. Give them what they want, but bury it in so much information that they'll never be able to find the pattern they're looking for.

Katherine Westfall smiled at the stars. And she thought that an astronomy display that showed all the myriad of stars one sees in space, but highlights the stars that one would see from Earth, might make a decent profit for an entrepreneur who knew how to bring a new product to market. She filed the idea away in her mind, alongside other ideas that she had stored there. It's never too late to make a profit, she reminded herself. I may be retired from the corporate world, but that doesn't mean I have to stick entirely to philanthropy.

Philanthropy. The word jogged her back to reality. You're not here to study astronomy, she told herself. You're spending six precious weeks heading for Jupiter to do what's needed out there. It's time to cut them off. No excuses. No mercy. Take a good look around their research station and then send them all packing back to Earth. Take Archer down before he can make his move against you.

Grant Archer was a threat. The head of the scientific team at Jupiter was on the short list to be appointed the next director of the IAA, the position Katherine wanted for herself. Not merely a council member; she had to be the director. Had to be. She heard her mother's voice in her mind: "Get to the top, Katie. Whatever you do, get to the top. You're not safe until you're on top."

She knew that Archer and his staff of scientists were feverishly trying to complete a new submersible craft and send a crew of volunteers down into that murderous ocean. To study the leviathans. It was supposed to be a secret, but the scientists could keep no secrets from her. She had her sources of information in place aboard the research station.

He thinks that a successful mission to study those creatures will guarantee his appointment to the IAA directorship. He thinks he'll be able to jump ahead of me.

Unconsciously, Katherine shook her head. Archer and his scientists may say they want to study those Jovian beasts, but what they're really going to do is kill more people. Like they killed Elaine.

It had been a shock to Katherine Westfall when she discovered that she had a sister. Her mother had never told her of it. Not in all the years they had lived together had her mother once mentioned that she'd had another daughter, years before Katherine: Elaine.

Katherine discovered her sister's existence the day after her mother's funeral, as she went through the pitiful remnants that her mother had left behind. A scattering of photos, most of them obviously taken many years earlier, when her mother had been young and pretty, long before the years of toil had ground her down to a hard, suspicious shell of a gray-haired woman.

Two images in the computer file showed her mother with a baby. Only two images out of hundreds that had accumulated over the years. But those two images sparked Katherine's lively interest because both dated from before her own birth. Who was this baby? Why was her mother cradling the infant so tenderly in her arms?

The advantages of wealth include the ability to buy information. Katherine used her corporate security office to hire private investigators and track down this mystery child.

She learned at last that her mother had borne a daughter to one of her earliest lovers, nearly ten years before Katherine had been born. The man was wealthy, powerful. He refused to marry her mother, but took the baby from her to raise as his own. Mother never saw her again, Katherine realized. That's what made her so bitter. That's why she was so wary when Katherine met Farrell Westfall. "Get him to marry you," Mother had insisted. "Marriage or nothing."

So she had married. And her mother had died wealthy and comfortable. And Katherine learned she had a sister.

Her sister was a scientist who had been at research station *Thomas Gold*, orbiting Jupiter. But now, Katherine had found, she was back on Earth. In a convalescent hospital in Ireland.

She had traveled halfway across the world to meet her sister and arrived exactly two hours too late. Elaine O'Hara had died at almost the moment Katherine had left Sydney. She had been in poor health physically and emotionally since she'd taken part in the ill-fated mission into Jupiter's deep, seething ocean.

Jupiter had killed Katherine's only sister.

No, she told herself as she lay on the bed in her luxurious state-room aboard *Australia*. It wasn't Jupiter that had killed her; it was the single-minded, blindly arrogant scientists who had sent her to her death.

She smiled to herself, coldly. The sister she had never known would become the excuse she needed to kill the scientists' investigation of Jupiter. One way or another, she was going to send them all packing back to Earth. And if anyone questioned her motives, she could always tell them about her dear, martyred sister and point the finger of accusation at Archer and all the other heartless scientists who willingly sent innocents to their deaths.

ELECTRONICS WORKSHOP

Andy Corvus was not smiling as he bent over the electronics components scattered across the worktable.

"Murphy's Law," he muttered to himself. "If anything can go wrong, it will."

"What seems to be the problem?" Dorn asked.

The cyborg was sitting easily on a swivel-topped stool a meter or so from Corvus, who was on his feet, staring unhappily at the hardware strewn along the table. The electronics workshop was small, hardly big enough for the two men. Its one workbench was fully equipped, though, with tools and diagnostic instruments. Corvus wondered how *Australia's* maintenance crew kept the ship going with such a minuscule workshop, but then he guessed that the ship's systems got inspected and overhauled regularly in port, after a trip was finished.

Corvus looked up at Dorn and his face went from a frustrated scowl to a sheepish expression. "I've been working on this rig since we left Selene and it's still not right." Pointing at a gray titanium cylinder resting on the workbench, no bigger than his fist, he said, "I've got to get all these components to fit into that container. Six kilos of goods in a five-kilo bag."

Dorn waved his human hand. "Get a bigger container."

"It's not that easy," Corvus said, looking chagrined. "The size of the container is dictated by the volume available in the dolphin's skull."

"Dolphin?"

Grinning crookedly, Andy said, "Sure. Didn't you know we're

carrying dolphins aboard the ship? Taking them out to the *Gold* station."

"Dolphins." Dorn seemed incredulous.

"It's part of my work," Corvus explained. "I'm brain-linking with the dolphins as a sort of preliminary test, to see if I can make contact with the leviathans."

"And we're carrying dolphins on this ship all the way out to Jupiter?"

Corvus nodded enthusiastically. "We sure are. Four whole decks have been converted into an aquarium for them."

Dorn shook his head in disbelief.

"I was going to try to make contact with them later today, but if I can't get my transceiver into the volume they've allowed for their skulls . . ."

"You'll have to make smaller components," Dorn said, quite matter-of-factly. Then he added, "Or make more room in the dolphins' skulls."

Deidre had slept poorly, her dreams filled with scenes of war and bloodshed. Dorn—Dorik Harbin—didn't appear in those dreams; at least she didn't remember his presence. But the dreams were horrifying, people being slaughtered, villages burned to the ground. And the old *Chrysalis* habitat methodically destroyed, slashing laser beams ripping its components apart, people blasted into the vacuum of space, not even able to scream as their lifeblood spewed out of them.

She was glad that Dorn wasn't in the dining room when she came down for breakfast. But as she slid her tray along the dispenser tables she saw Max Yeager sitting off in a corner by himself, as if he'd been waiting for her.

As soon as he saw Deidre the burly engineer got up from his solitary table and buzzed over to her.

"Good morning," he said, smiling widely. "I hope you slept well."

"Not very," Deirdre replied.

She filled her tray with a plate of eggs, a mug of fruit juice, and a dish of melon balls, Yeager beside her every step of the way. She found an empty table and Yeager immediately pulled out a chair in his meaty hands and held it for her.

"I didn't sleep all that well, either," he said as he sat across the table from her. "Strange surroundings, eh? Have you done much traveling?"

With a shake of her head, Deirdre admitted, "This is my first trip away from home."

"I've traveled a lot," Yeager said. "Been to Mercury twice, helping Yamagata Corporation design those big solar energy satellites they're putting up out there. Rumor is, they want to use some of 'em to power lasers that'll propel lightsail ships out to Alpha Centauri."

"Alpha Centauri?" she marveled.

Before Yeager could respond, Deirdre's pocketphone buzzed. She fished it from the pocket of her slacks and saw the text message on its minuscule screen: "DEIRDRE AMBROSE, PLEASE RE-PORT TO DR. POHAN IN THE INFIRMARY. AT ONCE."

Staring at her, Yeager wondered aloud, "What's that all about?"

Deirdre pushed her chair away from the table and got to her feet. "I have to go," she said.

"You haven't had any breakfast!"

"I'm not that hungry, really." And she hurried out of the dining room, glad to leave Yeager standing there alone.

Wrinkled, bald, mustachioed Dr. Pohan smiled at her as Deirdre stepped into his office, but somehow his smile seemed tense to her, forced. The wall screens showed images of medical scans, slices through her body, circles of intestines, interiors of lungs like budding, branching flowers, pulsing, beating organs.

That's what I look like inside, Deirdre said to herself as she sat, staring fascinatedly, in front of the doctor's desk.

Without preamble, Dr. Pohan said, "We have a puzzlement on our hands, young lady."

"A puzzlement?"

"You have rabies."

Shocked, Deirdre gasped, "Rabies? That's impossible!"

Gesturing to the wall screens, "Impossible or not, your scans show the rabies virus lurking in your bloodstream. It can infect your brain, you know."

"I can't have rabies," Deirdre insisted. "You get rabies from an animal bite, don't you? I haven't been bitten by any animal. We don't allow pets on *Chrysalis II*; not animal pets, anyway."

His strained smile still in place, Dr. Pohan said gently, "How you acquired the virus is puzzling, very puzzling. But the important thing at the moment is to neutralize the virus before it reaches your brain and you begin to show symptoms."

"Neutralize it? You mean kill it?"

"If possible," said the doctor. "There are injections that can eliminate the virus, but unfortunately we don't carry such medications aboard ship. Who would expect cases of rabies to show up on an interplanetary liner?"

Deirdre caught the plural. "You said cases?"

"Yes. The woman you are replacing, she died of rabies on the trip out from Earth."

INFIRMARY

could die?" Deirdre cried.

"If untreated," said Dr. Pohan.

"But you said you don't have the vaccine. . . ."

"The treatment requires human rabies immunoglobulin. We were able to fabricate a small amount of same in the ship's pharmacy but it wasn't enough to save my patient. The virus had spread through her nervous system and into her brain."

Deirdre fought down an urge to scream. Forcing her voice to stay calm, steady, she asked, "Could you produce enough of it to treat me?"

For a century-long moment Dr. Pohan did not reply. At last he steepled his fingers and said softly, "We can try, Ms. Ambrose. It's a rather difficult synthesis, but we can try."

"And if you can't . . . ?"

The doctor shrugged. "The alternative is to freeze you until we arrive at Jupiter. I've already contacted the medical officer at station *Gold* and he has instructed his staff to produce the medication. It will be ready for you when you arrive there."

"Rabies," Deirdre repeated, her voice trembling just a bit.

"It is very strange," said Dr. Pohan. "Neither you nor the unfortunate woman who died was bitten or scratched by a rabid animal. She was from Selene, a well-respected biologist. Of course, she frequently visited Earth. She could have contracted the disease there."

"And she died."

"Apparently she had been infected some time before boarding this ship. The preboarding medical examination missed her condition entirely. The automated scans were not programmed to check for rabies, unfortunately. By the time she began to exhibit symptoms, it was too late to save her."

"And she died," Deirdre repeated, in a whisper.

Dr. Pohan put on his professional smile once again. "Please do not worry unduly. We have caught your case early. You will not die from it, I am almost certain."

That word *almost* blared in Deirdre's mind.

Deirdre walked like an automaton from the infirmary to the elevators and went blindly, unthinkingly, back to the dining room. It was closed: too late for breakfast, too early for lunch. It didn't matter; she had no appetite.

How could I get rabies? she asked herself a few thousand times as she headed back to her stateroom. By the time she got there, the room had already been cleaned, the bed made neatly, the lavatory sparkling.

Deirdre plunked herself down on the spongy little chair in front of the compartment's computer. Rabies, she repeated silently. She told the computer to look it up.

She heard a thump on her door. With a sigh, she got up and slid it open.

Dorn was standing there, his broad body filling the door frame. Behind him Deirdre saw Andy Corvus, grinning shyly at her, and Yeager, his smile almost a leer. Corvus was clutching a large aluminum box, gripping the handles on its sides in both his hands.

"We're going down to the dolphin tank," Andy said enthusiastically before any of the others could speak. "Wanna come with us?"

Deirdre blinked at him. "The dolphin tank?"

Yeager piped up. "The ship's carrying six dolphins out to Jupiter. Andy wants to talk to 'em."

"Come on," Andy coaxed. "I'll connect you to the dolphins if you like."

The box he was holding was obviously heavy; she could see the tension in his arms. Why doesn't he ask Dorn to hold it for him? Deirdre wondered. Or at least to help him carry it?

Dorn spoke up. "If we're imposing on your privacy . . ."

"No," Deirdre decided, "it's perfectly all right. I could use a little diversion this morning."

The four of them started down the passageway toward the elevators, Corvus lugging the big case all by himself.

Katherine Westfall was deep in discussion with Grant Archer, at the research station orbiting Jupiter.

The discussion, though, was not a conversation. *Australia* was still so far from Jupiter that it took electronic communications, traveling at the speed of light, slightly more than twenty-one minutes to span the distance between the ship and the *Thomas Gold* station. So their discussion consisted of alternating monologues. One would talk and then, some forty-two minutes later, the other could respond.

Archer's serious, steady-eyed face filled the wall screen in Mrs. Westfall's sitting room. As she reclined in a softly yielding chaise longue, she studied the scientist's intense, oh-so-earnest expression. He's rather good-looking, she thought. Boyish, almost, except for that gray little beard. Married. Happily, from what his dossier says. At least, he's been married to the same woman for more than twenty years.

". . . and although we're considerably over budget in several areas," Archer was saying, as if reading from a text, "I feel certain that once you're here and have the chance to see what we're trying to accomplish, you'll agree that our work is too close to success to be inhibited by budget cuts."

She smiled at him. Naïve fool, she thought. Scientists are all alike. What I'm doing is so important that it mustn't be stopped or even cut back. Money is no object. Of course it isn't. It's not *their* money that they're spending.

Archer had stopped talking. His image stood frozen on her display screen. That meant that he was finished for the time being and was waiting for her reply to reach him.

Westfall did not need a prepared script. Keeping her smile in place, she said, "I'm sure that the work you're doing is very important, Dr. Archer, but the economic facts of life must be taken into account, whether we like it or not."

Sitting up a little straighter, she went on, "Your research work is funded out of the profits made by the scoopship operations, as you know. The market for scooping fusion fuels out of Jupiter's atmosphere has leveled off. We are no longer expanding our construction of new fusion powerplants on Earth, and even the market for fusion torch ships has gone rather flat.

"That means that the profits have leveled off, and you can't expect increases in your funding. I'm afraid there's nothing that I, or you, or anyone can do about that. You must cut back on your budget, just like the rest of us."

She hesitated, wondering inwardly, Should I let him know that I'm aware of this giant submersible he's building? No, she decided. I want to see the shock on his face in person, up close.

She spoke a few more meaningless words of farewell, ending the discussion. The screen went blank gray.

Katherine Westfall leaned back in the couch as if exhausted by the morning's exertion. But she was thinking, I know what he'll do now. He'll rush to get that submersible finished and send a crew back into the ocean before I can cut off his funding altogether.

He'll push his people to their utmost. He'll be in a sweat to go back into the ocean and kill more of his underlings. Just like his predecessor killed my sister.

Good, she thought. All to the good.

DOLPHIN TANK

t was like being underwater. The dolphin tank took up four entire decks of the torch ship: four levels had been ripped out and filled with salt water, their outer bulkheads reinforced to withstand the pressure. The central core, where the elevator and ship's plumbing and electrical conduits ran, passed through the giant glassteel-walled tank.

Deirdre gasped in awe as she and her companions stepped out of the elevator cab. They were standing on a narrow circular platform, surrounded by the aquarium and its gliding, sinuous, colorful fish. She shivered slightly; the place felt chilly, and it smelled of a salty tang—clean, she decided. The air was cool and fresh, not like the other decks where the human crew and passengers lived.

"It's like being inside the ocean!" she exclaimed.

Corvus nodded happily. "That's right. It's as self-contained an ocean environment as the best ecologists on Earth could produce in this limited volume." He put the square aluminum case he'd been carrying down on the bare metal deck and rubbed his arms. "That bugger is heavy!"

A pair of dolphins slid past, sleek, gray, squeaking and clicking, their mouths turned up in a perpetual silly grin. They reminded Deirdre of Andy.

"Well," Corvus said, "to work." And he began to tug off his coveralls.

"You're not going into the water with them?" Yeager asked, looking a trifle apprehensive.

"Just long enough to insert the transceiver into that youngster there." He pointed at one of the smaller dolphins. It seemed to be eying Corvus as it swam past.

Once he'd peeled down to black skintight trunks, Corvus opened the big aluminum case and began pulling out a pair of swim fins, a breathing mask, and a cylinder of compressed air. Dorn stepped over and helped him strap the air tank onto his back.

"How do you get into the water?" Deirdre asked.

Pointing behind her, Andy explained, "Easy. Up the ladder to the top of the tank, over the edge up there, then *kerplop!* into the water."

"You've done this before?" Yeager asked.

"Every day since we left lunar orbit, just to get acquainted with the dolphins."

Deirdre was impressed with Andy's agility as he scrambled up the metal ladder carrying his fins in one hand. He'd hung the palm-sized metal cylinder of his transceiver around his neck on a metal link chain.

"The water must be cold," she said to Dorn, standing beside her. Yeager had moved slightly away; he was staring into the tank, watching the fish swimming tirelessly past.

Corvus pulled on his breathing mask and slipped into the water with barely a ripple. One of the dolphins swam up toward him with a barrage of clicks and whistles. Andy jackknifed and dived down toward the smallest of the dolphins. It circled him twice, chattering madly, then dashed away. Two of the bigger dolphins glided alongside Andy, one on either side. The little dolphin obviously wanted to play, but after several minutes of gyrations, the dolphin finally eased into a steady glide and allowed Corvus to slide one arm along its back.

They swam together for several minutes. Deirdre saw that, baby or not, the little dolphin was slightly longer than Andy's lanky form, swim fins and all. The adults dwarfed him.

At last he was able to insert his transceiver into a slot that had been surgically implanted in the young dolphin's skull. The two larger dolphins hovered around the youngster, chattering off a rapid-fire clatter of clicks. That's their language, Deirdre said to herself.

After a few more minutes, Andy kicked up to the surface and climbed out of the tank. Dripping wet, he came down the ladder to join them on the deck.

Dorn pulled a big white terry cloth towel out of the capacious aluminum case and draped it over Andy's shoulders as soon as he slipped his air tank off. Deirdre couldn't help wondering if the puddles Andy was dripping onto the deck might be slippery.

Yeager, looking even more ill at ease, had the same thought. "These puddles could be dangerous," he half growled.

"There's a mini vac in here someplace," Corvus said, ducking his head into the case. He pulled the vacuum out and offered it to Yeager. "Here."

Yeager looked astonished, then almost angry. But he took the tool and sucked up the puddles without complaint. Deirdre was surprised at how loud the machine was; its buzzing noise seemed to echo off the walls of the tank.

Corvus didn't notice the noise at all. He was busy pulling a gray electronics box out of his carrying case. To Deirdre it looked almost like an old-fashioned notebook computer, perhaps slightly bigger. Sitting it on the lid of the big aluminum case, Corvus opened up the device, turned it on, nodded when its screen brightened.

Then he pulled out a slim metallic circular band that glittered with optronic chips, lifted it in both hands like a royal crown, and settled it onto his matted, still-wet hair.

"Okay," he said, looking up at Deirdre and the others. "Now we see if it works."

Corvus seemed to go into a trance. His eyes half closed, his slightly uneven face relaxed into a sleeplike softness as he crouched on his knees by the electronics box. Like a sleepwalker he turned to the curving wall of the aquarium, then pressed his fingertips against the glassteel.

Dorn was watching him intently. Yeager looked edgy. Deirdre stood over Corvus, not knowing what to do, or if she should even try to do anything. Unbidden, the memory of her visit to Dr. Pohan came back into the forefront of her mind. Rabies, she thought. If he can't synthesize the antidote I could die.

The baby dolphin glided up to Corvus, squeaking and chattering, its two parents hovering not far off. Corvus turned sluggishly and rested his back against the curving glassteel wall of the tank. His chin drooped to his chest, his eyes closed completely. But his fingers twitched slightly.

"Is he all right?" Deirdre wondered.

"He seems to be breathing normally," said Dorn.

For several nerve-stretching minutes they watched Corvus. Nothing happened. The baby dolphin hovered near Andy, but silently now. The two adults swam smoothly, their powerful tails rhythmically surging up and down. The fish scurried around and around the circular tank endlessly. The adult dolphins had gone quiet, too, Deirdre noticed.

She looked from Corvus's semicomatose figure up to the circling fish and the silent dolphins, then back to Andy again. "Should we do something?"

"Do what?" Dorn asked.

Yeager gave a disgusted snort. "This is like watching paint dry." He turned and punched the elevator button.

"You're leaving?" Deirdre asked.

"I've got better things to do with my time than watch him—"

Corvus stirred. His entire body seemed to spasm once, then his eyes opened and he smiled lazily. "Made it," he said. "How long was I out?"

Reaching down to help Corvus to his feet, Dorn replied, "We didn't time you."

"That's okay," Corvus said easily as he lifted the circlet off his head. "It's all in the computer log."

"You were in contact with the dolphins?" Deirdre asked.

"Sort of," he said. "It wasn't really all that good. I couldn't get much out of her."

"The little one?"

"Yeah. Baby." He pointed as the trio of dolphins glided past them, chattering again. "She's got the transceiver in her skull." Brightening, he said, "Well, it wasn't bad for a first try."

The elevator doors slid open and Yeager stepped into the cab.

"Hey Max!" Corvus called. "Don't you want to try it?"

"Hell no!" Yeager snapped as the doors slid shut.

"He's scared," Corvus said, as if it surprised him.

Dorn shook his head. "Merely cautious. He's an engineer, after all. He doesn't plunge into a new experience without checking all the possibilities first."

Corvus nodded, but he still looked disappointed.

"How about you, then?" he asked Dorn.

METAMORPHOSIS

Me?" Dorn seemed shaken by Andy's question.

Corvus nodded hard enough to make a lock of his wetly matted strawberry hair flop over his forehead. "See if you can make contact with them," he said.

Dorn looked up at the dolphins swimming past, then back at Corvus again. "I don't know . . ."

Corvus stepped toward him, holding the optronic circlet in his extended hand. The slim metal band, studded with many-hued ovals, gleamed like a jeweled tiara. "It ought to work fine: I mean, the metal of your head will make a terrific contact."

Dorn looked anything but willing, Deirdre thought. He accepted the ring with his human hand and slowly fitted it over the metal cap of his head. On him it looks like a crown of thorns, Deirdre thought.

Smiling with satisfaction, Corvus pecked at the computer's miniature keyboard.

"Okay," he said to Dorn. "Just relax. I'll set up the connection for you."

Dorn stood as rigid as a tightly pulled bowstring while Corvus tapped away on the laptop's keyboard.

"Might help if you close your eyes," Andy suggested.

Deirdre saw the cyborg's human eye close. The prosthetic eye seemed to go dim.

For several heartbeats nothing happened. The dolphins were chattering again, back and forth. Deirdre wished she could understand what they were saying to each other.

"Not everybody can make contact," Andy whispered to her, as if afraid he might break Dorn's concentration. "It's a sort of—"

"NO!" Dorn roared. He spasmed, his back arching, his arms flailing wildly, hands clenched into fists. His human eye snapped open, the prosthetic one glowered hot red.

"No!" he bellowed again. Corvus tried to duck beneath his wildly swinging arms and went sprawling onto the deck. Dorn spun around and took a tottering step toward Deirdre, his half-human face a mask of rage. She backed away, terrified.

Scrambling to his hands and knees, Andy banged a fist on the keyboard of the computer.

Dorn stopped in mid-frenzy. For a long moment he stood frozen, the human side of his face twisted in what might have been blazing anger, or agony. His chest heaved. Sweat rolled down his cheek.

Deirdre's back was pressed against the elevator doors. She, too, was panting, frightened. He could smash the wall of the aquarium with that metal arm of his, she thought; glassteel or not, he could crack the tank's wall and drown us all.

But Dorn seemed to regain control of himself. Slowly. He stood there unmoving while Andy clambered awkwardly to his feet and Deirdre stared fearfully at the cyborg. Slowly Dorn's arms slumped down to his sides. Slowly the terrible rictus that had twisted his face so horribly relaxed.

At last he said, almost sheepishly, "I'm sorry. I couldn't do it."

"Are you all right?" Deirdre asked, breathless.

Dorn nodded once, somberly. "I am now." He lifted the optronic band off his head and handed it to Corvus.

"What happened?" Andy asked, taking the rig from the cyborg's prosthetic hand.

"I failed to make contact with the dolphin," Dorn replied flatly.

"Yeah, but you . . . you sort of went berserk for a minute there."

"I apologize."

"What did you see?" Corvus persisted. "What did you feel?"

Dorn hesitated a fraction of a moment, then replied, "Nothing."

"Nothing? But what—"

"Nothing," the cyborg repeated. Then he added, "I'm afraid I'm not a good subject for your attempt to make contact with the dolphins."

With that he pivoted like a machine and took a step toward Deirdre. She slipped aside and Dorn leaned a finger of his prosthetic hand against the elevator button.

"I'm sorry if I frightened you," he said as he stood facing the elevator doors.

"Are you all right?" Deirdre asked again.

"Yes. As all right as I can be."

The elevator doors slid open and Dorn stepped inside the cab. He touched the control pad and the doors shut. Deirdre heard the faint hum of the electric motors that lifted the elevator upward.

"Wow," said Andy. "That was weird."

"It was scary," Deirdre agreed. "He's a very powerful man."

Shrugging as if to put the whole episode behind him, Corvus held the optronic circlet out toward Deirdre.

"Would you like to try it?"

Deirdre could feel her eyes go wide. "Me?" she squeaked.

"What happened to Dorn isn't normal, Dee," Andy said, his voice faltering, uncertain. "I've never seen the linkage affect anybody like that."

"Maybe it has something to do with his being a cyborg," Deirdre suggested.

Corvus shrugged. "Maybe." He offered the circlet to her again. "Do you want to try it?" he repeated. "Please?"

Deirdre decidedly did not. But as she looked at her friend's soft blue eyes and heard the pleading in his voice she heard herself say, "Sure, I'll try it . . . I suppose."

CONTACT

With considerable misgivings Deirdre settled the slim optronics band onto her auburn hair. Andy nodded, satisfied, and made a few adjustments on the little computer.

"Now just relax," he coached her. "Close your eyes and relax. Like you're going to sleep."

Easier said than done, Deirdre thought. In her mind's eye she saw Dorn raging and flailing like a madman. That won't happen to me, she told herself. It won't. It can't.

"Maybe you ought to sit down," Corvus said. Opening her eyes, Deirdre saw him gesturing to the big aluminum case. "Here," he suggested. "You can sit here."

Deirdre sat tensely on the case. It felt cold, even through the fabric of her slacks. She closed her eyes again and rested her chin in her hands. Cold and hard. Not like the water. The water's warm and soft, it covers you all over, smooth and warm and soft.

Small. Mother says this water is small. She remembers when she was young and the water stretched forever. You could swim for days and never see the same bottom. And out farther the bottom was so far away you couldn't see it at all.

Effortlessly, she glided to the surface for a gulp of air. Mother and Father swam behind her, and they breathed, too. Through the hard wall that was the end of the world she saw a strange creature, neither dolphin nor fish. Land creature, Mother told her. But it was swimming with us a few breaths ago, she said to Mother. It played with me.

Land creature, Mother repeated. Not one of us.

She saw another land creature resting on a square rock. That's me! she realized. But I'm here, safe with Mother and Father. It was confusing. How can that be me, outside the world, when I'm here where I've always been?

She decided to ignore the strange land creatures. They didn't really matter. The world was good. Filled with fish. No dangers. Mother had told her more than once about the dangers in the big water, fish with sharp teeth who liked to eat baby dolphins. None of them here in this water. This is good water. Small, but good.

She emptied her lungs, popping a trail of bubbles from her blowhole, and rose swiftly to the surface. Bursting through, she jumped exuberantly into the not-water and splashed down again, nose first.

Mother chattered unhappily. Father, too. Don't go off on your own, they warned.

But there's nothing to be afraid of, she replied. This little water has no dangers in it. You told me so yourselves.

Still, be careful. Someday we might reach the big water, and there will be dangers there. Learn to be careful.

She thought Mother and Father were being foolish. They remember the old fears, she told herself. But then she thought how exciting it would be to swim in the big water, to travel on and on, never seeing the same bottom twice, racing through the big water. Father told her that his family chased fast-swimming fish that were so numerous their schools were wider across than all the dolphins of the family put together. The family hunted those fish.

Not like here, where the water was so little that the fish were few, hardly enough to keep the hunger away. So few that they had no place to run to, no place to hide. Even when they formed a school it was small and easy to slice through.

She glided unhappily through the stupid fish. This water may be safe, she thought, but it's not much fun.

Maybe I can get Father to jump with me! She swam close to his sleek, powerful body and asked him. Mother immediately said no, but Father—

"That's enough," said Corvus.

Deirdre blinked and looked up at Andy. He was lifting the optronic circlet off her head, the expression on his face quite serious, almost grim.

"What . . . ?" Deirdre felt confused. This isn't Father, a voice in her mind said.

"You were under for five full minutes," Andy said somberly. He looked worried, almost.

Deirdre sat up straighter and took a deep breath. I'm sitting on Andy's case. I'm aboard the torch ship. We're heading for Jupiter.

"Are you okay?" Andy asked.

"I think so," said Deirdre. Then she smiled, remembering. "Yes, I'm fine."

"You made contact." It wasn't a question.

"I was the dolphin!" Deirdre said, suddenly aware of what had happened. "It was . . . I . . . it was like I was the dolphin, swimming in the tank!"

"Great!" he said. Pointing to the laptop, open on the floor beside the case she was sitting on, Andy said, "I was monitoring your vital signs on the screen. You made the transition without a hitch."

"It was strange," she said. "It was like . . . I wasn't me anymore. I was the dolphin. The little one."

"Baby."

Nodding, Deirdre said, "It's a shame to keep them in that little tank, Andy."

"Little? It's the biggest we could build for them."

"But it's little for them. They're used to swimming in the ocean, not a tank."

"They've never been in the ocean, Dee. These dolphins were raised in cetacean laboratories on Earth. Baby was born in La Jolla, California. Her mother was taken from the Pacific when she was younger than Baby is now. They were transferred here to this ship a week before we left Earth orbit."

"But Baby remembers the ocean," Deirdre insisted. "The adults have told her about being in water where they could go day after day and never see the same bottom twice."

Corvus ran a hand through his thick mop of hair. "Really? Baby remembers things she's never experienced for herself?"

"Yes, she does."

For a moment Corvus was silent. Then he said softly, "Dee, if

Baby can remember things that she's never seen, that means that she was told those things by the older dolphins. Like stories we pass down from one generation to the next."

Deirdre said, "I suppose it does."

Corvus licked his lips. "That means they're intelligent, Dee! The ability to pass information from one generation to another is one of the key indicators of intelligence!"

They had missed lunch. By the time Deirdre and Andy got to the main lounge, the doors to the dining area were closed, not to be opened again until the cocktail hour.

"I'm starving," Deirdre complained. "I haven't even had breakfast."

Pointing to the row of automated dispensers off to one side of the lounge's empty bar, Corvus suggested, "We can get a sandwich or something, I guess."

The dispensers' offerings were limited, but Deirdre was so hungry that she took a salad, a sandwich, and a square dark object that was purported to be a fudge brownie. Plus a large cola. Corvus settled for a salad and a cup of lukewarm tea.

"I'm a vegetarian," he explained when Deirdre looked questioningly at his meager tray.

The lounge was almost empty at this hour of the mid-afternoon. They found a table by the bulkhead, beneath a wide screen displaying a view of Saturn, with its gleaming broad rings.

As soon as they put their trays on the table and sat down, Corvus said urgently, "You've got to help me with this."

"With what?" Deirdre asked.

"The dolphins!" he fairly yelped. "You made contact with Baby so easily. You're a natural. You got more out of her in five minutes than I've gotten in two days. A lot more."

"Beginner's luck," Deirdre murmured.

"No, you're a natural. Wow! If we can show evidence that they're intelligent . . . wow! What a breakthrough that'll be!"

"I suppose it would be significant."

"Significant! It's monumental. Here we've been searching for intelligent extraterrestrial life for the past hundred and fifty years and there's an intelligent species right on Earth with us!" His grin was ear-to-ear.

"Is what we've done today enough to prove it?" she asked.

Wagging his head, Andy replied, "Nope. Not by itself. All we've got is your unsupported word about what Baby was thinking. That's not enough."

"Why not?"

He smiled gently at her. "I think it was Carl Sagan who said, 'Extraordinary claims require extraordinary evidence.'"

"Not just my word?"

"Nobody's accusing you of lying, Dee. But the scientific community will need more solid evidence than your unsupported word."

"So what—"

Her phone buzzed. Deirdre's first instinct was to turn it off, but then she realized that the most likely person to be calling her was Dr. Pohan.

"Excuse me, Andy," she muttered as she pulled out the phone and flipped it open.

It was indeed Dr. Pohan. And he was smiling broadly beneath his florid mustache. Without preamble he said, "I have good news, Ms. Ambrose. Please come to my office in the infirmary as quickly as you can."

Dierdre clicked the phone shut and got to her feet. Half her salad and all of her sandwich and dessert still remained on the table.

"I have to go, Andy."

"Who was that?" he asked, looking up at her.

"I'll tell you later," Deirdre said as she picked up her tray and headed for the disposal chute. She managed to gulp down two bites of the limp sandwich before she dumped what was left and hurried toward the infirmary.

Dr. Pohan was still smiling benignly when she sat down in front of his little desk.

"Good news, you said?" Deirdre asked.

"Indeed! Indeed." Dr. Pohan's head bobbed up and down.

"You can synthesize the vaccine?"

"It appears so," the doctor said cheerily. "We need a donation of blood of a type that is compatible with yours. I have scanned the records of everyone aboard ship and come up with a potential donor."

"A potential donor?" Deirdre asked. "Only one?"

"One should be sufficient, if he is willing to give us some of his blood. From a comparatively small amount we can synthesize the immunoglobulin you require."

Her pulse speeding, Deirdre asked, "And is he willing?"

"We will find out shortly. I have asked him to join us here."

At that, Deirdre heard a single sharp rap on the door behind her.

"Enter," cried Dr. Pohan.

She turned in her chair as the door slid open.

Dorn.

Back in the main lounge, Andy Corvus chewed thoughtfully on his salad.

She made contact with Baby, he was saying to himself, I'm sure of it. She couldn't just make up the impressions she told me about. The dolphins have language! They can actually communicate abstract ideas to one another!

But who's going to believe it, without solid evidence to back up her word? I'd be laughed out of the business—or worse, accused of fraud.

Got to make Deirdre's sensory impressions visible, recordable. Got to get her brain wave patterns into some form of reproducible data retrieval program.

But how?

Dorn took one step into Dr. Pohan's compact little office, saw Deirdre sitting before the doctor's desk, and froze into immobility.

"Come in, come in," Dr. Pohan urged him, gesturing to the only other chair in the room, beside Deirdre's.

He settled slowly, almost suspiciously, into the chair. It creaked beneath his weight.

Dorn said, "Your message said you required a blood sample from me."

"Require is too strong a word," said the doctor amiably, unconsciously brushing his curling mustache with one finger. "We request a blood sample. Request."

"We?"

"Ms. Ambrose has a medical condition that can be alleviated with a donation of your blood, sir."

Dorn turned his head toward Deirdre. "I'll give you as much blood as you need, of course."

"Why, thank you," she said.

"A few cubic centimeters should do nicely," said the doctor. "A few cc's will be more than enough, I'm sure."

Dorn nodded. Deirdre felt enormously grateful.

Katherine Westfall was on *Australia*'s bridge when her wristphone pinged. She glanced at its miniature screen briefly, saw that the message was from Dr. Pohan, and ignored it. The phone would automatically record his message for her to retrieve later.

Captain Guerra had invited her to the bridge and was showing it off to her with the glowing enthusiasm of a proud father.

She thought the bridge seemed surprisingly small, considering the size of the ship. The place seemed to vibrate subtly with the background thrum of electrical power. And it felt too warm, as if overly crowded. Yet only four officers were on duty, in addition to the captain. A cluster of display screens showed various sections of the ship's interior; she could see passengers walking along passageways, crew personnel working at machinery she could not fathom. The multiple views reminded Katherine of the segmented eye of an insect. There was even a view of the empty beds of the infirmary, and Dr. Pohan's office, with the wrinkled little leprechaun sitting at his desk.

On the opposite bulkhead a single broad screen showed a telescopic view of Jupiter's slightly flattened disk.

"We're getting closer every hour," the captain said grandly. "You can see the planet's oblateness clearly."

"It looks much paler than I had expected," Katherine said, remembering the pictures she had seen of vibrant bands of deeply colored clouds, swirls and eddies of storm systems the size of Earth and bigger.

The captain muttered something about false-color imagery.

The bridge had only half a dozen crew stations arranged in a shallow semicircle around the captain's command chair, and two of the curved, instrument-studded stations were unoccupied, at that. Standing beside Westfall, Guerra pointed out consoles for navigation, propulsion, life support, and communications. Uniformed officers, two of them women, sat at each console.

"And these other two?" she asked, pointing to the empty consoles.

"Backup stations," said Captain Guerra. "We don't need to man them unless there's some sort of emergency."

"Indeed?"

"As a matter of fact," the captain said, patting one hand on the arm of his command chair, "I could run the ship from my chair here, all by myself alone. The systems are so highly automated that I could do away with the crew altogether and she would still run perfectly well."

Westfall made herself appear impressed. But she couldn't resist asking, "Then why do you carry the crew along with you, Captain?"

Guerra's bearded face looked surprised at her question, then nettled. But almost instantly he broke into an accommodating grin. "You're joking, of course."

"Perhaps," Westfall said, permitting herself a slight smile. "But if I were heading the corporation that owns this vessel I'd want to know why I had to pay for crew members who aren't needed."

Obviously struggling to maintain his pleasant expression, the captain replied, "They are *needed*"—he emphasized the word—"for two reasons. One, in case the automated systems fail or conditions exceed their programming limits."

Westfall nodded.

"And two—well, frankly, it's for the passengers. Our psychology consultants tell us that the passengers would be afraid to travel on a completely automated ship."

"I see. It's public relations, then."

Guerra's genuine smile returned. "Exactly! Public relations." He paused, then added, "Besides, some of the passengers enjoy having dinner with a good-looking young ship's officer. Eh?"

With a knowing arch of her brow, Westfall said, "I prefer older men, myself. Men of experience."

The captain absolutely glowed. For a moment Katherine thought he was going to wink at her.

Instead, he asked, "In that case, would you join me for dinner this evening in my quarters?"

"Why not?" Westfall replied, thinking how predictable the captain was, how easy it was to get this man to do her bidding.

Once back in her own suite she immediately went to the desk in her sitting room and played Dr. Pohan's message. The gnomish little doctor's image looked very serious, almost grave, on the desktop screen.

"I met with Ms. Ambrose and the cyborg this morning. He has agreed to donate blood. He didn't even ask what the reason was. All I had to do was tell him that Ms. Ambrose had a medical problem and he agreed without hesitation."

Good, thought Westfall.

The doctor continued, "I should be able to synthesize enough immunoglobulin to sustain Ms. Ambrose until we reach the Jupiter station. She will still be carrying the rabies virus in her blood system, of course, but she will exhibit no symptoms."

Perfect, Westfall said to herself. Once we're at station *Gold* she'll have to depend on me to get enough of the serum to keep her alive. I'll have her under my control.

LEVIATHAN

The Kin searched for a down-welling current that would carry food particles to them. The Elders directed the Kin toward a new storm that recently had arisen, reasoning that its power would draw food down from the cold abyss above. Leviathan and the rest of the Kin could sense the storm's turbulence growing even though it was still too far away to see directly. But there was no infall of food to be found at this distance from the storm. The Kin pushed on, directed by the wisdom of the Elders.

Storms were dangerous, but the Elders decided that the Kin had no choice but to seek new currents of down-drifting food particles even if they had to go dangerously near the storm's turbulent power. Without the food, members of the Kin would starve. As death approached they would dissociate into their separate member parts, never to bud again and generate new members of the Kin.

And there were darters out there, as well, their voracious hunger never satisfied. They would never dare to attack the Kin in all its unity, but when an individual swam off to dissociate, the darters pounced. A lone member of the Kin, dissociating into its separate components, was prey to the darters. Before the components could bud and then coalesce to form a new leviathan, the predators would attack.

It was an ancient dilemma. Without dissociating and budding, new members of the Kin could not be generated. But by going off alone to dissociate, a lone leviathan was prey to the ever-lurking darters.

Leviathan remembered its own buddings, and the narrow escapes it had won from the slashing, insatiable darters. Its battles were painful memories, and the time for a new dissociation was approaching, Leviathan knew.

Time and again Leviathan had pictured the same question to the Elders: Why must a member go off alone to dissociate and bud? Why cannot some members of the Kin escort the individual through its dissociation and budding?

The Elders' response was always the same horrified revulsion. Dissociating in view of others! Disgusting! The images they flashed said that the Symmetry could only be maintained by continuing the ancient ways, the rituals that the Kin had observed from time immemorial. The darters are part of the Symmetry, they pictured. Accept them as you accept the food that drifts down from the cold abyss above.

Their answer did not satisfy Leviathan, but there was nothing to be done about it. The Kin would go about their lives, feeding, dissociating, budding, and coalescing to create new Kin members just as they always had. And the darters would feast on their weakest.

Unless the flow of food was permanently ended, the Symmetry completely broken. Then the Kin and the darters alike would starve.

The storm was growing stronger. Leviathan's eye parts could see the faint flicker of lightning far off. Faintly, faintly Leviathan's sensor parts reported that there were indeed currents of food swirling toward the storm's churning vortex.

Stationed out on the perimeter of the Kin, Leviathan kept its sensory parts keenly on guard against approaching darters. But it saw nothing. The sea was empty of their threat. Still, Leviathan felt uneasy. They were out there, it knew. Out beyond the range of our sensors, Leviathan reasoned, the darters are waiting for one of us to break away and begin dissociating. Alone.

How close to the storm will we go? Leviathan drew the image of that question on its flank, its luminescent members lighting up in response to the directions from its central brain. The image flickered from leviathan to leviathan, inward toward the core of their flotilla, where the Elders made their stately way.

As it waited for an answer, Leviathan thought again that the Kin who were about to dissociate should be at the Kin's center, protected from the darters. Yet the Elders regarded his suggestion with abhorrence. Do not attempt to change what has always been, they pictured in harsh blue images. Accept what must always be.

Accept. Leviathan had no choice but to accept the will of the Elders. But it thought that when the time came, many, many buddings from now, when Leviathan itself became an Elder, it would change these ancient ways. It would protect the members who now had to face the darters alone. It would make the Kin safer and better.

For now, though, Leviathan had to accept the Elders' decision. For now—

Leviathan's sensor members flashed a shrill warning. Darters! A huge pack of them out there, just on the edge of detection. Moving in the same direction as the Kin, but angling so that they were cutting across the feeble flow of food that was being sucked toward the growing storm.

The darters were placing themselves between the Kin and the needed current of food. This was something new. Leviathan had never seen such a maneuver in all the images the Elders had shown.

The darters were waiting to ambush the Kin. Not satisfied with attacking lone members, they were maneuvering to cut off the Kin from their food.

This was something new. And dangerous.

OBSERVATION BLISTER

As they left Dr. Pohan's office, Deirdre looked up at the cyborg and said, "Thank you so much, Dorn."

"*De nada*," he said, then translated: "It's nothing."

"It means a lot to me."

He said nothing.

She felt almost uncomfortable walking beside him along the passageway. She was not accustomed to having to look up at people, and he was almost ten centimeters taller than she, his shoulders broad, his torso like the thick body of a miner's digging torch. He's half metal, she kept thinking to herself. Half of his body is a machine.

At last she said, "You didn't ask what my medical problem is."

"Does it matter?" he asked. "You need my help. It's simple enough for me to give it."

They passed a pair of crewmen in gray fatigues coming down the passageway from the other direction. Both men smiled at Deirdre and glanced furtively at Dorn as they squeezed past the cyborg.

Deirdre wondered, "What happened to you when you tried to make contact with the dolphins?"

For several paces Dorn said nothing.

"I'm sorry," Deirdre said. "I shouldn't pry."

"I saw my own past," he said, his voice a low rumble.

"Your past? That made you go berserk like that?"

His voice heavy with misery, Dorn replied, "It was like all my nightmares at once."

Deirdre didn't know how to respond to that.

They walked on for a few more moments, then Dorn asked her, "Did you look up Dorik Harbin's dossier last night?"

Nodding, Deirdre replied, "Yes, I did."

"So you know who I was."

She thought about that for a moment, then said, "But who are you now?"

He looked down at her as they paced along the passageway.

"I mean," Deirdre explained, "the dossier stopped with the verdict at your trial. Dr. Yeager says you're some kind of priest. And when did you . . ." She couldn't finish the sentence.

"When did I disfigure myself? When did I become a cyborg?"

Deirdre nodded again. Another group of people were coming down the corridor toward them, five passengers, from the way they were dressed.

Dorn waited for them to pass, then suggested, "We need some privacy to discuss this without being interrupted."

Or overheard, Deirdre added silently.

She followed him as he headed for the elevator. He expects me to go to his quarters? she wondered.

But once they got into the elevator Dorn called out, "Observation blister." Turning to Deirdre, he said, "We should be able to speak freely there."

Australia's observation blister was a glassteel ring that ran around the circumference of the ship's outer hull. It was an adornment for passengers, where they could look out on the universe from the safety of the ship. To the surprise of the shipping company's management, hardly any passengers took advantage of the facility during midtransit. Despite highly advertised lectures and even cocktail parties hosted by the captain, most passengers had little interest in observing the all-engulfing black emptiness of the universe. It made them uneasy, even frightened. Only when the ship was approaching planetfall did passengers come to gape at the world they were approaching.

Dorn ushered Deirdre through one of the hatches that lined the circular passageway between the elevators and the blister. She stepped through and gasped.

As Dorn closed the hatch, Deirdre suddenly felt as if she were standing in space. The lights went out automatically when the hatch shut and there was nothing between her and the infinite universe but the transparent curving bubble of glassteel. Her knees went weak.

So many stars! The universe was filled with hard unblinking points of light: red, blue, yellow, it was overwhelming. Clouds of stars, swirls of stars, endless boundless teeming stars that sprinkled the blackness of space with color and beauty. Back at *Chrysalis II* they had observation ports, but nothing like this. This is like being outside!

Dorn heard her gasping breath. "Are you all right?"

"I . . ." Deirdre had to consciously remind herself that she was perfectly safe, standing on a glassteel deck, warm and protected from the vacuum out there that stretched to infinity. "I think so," she half whispered.

"I'm sorry," Dorn said softly. "I forgot how overwhelming it can be the first time. I've spent much of my life in spacecraft. This dark forever is like home to me."

She turned toward him, saw the starlight glinting off the etched metal side of his face.

"The Sun is behind us," Dorn began to explain, "on the other side of the ship. We're in shadow here. That's why you can see so much without the Sun's glare cutting down visibility."

"It's . . . it's the most awesome thing I've ever seen."

"The universe," Dorn said, as solemnly as if praying. "Infinity."

For several minutes Dorn pointed out the brighter stars for her, identified blue-hot Rigel and the sullen red of Betelgeuse.

At last she interrupted him. "You said we could talk in private here."

"Yes," he said, nodding gravely. "The blister goes all the way around the ship, but it's divided into compartments that are sound-proof." He hesitated. "I believe the ship's management thought couples might enjoy romantic liaisons here."

Making it under the stars, Deirdre thought. Not a bad idea, once you got accustomed to having all those unblinking eyes watching you.

"You asked me when I became a cyborg," Dorn said.

"I don't want to pry," said Deirdre. "If it's painful for you—"

"Pain is part of life. If we're going to work together at the Jupiter station, you deserve to know about me."

So he told her. Told her of his life as a mercenary soldier during the Asteroid Wars. How the corporation he worked for supplied their mercenaries with performance-enhancing drugs. How he had murdered a woman who loved him in a blaze of narcotic-driven jealous fury. How he destroyed the old *Chrysalis* habitat under the battle frenzy that the drugs induced. How he had held a minigrenade to his chest once his mind cleared and he realized what he had done.

"You tried to commit suicide?" Deirdre asked.

In the starlit shadows Dorn replied evenly, "I wasn't permitted to die. The corporations had invested too much in me. And besides, their medical technicians saw me as an interesting problem. So I was saved. I was rebuilt."

"That's how you became a cyborg."

"Yes. Not every scientist works for the benefit of humankind. Some of them—many of them, I think—work to solve problems that intrigue them. Work to achieve things no one else has achieved before them."

Deirdre remembered a quotation from her history classes. The physicist J. Robert Oppenheimer had said, "When you see something that is technically sweet, you go ahead and do it and you argue about what to do about it only after you have had your technical success."

DORN'S TRANSFORMATION

You became a priest?" Deirdre asked.

For a heartbeat Dorn remained silent. Then, "I had a life-altering experience. I encountered . . . an artifact. A work of an alien intelligence."

"In the Belt?" Deirdre jumped at his revelation. "The rumors are true? About an alien artifact in one of the asteroids?"

"True," said Dorn. "There is an alien artifact buried inside a small, stony asteroid. The rock is the property of Humphries Space Systems, Incorporated. I was still an employee of HSS when it was discovered. I was assigned to guard the asteroid and make certain that no one saw the alien artifact.

"But I saw it. Every day, for weeks. It changed me."

"It's really true?" Deirdre marveled.

"Really true. However, Martin Humphries guards the asteroid jealously. At first he wanted to keep it for himself alone. When he flew out to see it, though, the artifact drove him insane. He collapsed, jibbering, helpless."

Dorn stopped, as if the memories he was recalling were too painful to continue. But before Deirdre could think of anything to say, he resumed.

"Humphries recovered, eventually. But he would allow no one to see the artifact. And he wanted to eliminate those who saw his collapse, who heard his weeping, inconsolable pleadings."

"He wanted to kill you?"

"He tried. But I, too, had seen the artifact. Experiencing it changed my life. I stopped being Dorik Harbin, mercenary warrior. I became Dorn. A priest. I began to try to atone for my former life."

"Atone? How?"

"By finding the bodies of the mercenaries killed in the Asteroid Wars. Finding them and giving them proper death rites."

"You did this?"

"For years. Wandering through the Belt, finding the dead who had been left to drift alone endlessly in space. This I did, together with the woman you saw at my trial."

"My father exiled you."

Almost smiling in the dim starlight, Dorn said, "He wanted to execute me. He wanted to kill me with his own hands. He settled for exile. I was recruited by the scientists of the Jupiter station. They've been testing me at Selene University for the past two years, to see if I can help them make deep dives into the Jovian ocean."

"And here we are," Deirdre said, trying to make it sound light, "on our way to Jupiter."

"Yes."

"You've lived quite a life," she said. It sounded pathetically inane, she knew.

With a slight shake of his head, Dorn confessed, "But now I have no purpose for living. I've found all the dead from the Wars that I could. That doesn't atone for all those I killed."

"You're working for the scientists now."

"Yes, for the scientists. But serving their purposes doesn't give me any purpose to my life. I'm an empty shell, Deirdre. I have nothing to live for."

She reached out and touched the human side of his face. "You've gone through so much. You'll find some reason for living. Maybe at Station *Gold*. Maybe you'll find your true purpose there."

"Maybe," he echoed. It sounded hollow to Deirdre.

"Well," she said, "thanks for telling me about yourself. I hope you find what you're looking for."

She started for the hatch, but Dorn put up his metallic hand, stopping her.

"This conversation began," he said, "with you saying that I didn't ask what your medical problem is. May I ask you now?"

She bit her lip, hesitating. *He has a right to know*, Deirdre told herself. He's willing to give you his blood to help you. He has a right to know the truth.

"I have rabies," she said, so softly she could barely hear her own words.

"Rabies." Dorn appeared unshaken by the news. Then he asked, "I didn't realize that animals are kept in *Chrysalis II*."

"They're not," said Deirdre. "No pets. No meat animals. We get protein from soy substitutes and aquaculture."

"Then how did you contract rabies? It comes from being bitten or scratched by a rabid animal, doesn't it?"

Nodding, she answered, "That's what makes it so peculiar. Dr. Pohan hasn't been able to figure it out."

"Is the doctor certain that it's rabies? It seems totally unlikely."

She shrugged. "He's certain. The virus showed up in the blood sample he took."

Dorn looked out at the endless stars for several silent moments. At last he said to Deirdre, "He took a sample of your blood."

"Yes. He did it for all the passengers. Didn't he take a sample of your blood?"

"Weeks ago, just after I boarded at Selene."

"He must have taken samples from everybody."

"He extracted your blood with a hypodermic syringe?" Dorn asked.

"How else?"

"And you haven't been bitten or scratched by an animal before you boarded this ship?"

A little impatiently, she replied, "I told you, Dorn, there aren't any animals in *Chrysalis II* to bite or scratch me!"

"Then the only time your skin has been punctured is when the ship's doctor took your blood."

"Yes . . ." She finally saw where he was heading. Her eyes widening, Deirdre asked, "An infected needle?"

"How would it get infected with rabies here aboard the ship?"

"Dr. Pohan said there was a rabies case on the way out from the Earth/Moon system. A fatality."

Dorn shook his head slowly. "I've been aboard this ship since it left lunar orbit. As far as I know, none of the passengers who came aboard from Earth or Selene have died."

Deirdre felt confused. "He lied to me?"

"He not only lied to you," said Dorn. "He infected you with rabies."

Max Yeager looked around the compartment with narrowed eyes as Corvus ushered him into his quarters.

"Cripes, this place looks like the back room of an electronics lab. Where the hell do you sleep?"

Corvus waved toward the bed, which was covered with several laptops, a scattering of headsets, thumb-sized hard drives, diagnostic tools, and other gadgets. Two more laptops sat open on the compartment's tiny desk, their screens glowing, and a half-dozen more rollup screens were pasted to the bulkheads. The compartment's built-in wall screen showed a garishly colored image of what looked to Yeager like a canary yellow head of cauliflower. Or maybe a human brain. Tiny numbers pulsed on the imagery.

"What're you doing in here?" Yeager demanded. Inwardly he felt almost insulted at the cluttered, chaotic state of Corvus's room. You can't get any work done in such a turmoil, he thought. I'll bet he can't even find the toilet in this mess.

Scratching at his thick thatch of red hair, Corvus said goodnaturedly, "I'm trying to figure out a way to reproduce the visual imagery that Dee saw when she was in contact with Baby."

"Aha," said Yeager.

"Aha what?" Andy asked. "Aha, like you know how to do it, or aha, you think it's impossible."

Frowning slightly, Yeager said, "Aha, like now I understand what all these screens are showing." He jabbed a finger at the rollups on the bulkheads. "Brain scans."

"Right. The one on the wall screen is Baby's brain."

"And what are all these numbers blinking on top of the imagery?"

"Color identifiers," said Corvus. "I'm color blind, so I use the numbers to tell me what the colors are."

"Uh-huh." Yeager swung his gaze back and forth among the screens. "So this one is the dolphin's brain . . ."

"And all these," Corvus waved a hand, "are Dee's—Deirdre's brain." He stepped to the desk and sat on its springy little chair.

Yeager noticed that his feet were bare. He probably can't find his shoes, the engineer thought.

Pointing to the two adjacent laptops, Corvus explained, "And these two show Dee's brain activity in real time when she was connected with Baby."

Yeager bent over Andy's shoulder and peered at the two screens. He couldn't help worrying that the pair of laptops were too big for the compartment's desk. If he's not careful he's going to wind up with one of them on the floor, the engineer thought. Maybe both of them.

"See?" Corvus was saying. "When an area in one of their brains lights up, the other brain lights up, too."

"Not the same area," Yeager muttered.

"Well, they're not the same brains. Not the same species. One's a dolphin and the other's a human being."

"So how do you know they're connected?"

"They light up at the same time. And even though the regions of the brain showing activity aren't exactly the same, they're pretty darned close. I mean, we've made functional maps of human and dolphin brains for years. They're both lighting up in the same functional area."

Yeager grunted, "Huh?"

Looking slightly disappointed, Corvus explained, "This area here in Dee's brain is her visual cortex. The dolphin's visual cortex is here." Andy tapped the laptop's screen hard enough to make it wobble on the edge of the desk.

"They both light up at the same time," Yeager realized.

"Right! That means they're both seeing the same thing at the same time!"

Yeager rubbed his stubbly jaw thoughtfully. "I don't know if you could say that, Andy. I don't think you've got enough evidence to make that stick."

"That's why I called you. Can you help me?"

"Me? I'm not a neurotechnician."

"But you've got a lot of experience with sensors and transducers. I looked up your dossier, you know."

Yeager almost smiled. "My experience is with electronics and optronics equipment, not brains. There are lots of people who know a helluva lot more about this than I do."

"Is there anybody on the team with you that can help me?" Corvus's voice was almost pleading.

"What do you want to do?"

"I want to take these brain scans and convert them into visual imagery. I want to put what Baby and Dee were seeing into images that you and I can see."

Yeager gave out a low whistle. "That's a tall order, pal. I don't know if anybody knows how to do that."

"Well, then we'll be the first!"

Shaking his head, Yeager said, "You want to take the electrical impulses flickering through a brain and turn them into visual pictures?"

"Right!" Corvus bobbed his head up and down so hard his hair flopped down over his forehead. Pawing at it, he explained, "The brain receives electrical impulses along the nerve path from the retinas of the eyes. It transmutes those impulses into visual imagery. Pictures. Why can't we do that with the data we've got from their brain scans?"

Yeager looked around for a place to sit down. There was none. The bed was covered with gadgetry. The other chairs in the compartment were also loaded with junk. Corvus himself was sitting on the only available chair.

Looking down at Andy, Yeager said, "You're dealing with the difference between the brain and the mind."

Corvus nodded.

"We can scan the electrical activity of the brain. Been doing that for more than a century. But how those pulses get translated into pictures is something that the human mind does, and we don't have any idea of how that works."

"Not just the human mind," Corvus maintained. "The dolphins see pictures in their heads, too."

"You have any hard data to back up that statement?" Yeager demanded.

"Behavioral data."

Shaking his head, the engineer objected, "Not good enough, friend. You don't know what goes on in a dolphin's mind. You'll probably never know."

Almost defensively, Corvus said, "Well, that's what I want to find out. We've got to figure out a way to do it. How can we ever make any meaningful contact with the leviathans if we can't even make real contact with a species from our own planet?"

Yeager shook his head sadly. "Beats me, Andy. Beats the hell out of me."

infected you?" Dr. Pohan slowly rose from behind his desk, like a cloud of smoke boiling up. "You accuse me of deliberately infecting you?"

"Not deliberately, perhaps," Deirdre said placatingly.

Dorn, sitting beside her, was unimpressed with the doctor's ire. "How else could she be infected, except by the needle you injected into her arm? Her skin hasn't been broken by anything else."

Visibly trembling, the doctor hissed, "This accusation is monstrous. Outrageous!"

Deirdre could see that Dr. Pohan's face had turned beet red. His mustache fairly quivered with fury.

"You told me," she said, in a low, calm voice, "that another passenger had died on the trip between Selene and *Chrysalis II.*"

Slowly settling back in his chair, Dr. Pohan glared at the two of them. Finally he nodded curtly. "That is true."

"I've been aboard this ship since it left lunar orbit," Dorn said. "I've heard nothing about a passenger dying."

His voice dripping with scorn, Dr. Pohan said, "Do you think that we would *advertise* the death of a passenger? Our executives in Selene ordered us to keep it as quiet as possible, while we and they investigate the circumstances of the unfortunate woman's death."

Unmoved, Dorn said, "May we see her file?"

"To what purpose?"

"To prove to ourselves that she existed."

Deirdre expected the doctor to explode again. Instead, he simply glared at Dorn for a long, fuming moment. Then he snapped, "Computer. Display file of Frieda Nordstrum."

The screen on the bulkhead to one side of Dr. Pohan's desk glowed to life. It showed an ID image of a blond, ruddy-faced woman. Deirdre thought she looked at least twenty years older than herself, although with modern rejuvenation therapies it was difficult to guess ages. The dossier accompanying the image said that she was a Norwegian microbiologist, aged thirty-eight, a graduate of Uppsala University in Sweden. She had left her most recent post at Selene University, on the Moon, to accept a position on the research staff at station *Thomas Gold*, in Jupiter orbit.

"And she died?" Deirdre asked.

"Aboard this ship," said Dr. Pohan. "Under my care."

"Of rabies."

The doctor glowered at Deirdre, but called out, "Computer, display medical record of Frieda Nordstrum."

The dossier disappeared in an eyeblink, replaced by a brief medical record, which ended in a death certificate. Deirdre supposed that the signature scrawled at its bottom was Dr. Pohan's.

"Are you satisfied now?" Dr. Pohan growled.

Dorn said nothing, but Deirdre got to her feet as she apologized, "I'm sorry we bothered you, Doctor. It's just that . . . none of this makes sense!"

Dr. Pohan rose also. In a gentler tone he said, "I know it must be very frightening to you. But we will have your condition under control within the next twenty-four hours."

Under control doesn't mean cured, Deirdre thought.

Standing up beside her, Dorn said, "This still doesn't explain how Ms. Ambrose contracted rabies."

The doctor's face flushed momentarily, but he brought himself under control with an obvious effort. "I have no explanation as yet," he said stiffly. "It seems clear that Dr. Nordstrum was infected while visiting Earth and carried the infection back to Selene where she boarded this ship before her illness was detected."

Turning toward Deirdre, Dorn began, "But how—"

"How Ms. Ambrose was infected is under investigation, intense investigation. Perhaps the virus has found a new pathway between one victim and another. A new vector. I am studying that possibility, with consultation by the corporation's medical staff in Selene."

"I see," said Dorn.

Leaning the knuckles of both hands on his desktop, Dr. Pohan said firmly, "I can assure you, I do not appreciate being accused of infecting my patient, either accidentally or deliberately."

"I understand," Deirdre said. With that, she and Dorn left the doctor's office.

Once outside the infirmary, in the passageway leading to the elevators, Deirdre said, "He's doing his best to track down the way the virus infected me."

Dorn seemed unimpressed. "Perhaps he sees a chance to make an important discovery, tracking down a new vector for the rabies virus. It could be a considerable feather in his cap."

"You think that's what he's after?"

"It could be a considerable feather in his cap," Dorn repeated.

Deirdre broke into a giggle. "He won't get any feathers in his cap if he doesn't learn how to control his anger. I thought he'd have a stroke!"

Nodding thoughtfully, Dorn agreed, "He did get very incensed, didn't he?"

"Well, we did accuse him of deliberately infecting me. I don't blame him for getting furious."

"Methinks," Dorn muttered, "that he doth protest too much."

Katherine Westfall did not like having this excitable little man in her sitting room, but she felt that it was better to see him face-to-face rather than communicate over the ship's phone system. Phone conversations are supposed to be private, she knew, but they go through the ship's communications system and systems can always be tapped.

Dr. Pohan could not sit still. Katherine had offered him a glass of wine, even poured him a long-stemmed goblet of beautiful Sancerre with her own hand, but the doctor hardly took a sip before he bounced to his feet and began pacing across the thick carpeting.

"They know!" he said, mopping his bald pate with one hand while his other nearly spilled the wine, it was shaking so badly.

"They know nothing," Westfall said calmly.

"But they suspect! They accused me of infecting her! In my own office! She and that lumbering cyborg, they realize that the only way she could be infected was by the needle I used to take her blood sample."

He looks ridiculous, she thought, a stubby little bald man with that ludicrous mustache, his clothes all wrinkled and sweaty. Struggling inwardly to hide her disdain, Westfall replied, "You showed them the Nordstrum dossier?"

Dr. Pohan stopped his pacing. "Yes. That seemed to placate them. For the moment."

With an unruffled smile, Westfall said, "There you are. Crisis resolved."

"Is it?" Dr. Pohan returned to the sculpted chair facing Westfall's but stopped short of sitting in it. "How long do you think it will take them to think of checking with Selene University? How long before they find that Frieda Nordstrum never suffered from an animal bite, that she did not contract rabies until she came aboard this ship! How long before they discover that the woman died of a genetically engineered mutation of the virus!"

Katherine took a sip of her wine as she thought about that. Putting the stemmed glass down on the little table beside her chair, she said, "I can see to it that the university's personnel files are unavailable for their scrutiny. Privacy laws and all that. The ship's files, as well. They'll never be able to find that she wasn't infected while visiting Earth, that she wasn't carrying the virus in her when she came aboard this vessel."

The doctor wagged his head. "We committed murder!"

"You conducted an experiment," Westfall countered. "The experimental subject died. It happens all the time. Scientists are always doing things like that."

Dr. Pohan looked horrified. "But you . . . you told me . . . you *ordered* me . . ."

With the sincerest smile she could generate, Katherine Westfall said reassuringly, "As long as you keep Ms. Ambrose's condition under control she will be satisfied. You've told her that the medical staff at *Gold* has the facilities to cure her?"

"Yes."

"Good. Let her continue to think that. Once we get to Jupiter she'll find out differently, but by then she'll no longer be your problem."

The doctor stared at her perplexedly. For several heartbeats he said nothing. Then, "May I ask . . . why are you doing this? Why did you have me infect her? After all, rabies can be dangerous. . . ."

Smiling truly now, Katherine Westfall said, "Not as dangerous as curiosity, Doctor."

Dr. Pohan's eyes went wide. *He understands my meaning,* Westfall saw. *He understands me perfectly.*

Max Yeager was glad to be out of Andy's junkyard of a compartment. The two men were in the dining room, munching on soymeat patties as they argued about Corvus's hopes.

"The human mind is the transducer," Yeager was saying, waving a forkful of salad in midair. "It takes the electrical impulses from the eyes and makes pictures out of them."

Corvus shook his head. "But how? How does it work? How can the brain turn electrical impulses into visual imagery?"

"We do it with display screens," Yeager mused. "Electrons paint pictures on the screens."

"Is that how it's done in the visual cortex?"

"How would I know?"

Corvus began to reply, but as he looked up from his dinner plate he saw Deirdre and Dorn heading toward their table.

Once they were seated and had spoken their dinner orders to the robot that had immediately rolled up to the table, Corvus and Yeager fell into their argument again.

"It can't be done," Yeager insisted.

"You mean you don't know how to do it," said Corvus.

"Same thing," Yeager rejoined, with a knowing grin. "If I don't know how to do it, nobody knows how to do it."

"Do what?" Dorn asked.

"Translate the electrical activity in Dee's brain into visual imagery while she's in contact with Baby," Corvus explained.

The argument between the two men swirled on. It wasn't until their desserts were served that Deirdre said, "Maybe we can go around the problem."

"Go around it?" Corvus and Yeager asked in unison.

Deirdre hesitated a moment. "This may be silly . . ."

"Go ahead," said Corvus. "We're open to any and all ideas."

"Well, why don't I just tell you what I'm seeing while I'm in contact with Baby?"

Dorn objected, "But you seemed to be sleeping when you made contact with the dolphin."

"If I could stay awake," Deirdre said, "I could tell you what I'm seeing while you're recording my brain wave patterns. That would help, wouldn't it?"

"It sure would!" Andy said.

"But you weren't awake," Yeager objected. "Not fully conscious, anyway."

Deirdre said, "Well, that was just my first experience with the equipment. Maybe with practice I could stay conscious, aware."

"Come to think of it," Corvus said, "I stayed conscious when I was in contact with the elephant, back Earthside."

Yeager objected, "But here with the dolphins you both went into a trance."

"Yeah, but that might just be an initiation reaction."

"You think with practice you could stay awake?" Yeager asked, looking from Corvus to Deirdre and back again.

Corvus shrugged. "It's worth a try."

With a nod, Yeager agreed. "What've we got to lose?"

Katherine Westfall felt relieved when Dr. Pohan finally left her quarters. *He's on the verge of babbling it all out to that Ambrose woman and her friend,* she thought. *But I can't get rid of him, it would look too suspicious.*

No, she told herself as she got up from her chair and headed for the bedroom, *I'll have to keep bucking him up and showing him that Deirdre Ambrose is no threat to him. As long as he keeps her condition under control, she'll be satisfied. She won't snoop any farther. Even if she tries to contact Selene to check on Dr. Nordstrum's medical file, all she'll get is a polite refusal to show faculty records.*

Then she got a better idea. *Freeze her! Tell her the treatment isn't working and she'll have to be frozen until we reach Jupiter and the research station. It would only be for a little more than a week. That would keep her from snooping around and satisfy Pohan that he's not under any threat from her.*

Nodding happily as she headed for her closet, Westfall told herself, *Keep her frozen and we'll be all right until we reach the* Gold *station. Once we're there, I'll have young Ms. Ambrose revived and totally under my control.*

Katherine Westfall smiled at that thought as she began to dress for her dinner with Captain Guerra.

DOLPHIN TANK

Andy Corvus stood disconsolately over Deirdre, who appeared to be dozing as she sat on Andy's big aluminum case, the optronics circlet over her auburn hair. Her eyes were closed, her breathing slow and regular, her hands relaxed in her lap.

Standing beside Corvus, Dorn said, "Has she made contact again?"

Andy said nothing, but pointed to the two laptop screens on the deck at Deirdre's feet. Each showed an image of a brain: Deirdre's and the dolphin Baby's. Each image flickered with electrical activity, in close unison.

"Looks that way," Corvus said forlornly.

"That's good, then," said Dorn.

With a shrug of his shoulders that seemed to flex his entire arms and his whole back, Corvus replied, "She can't seem to stay conscious while she's in contact."

Dorn nodded.

"That means she can't tell us what she's seeing, what she's experiencing. Not in real time."

"She'll tell us when she regains consciousness."

Shaking his head, Corvus murmured, "Not good enough. All we'll have is anecdotal evidence. She could be making up the whole thing."

"You don't believe her?" Dorn challenged, a hint of truculence in his voice.

"I believe her, but the scientific community's going to want more than her unsubstantiated word. If she could stay awake and give us a real-time narrative, then we could compare her time line with her brain activity and Baby's. That would be real proof that she's in contact with the dolphin."

Dorn rubbed the flesh side of his jaw. "Andy, are you interested in making meaningful contact with the dolphins or in publishing a paper that will enhance your scientific reputation?"

"Both," Corvus answered without a flicker of hesitation.

"You may have to settle for just the one of them."

"You don't understand," Corvus said earnestly. "Science depends on publishing your results so others can duplicate them. Every observation, every measurement, every claim has to be subject to test. You publish something new and the rest of the community tries to duplicate what you've done. If they can get the same results you did, your work becomes an accepted part of science. If they can't, if they don't get the same results that you reported, your work goes into the trash bin."

"But the important thing," Dorn insisted, "is that she is making meaningful contact with the dolphin. Which means your equipment might allow you to make meaningful contact with the leviathans, once we reach Jupiter."

"The important thing," Corvus replied, "is that the scientific community believes that I've done it. I can spend the rest of my life chatting with those giant whales on Jupiter, but if the scientific community doesn't believe I've done it, what good is it?"

"What good is it to who? You personally? The scientific community? The human race in general?"

Corvus rolled his eyes heavenward. "Look, Dorn, my work won't do the human race any good at all if the scientific community says it's doggie doo."

For an instant Dorn said nothing. Then he broke into a deep, chuckling laugh. "Doggie doo? Is that the technical name for it?"

Corvus grinned back at him sheepishly. "You know what I mean."

At that moment, both laptops chimed and they turned to look down at Deirdre. She stirred, her eyelids fluttered, then she opened her eyes fully. Corvus realized for the first time that there were glints of amber in her light brown eyes. Beautiful eyes, he thought.

"I fell asleep," Deirdre said apologetically.

"That's all right," said Dorn, extending his human hand to help her to her feet.

"You made contact again?" Corvus asked.

Deirdre nodded absently. "Baby's mother told us a story."

"What?"

"A story?"

"It was kind of strange," Deirdre said. "Not like a story so much as a . . . a prediction, I guess you'd call it. Maybe a warning."

Swimming effortlessly in the tank, Deirdre heard Mother's clicks and whistles as if the dolphin were talking to her.

It seems safe and easy now, Mother was saying, in this water where there are no sharks to threaten us and the fish are always close to our teeth.

But sometime we may find our way out to the true waters again, the waters where our mothers and fathers of old swam and hunted. Waters that are so deep they have no bottom. Waters that have treacherous currents that can carry you far, far away.

The sharks are always there, waiting for a lone dolphin with their sharp teeth. They are always hungry. They never rest.

Baby flipped her tail and rose gracefully to the surface for a gulp of air. Mother followed her while Father swam below.

You must be ready to face the sharks. Ready to swim in the big water. Ready to hunt. Now the fish have nowhere to hide from us. But in the big water the fish can run far, far away.

How big is the big water? Baby asked.

A hundred feedings would cover only a small part of it, Mother replied.

Have you seen this?

Mother said, I have seen bigger water than we are in now, but no, I have not swum in the truly big water. My mother, and her mother, and their mother's mothers have told about it.

Schools of fish that blot out the light, Baby said.

Yes, and sharks that eat baby dolphins.

Baby said, Sharks are bad.

Very bad, Mother agreed. My sister lived in the big water long ago. She was attacked by sharks. The others of the family tried to drive the sharks away but we were too late. They killed her.

Sharks are bad, Baby repeated.

Very bad. Be on your guard against them.

But there are no sharks in this water.

Not now. But they could come to this water. And they like to eat nothing better than baby dolphins.

"The mother was warning Baby about sharks?" Corvus asked.

"Yes," said Deirdre. "I don't think Baby believed her. At least, I didn't feel any sense of fear in Baby."

Dorn said, "Perhaps you could check the mother's history and see if she had a sister who was attacked by sharks. That could verify Deirdre's contact, couldn't it?"

Andy grinned brightly. "It might at that."

I t was two days later when Deirdre sat on the medical couch in the infirmary waiting for her daily injection from Dr. Pohan, still wondering about how she might have contracted rabies.

Dr. Nordstrum was from Earth, she thought. She worked at Selene, but she could've gone back to visit Earth easily enough; it's only a few hours' flight. Okay, she might have been bitten or scratched by some rabid animal. There's all sorts of wild animals on Earth. Twenty billion people and woods and grasslands and everyplace teeming with bacteria and feral beasts. Earth is like a zoo. A jungle.

But then she reasoned, Still, if Nordstrum was a microbiologist, wouldn't she have recognized the symptoms of rabies? Especially if she'd been bitten by an animal out in the wild. Wouldn't she have taken the precaution of the proper treatment instead of letting the infection grow in her body until it killed her?

Maybe she was so eager to get out to the research station at Jupiter that she ignored the early symptoms. They're not much. Just a rash, according to what the medical files say. Maybe some mood changes; irritability. Maybe that's what made her ignore—

The accordion-fold door to the treatment cubicle clattered open and Dr. Pohan stepped in. Deirdre saw that he wasn't smiling.

"Good morning," the doctor said flatly.

"I'm ready for my injection," said Deirdre, pushing up the sleeve of her blouse.

Dr. Pohan shook his head as he commanded, "Computer, display Deirdre Ambrose's record."

The screen on the partition beside the couch showed a single rising red curve against a grid of thin yellow lines.

"The treatment is not working," said Dr. Pohan. "At least, it is not working fast enough."

Deirdre stared at the curve. The virus is growing inside me, she realized. Multiplying.

"What should we do?" she asked, suddenly breathless with anxiety.

Tugging at one end of his mustache, the doctor replied curtly, "Freeze you."

"Freeze me? Cryonics?"

Dr. Pohan raised both his chubby little hands. "No, no, no. Not cryonics. Not liquid nitrogen. We only have to chill you down enough to slow your body functions sufficiently so that the disease will not grow while we're in transit to Jupiter. A matter of some nine days, that's all."

"Will I be conscious?"

Shaking his head slightly, the doctor said, "You will be asleep. Your metabolic functions will slow to less than one-third of their normal pace. You will be fed intravenously."

"I see," Deirdre said. But she had her doubts about the procedure.

Dr. Pohan put on a reassuring smile. "It will be like taking a long, refreshing nap. When you wake up you will be aboard station *Gold*, where the medical staff has much better facilities for your treatment."

"I see," Deirdre said again. But she still felt terribly unsure about the entire matter.

Pohan slid the door back again. Two white-smocked medical technicians were waiting there, both women, both short, slender Asians. The whole crew must be Asian, Deirdre thought idly as they wheeled up a gurney and helped her lie down on it.

Andy Corvus was in his quarters, reviewing Deirdre's last session with the dolphins. Max Yeager was sitting on one of the cluttered room's chairs; he had cleared the junk Corvus had deposited on the chair and simply dumped it on the thickly carpeted floor.

"So you can get Dee to narrate what she experienced and play her words alongside the DBS data," Yeager was saying.

"That's the best we can do," Corvus said despondently, "unless we can figure out how to visualize these nerve impulses."

"It's better than nothing," Yeager said.

"Not much," Corvus said.

"You've checked about the sister that was killed by sharks?"

Nodding, Corvus said, "They're checking the files back Earthside, but if it happened in the wild they probably won't have any record of it."

"Well, you've got Dee's narration."

"I don't see how—"

Corvus's pocketphone jingled. Yeager thought the tune it played sounded familiar, but he couldn't place it.

Andy flicked the phone open and pointed it at the compartment's wall screen. Deirdre's lovely face appeared. She looked distraught.

Without preamble she said, "Andy, I won't be able to work with the dolphins today."

"What's wrong?"

"I'm going to be frozen."

"Frozen?" Yeager and Corvus yelped together.

"To slow down the rabies," she said. "I'll be kept frozen until we reach Jupiter."

Leaping to his feet, Corvus shouted into the phone, "Don't let them touch you! I'll be right down there." Then his brows shot toward his scalp and he asked somewhat sheepishly, "Uh . . . where are you?"

Yeager went with Corvus. The two men hurried down the passageway toward the elevator, grasping the big aluminum crate between them. They put it down on the deck as they waited for the elevator.

Once the doors slid open they saw that Dorn was already in the cab.

"What's happening with Deirdre?" he asked as Corvus and Yeager tugged the box into the elevator with them.

They swiftly explained. "I can put her under with the DBS equipment," Corvus said, almost breathless with exertion and excitement. "I don't want them to freeze her if they don't have to."

Dorn thought about it as the elevator rose toward the infirmary's level. "The brain stimulator can put her into a comatose state," he said calmly, "but will it slow her metabolic rate?"

"Huh?" Corvus blinked. "No, it won't."

"That's why they want to freeze her, isn't it? To slow her metabolism so the disease doesn't spread inside her body."

Yeager looked digusted. "We didn't think of that."

"We just wanted to save her from being frozen," Corvus muttered.

Dorn shook his head. "Good intentions. But it won't help her."

The elevator stopped and the doors slid open. Dorn bent down and lifted the aluminum box in one hand while his two friends watched glumly.

INFIRMARY

Dr. Pohan was not happy to see the three of them as they burst into the infirmary, Dorn lugging the aluminum box under his prosthetic arm.

"This is a restricted area!" he snapped at them. "No visitors allowed."

Before either of the others could reply, Yeager said firmly, "We're friends of your patient and we're not leaving until we see her."

Pohan tried to glare at them, but he was too small to be intimidating. The three men towered over him. Yeager could see beads of perspiration break out on the doctor's bald pate.

"Very well," Pohan said, almost in a whisper. "Just for a moment."

The cubicle was small and felt chilly. It smelled of disinfectant and something with a flat, acrid tang to it. Deirdre was lying on what looked to Andy Corvus like a high-tech couch. Three sides of the bed were surrounded by blinking, beeping electronics gear. Off in the corner a white boxy refrigerator gave off a faint wisp of condensation. Two Asian women in white medical gowns and soft blue masks stood to one side, silent, their dark eyes appraising the trio of interlopers.

Deirdre smiled up at them. "Hi," she said groggily.

Dr. Pohan half whispered, "She has already been sedated. She will lose consciousness soon."

Awkwardly bending his lanky frame over Deirdre, Corvus asked, "How d'you feel, Dee?"

"Sleepy."

"Are you all right?" Yeager asked.

"Guess so."

Dorn stepped up, still grasping Corvus's equipment box in his prosthetic arm, and offered his human hand to her. She reached up and clasped it.

"We'll be waiting for you," he said. Then, looking sternly at Dr. Pohan, he added, "We'll be right here when you wake up."

Dierdre smiled at the three of them. "Good," she whispered. "Good."

She closed her eyes and her face relaxed into sleep.

Dr. Pohan hissed, "She is sedated. Now go! We have work to do."

Dorn glanced at his two companions, then said to the doctor, "One of us will be here in your infirmary at all times."

"Impossible!" snapped Pohan. "We have no waiting room, no facilities for—"

Yeager interrupted him. "At all times, like the man said. Even if we have to wait out in the passageway."

"Yeah," said Andy. "We'll keep watch over her night and day."

Dr. Pohan looked as if he might burst: red-faced, mustache quivering, scalp covered with beads of perspiration. But he admitted defeat. "Out in the passageway, then. Do not interfere with medical procedures."

"We wouldn't dream of it," said Yeager, straight-faced.

"We merely want to look in on our friend from time to time," said Dorn.

"Every day," Corvus emphasized.

LEVIATHAN

Leviathan's eye parts could see the darters clearly now, a huge swarm of them lurking upcurrent, between the Kin and the flow of food sifting down weakly from the cold abyss above.

Darters had never done this before, as far as Leviathan knew. They hunted in small packs and attacked individual members of the Kin, usually when one went off alone to dissociate and bud. But now the darters had grouped together and were apparently willing to attack the Kin en masse.

It flashed a question to the Elders, deep in the core of the Kin's formation. Have the darters ever shown this behavior before? Have they ever displayed such planning, such cunning?

Leviathan's question was relayed from one member of the Kin to another, inward toward the Elders. Leviathan watched the displays flashing yellow and green, briefly lighting the water, fainter and fainter as the message moved inward toward the Elders. Waiting, Leviathan saw that the darters were trying to cut the Kin off from the flow of food. If they wished to reach the downcurrent they would have to fight their way past the darters.

And if they failed to reach the flow of food, members of the Kin would begin to disintegrate involuntarily, hunger driving their primeval instinct to dissociate and reproduce. Then the darters would feast.

At last the Elders' answer flashed from the display of the member nearest Leviathan. None of the Elders could recall the darters showing such organization and forethought before. Not even the most senior of the Elders had seen anything like this, even from its first budding, long ages ago.

Something new! Despite the danger Leviathan thrilled at the concept. Something new and different was happening. Perhaps it would lead the Elders to change their ancient ways.

Another message flashed from the display cells of the member nearest Leviathan. The Elders have decided that the Kin will turn away from the darters.

Leave the food stream? Leviathan was stunned by the Elders' decision. Before it could question the command, though, the message from the Elders continued:

There are other food streams. The world is wide. There is no need to confront the darters over this one stream. We will find another.

As the huge spherical formation of the Kin slowly turned away, Leviathan wondered if the Elders knew what they were doing. The darters aren't going to remain where they are and let us get away from them. They will follow us and attack, sooner or later.

Leviathan flashed that message inward toward the Elders. In time their reply flared from the hide of the member nearest it. The darters would never dare to attack the assembled Kin. We would destroy them and they know it. Stay together and we will leave them far behind us while we find another food stream.

Leviathan wondered about that. The darters have changed their ways, but the Elders do not recognize it. Nor do they realize that we must change our ways, as well.

But decisions of the Elders must be obeyed, or the Symmetry will be damaged beyond repair. Reluctantly, Leviathan swam with the rest of the Kin, away from the food stream, away from the waiting darters.

Its eye parts saw that the darters turned, too, and began to follow the Kin on their new course. They could be patient, Leviathan thought, and wait until starvation forces us to begin dissociating.

II
JUPITER ORBIT:
RESEARCH STATION *GOLD*

We are not to imagine or suppose, but to discover,
what Nature does or may be made to do.

—Francis Bacon

RECOVERY

Deirdre was dreaming about the dolphins. She was a dolphin herself, swimming easily in a world filled with fish, sunlight streaming from above, water sparkling and warm.

"Ms. Ambrose? Can you hear me?"

The voice was gentle but annoying. She dived deeper into the sea, searching for the bottom where the tasty squid jetted among the rocks and coral formations.

"Ms. Ambrose. Open your eyes, please."

Go away, Deirdre thought. Leave me alone, won't you?

"Dee," a different voice called. "It's me, Andy. Can you wake up now?"

Andy. She pictured his boyish, grinning, slightly crooked face. Reluctantly Deirdre opened her eyes. It took an effort: Her lids were gummy, as if someone had pasted them together.

"Hey, that's good! How d'you feel?"

Blinking, she made out a fuzzy form leaning over her. A few more quick flickers of her lids and Andy Corvus's face came into focus. He was grinning in his lopsided, easygoing way.

"Hi! Welcome back."

Dorn's half-metal form came into view. "Welcome to station *Gold*."

"We're here?" Deirdre's throat felt parched, her voice was scratchy.

"We are always here," Dorn said gravely, "wherever that may be."

Andy said, "What he means is—"

"Never mind what he means." Max Yeager's burly form pushed into view, behind the other two. "How are you, gorgeous? How do you feel?"

Swiftly taking stock, she said shakily, "Okay, I guess." Then, stronger, "Fine, actually. I feel fine. Like I've had a good, long nap."

"Nine days, just about," said Corvus.

Deirdre pushed herself up on her elbows and the thin sheet covering her slipped away. With a shock, she realized she was wearing nothing. Corvus gulped as she grabbed the sheet and pulled it up to her chin. Dorn looked away. Yeager turned flame red.

A medical orderly, young and male, offered Deirdre a small cup of water. Clutching the sheet with one hand as she sat up on the bed, Deirdre accepted the water gratefully. The bed rose automatically to support her.

"We have fruit juices, if you prefer," said the orderly.

"This will do, thank you."

Glancing around as she drank, she saw that they were obviously no longer in *Australia*'s pocket-sized infirmary. This was an actual room, with walls instead of flimsy partitions and display screens that showed vivid swirls and streams of color. Those are Jupiter's cloud tops, Deirdre recognized. They must be real-time views.

"So we're on station *Gold*," she said.

"It's big," Corvus replied, grinning widely. "A lot bigger than the torch ship. Got lots of labs, workshops, even an auditorium where they hold conferences and such."

Yeager said, "The living quarters aren't as spiffy as *Australia*'s, but they're not all that bad."

"Wait until you go out to the observation deck," said Dorn, "and see Jupiter close-up. It's overwhelming."

Deirdre nodded. "You guys will have to show me around the station."

All three of them nodded happily.

Sitting in a virtual reality chamber, her face masked by molecule-thin goggles and a speaker bud in one ear, Katherine Westfall was getting a tour of *Gold* from the station's director, Grant Archer.

Archer had been at the arrival lounge's airlock to welcome her aboard the station.

"We'll take care of your staff, Mrs. Westfall," he had told her. "Once you're settled in, I'd like to give you a tour of the station."

Except for his silvery little beard and close-cropped hair, Grant Archer appeared deceptively youthful. Good shoulders, Westfall saw, and steady brown eyes that looked as if they could be stubborn.

"My people will see to my luggage," she had said. "Why don't we start the tour right now?"

Archer had smiled at her, a warm, personable smile. "That will be fine." He gestured down the passageway leading from the arrival lounge. "This way, then."

She was surprised when he led her to a small, dimly lit chamber, empty except for a high-backed chair standing in its center. It looked to her more like an interrogation room than anything else. Except that its walls were covered with gauges and dials and there was a bulky electronics console in one corner.

"The station's pretty big," he said, leading her to the chair. "We've learned that going through it in virtual reality is a lot easier than actually walking into every nook and cranny."

"Oh," she said as she sat in the chair. It felt cold, hard.

"I'll run the simulation myself," Archer said, going to the console. She had to turn around in the chair to see him leaning over the console's desk front and switching on the power. A row of green lights sprang up.

Archer opened a drawer and pulled out what looked to her like a limp cloth and a tiny blob of plastic.

"If you'll slip the viewing screens over your eyes and put the speaker into one of your ears, we'll be ready to go."

Wordlessly Katherine did as he asked. A pang of alarm surged through her. Suddenly she was alone in darkness. She couldn't see a thing.

But then she heard Archer's calm tenor voice: "Okay, everything's in the green. Here we go. Welcome to research station *Thomas Gold*."

olors swirled briefly before her eyes. They coalesced to show Katherine Westfall a view of the station as it orbited the giant planet Jupiter. She seemed to be hanging in space, yet she felt perfectly warm and comfortable; the solidity of the chair she was sitting upon felt reassuring.

She saw that the station consisted of three wheels, one on top of another, connected by a central spine. The outer skins of the wheels were studded with viewport bubbles, airlock hatches, antennas, sensors, and other paraphernalia that Katherine could not identify. As she drifted closer to the orbiting station she could see elevator cabs running up and down the central shaft. The entire station was spinning slowly. Of course, she told herself: That's how they get a feeling of gravity inside, even though it's only one-sixth of normal.

Archer's calm, steady voice sounded in her ear. "Station *Gold* originally was just one wheel, the one on top. We've named that one after the station's original director, Dr. Li Zhang Wo. The other two wheels are too new to have been named yet."

That's where most of his funding has been spent, Westfall said to herself. On construction.

Archer's voice droned on, "The first wheel is now devoted completely to research operations. We have teams working on the four big moons of Jupiter, the Galilean satellites . . ."

And Westfall saw a building on the ice surface of Europa, built like a fortress in that frozen wilderness. The sky was dark and empty except for a scattering of stars. Archer's voice explained that glare from sunlight reflecting off the ice blotted out all but the brightest of stars. The scene looked bleak and cold and somehow frightening to Katherine. She shuddered involuntarily.

"The surface structure has to be heavily insulated not only against the cold," Archer was explaining, "but also against the tremendous radiation flux from Jupiter's Van Allen belts."

At that, she saw the immense multihued planet climbing above Europa's ice-covered horizon, like a huge all-encompassing monster rising out of the black infinity. Jupiter was enormous, streaked with ribbons of color that eddied and swirled while she watched, suddenly gasping for breath.

"Of course," Archer's cool, unruffled voice continued, "the real work on Europa goes on beneath the ice mantle, in the buried ocean."

Katherine watched submersibles nosing through the dark waters, their lights illuminating a nightmare world of long stringy swaying things, dead white, tentacle-like arms waving in the currents. Sheets of rubbery expanses floated into the light and out again, as if trying to flee to the safety of darkness.

"There's plenty of life in the oceans of Europa, Ganymede, and Callisto. Most of it is comparable to terrestrial life-forms such as algae, plankton, kelp, and such. All the forms we've found so far are autotrophic, like green plants on Earth, although they don't use sunlight as their energy source. They produce their own foodstuffs using the heat energy from the moon's gravitational flexing as it orbits Jupiter."

On and on Archer explained. Though she knew perfectly well that she was sitting safe and warm in the VR chamber, Katherine Westfall felt jittery, almost frightened at the frigid and utterly alien worlds she was experiencing. Even when the scene shifted to Io with its colorful volcanic eruptions of bright molten sulfur, she felt cold and frighteningly alone.

Abruptly the scene changed again to show an ugly, irregular, pockmarked chunk of rock floating in the emptiness of space.

"Some of our researchers are studying the smaller moons of Jupiter, as well," Archer explained. "They've identified seventy-three of them so far. Most of them are asteroids or cometary bodies that have fallen into Jupiter's huge gravity well and been pulled into orbits around the planet."

The scene shifted to show Jupiter's colorful, churning cloud tops again.

"Occasionally an asteroidal or cometary body is pulled into Jupiter itself," Archer narrated. Westfall saw an oblong chunk of what looked like dirty ice tumbling through space, heading smack into the clouds, a trail of vapor boiling off it as it fell. "Less than two months ago Comet McDaniel-Lloyd was pulled into the planet."

The comet disappeared into the bright-colored clouds. Then the region brightened briefly with what might have been an explosion below the top of the cloud deck.

"The comet exploded with the force of thousands of megatons," Archer was saying, still as calm as a grandfather reading children's stories. "We are, of course, studying the effects the explosion has had on the local ecology."

Once more she saw the three-wheeled station. "The station's orbit is close enough to Jupiter so that we're below the most intense radiation of the Van Allen belts. Our second wheel is taken up by the commercial gas scooping operations that extract fusion fuels such as helium-three out of the upper layers of Jupiter's atmosphere and sell them to fusion power companies on Earth, the Moon, and elsewhere in the solar system. For more than twenty years, Jupiter has been the main energy source for the human race's fusion power systems."

Westfall saw a sleek, bullet-shaped vessel detach itself from the station's middle wheel and hurtle downward toward the colorful cloud tops of the giant planet.

"The scoopships are remotely controlled, of course, by personnel in the station." The view changed to show a team of men and women in sky blue coveralls sitting at a row of consoles.

"The fusion operation consists of remote operators, maintenance and service personnel, and the usual corps of administrators and directors," Archer was saying, as if reading from a prepared script.

"Without these scooping operations, fusion powerplants throughout the solar system would be deprived of the fuels they need to provide the human race's main source of clean, efficient energy."

The market for fusion fuels has leveled off, Westfall knew. The scientists don't want to face the fact that their budgets will have to level off, as well.

Now the scene before her eyes was from a camera mounted on one of the scoopships. She watched, suddenly fascinated, as the ship plunged toward those roiling, racing cloud tops.

"Wind speeds at the uppermost levels of the clouds routinely exceed five hundred kilometers per hour," Archer was saying, without a trace of emotion. "The clouds are composed mainly of diatomic hydrogen molecules and helium atoms: The fusionable isotopes such as helium-three comprise only a small fraction of the total."

The ship plunged into the clouds. Katherine watched, wide-eyed, as her view was enveloped in swirling multicolored mists.

"The colors, of course, are from minor constituents in the clouds: sulfur, oxygen, carbon, and such. The ships separate out those impurities in flight and carry back only the fusionable isotopes that are needed."

Abruptly, they broke out of the clouds. Katherine could again see the research station rotating slowly, almost majestically, as the scoopship returned with its cargo of fusion fuels.

She thought that her tour was finished, but instead the scene shifted to show the insides of a laboratory with serious-looking men and women working at some elaborate network of glass tubing while Archer's voice cheerfully began to explain what they were doing.

It seemed like hours, but at last the tour ended and Archer helped her remove the mask and earbud.

"That's about it," he said, smiling as he helped her to her feet. "You've seen just about our entire operation, in less than two hours."

Katherine Westfall nodded as she stood up. She felt tired, almost exhausted, her legs stiff. But then she realized that Archer's tour did not mention the studies of Jupiter itself, of the airborne life-forms in the giant planet's atmosphere, nor the creatures living in the huge globe-encompassing ocean. He didn't show me the station's third wheel at all, she said to herself. What's going on there? she wondered. What's he trying to hide from me?

INTELLECTUAL COUSINS

As they left the virtual reality chamber, Katherine Westfall told Grant Archer, "It's not necessary for you to escort me to my quarters."

"It's my pleasure," he said, smiling gently at her. "It's not every day that we have such a distinguished visitor."

She realized with some surprise that Archer was nearly a dozen centimeters taller than she. He doesn't look that big, she thought. He's built very compactly.

"I hope you'll have dinner this evening with my wife and me," Archer was saying as they walked along the passageway. "She's very anxious to meet you."

"Of course," said Westfall. Then, choosing her words with special care, she added, "And when do you show me the station's third wheel?"

His smile actually brightened. "Ah! That's where the team studying Jupiter itself is housed. Along with the dolphins and the engineering crew."

"Dolphins?"

"It's a holdover from Dr. Wo's original work," Archer said. "He had the idea that we could use dolphins to learn how to communicate with an alien species. He called them our intellectual cousins."

"But dolphins are from Earth."

"Yes, but they're quite a bit different from us. Intelligent, no doubt, but they live in such a different environment that they might as well be from a different world."

"Dolphins," Westfall repeated.

Chuckling, Archer told her, "At one point, Dr. Wo had a gorilla here. Enhanced her intelligence with a brain implant. It used to be a regular hazing ritual for new scooters to be introduced to her."

"Scoopers? The people who run the scoopships?"

"Scooters," Archer replied, pronouncing the word with deliberate precision. "It's a slang term for scientists."

"You actually keep a gorilla here?" Westfall could see the points she could score with the IAA council when she told them Archer was spending money on a gorilla in the Jupiter station.

"Oh, Sheena's long gone," he said. "She lived happily in a preserve back in Africa. Died several years ago, of natural causes."

Westfall felt disappointed. "But you still keep dolphins."

Nodding, "A new batch came in on the torch ship with you. We've been making some progress in translating their language. We can talk back and forth with them, to some extent."

"Can you?"

"It's slow, but we're making progress. The work goes back more than twenty years. Elaine O'Hara was one of the earliest researchers in that area."

Elaine O'Hara! Westfall could feel her eyes flare at the mention of her sister's name. She immediately clamped down on her emotions and said merely, "How interesting."

Deirdre slid back the door to her new quarters. Corvus, Dorn, and Yeager stood behind her, peeping through the doorway.

She stepped in and looked around. "Very nice," she murmured.

The compartment was adequately furnished with a comfortable-looking bed, a small couch and two smaller reclinable chairs, a desk with a spindly typist's chair, bureaus on either side of the bed, doors that Deirdre figured opened onto closets, and a lavatory. A built-in bar separated the minuscule kitchenette from the rest of the room. Deirdre's one travel bag rested on the bench at the foot of the bed.

"Not bad," Yeager said, striding past her to stand in the middle of the room. He turned a full circle, then grinned at Deirdre. "Much nicer than the cubbyhole they stuck me in."

Dorn said, "All our quarters are quite similar, almost identical.

This is a standard accommodation, according to the indoctrination video."

"You really watch that kind of stuff?" Yeager scoffed.

"Our rooms are further along this passageway," Corvus said. "We'll be neighbors."

Yeager went over to the bed and sat on it, bounced up and down a few times. "This is going to be fun."

Deirdre decided he'd gone far enough. "Off my bed, please, Max. Go find your own. I've got to unpack."

"I could help you." Yeager leered.

Dorn took a menacing step toward the engineer.

Corvus said, "I think we ought to get back to our own rooms and let Deirdre unpack." He waggled a finger at Yeager. "C'mon, Max. Let's go."

Yeager grumbled, "Spoilsports. You guys act like a couple of chaperones. I don't need a chaperone."

"No," said Dorn gravely. "You need a keeper."

They all laughed, Yeager the loudest, and filed out of the room, leaving Deirdre alone. For a long moment she smiled at the closed door, then remembered that she still carried the rabies virus inside her.

The medical staff here will take care of it, she told herself, wishing she really believed that.

As she began to unpack, a chime sounded. Looking up from her travel bag she saw that a yellow light was blinking beneath the smart screen on the wall above the desk.

A message, she thought. Maybe from Dad?

Still standing at the foot of the bed, she called out, "Computer. Display incoming message."

A man's face appeared on the wall screen. He looked fairly young, except for his skullcap of silver hair and trim little beard.

"Ms. Ambrose," he said, "I'm Grant Archer, director of this station. I'd like you to meet me in my office at sixteen hundred hours. You can find the way with your pocketphone. If you have any problems, please call me."

His image winked out, immediately replaced by the figure of a woman's face, sculpted, taut-skinned, her hair a perfect golden honey shade clipped like a helmet framing her countenance.

"Deirdre Ambrose, this is Katherine Westfall. Please come to my quarters. At once."

KATHERINE WESTFALL'S QUARTERS

Deirdre knew who Katherine Westfall was, and she saw that it was only 1410 hours: plenty of time to call on Mrs. Westfall and still make her appointment at Dr. Archer's office.

Why does she want to see me? she wondered as she swiftly changed into one of the few dresses she had brought with her, a short-sleeved flowered frock that her father had bought for her on her last birthday.

Mrs. Westfall sounded very imperative, Deirdre thought. She said please, but she also said *at once.* With a shrug of acceptance, Deirdre said to herself, Well, I suppose a woman in her position is used to having people jump when she snaps her fingers.

Using the map display of her pocketphone, Deirdre hurried along the station's main passageway. She knew it ran along the circumference of the station's wheel, but the structure was so large that the passageway seemed almost perfectly flat. It was only when she looked far ahead that she saw the deck curved upward and disappeared.

She was grateful that the station was at lunar gravity, like *Chrysalis II*, one-sixth of Earth's. After two weeks of a full *g*, it felt good to be back to normal again. Still, she appreciated the chance to exercise her body after lying asleep for more than a week.

At last she found the door modestly marked K. WESTFALL and tapped on it.

A lean, almost cadaverous young man in a dark tunic and slacks slid the door back. His head was shaved bald, his cheeks were hollow, gaunt.

"Ms. Ambrose," he said in a ghostly whisper, before Deirdre could speak a word.

"That's right."

The young man stepped aside to allow Deirdre to enter. The compartment looked more like an anteroom than living quarters. A desk, several sculpted plastic chairs, a display screen showing an image of a painting of a mother and child that Deirdre recognized from her art classes: a Renaissance master, she thought, Michelangelo or Titian or one of those. Then she remembered clearly: Raphael, the *Madonna del Granduca*. It had been in the Pitti Palace in Florence until the greenhouse floods.

"Mrs. Westfall will be with you momentarily," the young man whispered. Gesturing to the chairs, he added, "Please make yourself comfortable."

Deirdre sat, wondering why Mrs. Westfall had told her to come at once if she was going to have to wait. The young man sat behind the desk and stared into his computer screen, ignoring Deirdre entirely. There was an inner door beside his desk, tightly closed.

"Mrs. Westfall asked me to come right away," she said to him.

Hardly glancing up from his screen, the young man said, "Mrs. Westfall is a very busy woman. I'm sure that she's made a special disruption in her schedule to see you."

"But I—"

The computer chimed. The young man pointed to the inner door and said, "Mrs. Westfall will see you now." Without a smile, without a hint of warmth.

Deirdre rose and went to the door. "Thank you," she said to the man. Silently she added, You flunky.

The door opened onto a compartment not much bigger than Deirdre's own quarters. But this was obviously merely the sitting room of a much larger suite. Comfortable couches, deep upholstered armchairs, an oval glass coffee table set with a tray that bore a beaded stainless steel pitcher and several metal cups. But no Katherine Westfall.

Deirdre felt her brow knitting into a frown. Where could she be? Why did she—

Katherine Westfall swept into the room from the door in the far wall, looking resplendent in a sheathed lounging suite of carnation red. She's tiny, Deirdre realized. Petite. But she seemed to radiate self-confidence, poise, power. She was smiling graciously, but there seemed no warmth to it. Deirdre couldn't help thinking that asps are tiny, too, but deadly.

Mrs. Westfall reclined on the couch behind the coffee table, looking as if she were posing for a fashion 'zine.

Deirdre picked up an aroma of . . . flowers? There weren't any flowers in the room. Deirdre thought there might not be any flowers anywhere aboard the research station. But when you're rich, she understood, you can have the scent of flowers wherever you go. Or anything else you want.

"Deirdre Ambrose," Westfall said, from the couch. "I am Katherine Westfall."

"I recognized you from the news nets," said Deirdre.

"Please do sit down. Would you like some juice? It's a mix of orange and mango. Quiet nutritious, and very tasty."

"Thank you."

When Mrs. Westfall made no move to pour the juice, Deirdre picked up the pitcher and did it herself.

"I'll join you," said Westfall. Deirdre poured a cup for her.

Katherine Westfall took a measured sip of the juice, then said to Deirdre, "I've heard about your medical condition."

"Oh?"

"Rabies. Very unusual. It could be troublesome if it's not treated."

"It could be fatal," Deirdre said, in a low voice.

Westfall nodded. "Back on Earth there was some rumor about a biology laboratory that developed a genetically engineered form of rabies."

Surprised, Deirdre asked, "Why would anyone do that?"

Westfall smiled thinly. "Scientists. They're always into something. Like little boys digging in a mud puddle."

Do I have a gengineered version of rabies? Deirdre wondered.

Westfall's smile faded. "I understand that you accused Dr. Pohan of deliberately infecting you."

"Oh! Well, I'm not sure it was deliberate. But the only way I could have contracted the infection was from the needle he used for my blood test, when I first came aboard the *Australia*."

"The accusation upset him terribly."

Not knowing what else to say, Deirdre murmured, "I'm sorry for that."

More forcefully, Westfall said, "He'll get over it. The question now is, how can we treat your condition? Especially if it's an artificially mutated form of the virus?"

"I discussed that with the medical staff earlier today," Deirdre said. "They're developing the necessary vaccine. Dorn has volunteered his blood."

"The cyborg," Westfall said, with obvious distaste.

Deirdre nodded.

"Well," Westfall said, "I want you to know that I am personally looking into your problem. If there's anything you need, anything I can do for you, don't hesitate to ask."

"Why . . . that's very kind of you."

"Not at all."

"Thank you, Mrs. Westfall."

Katherine Westfall nodded graciously. Then she said, "Now tell me what your own work is all about."

Thrown off-kilter by the sudden change of subject, Deirdre confessed, "I don't really know. Not yet. I have a meeting with Dr. Archer in about an hour. . . ."

Her face hardening slightly, Westfall said, "Do you mean that you've come all this way without knowing what you are expected to do? Or why?"

"It seems strange, doesn't it? We got a message that they needed a microbiologist here at station *Gold* and I was asked to fill the position."

"But what will you be doing? Why does Archer want a microbiologist?"

Deirdre shook her head. "I don't know. Not yet."

Her flawless brow wrinkling, Westfall said, "I'd appreciate it if you told me about it, once you find out. As a member of the IAA council, I want to be kept informed about the work going on here."

"I'm sure Dr. Archer will—"

"Not Dr. Archer," Westfall said, steel in her voice. "You. I want you to keep me informed on what's going on here. Fully informed."

"Me?"

"You. And don't let Archer know that you're reporting to me."

"But I—"

Westfall's cobra smile returned. "Keep me informed and I'll do everything I can to help cure your infection. Do we understand one another?"

Her mind still spinning from Katherine Westfall's demand, Deirdre realized as she sat facing Dr. Archer that his beard made him appear older than the rest of his face suggested.

Grant Archer's office looked more like a comfortable sitting room than an executive's headquarters. No desk, just an eclectic scattering of chairs, two of them recliners—which Deirdre instinctively avoided. The walls were glowing, soft gray smart screens.

The station's director was sitting in a slightly tattered old armchair, his feet propped on a round ottoman that looked to Deirdre as if it might originally have been a small oil drum. Now it was covered in putty-gray upholstered faux leather. A little table of clear plastic stood beside his chair; what looked like an electronic remote-control wand rested on it.

"I really appreciate your coming all the way out here on such short notice," Archer was saying.

"The scholarship you're offering is a very strong incentive," she said.

Archer shrugged. "It's the least we can do. We're in something of a bind. We suddenly lost the microbiologist who was scheduled to join our staff and—"

"Frieda Nordstrum?" Deirdre asked.

He looked surprised. "From Selene University, yes. Did you know her?"

Deirdre hesitated, then said, "Only by reputation."

"Her death was a surprise to us all," Archer said.

"Rabies," said Deirdre.

He nodded somberly.

"I've come down with it, too."

"Yes. I saw your medical file. How in the world did you ever contract rabies?"

Deirdre hesitated. "I don't know," she said. That was the truth, she told herself. The rest is suspicion, guesses.

"Our people here will take care of you, don't worry," Archer said easily.

Deirdre wondered if she should ask him about Katherine Westfall's mentioning a genetically engineered form of the virus.

Before she could make up her mind, though, Archer brightened and said, "Well now, we ought to talk about what you'll be doing with our team."

"I was wondering why you want a microbiologist."

"To tell you the truth, Ms. Ambrose, I'm clutching at a straw. And I have an ulterior motive for asking specifically for you, as well."

"I don't understand."

"You've done some work on *Volvox*, haven't you?"

Deirdre replied, "*Volvox aureus*, yes. I did my master's thesis on that."

"That's why you're here," Archer said. "One of the reasons, at least. Frieda Nordstrum was the world authority on *Volvox*."

Blinking with surprise, Deirdre objected, "*Volvox* are colonies of single-celled algae. What makes you so interested in them?"

"The leviathans," said Archer.

"Those giant whales in Jupiter's ocean? I don't see what they've got to do with *Volvox*."

"Those giant whales," Archer said, "are colonies of smaller units. It's hard to believe, but they are actually like *Volvox* and the Portuguese man-of-war: creatures that are composed of specialized independent organisms, living together cooperatively. I believe it's called symbiosis."

It took Deirdre a moment to digest that idea. Archer was smiling at her. It makes him appear quite youthful, Deirdre thought, gray hair or no.

Mistaking her silence for disbelief, Archer said, "I'm not a biologist of any stripe, but I was hoping that you might use what you know of *Volvox* to help us understand the leviathans."

Deirdre had to suppress a laugh. With a shake of her head, she replied, "A colony of fifty thousand *Volvox* algae might make a ball about half a millimeter in diameter. Those whales—"

"Leviathans," Archer corrected.

"Those leviathans are *kilometers* across, aren't they? The size of mountains?"

"And then some."

"So where's the connection?" Deirdre asked. "How can microscopic algae help you understand those enormous Jovian creatures?"

Archer's face settled into a thoughtful pucker. "As I understand your little bugs—"

"Algae."

"Algae," he conceded, with a dip of his chin. "As I understand it, their colonies have some specialized cells: flagella for propulsion, eyespots that sense light, that sort of thing."

"They have sexual cells, too," said Deirdre.

"They do? I thought they reproduced by fissioning."

"Also through sex. But alone. One colony can contain both sexes. They don't have to find a partner."

Archer rubbed at his beard. "We've seen the leviathans disassembling, coming apart into component units which then bud off new units. And then they all reunite to form two beasts where there's been only one before."

"You've observed that?"

Without answering, Archer picked up the remote control unit on the table beside his chair and pointed it at one of the wall screens.

"It's very rare," he said. "We've been studying the leviathans for more than twenty years and we've only seen this once. Of course, we can't get down into that ocean and watch them continuously . . ."

The screen showed a murky expanse. Deirdre could barely make out several shadowy forms moving through the gloom.

"Leviathans," Archer said, in a voice that was little short of awestruck.

A tiny red line appeared at the bottom of the screen, no more than three millimeters long, Deirdre judged.

"That scale line represents a hundred meters," Archer said. "A little longer than the length of an American football field."

Deirdre blinked. "Then the animals must be . . ."

"On the order of ten kilometers long. Roughly the size of Manhattan Island."

"Oh my!"

Archer smiled tightly. "Indeed."

The picture suddenly cleared considerably. Deirdre could see the nearest animal in some detail now.

"Switched sensors to the sonar. We get better imagery with sound than we do with any frequency of light."

"How deep are they?"

"This is about seven hundred kilometers below the surface."

"Seven hundred . . ." Deirdre began to understand the awe in Archer's voice.

"This was recorded by one of our submersibles. Unmanned, of course."

Seven hundred kilometers deep, Deirdre thought. No human being could survive at that depth, not even in the best submersible anyone could build. But then she remembered that Max Yeager boasted of designing a sub that could carry a human crew down to the depths where the leviathans swam.

As if he could read her thoughts, Archer said, "We've just about completed a new submersible that will be crewed. Five people, maximum."

"Dr. Yeager designed it," Deirdre said.

"That's right. He's come out here to check out the final details of the construction. He was on the ship coming in with you, wasn't he?"

She nodded. On the screen, the massive leviathan seemed to be falling apart. As it swam through the dark sea it began to break up.

Deirdre saw bits and pieces of the animal floating off independently. What looked like flippers slipped away first, then broad chunks of the beast's hide and inner parts that she could not identify.

"Disassembling," Archer said. "This is when they're vulnerable to the sharks. Predators. They're much smaller than the leviathans, but very fast. Big teeth."

A trio of what had been fins floated closer. Suddenly they began to shudder; the shaking grew more and more violent.

"The waves they send through the water when they bud like that is what attracts the sharks," Archer said.

They watched for more than an hour as the individual bits fissioned, dividing into two. And then began to unite again, to reassemble.

"Endosymbiosis," Deirdre murmured.

She stared at the screen, fascinated, as the hundreds of separate units slowly linked together into two complete leviathans and finally swam off side by side into the murky distance. The screen went blank.

"That was a lucky one," Archer said, sitting up straighter in his chair. "No sharks found them."

"That's how they reproduce," Deirdre said.

"But how do they accomplish it?" Archer asked, staring intently at the empty screen. "How do they know when to dissociate? How do the separate units know how to get together to form a new animal? Do both of the new ones share the knowledge, the memories of the original?"

She shook her head. "I still don't see how studying *Volvox* could help you. They're so different. . . ."

With a smile that was almost shy, Archer admitted, "Well, now we come to my ulterior motive for picking you."

"Your ulterior motive?" Deirdre asked.

"You have something of a reputation in *Chrysalis II* as a visual artist."

She felt her jaw drop. "Visual artist? You mean those little murals I've painted?"

"And the digital imagery you've created," Archer said. "I've seen those, too. You're quite good."

Confused, Deirdre asked, "You want me to decorate the station?"

"No, no." Archer laughed. Hunching closer to her, he said, "You see, the leviathans apparently communicate in visual imagery. I thought a woman with your talents for visual imagery might be helpful to us."

With that, Archer picked up the remote control again. The wall screens on both sides of the office suddenly were filled with images of the leviathans flashing colors at one another: cool green, bright yellow, intense red. It was like being in the dolphin tank again, Deirdre thought. They were surrounded by the immense leviathans, swimming placidly in Jupiter's ocean, flashing colored lights back and forth.

"That's how they communicate?" she heard herself ask as she stared at the screens.

Archer said, "It seems obvious. They're not simply making displays. They're *communicating*. Intelligent communications. The way we use speech, they use visual imagery."

"And you want me to study their imagery and see if I can make any sense out of it," she said, her eyes still fastened on the screens.

"That would be a good beginning," Archer said. "We've recorded hundreds of hours' worth of their imagery."

Deirdre murmured, "You know that I've been working with Dr. Corvus and the dolphins. He wants to use DBS equipment to make contact with the leviathans."

"I didn't realize you were working with him," Archer admitted. With a slight shrug, he added, "Well, that's another avenue of approach to the problem."

Deirdre saw the burning eagerness on his bearded face. He wants to understand those gigantic creatures, she recognized. He's dying to know, she thought. And he's willing to risk lives to find out. He's willing to send people down into that alien ocean to find out, no matter how dangerous it is.

Deirdre hesitated, then plunged, "I don't know if I can do that for you, Dr. Archer."

With a visible effort, the station director blanked the wall screens and turned to Deirdre. Smiling gently, he said, "Well, you think about it, Ms. Ambrose. It's very important to us, to our understanding of these alien creatures. To our ability to make meaningful contact with an intelligent extraterrestrial species."

"You think they're intelligent?"

"I'm certain of it."

Deirdre's mind was spinning. Intelligent. Communicate through visual images. He wants me to go down into the ocean.

"And don't forget about little *Volvox*," Archer added, less intensely. "Any ideas or information will be welcome. We're pretty desperate for new ideas."

"I'll try," she said, pulling herself to her feet.

Archer stood up, too. As he walked to the door with her he said, "I'm giving a little dinner this evening for the new arrivals. Nineteen hundred hours, in conference room C. I hope you haven't already made other arrangements."

Knowing that an invitation from the station director, even a casual one, was more like a command, Deirdre replied, "I'd be happy to come."

"Good," he said as he slid open the door to the passageway. "Nineteen hundred. Mrs. Westfall will be joining us, too."

When Deirdre got back to her own compartment there was a message from Andy Corvus waiting.

"Hi there, Dee," he said, his slightly mismatched face grinning boyishly from the wall screen. "We're all invited to dinner with the station director tonight. Can I pick you up around eighteen forty-five?"

She returned his call immediately. Andy wasn't in his quarters, so she left a message.

Precisely at eighteen forty-five she heard a rap on her door. Still wearing the flowered dress, she slid the door back and saw that Andy was accompanied by Yeager and Dorn. Yeager had obviously shaved; he smelled of cologne.

"The three musketeers," she said, smiling brightly at them.

Yeager elbowed Corvus aside and offered his arm to her. "Then you must be the Queen of France," he said grandly.

She politely stepped past Yeager and slipped her arm around Corvus's. "Andy asked me first," she said sweetly to Yeager.

"Yeah," he grumbled, "but I'm better-looking."

Dorn said, "And more modest, too."

They all laughed, linked arms, and strode along the passageway toward conference room C.

It was a small room, almost intimate, its oblong central table set for eight. Grant Archer was already standing at the side table set up on the far end of the room with an array of bottles and glasses and a large silvery bucket of ice.

"The newbies!" Archer called out to them. "Welcome."

He introduced the buxom dark-haired woman beside him as his wife, Marjorie. Deirdre quickly learned that she was a biochemist.

"Are you working on the leviathans?" Deirdre asked as she poured herself a glass of fruit juice.

Marjorie smiled tolerantly. "We're all working on the leviathans, whether we want to or not."

Deirdre felt her brows go up. But before she could think of anything to say, the double doors slid open and Katherine Westfall swept in, accompanied by a beefy-looking young man in a sky blue blazer and tight slacks. A boy toy! Deirdre said to herself. He was good-looking, in a muscular bodyguard way. At least he's not that zombie I met earlier, Deirdre thought.

Archer went the length of the room to welcome Mrs. Westfall and her escort, then introduced them to each of the others. The boy toy claimed to be an accountant; he looked more like a security guard to Deirdre. Westfall gave no hint that she'd already met Deirdre.

"We don't normally serve alcoholic drinks here," Archer said, once he had led Mrs. Westfall to the makeshift bar, "but in honor of your presence, we've figured out how to make a dry martini." He poured a clear liquid into a stemmed, wide-brimmed glass and handed it to her. "I hope it meets with your approval."

"I'm sure it will," Westfall said, the corners of her lips curving ever so slightly. She sipped, then pronounced, "Perfect! How did you ever do it?"

Archer looked almost sheepish. "Well, the head of our food service group claims that he once tended bar in Sydney, Australia. I'm not certain that I believe him, but Red is a very resourceful person."

"He certainly knows how to mix a martini," Westfall said. But Deirdre noticed she didn't take another sip.

"Speak of the devil," said Marjorie, as the double doors opened and a short, wiry red-haired man with a bushy red mustache and a bristling skull-hugging crew cut entered, leading a quartet of serving robots, their flat tops laden with covered dishes.

"Rodney Devlin," Archer announced. "Our chief cook and bartender."

Devlin was wearing a sparkling white chef's jacket and a big grin on his lantern-jawed face. He made a little bow as the robots rolled along the side wall like a quartet of well-trained waiters, then stopped in unison.

"Greetings and salutations, folks," said Devlin. "Who's for steak and who's for fish? It's all soy-based, o'course, but I think I got the flavors right."

Devlin disappeared once everyone sat at the table and began eating. By the time the diners were picking desserts off the robots that maneuvered slowly around the table, Archer said, "I'm looking forward to working with all of you and learning more about the leviathans."

Andy Corvus, halfway down the table, replied, "I'm looking forward to making contact with the beasts."

"Contact?" Marjorie Archer asked.

With his usual vigorous nod, Andy explained, "If they're intelligent, we should be able to communicate with them."

"*If* they're intelligent," Mrs. Westfall said.

"I'm sure that they are," said Grant Archer.

"How so?" Westfall asked. Her voice was soft, but everyone turned toward her.

"Because they communicate with each other," Archer replied. "They flash signals back and forth. They have language—"

"Flashing lights don't necessarily mean language," Westfall objected. "Fish in Earth's oceans make luminescent glows and they're certainly not intelligent."

"The leviathans are," Archer insisted. "I'm sure of it."

Westfall smiled thinly, but said nothing.

PLANS

Well," said Yeager, loudly enough to make all heads along the table turn toward him, "I'm here to see that you can send a team of people down into that ocean with the leviathans, whether they're intelligent or not."

Westfall raised a brow. "Really?"

Archer cleared his throat, then started to explain, "I was going to tell you about that tomorrow, when we go through the station's newest wheel."

"The area that's dedicated to studying the leviathans," Westfall said. It was not a question.

"The area that's dedicated to studying the planet Jupiter, including its indigenous life-forms," Archer replied evenly.

"And you intend to send a human team into the ocean?"

"Yes, I do."

"There hasn't been a human probe into the ocean in twenty years," Westfall said. "Not since you yourself went down there."

"I'm quite aware of that."

"You'll need IAA approval for such a dangerous mission. I doubt that you'll get it."

Archer seemed to square his shoulders without moving from his chair at the head of the table. Deirdre noticed that his wife slid her hand over his.

"As I read the regulations," Archer said, forcing a smile for Mrs. Westfall, "IAA approval is necessary for funding allocations, not for approving specific missions."

"For such a dangerous mission—"

"It won't be all that dangerous," Yeager said.

Deirdre turned toward the engineer, who was sitting on her right. Everyone else looked at him, too.

"Not dangerous?" Westfall asked, clearly disbelieving him.

Yeager spread his hands grandly. "No more dangerous than working out on the surface of Europa. Or Io, with those volcanoes spouting off."

"But you'll have to dive hundreds of kilometers deep into that ocean. The pressures—"

"No problem," said Yeager.

"But the earlier missions all suffered terrible damage. Casualties. People died!"

Yeager gave her a condescending grin. "The earlier missions were sent out before we had a firm understanding of just what the conditions are down there. We knew the pressure would be tremendous, but how tremendous? We didn't have any firm numbers. You can't design without firm numbers to work with."

Still looking incredulous, Westfall said, "You're saying that—"

"I'm saying that the past twenty years' worth of uncrewed missions into the ocean have given us enough data about the pressures and other conditions down at that level so that we can design a vessel that can safely carry people there."

Dorn spoke up. "Those pressures were calculated long before the first human mission went into the ocean, weren't they?"

"Sure they were," Yeager agreed. "But those calculations were based on theoretical work. Models that made a lot of assumptions. There wasn't any actual data. Now we have real data and we know to several decimal places what the conditions are." Before anyone could respond, the engineer went on, "And when you know what you're working against you can design a vessel that will work in those conditions. Work just fine."

Westfall turned to Grant Archer. "So you've built such a vessel, haven't you?"

"It's waiting for its final checkout," Archer said. "It's co-orbiting with this station. I'll show it to you tomorrow."

"I didn't see it in the virtual reality tour you gave me," Westfall said. Her voice was not accusing, not sharp, but Deirdre could hear the icy distrust in her tone.

For a couple of heartbeats Archer said nothing. Then, "No, the vessel hasn't been included in the VR tour. Not yet."

Deirdre imagined she could see the wheels spinning inside Westfall's perfectly coiffed head.

At last Westfall said, "As a member of the IAA's governing council, I could get the council to issue an order forbidding a human mission into the ocean."

Taut-faced, Archer replied, "You couldn't get the council to act before the mission is launched."

Anger flared on Westfall's face for an instant, but she immediately suppressed it. "I think you underestimate the speed with which the council can act—when properly motivated."

Archer glanced at his wife, sitting beside him, then returned his focus to Westfall. "Mrs. Westfall," he said with deliberate formality, "I intend to send that vessel into the ocean of Jupiter. You can fire me from my post afterward, but that's what I intend to do."

"I won't allow it," Westfall said.

Andy Corvus piped up. "Hey, wait a minute. I've got to get down into that ocean. I've got to make contact with those critters."

"You've *got to*?" Westfall practically sneered the words.

"That's right," Corvus snapped back at her. "I've got to. I'm a neurophysiologist. I believe I can make a meaningful communications contact with an alien life-form. I might be wrong about that, but I'll never know unless I get the chance to try."

Marjorie Archer asked softly, "But why do you say you've got to do that?"

Corvus turned toward her. "You're a scientist. You know why."

"Please, tell me," Westfall said.

Andy ran a hand through his thick red mop before saying, "I'm a scientist. I do science. That's my life. Michelangelo carved statues. Beethoven wrote symphonies. I do science. If you prevent me from doing it, it's like . . . well, it's like chopping off my hands. You haven't killed me, exactly, but you've put an end to my life."

Westfall shook her head slightly.

Deirdre said, "It would be as if someone prevented you from doing the work you love. Stopped you from being who you are, turned you into a hollow shell."

Looking slowly from face to face, Westfall asked, "Is that the way all of you feel? You're all scientists, do all of you—"

"I'm an engineer," Yeager interrupted. "But, yeah, that's what it's all about. Birds gotta fly, fish gotta swim, and once you get hooked into this kind of research, you've got to do it. Or life becomes meaningless."

Westfall turned to Dorn. "You're not a scientist, are you?"

"No, I'm not," said the cyborg. Then he added, "Scientists are curious people. I'm merely a curiosity."

Archer tapped a fork against his water glass and everyone turned toward him. "I didn't intend for this dinner to turn into a confrontation." With a grin, he added, "Or a symposium on the philosophy of science."

Westfall allowed herself a slight smile.

Archer continued, "Tomorrow, Mrs. Westfall, I'd like to show you what we're doing in our studies of Jupiter and its life-forms. Show you how far we've come—and how very far we still have to go."

Westfall nodded regally. "Until tomorrow, then."

CONTROL CENTER

D eirdre was awakened by the insistent buzzing of the phone. She sat up in bed, rubbed her eyes, and asked the communications system's computer, "Who's calling?"

G. MAXWELL YEAGER appeared on the screen above her desk. Deirdre saw that the time was only 0600.

"Voice only," she commanded the phone.

"Dee!" Yeager's voice sounded urgently. "You awake?"

"I am now, Max."

"C'mon, get dressed and meet me in the galley. We'll grab some breakfast and then go down to the third wheel and inspect *Faraday* before Archer brings Westfall down there."

"I can't," she said, rubbing sleep from her eyes. "I have to be at the clinic at eleven hundred hours," she said.

"I'll have you back before then, don't worry."

"Who's Faraday?" Deirdre asked.

"Not who. What. My ship. The baby that's going to take Andy down to the leviathans."

"Why do you want me to—"

"I've gotta give her the once-over before Westfall sees her," Yeager explained, "and I'd really like you to see her."

"But I—"

"I want to show off!" Yeager's voice sounded eager, excited. "You're the prettiest lady on this merry-go-round so I thought it'd be fun to show off to you. Okay?"

Grinning at his explanation, Deirdre said, "Okay. I'll meet you in the galley in half an hour."

"Fifteen minutes," Yeager said.

"Thirty," said Deirdre firmly. "It takes time to look beautiful."

"Why did you name it *Faraday?*" Deirdre asked as she and Yeager rode the elevator down the station's central shaft toward the third wheel.

For a moment Yeager didn't reply. Deirdre thought he looked almost embarrassed. The only sound in the slightly swaying elevator cab was the swish of its rush down the tube.

At last Yeager explained, "Well, he's always been a kind of hero of mine. Michael Faraday. Son of a cobbler, back early in the nineteenth century. Made himself into one of the great scientists. An experimenter. A hands-on guy."

Deirdre nodded, beginning to understand.

"He invented the electric power generator. Called it the dynamo. Edison and the whole electric utility industry was based on his little contraption. Even the earliest nuclear power plants still used the kind of generator he invented."

"I can see why you admire him," Deirdre said.

Yeager broke into a grin. "There's a story about Faraday. He gave a big public lecture in London about his little dynamo and after it was over a lady from the audience came up and asked him . . ." Yeager broke into a wavering falsetto, "'Mr. Faraday, your invention seems very interesting, but tell me, of what use is it?' Faraday answered her, 'Madam, of what use is a newborn baby?'"

Deirdre said, "I've heard that story. In school, one of the professors told that story as an example of what scientific research is all about."

"You betcha," Yeager said. "But there's a different version of the story, one that I like better."

The elevator stopped with a *ping!* and its doors slid open. They stepped out into a passageway much like the main passageway up in the top wheel. But this one looked new, raw, almost unused to Deirdre's eyes. Its deck was uncarpeted and it smelled of fresh paint.

Yeager fished his pocketphone from his tunic, then pointed toward their right. "This way," he said.

"What's the other version of the story?" Deirdre asked as they started along the sloping passageway. The doors along the corridor were unmarked, and Deirdre got the impression that the rooms behind them were empty.

"Oh, the other version," Yeager said. "Well, it's the same setup: Faraday gives his lecture to the public, but afterward it's a member of Parliament who comes up and asks him what good his little dynamo might be. And Faraday tells him, 'I don't know, sir. But someday you will put a tax upon it.'"

Yeager laughed loudly. Deirdre smiled at him.

He stopped at a double door that was marked CONTROL CENTER—AUTHORIZED PERSONNEL ONLY.

"Are we authorized personnel?" Deirdre asked.

As he tapped on the door's security pad Yeager said, "We are if I know the lock's combination."

"But I'm not—"

"You're with me, kiddo."

The door slid open and they stepped into what looked to Deirdre like a mission control chamber. A horseshoe of consoles ran around a central chair whose padded arms were studded with colored buttons. The walls were smart screens from floor to ceiling, all of them blank. Deirdre counted an even dozen consoles, their cushioned chairs all empty, their screens and dials all dead.

Without an instant's hesitation, Yeager went to the central chair and settled himself in it. His fingers began playing along the buttons in the chair's arms and, one by one, the consoles hummed to life. Deirdre stood to one side, half leaning against the chair's padded back.

"Okay," Yeager said, nodding as if satisfied with what he saw, "now watch the middle screen, right in front of us."

The screen ran the entire length of the chamber's front wall. It began to glow and then sharpened to show a curving metal surface with an airlock hatch in it. Closed.

"That's *Faraday*," Yeager said. "A slice of it, at least."

"That's the vessel that's going to take people into the ocean?"

"Yep. That's her. Him. Whatever." Yeager was still pecking at

the buttons on the control pads. The consoles' screens were displaying graphs and images, the gauges were all alight.

"Ships are referred to as 'she,'" Deirdre said, "no matter who
they're named after."

"Because it costs so much to keep 'em in paint and powder,"
Yeager wisecracked.

"That's an old sexist cliché," Deirdre said, with a disapproving
click of her tongue.

But Yeager's attention was totally focused on the vessel. "She's a
beauty, isn't she? This is the first time I've seen her. After all the
drawings and plans and simulations, there she is. She's *gorgeous!*"

"It looks big."

Yeager grunted. "As big as this whole station, almost. So big we
can't attach it to the station, it'd throw the center of mass entirely
out of whack and we'd start wobbling like a drunken sailor."

"It's not connected?"

"Co-orbits with the station. To get to it you have to get into a
spacesuit and go EVA."

"Goodness."

Grinning tightly, Yeager said, "Goodness has nothing to do
with it." Looking up into her face, the engineer asked, "Want to go
aboard her?"

RESEARCH VESSEL *FARADAY*

A board your *Faraday*?" Deirdre asked. "I've never been in a spacesuit. I don't know—"

"Not in actuality," Yeager said, almost impatiently. "VR."

"Virtual reality."

"Yeah." Pointing, "Take that console, the one on the end. You'll find goggles and ear plugs in the top drawer. Should be feelie gloves in there, too."

Deirdre sat at the humming console, wormed a plug into her ear, pulled on the fuzzy-looking tactile gloves, then slid the goggles over her eyes. The goggles made everything look slightly greenish.

"Okay," Yeager's voice muttered in her ear. "Just a minute now while I power up the system . . ."

The world went blank for a moment; Deirdre could see nothing. Abruptly she was hanging in space between the station and the gigantic sphere of *Faraday*. She gasped with surprise.

"It's *huge*! Almost as big as the station!"

She heard Yeager chuckle. "Yep."

"What are all those fins sticking out from it?"

"Steering vanes," Yeager answered. "For maneuvering, either in Jupiter's atmosphere or its ocean."

Deirdre nodded silently.

"Now we activate your propulsion unit," Yeager said.

Although she felt no force upon her, Deirdre saw that she was moving through empty space toward the airlock hatch on *Faraday*'s curving surface. She saw a nine-unit keyboard on the hull next to the airlock.

"Combination's one-two-three," Yeager told her. "I like to keep things simple."

Reaching out with her gloved hand, Deirdre tapped out the combination. She could feel the solidity of the keys against her fingertip. The hatch slid open silently.

"Go right in, kiddo."

Somewhat hesitantly, Deirdre stepped into the airlock. She waited while the outer hatch closed, the chamber filled with air, and finally the inner door opened. She saw a long tunnel made of gleaming metal, a tube, with a six-seated cart waiting empty.

"Sit down and strap in," Yeager instructed her. "This buggy goes fast."

It felt odd: Deirdre knew she was still sitting at the console in the control center, but like a dreamer she climbed into the cart's front seat and clicked the safety belt across her lap. Without warning the cart shot down the tunnel like a bullet. The curving walls blurred, but Deirdre felt no sense of motion at all.

"You're diving through an even dozen layers of reinforced compression shells," Yeager explained as she whizzed through the tunnel, "down to the crew station at the vessel's center."

The cart slowed, then stopped at another hatch. Following Yeager's instructions, Deirdre got out of the cart, opened the hatch, and stepped into a small, cramped chamber, packed tight with consoles and sensor screens.

"This is it?" she asked, feeling disappointed. The place was so small. Barely room for five people, cheek by jowl. I've seen bathrooms bigger than this, she thought. People are supposed to live and work in here?

"That's it," Yeager's voice told her. "That's the bridge. The crew will work there for two weeks—if everything goes according to plan. Which it won't."

"Where do they sleep? Eat?"

Yeager guided her past a tall, square unit that he identified as the galley; it looked like an oversized snack dispenser to Deirdre. Then she went through another hatch into the sleeping quarters, even smaller and more compact than the bridge. The individual bunks were mere drawers set in a metal bulkhead. It reminded Deirdre of videos she had seen of morgues, on Earth.

"You'd better test your crew for claustrophobia before you let them in here," she said.

She could sense Yeager nodding. "Yeah, it's kinda tight, isn't it?"

"Not much privacy."

She heard Yeager grunt. Then he said, "Okay. Seen enough?"

Deirdre nodded. Abruptly her vision went black, but before she could utter a sound she saw the control center aboard the station again, still tinted slightly green.

She pulled the goggles off her head, brushed a hand through her hair. "The vessel's so big and the crew area is so small."

"Gotta be that way," Yeager said, still sitting in the command chair. "Pressure. The ship's got to be able to take enormous pressure."

"The crew, too," Deirdre said.

"Guess so," said Yeager.

It was nearly 1000 hours, Deirdre saw.

"I've got to get back," she said to Yeager. "My appointment at the clinic."

Sitting in the command chair, the engineer nodded without looking up from the buttons he was pecking at. "Okay. You can find your way, can't you? I've gotta double-check all these systems before Archer brings Westfall down here."

Deirdre said, "I'll be fine." She started for the hatch, then turned back to Yeager and said, "Thanks for the tour."

"Uh-huh," he said absently, still fiddling with his controls.

Deirdre saw that his attention was on his work. He had shown off to her and now he was all business. With an understanding shrug she left the control center and headed for the elevators. *Max is in his element,* she told herself. *He wanted to impress me, but he wants to play with his gadgets even more.*

The elevator doors slid open even before she reached for the call button, and Dr. Archer stepped out, with Mrs. Westfall a step behind him. Deirdre marveled again at how diminutive Westfall was. Small physically, she thought, but that little body of hers carries enormous power.

"Hello!" Archer said, surprised. "I didn't expect to see you here."

"Dr. Yeager asked me here to see the vessel he's designed. He's inside, checking out its systems."

Westfall said nothing, but she gave Deirdre the slightest of nods as she brushed past. As if she approves of my looking things over down here, Deirdre thought. As if she thinks I'm spying for her.

Deirdre felt nervous as she entered the clinic. It was much larger than the infirmary on *Australia*. Even the anteroom was bigger than Dr. Pohan's cubbyhole of an office. A white-smocked receptionist sat at a desk that curved around her chair like the pseudopods of an amoeba reaching for its prey. The receptionist was a smiling, slightly overweight gray-haired woman. She glanced at her desktop screen and then looked up at Deirdre.

"Deirdre Ambrose. You're scheduled to see Dr. Mandrill. Right on time. That's good."

Dr. Mandrill turned out to be a puffy-faced, laconic Kenyan. His office walls were covered with old-fashioned photographs of himself with adults and children whom Deirdre assumed were his family, back Earthside. His voice was a deep, rich baritone.

"Your condition is very serious," he said, almost accusingly. Then he broke into a dazzling smile. "But we'll take care of you, never fear."

Deirdre expected to be put through more examinations and scans, but Dr. Mandrill apparently was satisfied with the file from *Australia*. He nodded and muttered to himself as he read Dr. Pohan's report, then finally looked up at Deirdre.

"As long as your friend keeps volunteering his blood, you'll be fine."

"Dorn," Deirdre breathed.

"Yes. He's a cyborg, I understand. Interesting case." Tapping his computer screen, the doctor added, "We're running a series of experiments on him, I see."

ULTRAHYPERBARIC CHAMBER

The pain was bearable. So far.

Dorn sat alone in the bare, metal-walled chamber. Benches ran along its curved walls, enough room to seat six people. But Dorn was in the chamber alone.

"How do you feel?" The technician's voice coming through the speaker grill in the overhead sounded strangely deep, distorted. It must be the pressure, Dorn told himself.

Aloud, he reported, "Some discomfort in my chest and abdomen."

His head and body were plastered with sensors, both his metal half and his flesh. Outside the chamber the technicians were monitoring his physical condition: heart rate, breathing, brain wave patterns, electrical conductivity of his wiring, lubrication levels of his servomotors, activity of the digital processors in his prosthetics.

"Can you stand up and walk a few paces, please?"

Dorn got stiffly to his feet and stepped along the narrow aisle between the benches, surprised at how much effort it took. His leg ached; even the prosthetic leg seemed stiff, arthritic.

"Very good. We're going to notch up the pressure slowly. You tell us when you want us to stop."

Dorn sat down again and gripped the edge of the bench with both his hands. His head began to thrum. It became difficult to draw a breath. The pain ramped upward, slowly but steadily, always worse. Closing his human eye, Dorn sat quietly and took it without complaint.

Suddenly the bench splintered beneath him with an oddly deep crunching noise. Dorn looked down and saw that his prosthetic hand had crushed the plastic.

"That's enough!" the technician's slurred voice bawled. "Take him down."

They did it slowly, very slowly, but at last the pain eased away entirely. After nearly another hour of sitting alone in the bare, claustrophobic chamber, the hatch creaked open and the chief technician stuck his head in.

"You can come out now, Mr. Dorn. Test's over."

Dorn got slowly to his feet. He felt a little unsteady. His human leg tingled as if pins and needles were being jabbed into the flesh. Even the prosthetic leg felt balky, stiff, as if somehow its bearings had become infiltrated by grit.

He ducked through the hatch and stepped out onto the laboratory floor. Four technicians were bent over their console screens. Their chief, a round, ruddy-faced man with closely cropped blond hair, gazed at Dorn with unalloyed admiration.

"You took six times normal atmospheric pressure without a peep," he said, smiling toothily.

"Is that good?" asked Dorn.

"Damned good. Damned good. And that's in air, not the gunk."

Dorn started to ask what "the gunk" might be, but the tech chief didn't give him time to frame his question.

"Perfluorocarbon," he explained, still smiling. "They immerse you in the stuff. You breathe it instead of air. Allows you to work in much higher pressures. Much higher."

Dorn bit back a sardonic reply. Then he remembered that he was expected at the clinic to donate more blood to Deirdre.

Andy Corvus, meanwhile, was swimming lazily in the dolphin pool. Fish glided by him, all the colors of the rainbow, swishing their tails mindlessly. Turning his head slightly, Andy saw through his breathing mask two of the dolphins, big as moving vans, sleek and gray, their mouths curved in perpetual grins. Andy waved to them and they chattered and whistled as they effortlessly swooped past him.

Where's Baby? he wondered. Baby and her parents had been transferred from *Australia* to this tank in the station. It was much bigger than the tank aboard the torch ship: It took Andy nearly a quarter of an hour to swim its full length.

At last he spotted Baby, down near the bottom, nosing among the artificial coral formations there. Got to think in three dimensions, he told himself. The world of humans is a flatland; dolphins live in three dimensions.

"Hello, Baby," he said inside his mask. The chip-sized computer built into the mask translated his words into a series of high-pitched chirps.

Baby zoomed up toward him, then swam a circle around Corvus, chattering back at him.

"Hello, Andy," the computer translated. "Good fishing?"

"I'm not hungry," Corvus said.

"I am." And Baby flashed away with a flick of her powerful flukes.

Corvus looked around for Baby's parents. The youngster's moving around without them now, he realized. She's growing up. I wonder if dolphins have a teenaged phase, when they rebel against their parents. Or try to. He remembered his own teen years, how ancient and conservative his parents had seemed.

His wristwatch buzzed. The vibration told Corvus that he'd been in the water with the dolphins for three full hours. He sighed inwardly. Time to get out. Time to return to the dry world of his fellow humans.

Reluctantly he swam to the surface. Suddenly Baby was beside him, smoothly spouting and then sucking in a gulp of air. She chattered briefly.

"More fish?" the computer translated.

Corvus smiled inside his face mask. Yep, he replied silently, I'm going to get me some lunch. Maybe the cooks have made some pseudofish today, instead of the usual soyburgers.

Aloud, he said to the young dolphin, "Time to leave, Baby. I'll be back soon."

It took a moment for the computer to translate his words into clicks. Then Baby replied, "Good hunting, Andy."

"Good hunting, Baby."

Corvus was surprised at how physically tired he felt once he'd climbed out of the water and planted his feet on the solid deck that ran the circumference of the huge tank.

Lunch sounds like a good idea, he thought as he slowly pulled off his air tank and stowed it in the locker where he kept his swimming gear. The floor of the deck was porous: The water dripping from his body disappeared as the permeable tiles wicked it up. Corvus showered, toweled off, and pulled on his shapeless coveralls. Deirdre had told him they were olive green and didn't go well with his red hair and fair complexion. The colors meant nothing to him.

He was closing his locker door when he heard voices drifting down the passageway from the direction of the elevators. A woman and a man, he recognized.

Around the curve of the passageway came Dr. Archer and that Mrs. Westfall. Andy instinctively distrusted Katherine Westfall. She had a superior air about her that raised his hackles. Like she thought herself better, more important, than anyone else. Shrugging to himself, he admitted, Well, she sure is more important. But does she have to throw it in your face?

"Ah, Dr. Corvus," Archer called as they approached. Andy saw that three dark-suited young men trailed behind the pair of them. Westfall's flunkies, he guessed.

"Dr. Archer," Corvus replied. "And Mrs. Westfall. Hi. How are you?"

Westfall said, "Dr. Archer has been telling me that you can actually talk with the dolphins." The tone of her voice clearly said she didn't believe it.

"Um, to a limited extent, yes."

"Really?"

Archer, standing slightly behind Westfall, raised his brows in an expression that looked almost beseeching to Andy. Corvus understood: Don't start an argument with her. Don't let her get under your skin.

Making himself smile for the IAA councilwoman, Corvus said genially, "Would you like to talk with them?"

DOLPHIN TANK

Me?" Westfall's hazel eyes went wide. "Talk with a dolphin?"

Corvus opened his locker and pulled out his breathing mask. "The translator's built into the mask. You'll have to put it on."

As she accepted the mask from Corvus's hand, Westfall asked guardedly, "How does it work?"

"We've built up a vocabulary of dolphin sounds and translated some of them into human language. The translator's set for English, but we can switch it to something else, if you like. Spanish, Chinese, a few others."

"English will be fine," Westfall said.

"Just slip the mask over your head," Corvus said, gesturing.

"But how does it work?" she insisted. "I mean, how can you translate the noises those fish make into meaningful human words?"

Corvus glanced at Archer, then focused again on Mrs. Westfall. "In the first place, ma'am, they're not fish. They're mammals, just like you and me. They breathe air. They have brains that are just as complex as our own; a little bigger than ours, actually."

Archer stepped in. "Over many years we've built up a dictionary of dolphin vocalizations and correlated them with human words. It's been very slow work. The two species live in very different environments."

"But we're able to talk back and forth," Corvus said. "At least, a little bit." With a little chuckle, he explained, "We don't discuss philosophy or any abstract subjects. But we can talk about fish, heat and cold, solid objective things."

Archer added, "This work goes all the way back to when Dr. Wo was running this station, more than twenty years ago. He believed that learning to communicate with the dolphins would help us learn how to communicate with a completely alien species, such as the Jovian leviathans."

Westfall looked down at the breathing mask she held in her hands. It was still slightly wet, Corvus saw, but he decided not to take it back and wipe it off.

"Do you really believe that you can have a meaningful dialogue with dolphins?" she asked.

"They're pretty darned smart," Corvus said. "Of course, we're dealing with tame ones, dolphins that have been raised in captivity. I'll bet the wild ones are even smarter. I mean, they've got to deal with sharks and all, they have to navigate across whole oceans. Lots more problems for them to handle. And they live in bigger family groups, too."

Westfall seemed to be trying to digest these new ideas. Corvus thought she looked like a kid facing a plate of spinach.

"You don't have to try it if you don't want to," he said.

That moved her. Without another word Westfall slipped the mask over her tawny hair. Very carefully, Corvus noted. She doesn't want to mess her 'do.

The mask was loose on her face, but Andy thought that it didn't matter as long as she wasn't actually going into the water.

"Now what?" she asked, her voice muffled somewhat by the mask.

Corvus beckoned her to the glassteel wall of the tank, where the fish were swimming by and the dolphins gliding sleekly among them.

"It'll work best if you press the mask against the tank," he said to Westfall. "That'll conduct the sound better."

Still looking uncertain, Westfall leaned forward until the mask was firmly against the glassteel. Corvus saw one of the adult dolphins swim toward her, curious. Then he caught sight of Baby, a dozen meters or so deeper.

"Say hello to Baby," he prompted.

"Hello, Baby," said Westfall.

The young dolphin chattered and Westfall flinched away from the tank.

"He answered me!" she exclaimed.

"She."

"Yes. She's a female, isn't she?" Westfall pressed against the glassteel again and asked, "How old are you, Baby?"

Corvus knew that dolphins didn't keep time the way humans did. Baby clicked and chattered.

Westfall said, "She asked me if I've eaten today."

"Feeding's important to them," Andy said.

"Ask her where her mother is," Archer suggested.

"Where's your mother?"

More chattering, and an adult dolphin swam up beside Baby, clicking and whistling.

"That's her mother," said Westfall.

Corvus watched happily as Baby and Westfall exchanged a few more words. At last the woman stepped back from the tank and pulled the mask off.

"That was . . ." She seemed to search for a word. ". . . fascinating."

Taking the mask from her hands, Andy said, "We're trying to enlarge our vocabulary of dolphin speech. I wish we could get back to Earth and start talking to some of them in their natural habitat."

"We?" Westfall asked.

With a self-deprecating little smile, Corvus said, "I'm just the tip of the iceberg in this. There's a whole slew of people back at the University of Rome and a half-dozen other research institutions."

Archer said, "Scripps, Woods Hole, several others."

Westfall's expression hardened slightly. "But how do you know you're really communicating with them? Mightn't your so-called vocabulary simply be words you've placed as definitions of their noises? Mightn't you be fooling yourselves?"

Shaking his head, Andy countered, "We've done some pretty strict tests. Not just gabbing at each other, but asking the dolphins to find specific objects in the water, asking them to perform some acrobatics. It's a real language and we're getting the hang of it. It's pretty slow, I admit, but we're learning."

Before Westfall could reply, Archer said, "This work goes back more than twenty years, as I said. Dr. O'Hara was really the pioneer in this area."

"Elaine O'Hara." Westfall's expression suddenly turned glacial.

"Lane O'Hara," Archer said. "She was a fine, wonderful person. Do you know her?"

"I never had the chance to meet her," Westfall said, her tone dripping acid.

GRANT ARCHER'S OFFICE

Max Yeager felt nervous.

"I appreciate your coming with me," he said as he and Dorn headed along the passageway toward Dr. Archer's office.

The cyborg replied gravely, "I have nothing to do this afternoon. The medics are reviewing the data on the pressure tests they ran on me."

Yeager had his pocketphone in one hand and every few steps glanced at the colored map it displayed to make sure they were on the right path. They passed a solitary woman in drab coveralls walking in the other direction. Up ahead a pair of men in virtually identical dark blue tunics and slacks were heading in the same direction as they. Yeager guessed that they too were looking for Archer's office.

The doors along the passageway bore small nameplates next to their keypads. This whole section of the station looked obviously older than the third wheel, worn, almost shabby. A quarter century of hard use, Yeager said to himself. It shows.

"May I ask why you want me to accompany you?"

Yeager was on Dorn's mechanical side. There was no discernable expression on the etched metal of his face, but the engineer heard the curiosity in his tone.

Feeling more fidgety as they got closer to Archer's office, Yeager admitted, "I . . . uh . . . I get kinda jumpy when a big shot like Archer calls me into a meeting. I'm a lot happier down in the labs, or getting my hands dirty on the hardware."

"You want moral support," Dorn said emotionlessly.

Yeager bobbed his head up and down. "Yeah. Something like that."

Sure enough, the two suits ahead of them stopped at a door and tapped on it for entrance.

As the two of them stepped in, Yeager and Dorn got close enough to see Grant Archer standing inside, welcoming them.

Licking his lips nervously, Yeager said, "This is it."

Dorn agreed with a solemn nod, and gestured with his human hand for Yeager to go in ahead of him.

The engineer hesitated. "Maybe we oughtta knock or something."

Before Dorn could reply, Archer looked past the two arrivals and spotted Yeager just outside the doorway.

"Dr. Yeager," he called. "Right on time. And you brought Dorn with you. Good!"

Archer came up and shook hands with Yeager, then with Dorn. Yeager saw there was no desk in the office, no hierarchical arrangement of any sort. Just an assortment of chairs that looked as if they'd been cribbed from a used furniture store.

"Make yourselves comfortable," Archer said, taking one of the recliners. He introduced the two other men as Michael Johansen, head of the station's Jovian studies department, and Isaac Lowenstien, chief of the safety and life-support department.

Mike and Ike? Yeager asked himself. Is this supposed to be some kind of joke?

It wasn't. Johansen was tall, his long legs stretching under the coffee table in the middle of their chairs. He had a long, narrow face with sharp, angular features and a scattering of freckles so pale they were almost yellow. His hair was the color of straw and baby-fine, wispy. His eyes were steel blue. A Viking's eyes, Yeager thought. Piercing. No nonsense.

Lowenstien, on the other hand, was a small, swarthy, intense man with tightly curled midnight-dark hair, smoldering jet-black eyes and a six-pointed star tattooed on the back of his right hand. Refugee, Yeager recognized. Must be third generation: His grandparents probably got killed when Israel was wiped out. They never forget.

Both Mike and Ike were staring hard at Yeager, like a pair of police detectives about to grill a suspect. Yeager felt as if he were sitting on a hard cement block instead of a cushioned armchair. Perspiration trickled down his ribs. This is going to be an inquisition, he knew.

Archer was sitting straight up in his recliner. But he smiled easily as he said, "We're here to review the status of the submersible and see if it's ready for a crewed mission."

Lowenstien immediately said, "The vehicle hasn't been flown yet. You can't risk a human crew in an untried vehicle." His voice was sharp, cutting.

Before Yeager could object, Johansen clasped his bony hands around his knees and looked up at the ceiling as he said in a slow drawl, "We've obtained as much data as we can from uncrewed missions. If we're to make any progress in understanding the leviathans we need a human mission."

Archer scratched at his trim little beard. "I find that I agree with both of you." He turned to Yeager. "Dr. Yeager, what do you have to say?"

Max had to swallow hard before he could find his voice. So what do I have to say?

"As you know," he began, stalling for time to arrange his thoughts, "I've spent the past five years in Selene designing the *Faraday* and supervising its construction."

"From four hundred million kilometers away," said Lowenstien.

"The data's the same, no matter what the distance," Yeager shot back. "But, you're right, yesterday was the first time I've seen the ship firsthand."

"And?" Archer prompted.

"She's a beauty," said Yeager.

"Have you gone aboard it?" Lowenstien demanded.

"Not yet. But I checked out all her systems from the command center. She's ready to fly."

Johansen said, "Then we should start the procedures to pick a crew."

Lowenstien objected. "We shouldn't risk a crew until the vehicle has demonstrated that it's safe to operate."

Archer said, "There's some urgency in this. We need to get a team down there before the IAA decides to hold us up."

"For very valid safety reasons," Lowenstien said.

"But if all the ship's systems check out," Archer countered, "then why should we hesitate? This isn't the dark ages, when test pilots had to try out new aircraft because they didn't have computers to simulate their performance."

"Simulations," Lowenstien said, "are not actualities."

Yeager said, "Now wait a minute. The whole point of this exercise is to send a human team down to the level where those giant whales live."

"And get them back alive," Lowenstien added. Johansen nodded.

"And get them back alive," Archer said, "before the IAA steps in and strangles us with red tape."

Johansen looked worried. "Do you think they would really try to stop us? Why?"

"We're risking human lives here," Lowenstien said.

Archer said, "Mrs. Westfall seems to be afraid of that. She's just as much as told me that she'll do everything she can to stop us from sending a human team in."

"May I say something?" Dorn asked.

They all turned toward the cyborg.

"I presume that I will be one of the crew," he said.

"You don't have any scientific training," Johansen objected.

"Yes, but I've had considerable experience piloting spacecraft."

"Not the same thing at all," said Johansen.

"And," Dorn added, "I apparently am better able than others to withstand the pressures that the crew will face."

That stopped them. For several moments the office was dead quiet.

Then Archer asked, "What is it you want to say?"

"I'm willing to ride in Dr. Yeager's vessel. I have confidence in his design."

Johansen smiled palely at the cyborg. Lowenstien looked faintly disgusted.

"We appreciate your courage," said Archer.

"Not courage," Dorn corrected. "Curiosity. I want to learn about those gigantic creatures. I want to see them face to face."

The discussion droned on for more than an hour. Johansen even began to argue that they should be spending more time on classifying the various species living in Jupiter's atmosphere, rather than focusing all their efforts on the leviathans. Yeager decided to head them off before they got themselves too deeply involved in what he considered to be a sideline issue.

"All right," he said, his nervousness gone now that he knew what had to be done. "We send the vessel into the ocean on an automated mission. No crew. We put her through the exact conditions she'll have to face with a crew aboard. If she gets through that without a problem, then we'll be ready for a human mission. Right?"

Archer turned from Yeager toward Johansen and Lowenstien. Each of them nodded agreement. Johansen seemed reasonably compliant about the idea, Yeager thought; Lowenstien wary, almost suspicious.

KATHERINE WESTFALL'S QUARTERS

S o they're going to send the submersible down there unmanned?" Katherine Westfall asked.

Deirdre nodded. "That's the plan."

Westfall had draped herself across the sitting room's chaise longue, clad in a skintight pair of glittering gold toreador pants topped by an emerald green silk jacket. Her sandals were crusted with gems: Deirdre wondered if they were real jewels. As usual, Westfall looked as if she had arranged herself to have her portrait snapped.

Sitting in an armchair facing her, Deirdre felt almost scruffy in her dark gray pullover blouse and lighter slacks. The coffee table between them was bare. Westfall had offered no refreshments of any kind for this midnight meeting.

"You're certain of this?" Westfall asked, almost accusingly. "This information is reliable?"

"I got it from Dr. Yeager, the man who designed the vessel. He'll be in charge of the mission."

"I see," said Westfall. A hint of a smile curled the corners of her mouth. "I presume you have Yeager suitably enamored of your charms."

Deirdre almost laughed in her face, remembering how easy it had been to get information out of Max.

Dorn had told her about the meeting in Archer's office when he'd met Deirdre in the clinic for her immunization therapy. The cyborg didn't have to be there, the clinic had a sufficient sample of his blood on hand, but somehow he seemed to show up whenever Deirdre had to get her shots.

"I appreciate your moral support," she'd said to him as they left the clinic.

"That seems to be my main function these days," said Dorn. He told her about Max's need for support in the meeting with Dr. Archer.

Once she was alone in her quarters Deirdre phoned Max.

"I hear you had a big meeting," she said to the engineer's image in her phone screen. "I hope it went well."

Yeager put on a toothy smile. "I'll tell you all about it over dinner."

"Fine," said Deirdre.

Yeager looked surprised, but he broke into his usual leering grin and replied happily, "I'll pick you up at eighteen hundred hours. Okay?"

"Fine," Deirdre repeated.

The station's galley was hardly a romantic trysting place, but Yeager found a table for two and spent most of dinner talking about the meeting and the decision to send *Faraday* into the Jovian ocean without a crew aboard.

"Can you do that?" Deirdre asked. "I mean, can the ship function without a crew?"

Yeager popped a forkful of apple tart into his mouth and nodded wordlessly as he chewed it quickly and then swallowed it down.

"She'll run fully automated," he said at last. But his expression was far from happy.

"Is there something wrong with that?"

He looked down at his plate. Nothing there but crumbs. Without looking up at Deirdre he muttered, "I don't like it."

"Your dessert?" She giggled. "You didn't leave much of it."

"Not the dessert," he said, meeting her eyes at last. "I don't like sending her down there alone. Without a crew."

"Why not?"

He hesitated a couple of heartbeats, then explained, "She'll have to go down so deep we'll lose contact with her. We won't be able to run her remotely, from here in the station. She'll have to run fully automated, completely on her own. She'll be all alone down there!"

"But you said the ship's designed to operate that way, if it has to."

Shaking his head, Yeager said, "Yeah, yeah, I know. Hell, I designed her! I know what she can do! I even set up a human analog file into her main program; silly thing to do, but I did it anyway."

"A human analog program?"

"Yeah." Yeager looked almost ashamed of himself. "Aphorism, adages . . . that sort of thing. So she wouldn't feel all alone down there."

Deirdre smiled at him. "Max, you're just a big softie. That program isn't going to make the computer feel better. Computers don't have emotions."

"I know. But I do."

"The ship will do fine, Max."

"I know. I know."

"So what's the problem?"

"I just don't like it. I worry about her. I'd feel a lot better if I was there with her."

"Golly, Max, you sound as if you're talking about a child of yours."

"I am," he said. "She's my baby, Dee. I'm scared for her."

Once they'd left the galley and walked along the passageway toward their living quarters, Yeager fell silent. Deirdre thought that all his bluster and loud confidence in his design was really a front. He was worried that his vessel might fail, that it might never return from its uncrewed mission into the Jovian ocean.

Are his insinuations about me nothing more than bravado, too? she wondered. She realized that she was going to find out.

"Well," she said, once they'd reached her door, "thanks for an interesting dinner, Max."

His familiar lecherous smirk returned. "The night is young, fair one."

Deirdre decided to follow her hunch. "That's true, it is."

Yeager was a big, burly man, she realized. But his eyes were a meltingly soft brown. He stood before Deirdre, suddenly tongue-tied.

"Would you like to come in?" she asked, in a breathy whisper.

"I . . . uh . . ."

"I'm afraid I don't have anything to drink."

"Yeah, well . . ."

"We could just sit and talk for a while. Or watch videos."

Yeager licked his lips, shifting slightly from one foot to the other, like a little boy.

Deirdre stepped so close to him that her body touched his. "Or whatever," she whispered.

"Uh . . . Dee . . ." Something close to panic flashed in Yeager's eyes. "I'm old enough to be your father, you know."

"Do you want me to call you Daddy?"

He gulped hard. "I . . . I've got two kids your age . . . older," he stuttered. "My ex-wife has custody of them. Back in Arizona."

"That's a long way from here," Deirdre murmured.

"I gotta go!" Yeager said. "I gotta review the simulation data and get ready for a meeting tomorrow with the launch crew."

"Do you have to?" Deirdre importuned.

"See you!" said Yeager. He turned and hurried down the passageway. Deirdre smiled knowingly as she watched him, a big hulking figure shambling along, running away from her. The more they talk, she knew, the less they act.

Katherine Westfall misunderstood her smile.

"You enjoyed your time with Dr. Yeager, it seems," Westfall said.

Deirdre sighed. "He's a dear man. A very dear man."

Westfall eyed her carefully for several silent moments. Then, "How's your therapy going?"

Startled by the sudden change of subject, Deirdre said, "Dr. Mandrill says my condition is under control."

"That's good. And as long as you continue to keep me informed about your colleagues' progress, we'll be able to keep your condition under control."

Deirdre saw perfectly well what she really meant. She'll be able to keep *me* under control.

LAUNCH

You're the launch director?" Max Yeager asked, his eyes wide with disbelief.

"I am," said Linda Vishnevskaya, standing before Yeager and looking up at him with unflappable tenacity. She was a tiny woman, barely as tall as Yeager's shoulder and elfin slim. Her curly golden hair was like a sunburst in the drab control center, her violet eyes calm and steady.

Almost truculently, Yeager asked, "How many launches have you directed?"

"Every one of them, since I first came to the station four years ago."

Yeager blinked at her. *This little pixie of a girl is the launch director?* It was hard for him to accept.

"My team has a perfect record," she said. "We haven't lost a single craft. Not on launch. Several have disappeared down in the ocean, of course, but that was after they were out of contact with us, beyond our control."

Nodding, Yeager admitted, "That's what I'm worried about."

Vishnevskaya's steely expression warmed slightly. "Not to worry, Dr. Yeager. We will treat your vessel with great tenderness. We won't hurt her, I promise you."

Yeager almost smiled. "She's a very valuable piece of equipment, you know. I've spent a lot of years working on her."

"I know," said the launch director. She reached for Yeager's hand. "You care very much for your baby. But now it's time for her to leave you and go out into the great big world."

Tugging at Yeager's arm like a toy doll pulling a big stuffed teddy bear, Vishnevskaya said gently, "Come, let me introduce you to my team."

Yeager followed her dumbly.

Grant Archer escorted Katherine Westfall through the double doors and into the control center's upper level. He showed her to one of the chairs built into the circular wall, several steps above the consoles arrayed along the center's deck.

"Isn't this rushing things?" Westfall asked once they were seated side by side. "Launching that enormous vessel on such short notice?"

Archer shook his head. "No, Mrs. Westfall. We're not rushing anything. In fact, we're slowing down from the plan I originally had in mind."

"Really?"

"I had wanted to send a human crew as soon as we could."

"Before I could get the IAA to stop you," Westfall said.

Archer conceded the point with a dip of his bearded chin. "There is that. But our technical people insisted that we test the vehicle with an uncrewed mission."

"Even so," Westfall said, "it's only been two days since you made that decision. And now you're actually going to launch it? Into the ocean?"

Pointing to the petite golden-haired woman sitting at the central console, Archer said, "This isn't like the old days, when it took weeks or even months to get a major launch under way. Our equipment is highly automated. And we have the best team in the solar system, if you ask me."

Westfall said nothing, but the cynical expression on her sculpted face showed that she was unconvinced.

"Besides," Archer went on, "we have the benefit of the scoopship operations. They launch vehicles into Jupiter's atmosphere every week, just about. They've got launch procedures down to a routine."

"The scoopships don't go into the ocean," Westfall pointed out.

"But the launch operations are pretty much the same," Archer countered.

Westfall decided to let the matter rest there, thinking, Archer's doing his damnedest to get his people down there with the leviathans before I can prevent him from doing it. The IAA governing council is taking its usual time about making a decision to prohibit a human mission. Two dozen windbags: It's a miracle that they make any decisions about anything at all.

But if this test mission goes well, Archer will have the ammunition to make the council back his play. He doesn't need the council's permission for his human mission. All he needs is for the council not to prohibit it. Unless I can get the council to act, and act soon, he'll send a human crew down there. And if the mission is successful, Archer will be handed the chairmanship of the governing council. I can't let that happen! His mission has to be a failure. A terrible, tragic failure.

Yeager was sitting alone in the control center's upper level across the circular chamber from Archer and Westfall. He barely noticed their presence. His attention was totally focused on the launch team as they began the countdown.

That little Russian kid seems to know what she's doing, Yeager told himself. The rest of the team is experienced, too. Some of 'em do double duty with the scoopship operations. They know what they're doing. They won't screw it up.

Still, his stomach was in knots as the countdown proceeded. At first everything seemed to rush by at hyperkinetic speed: One instant they were an hour from launch and a breath later they were on the final ten seconds.

Time stretched like warm taffy now. Ten seconds. Nine. Yeager knew exactly what was going on in *Faraday*: internal power on; communications on; propulsion system activated.

Eight seconds. Seven. Six.

At five seconds *Faraday* became fully autonomous: The ship no longer needed directions from the launch team's computers.

Four seconds. Three. Two.

Yeager unconsciously rose to his feet, his eyes fixed on the big screen that showed his vehicle, his baby, the pride of his career, hanging in the empty black of space.

One second. Launch.

For an instant nothing happened. *Faraday* just hung there, unmoving. Something's gone wrong! Yeager screamed silently.

Then the gigantic sphere rotated half a turn and began to move away from the station. It pushed off slowly for the first few seconds, then flashed away like a child's kite ripped into the blue by a sudden gust of wind.

She's gone, Yeager said, standing there on trembling legs. I might never see her again.

PERFLUOROCARBON

t's not like the old days," the technician was telling Dorn. "Back then they took off all your body hair and implanted electrodes in you surgically and whatnot. It was a real mess."

The cyborg listened without comment, thinking, I have no body hair to remove. He had been instructed to wear nothing but swim trunks, but had found an emerald green hooded robe in the station's quartermaster supplies and covered himself with it.

They were down in the third wheel. The technician was leading Dorn down a blank-walled corridor, toward a door marked IMMERSION CENTER. He looked like a teenager, almost Dorn's own height but gawky, awkward, as if his body hadn't yet become accustomed to his long limbs. His hair was sandy brown, his eyes sea green, his long face marked by prominent teeth in a narrow jaw.

"I mean," he went on, "now all they have to do is dunk you in the gunk and let your body adjust to breathing it. Simple."

"Have you tried it?" Dorn asked calmly.

The kid's eyes flashed wide. "Me? Uh, no, they don't need to dunk me."

"I see."

They pushed through the door and into the immersion center. It was a circular room with what looked like a large sunken bathtub in its center. Two more technicians were waiting by the railing that went around the tub's perimeter. One was a dark-skinned, round-faced man with frown lines etching his forehead. He was short and stocky; his skin seemed to glow, as if sheened with perspiration. His partner was a rather good-looking brunette woman, her complexion the golden brown of Polynesia. Both wore tan coveralls.

The frowning man looked up from his palmcomp. "I'm Dr. Vavuniva, the chief technician here. You are Mr. Dorn?"

"Just Dorn."

"Dorn," the chief technician said. "No first name?"

"Not anymore."

The tech's brows shot up and he cast a questioning glance at the woman. She said, "It's all right. We have his dossier. All the data we need is on file."

Turning to Dorn, she said, "You've been briefed, I presume."

"Fully," he said. She was on the tall side, he noted, barely a couple of centimeters shorter than he. Oval face, with a discreet tattoo of a flower on her left cheekbone.

"Is that a dahlia?" Dorn asked her.

She smiled. "Yes. My given name is Dahlia."

"I have no given name," he said.

"So I see from your dossier."

The chief tech said, "Well, let's get on with it." He turned to the younger technician. "You wait here. We might need you to help bring him back."

The kid nodded. He looked nervous, Dorn thought.

The woman said, "You understand that you're going to be immersed in liquid perfluorocarbon. You'll be able to breathe it just as you breathe air."

Dorn stepped to the railing at the edge of the tub. "I'll be immersed in there? Fully immersed?"

Dahlia smiled at him. "It's quite deep."

The chief tech said, "The tank goes down twelve meters. You'll be in over your head, don't worry."

Following their instructions, Dorn took off his robe while the youngster opened the gate in the railing. Dorn saw the three of them gazing at his body. They're trying not to stare, he realized. But his half-metal body seemed to hold their eyes like a magnet holds iron filings.

The young tech wondered, "How will the gunk react with . . . uh, with his . . ."

"Shouldn't be a problem," Dr. Vavuniva said. "The perfluorocarbon won't react with his metals, we checked that several times."

Dahlia picked up a belt of weights from the deck and offered it to Dorn. "You'll need this," she said.

"You've got to go down to the bottom," the chief tech explained, "and stay there for at least fifteen minutes."

Dorn nodded and accepted the belt from Dahlia, with a murmured, "Thank you." He fastened it around his waist.

"The belt has a built-in phone. Once you're fully immersed you'll be able to speak almost normally. And with the phone you can talk to us while you're down there."

Dorn thought, Call for help, she means. But she's too kind to say it.

Vavuniva turned to a screen set into the chamber's curving bulkhead. He touched it once, and a display of alphanumerics lit up.

Nodding as if satisfied, he turned back to Dorn and said, "Very well then, in you go."

Dorn saw that there was a ladder built into the side of the tank. He stepped into the perfluorocarbon, prosthetic foot first.

Dahlia leaned over the rail. "You'll gag on it. Everybody does, at first. It's a reflex. Don't panic."

Dorn smiled at her as best as he could. "Thanks for the advice. I'll try not to panic."

He climbed slowly down the ladder. The liquid felt cold, slimy to the human half of his body. Up to his waist. Up to his shoulders. Another step and the liquid rose over his head. He held his breath automatically. Down another step. Immersed in the liquid, Dorn could hear the tiny whining of the servomotors that moved his mechanical half. But the noise sounded deeper, lower.

He couldn't hold his breath any longer. His lung was burning. He couldn't help himself, he sucked in a deep breath. And gagged. Don't panic! he commanded himself.

For ageless moments he hung on the rungs of the ladder, feeling the cold oily fluid in his nose, sliding down into his lung. He closed his human eye, gripping the ladder, shuddering as he tried to breathe the liquid. His prosthetic hand bent the rung's metal.

With dogged resolution Dorn pushed himself off the ladder

completely and slowly sank deeper into the tubular tank. His feet touched bottom, his knees flexed slightly.

And he was breathing. It wasn't pleasant, but Dorn found that he could breathe almost normally in the all-pervading liquid perfluorocarbon. The fluid was almost as transparent as air; he could see the welded seams of the tank's metal walls quite clearly.

"I'm at the bottom," he said, his voice sounding strangely deep and slow in his ears.

"Fifteen minutes," came the chief tech's voice, also distorted. "Starting now."

Dorn waited, trying not to think about the past as the minutes ticked slowly by. When you go into Jupiter's ocean in the submersible you'll be immersed in this liquid, he thought. You'll have to spend days breathing this slime.

Unbidden, memories of his past life surged to his consciousness. His first raid, when he was twelve, destroying the village, killing everyone, everything, even the cattle and dogs. Strange that the mangy, half-starved dog still stuck in his memory. He had tried to kill it cleanly, with one shot, but only crippled its hind legs. The mutt crawled painfully away, yowling until he emptied the whole clip of his assault rifle and blew it to bloody scraps.

Dorn's pulse was thundering in his ears when at last the chief tech announced he could come back up.

Dahlia's voice added, "Climb the ladder slowly. Don't try to float to the surface, please."

Dorn followed her orders, glad to have something, anything, that papered over the memories of his past. When he broke to the surface, he gagged again. He began to cough uncontrollably as the younger technician leaned over the railing to help him out of the tank. Dahlia reached out both her arms to help steady him. Dorn's body spasmed. He bent over and coughed up oily, greenish liquid.

"You must lie down now," the chief tech said sternly. "We have to pump the perfluorocarbon out of your lungs."

Lung, Dorn replied silently, his body racked with coughing. I only have one lung.

The pumping procedure is worse than the immersion, Dorn

thought. But at last it was finished and he was breathing air once again. His chest hurt, his head was spinning, but he was breathing normally at last.

As he got slowly to his feet the chief tech looked at him unhappily. "Good enough for the first time," he said, as if it hurt him to admit it. "Tomorrow we start the high-pressure tests."

Even Dahlia looked sorrowful at that.

FARADAY

Linda Vishnevskaya pushed herself wearily from the control center's main console.

"That's it," she said, loudly enough for her six teammates to hear her even through the earbuds they were wearing. "The bird's on automated programming now. She's on her own."

It had been another routine day, which somehow made her all the more tired. Sitting at the console yesterday while *Faraday* ran through its internal checks during its initial orbits of Jupiter had been stupefyingly dull. The bird behaved beautifully: everything on the tick. Vishnevskaya had been a little edgy earlier this morning when *Faraday* plunged into Jupiter's thick swirling clouds, as programmed, but telemetry showed all systems were operating nominally.

Then came the entry into the ocean. Even that had been virtually letter perfect. And exactly as calculated, *Faraday*'s telemetry signals cut off. The bird was too deep in the ocean for electronics signals to reach station *Gold*; not even tight-beam laser communications could get through that depth of ocean, and the clouds that wreathed the giant planet perpetually.

"She's on her own," Vishnevskaya repeated, in a muttering whisper.

She looked across the chamber and up to the empty visitors' gallery. Empty except for one person: G. Maxwell Yeager was still sitting up there as he had sat through all day yesterday, watching, listening, as the controllers monitored *Faraday*'s plunge into the sea.

Tiredly she plodded up the stairs toward Yeager. He looked as if he hadn't moved a muscle in the past forty-eight hours. He was unshaven, pouchy-eyed, his tawny coveralls rumpled. Her nostrils twitched slightly as she neared him; obviously Yeager hadn't bathed recently.

"There's no sense staying here any longer. There's nothing we can do for her until she comes back up out of the ocean." She bit back the impulse to say "*If* she comes back."

Yeager shook his head and sighed. "I know. I know. It's just . . . I hate to leave her alone."

"She'll send up a data capsule tomorrow," the launch director said, trying to sound cheerful. "You'll see then that everything is going well."

"If she pops the capsule on schedule," Yeager replied morosely.

Vishnevskaya patted him on the shoulder. "Come with me, little father. I'll buy you a drink. We both could use some vodka."

Yeager slowly got to his feet.

"You've designed a good vehicle. She works beautifully. There's nothing else for us to do until she sends that first data capsule to us, Dr. Yeager."

Yeager admitted the truth of it with a rueful nod. "Well," he said, "if you're going to buy me a drink, at least you should call me Max."

Deirdre watched as the nurse pressed the hypospray gun against the bared skin of her arm. She felt a slight tingling, nothing more.

"Dr. Mandrill wants to see you now," the nurse said as Deirdre got up from the chair. She pointed toward the treatment room's open door. "Take a left; he's the third door on your right. His name is on the door."

Deirdre nodded absently as she rolled her sleeve down and buttoned its cuff. Dr. Mandrill. Maybe he has good news.

One look at the doctor's face showed that the news was not good. His dark eyes were rimmed with red, as if he'd been crying.

"Ms. Ambrose," he said, once Deirdre had seated herself in front of his desk, "we seem to be fighting a losing battle."

Trying to stay calm, Deirdre asked, "What do you mean?"

"The immunoglobulin therapy is holding your infection in check, but not making any progress in eliminating it."

"Oh?"

"Ordinarily, after a week of treatments, the virus would be virtually eliminated from your system," the doctor said, his fleshy dark face morose, his tone gloomy. "In your case, however, the virus shows no sign of decreasing. It is still in your nervous system, as strong as when you first came to me. Most puzzling. Most extremely puzzling."

Fighting down the tide of fear edging up from the pit of her stomach, Deirdre asked, "What can we do?"

With a massive shrug of his heavy shoulders, Dr. Mandrill said, "Continue the immunization therapy. Without it your disease will grow and spread. Perhaps if we continue the therapy long enough the virus will succumb to it."

"And if not?"

Another shrug. The doctor looked away from Deirdre as he said, "There is always the possibility that all we are doing is building up the virus's immunity to the immunoglobulin injections. In that case, the disease will grow worse."

"And there's nothing else you can do?" Deirdre was surprised by how small, how childlike, how pathetic her voice sounded.

Forcing a toothy smile, Dr. Mandrill said, "I have put in a call to Massachusetts General Hospital, on Earth. Perhaps they can suggest something."

Faraday reached the depth prescribed by its mission profile and adjusted its internal density to achieve neutral buoyancy.

Floating easily, the vessel's sensors showed that the sea was teeming with life at this level. *Faraday*'s central computer reviewed the data flooding in from the ship's sensors, checked them against earlier inputs from previous missions, and stored the new information in its capacious memory core.

Streams of organic matter flowed on turbulent currents that swept downward through the ammonia-laced water. Creatures of all sizes followed the currents, eating and being eaten. If a computer could feel excitement, *Faraday*'s central processor would have tingled with joy.

All the ship's systems were performing within nominal limits. The main fusion drive had switched from internal propellant to intake mode, sucking in water from the surrounding ocean, boiling it plasma hot, and expelling the superheated steam through the propulsion jets.

Heterotrophic life, the computer's biology program noted. No autotrophs at this depth, no creatures that manufacture foodstuffs for themselves, as green plants do on Earth. No, this ecosystem is based around the constant infall of organic particles from the clouds high above the ocean's surface.

The computer's primary assignment was to find one or more of the gigantic creatures defined as leviathans. These Jovian behemoths fed on the tiny organic particles sifting through the sea. They lived directly off the base of their food chain, like the largest animals of Earth, the great baleen whales.

Visual and even infrared sensors were pitifully limited in this deep, dark sea. *Faraday* depended on sensors that detected sound waves, like sonar, and pressure waves in the water made by the movements of living creatures. The most sophisticated transducers and display systems that the human mind could produce translated these waves into moving images that human eyes could see, human brains could interpret.

All the data streaming in from the sensors were being stored in *Faraday*'s memory on a picosecond-by-picosecond basis, to be transferred to the data capsules due to be sent back to the orbital research station, and finally to be uploaded once the vessel regained contact with the controllers aboard the station.

Faraday extended its sensors' range to their limits, but there was no sign of the mammoth leviathans. Logic tree concluded that this meant that none of the creatures were at this depth. Mission protocol called for following the most abundant stream of organics, in the expectation that this would lead to one or more of the leviathans feeding.

Faraday activated its secondary propulsion system and began to follow the richest organic stream, diving deeper into the ocean, adjusting its buoyancy as it sank downward. Its external temperature sensors reported that the outer hull was rapidly becoming hotter, but internal monitors showed that the temperature rise was not threatening.

Not yet.

think they're laughing at me," Andy Corvus said disconsolately.

This late in the evening, the galley was nearly empty. The dinner hour was long past, and only a few of the neatly lined-up tables were occupied. The usual noise and clatter of the place had transformed into a scattering of quiet conversations as people finished their desserts or sipped synthetic coffee.

"Who's laughing at you?" Deirdre asked.

"The dolphins," said Corvus.

"Laughing at you?"

He exhaled an unhappy sigh. "I've been in that tank with them every day, just about all day. Trying to learn more of their language. They swim around me and chatter to each other and I can't figure out what they're saying. Even Baby isn't as friendly as she used to be."

Deirdre could see the wretchedness on his usually happy face.

Corvus went on, "I mean, they talk to each other but they're not talking to me."

"Not at all?"

"Aw, they say hello and good hunting and things like that. But they say a lot more to each other and they're not letting me know what they're talking about. I think they're laughing at me: dumb two-legs trying to learn their language."

Deirdre reached for her nearly empty teacup as she said, "I don't think they'd behave that way, Andy. Maybe you've just reached a level that's going to take more work, more effort."

Suddenly insistent, Corvus asked urgently, "Dee, would you come back to the tank with me? You made contact with them so easily. They like you!"

"They don't dislike you, Andy."

"Maybe not," he conceded, "but I'm up against a stone wall. Will you help me, Dee? Please?"

She saw the pleading in his wide blue eyes, but heard herself say, "I can't, Andy. I'm working full time on the *Volvox*, trying to find the chemical signals that trigger their reproduction."

"Yeah. I guess that's important, too."

"Dr. Grant himself gave me the assignment. I report directly to him."

"What assignment?"

They looked up to see Max Yeager approaching their table. He pulled out a chair and sat between the two of them.

"Hope I'm not too late for dinner," Yeager said as he sat down. He looked tired, rumpled, unshaven. He smelled unwashed.

"Where've you been?" Corvus asked the engineer. "Haven't seen you for the past two days."

Yeager scratched at his stubbled jaw. "Down in the control center, waiting for my baby to talk to me."

"*Faraday?*" Deirdre asked.

Yeager nodded as a robot waiter glided to their table, the evening's menu displayed on its touch screen.

"Who else?" he said. "She's been on her own for more than fifty hours now. Too deep to maintain a link with us. She's supposed to fire off a data capsule tomorrow."

"So you'll know then how she's doing, right?" Corvus asked.

"Maybe," Yeager replied. He methodically pecked out his dinner order and the robot trundled away.

"What assignment were you talking about, Dee?" the engineer asked.

"For Dr. Archer. I'm studying *Volvox aureus*. He thinks it might give us some insights into the way the leviathans reproduce."

Yeager's old leer reappeared. "I like the way we reproduce."

"Oh, Max," Deirdre said.

"I need Dee down in the dolphin tank," Corvus told the engineer. "They've stopped talking to me."

Still grinning, Yeager said, "Well, I don't blame them for prefer- ring our beautiful one to you, Andy."

Deirdre looked past Yeager's dark-jawed face and saw Dorn en- tering the galley. He walked slowly, as if utterly weary.

Corvus saw him too and waved the cyborg to their table.

"How are you?" Deirdre asked as he sat down.

"Fatigued," Dorn said. "I have been many things in my life. Now I am an experimental animal."

"Pressure tests?" Yeager guessed.

"Pressure tests," Dorn acknowledged. "The scientists are very happy with me: I've withstood higher pressures than any other sub- ject they've ever worked with."

"They dunk you in that liquid?" Corvus asked.

"Perfluorocarbon. Yes."

Deirdre suppressed a shudder as Corvus asked, "What's it like?"

"Not comfortable," said Dorn. "Not enjoyable at all."

"I heard it's cold and slimy," Corvus said.

Nodding, Dorn added, "And then some."

"Great," Corvus said. "I'm going to have to live in that stuff for days on end when I go down on the crewed mission."

"I'll be with you, apparently," said Dorn.

Yeager made a sour face. "First we've got to get *Faraday* back and check out how she performed."

"Your vehicle is still in the ocean?" Dorn asked.

"Another two days," Yeager answered.

The waiter came back with Yeager's dinner tray. Dorn did not order anything.

"I'm too tired to eat," he said.

"You ought to keep up your strength," Deirdre said.

He made a noise that might have been a grunt. "The scientists check my physical condition at the start of each day. If they feel I lack sufficient nutrition they pump nutrients into me through an IV tube."

"Yuck!" said Corvus.

Yeager picked up his fork, hesitated, then looked at each one of them in turn.

"We make quite a quartet," the engineer said sardonically. "Andy can't get his dolphins to talk to him. Dorn's being used as a guinea pig. I'm hanging around like an expectant father in a maternity ward." He turned to Deirdre. "You're the only one without a problem, Dee."

"I have my problem," she said quietly.

"Anything I can do to help you?" Yeager asked, his usual smirk gone; his expression was almost fatherly.

"Or me?" Corvus said.

"Or me?" added Dorn.

Deirdre smiled at the three of them. "You're all very kind. But my problem is medical. Rabies."

"Aren't the medics helping you?" Corvus asked.

With a slight shake of her head, Deirdre replied, "The immunization shots aren't working the way they should. The virus is still infecting my nervous system."

"You're not showing any obvious symptoms," said Dorn.

"Not yet," Deirdre replied.

"Why aren't the shots working?" Corvus wondered.

Deirdre started to answer, hesitated, then decided to plunge in. *If I can't trust my three friends I'm really all alone,* she said to herself.

Aloud, she told them, "The virus might be genetically engineered. I think it is."

COUNTERMOVE

enetically engineered?"

"By whom?"

"What do you mean?"

Deirdre raised both her hands and tried to calm them down, surprised at how angry and distressed all three of them seemed.

"Mrs. Westfall told me—"

"Katherine Westfall?" Corvus gaped at her. "What's she got to do with it?"

"She's the one who raised the possibility," Deirdre said.

"I don't get it," said Yeager. "Why would a member of the IAA's governing council be involved in something like this?"

Deirdre closed her eyes briefly, remembering Katherine Westfall's exact words.

"She told me, quote, 'Back on Earth there was some rumor about a biology laboratory that developed a genetically engineered form of rabies.'"

"She said that?" Yeager asked.

"Word for word."

"That doesn't mean—"

Deirdre interrupted, "Then she told me that she wants me to keep her informed on what Dr. Archer is doing. She particularly wants to know what's going on with his plan to send a crewed mission into the ocean, Max."

"Well, she would, wouldn't she?"

"She wants me to spy on Dr. Archer for her."

Yeager's face showed clear disbelief. Andy looked doubtful, too. It was hard to read Dorn's impassive features.

Deirdre went on, "She told me, quote, 'I want you to keep me informed on what's going on here. Fully informed. Keep me informed and I'll do everything I can to help cure your infection. Do we understand one another?' "

The three men glanced at each other uneasily.

"That's exactly what she said to me," Deirdre assured them. "And you should have seen the expression on her face! Like a snake!"

"This is very serious," said Dorn.

"Why would she do it?" Yeager wondered aloud.

"What should I do about it?" Deirdre asked.

"Not 'I,' " said Dorn. "Us. What should *we* do about it?"

"We've got to do something," Yeager said.

"Yes, but what?" asked Dorn.

"Use your head," Corvus said, looking impatient. "Go to the top. Tell Archer about it. He's the only one who can help us."

First thing the next morning, the four of them trooped over to Grant Archer's office. The station director looked surprised as they came in, unannounced, and asked for his attention.

Archer stroked his beard absently as he listened to Deirdre's recital. When at last she finished, he leaned back in his recliner and was silent for several moments. Deirdre, Corvus, Yeager, and Dorn sat arrayed around him, waiting for the station director to say something.

At last Archer sat up straighter and murmured, "It never ends."

Corvus blinked at him. "What never ends?"

Leaning his hands on his thighs, Archer said softly, "When I first came here, more than twenty years ago, I was asked to spy on the station director."

"What?"

His light brown eyes focused on the past, Archer told them, "When I came to station *Gold,* I was a grad student working toward my doctorate in astrophysics. The New Morality sent me here as part of my public service obligation."

"The New Morality?" Deirdre asked.

"They're a religious outfit back in North America," Yeager explained. "Fundamentalists."

"They were a very powerful political force back then," said Archer. "They thought that the studies of extraterrestrial life that were being conducted here on *Gold* conflicted with their views of the Bible. They sent me here to find out just what the scientists were doing and report back to them."

"They thought that studying ET life contradicts the Bible?" Corvus said. "That's nutty."

"Not to them," Archer replied. "They were very powerful in those days. They practically ran the government."

Dorn said, "When a religious group gains political power, both the religion and the political system suffer."

Archer shook his head, as if trying to clear his mind. "That was more than twenty years ago. Things have changed. For the better, I think."

Yeager said, "There're still lots of people back Earthside who believe all that fundamentalist bullshit."

"But Mrs. Westfall isn't one of them," Deirdre pointed out.

Archer agreed. "No, I don't believe she is."

"Then why does she want Dee to spy on you?" Corvus asked.

Archer almost smiled. "Beats me. She must have her reasons. I've shown her everything we're doing here. I've been quite open with her."

Dorn said, "Conspiracy theory."

"What?"

"People who believe in conspiracy theories are never satisfied with the information you give them—unless that information confirms their beliefs."

"Like the UFO believers," Yeager said.

"Well, the solar system really has been visited by intelligent extraterrestrials," Corvus said. "We know that."

"Millions of years ago, most likely," Yeager countered.

"Maybe not," said Deirdre, turning to Dorn.

The cyborg nodded to her, then told the others, "There is an artifact that seems quite beyond human capabilities, hidden out in the Asteroid Belt. I've seen it. It changed my life."

"But we've got no idea how long it's been there," Yeager insisted.

"The point that I originally intended to make," Dorn said, looking squarely at Archer, "is that no matter how much information you give to someone who believes in conspiracy theories, that person will remain convinced that you are hiding vital facts from him."

"Or her," Deirdre added.

Archer's face showed he understood Dorn's point. "So you think that Mrs. Westfall believes I'm hiding something from her."

"And she's enlisted Deirdre to pry that information out of you," Dorn said.

"But I'm not hiding anything!"

"That means that Deirdre can't tell her anything more than she's already learned directly from you."

Yeager said, "Which means she'll think Deirdre's holding out on her."

Corvus picked up, "Which means she won't let the medics cure the gengineered virus."

They all turned toward Deirdre.

"I could die of rabies," she said, in a choked whisper.

"No!" Corvus snapped. "Never!"

"We'll get her to produce the cure," Dorn said, folding his prosthetic hand into a tight fist.

"Maybe there isn't a cure," Yeager said. "Just because some lab manufactured an engineered virus doesn't mean they've also made a way to kill it."

Deirdre felt her insides simmer with sudden fear.

Archer saw the expression on her face and said gently, "Don't worry. I'll send all your medical files and a sample of your blood to the nanotech lab at Selene University. They'll design a nanomachine specifically to track down that virus and tear it apart."

"That . . ." Deirdre's breath caught in her throat. "That would be very expensive, wouldn't it?"

Archer smiled at her. "We've already paid for your passage here.

And your scholarship. This would simply be protecting our investment in you."

"And do you think that would work? The nanobugs could wipe out the virus?"

"Certainly. I'll send the data today. Your current therapy is maintaining you; the virus isn't spreading through your nervous system. Selene will produce the nanomachines to cure you."

"And what do we do in the meantime?" Corvus asked. "Westfall will expect information from Dee."

"We'll give you information to feed her," Archer said. "For example, *Faraday*'s first message capsule is due to pop out of the ocean later today. Isn't that right, Dr. Yeager?"

"Max," Yeager corrected automatically. Then he added, "You're right. Data capsule's due in"—he glanced at his wristwatch—"two and a half hours."

"Make a copy of the capsule's upload and give it to Deirdre," Archer directed. "That should keep Mrs. Westfall happy for a while."

Corvus grinned. Dorn nodded thoughtfully.

But Yeager said, "If the capsule comes up. If everything's going right down there."

ensor data: No leviathans observed.

Central computer: Extend search to maximum sensor range.

Sensor data: No leviathans observed.

Program time line: Data capsule to be launched in 60.0000 seconds.

Central computer: Query logic tree. Launch data capsule despite lack of data?

Logic tree: Command protocol dictates data capsule launch according to preprogrammed schedule, regardless of contents of data storage.

Human analog subprogram: Aphorism, "No news is good news." Aphorism, "It is always darkest before the dawn."

Central computer: Launch data capsule on schedule.

Mission objectives program: Data capsule launched.

Sensor report: Pressure waves indicate presence of large organisms at extreme range of sensitivity.

Time line: 17.3318 seconds elapsed since launch of data capsule.

Sensor report: Detected organisms moving at depth deeper than mission profile cruise depth.

Central computer: Mission profile cruise depth can be exceeded if necessary.

Sensor report: Detected organisms' depth estimated at 900 kilometers below ocean surface.

Central computer: Nine hundred kilometers is within nominal performance limits. Change course to dive to depth of detected organisms.

Navigation program: Course correction implemented. Diving.

Sensor report: Detected organisms not leviathans. Signature indicates organisms to be predators.

Memory bank: Sharklike predators attack and feed on leviathans. Voracious. Extremely dangerous. Have attacked research vessels from time to time.

Central computer: Query, How many predators have been detected?

Sensor report: Eighty-two.

Memory bank: No previous observation of more than fifteen predators at one sighting. Eighty-two predators an unprecedented number.

Central computer: Query decision tree: Launch additional data capsule?

Decision tree: Not enough data to determine if this is new behavior of predators or normal behavior not heretofore observed.

Logic program: Large assemblage of predators an indication that large assemblage of prey must be near enough to be attacked. Since predators prey on leviathans, conclusion is that leviathans must be within sensory range of predators.

Mission objectives priority: 1. Self-preservation. 2. Observation of leviathans. 3. Report accumulated data on schedule. 4. Report new phenomena immediately. 5. Observation of predators.

Central computer: Follow predator swarm, assuming that they will lead to leviathans.

Mission protocol program: WARNING. Predator swarm near mission profile depth limit. Leviathans may be below mission profile depth limit.

Central computer: Follow predator swarm to depth limit of mission profile.

"No leviathans?" Andy Corvus asked, wide-eyed with disbelief. "Not even one?"

Max Yeager shook his head. "Not even one."

Corvus had dropped in at the control center after another disappointing swim with the dolphins. Only one of the consoles was manned; even the cute little Russian chief controller had taken off. Yeager sat at one of the consoles, looking weary and rumpled, his long hair tangled, his chin dark with several days' growth of stubble.

"Where are they?" Corvus asked.

Irritated, Yeager jabbed a finger at the console's central screen. "You see any? They're not there! Nowhere in sight!"

Corvus stared at the screen as if he could make the leviathans appear by sheer willpower.

"I've checked all the data sixteen times from Sunday," Yeager grumbled. "*Faraday* entered the ocean smack in the middle of their usual feeding grounds. But they aren't there." With a shake of his shaggy head he added, "They must be down lower, maybe too deep for her to reach them."

"Maybe the ship scared them off?"

Yeager gave him a sour look. "My baby might look big to you, Andy, but to those damned whales it's just a little minnow. She didn't scare them."

Frowning with puzzlement, Corvus muttered, "Maybe something else did, then."

Faraday Central computer: Query core memory *re* attacks on submersible vessels by predators.

Core memory: Attacks by predators not unusual. Two earlier submersible vessels lost, presumably due to predator attacks.

Mission objectives priority: 1. Self-preservation. 2. Observation of leviathans. 3. Report accumulated data on schedule. 4. Report new phenomena immediately. 5. Observation of predators.

Mission protocol program: WARNING. Approaching depth limit of mission profile.

Systems check: All systems functioning within design parameters.

Central computer: Do not exceed depth limit of 1000 kilometers.

Logic tree: Prime directive of self-preservation can be achieved by maintaining sufficient distance from predators to forestall their attacks.

Central computer: Follow predators while maintaining existing distance from them.

Logic tree: Why do predators attack inanimate vessels? Possibility one: Predators do not have enough intelligence to recognize inanimate objects from potential edible prey. Possibility two: Predators behaving analogously to predators of Earth by staking out hunting territory and resisting encroachment by others.

Question: Are predator attacks simple reflex action or territorial behavior? Not enough data to decide.

Subsidiary question: If behavior is territorial, how do predators distinguish particular locations? Are there characteristics of the ocean environment undetected by ship's sensors but clearly discernable to predators?

Central computer: Insufficient data to derive meaningful solution. Continue following predators; maintain existing distance; do not exceed depth limit.

Safety subprogram: WARNING. Increasing depth causing rising internal temperatures.

Query: Are rising internal temperatures causing system malfunctions?

Safety subprogram: All systems operating within nominal limits.

Central computer: Continue existing course.

Sensor report: Predator pack has divided into two segments. One is continuing on course. The other has reversed course and is heading toward this vessel.

OBSERVATION DECK

Deirdre felt her breath catch in her throat.

She had agreed to meet Mrs. Westfall in the observation deck of station *Gold*, a special section of the second wheel with a long window of glassteel looking out into space. The deck was empty and dark when Deirdre entered; like the observation blister aboard *Australia*, once she closed the hatch she seemed to be hanging in the middle of infinity, swarms of stars gleaming all about her, solemn and unblinking, stars of all colors blazing their light across the universe.

Deirdre took an unsteady step across the glassteel floor. It was like walking on the face of the deep. And then, as the station slowly rotated, massive Jupiter rose majestically into view. The planet loomed huge, immense, its varicolored clouds churning and whirling before Deirdre's staring eyes. It filled her vision, engulfed her senses like a true god, encompassing everything. Deirdre felt herself trembling. Jupiter, king of the gods, mightiest of all the planets of the solar system.

She reached out her hand as the incredible swirling beauty of the planet slid unhurriedly before her amazed eyes. Her fingertips touched the cold solidity of the glassteel window. For long minutes she stood there, transfixed, watching the giant planet's roiling, eddying clouds. Close enough to touch, she thought. Almost close enough to touch.

Then the station's rotation swung Jupiter out of her view. She watched the curve of the planet's limb, brilliant against the blackness of space, slowly swing out of sight. How pale the stars seemed! How distant and cold.

The hatch opened and the floor lights glowed faintly. Deirdre could see Katherine Westfall's slim figure reflected in the window, outlined within the frame of the hatchway.

Reluctantly she turned to face Mrs. Westfall. The woman was only shoulder high to Deirdre, but her form-fitting metallic jumpsuit once again made Deirdre feel shabby in her everyday gray coveralls. Once the hatch closed and the lights dimmed again, she heard Westfall's breath puff out of her.

"Goodness!" Westfall gasped.

Deirdre smiled knowingly. "It's like being in outer space," she said, extending a hand to Westfall.

Quickly recovering, Westfall disdained Deirdre's hand as she stepped up beside her. "It is rather spectacular, isn't it?"

"The universe," Deirdre murmured.

"All those stars. Clouds of them. Oceans of them."

"Yes."

"Can you identify them?"

"Some," Deirdre said. "That bright blue one is Sirius, I think. And over there, the yellowish one, that's probably Canopus."

Westfall said, "When we were children we always tried to find 'Beetlejuice'."

"You grew up in Australia?"

"The Outback. I thought we saw plenty of stars back there, but this . . . this is rather much, isn't it?"

"Rather," Deirdre agreed.

"Now then," Westfall said, her tone turning businesslike, "what have you found out?"

Knowing that Dr. Archer would tell her about *Faraday*'s first data capsule within a few hours, Deirdre reported, "The vessel sent its first data capsule on schedule."

"Data capsule," Westfall repeated, uncertainly.

"The vessel is down so deep in the ocean that it can't transmit messages by radio or laser, so it's programmed to send capsules up into orbit."

"Ah! I see. And the capsules contain information about what the ship has been doing."

"Exactly. The first capsule came out of the clouds and established an equatorial orbit late yesterday."

"And what information did it carry?"

Deirdre shrugged slightly. "All the ship's systems are performing as designed. *Faraday's* down at the depth where the leviathans are usually found."

"And?"

"No leviathans yet. None of the creatures have been detected."

"None? Not one?"

"Not one."

"What do the scientists have to say about that?"

Hearing the impatience in her voice, Deirdre thought, She'd never be able to be a scientist; she wants results too soon.

"Well?" Westfall demanded.

"They're sort of surprised. The vessel was sent to a region where there's always been leviathans swimming and feeding. But right now there's nothing."

"How can that be?"

"That's what they're trying to figure out. The vessel's following a stream of organics, the stuff the leviathans feed on. Sooner or later they'll find some of the creatures, unless . . ."

"Unless what?"

"Unless the creatures have gone so deep the vessel can't follow them."

Even in the starlit dimness Deirdre could see unalloyed anger twisting Westfall's usually composed features.

"They're hiding something!" she snapped.

"No, that's what the data capsule showed," said Deirdre.

"Either they're hiding vital information from you or you're hiding it from me. Either way, I want to know everything they've found. Everything! Do you understand me?"

"But that *is* everything!" Deirdre said.

"I don't believe you. I don't believe any of you! You're hiding the truth from me and—"

Westfall stopped in mid-sentence. Deirdre saw a reddish glow starting to light her face. Turning, she saw that Jupiter was sliding into view once again.

Westfall stood open-mouthed, staring.

"My god," she whispered. "My god."

Deirdre fought down the urge to snicker at Westfall's sudden awe.

"It's overpowering, isn't it?" she whispered, extending her hand toward Westfall once more.

"Overwhelming," Westfall said, in a little girl's frightened voice. "As if it's going to fall down on us, crush us . . ."

She turned and bolted for the hatch, fumbled with the keypad lock, and pushed out into the passageway as soon as the hatch clicked open.

Deirdre went after her. Westfall was standing pressed against the passageway bulkhead, eyes closed, breathing hard.

"Are you all right?" Deirdre asked.

With an obvious shuddering effort, Westfall pulled herself together. She took in a deep breath, opened her steel gray eyes, ran smoothing hands along the thighs of her metallic jumpsuit.

"I'm fine," she said calmly. "I was merely . . . surprised. I've never seen Jupiter like that before. It seemed . . . so close . . . so . . . so immense."

Deirdre nodded. "It's a powerful experience."

Straightening her spine, Westfall said, "Be that as it may, I expect you to find out what the scientists are hiding."

"But they're not—"

"They are," Westfall snapped. "And if you value your life you will find what it is and report it immediately to me. Immediately!"

With that, Westfall turned and strode up the passageway, leaving Deirdre standing there, stunned and frightened.

ATTACK

araday watched as the group of predators split precisely in two. Half of the sharklike beasts continued on the course that the pack had been following; the other half was speeding directly toward *Faraday*.

Calculating their speed as they approached, *Faraday*'s central computer estimated that it could outrun the predators, if necessary. The beasts were big, several of them slightly longer than *Faraday*'s own diameter. The programming's primary directive of self-preservation flared to the top of the computer's priorities, replacing the directive to find and observe the leviathans. The human analog program pulled up another aphorism: "Those who fight and run away live to fight another day."

Faraday awaited the predators' attack.

The beasts swarmed all around *Faraday*, completely englobing the vessel as they swam sleekly in slowly tightening circles. *Faraday* made no effort to evade them; the vessel merely maintained its course heading and speed.

Closer and closer the predators glided. *Faraday*'s sensors studied them intently while the central computer ordered a fresh data capsule be prepared for launching.

Each of the predators had a row of glistening circular objects running the length of its body. *Faraday* assumed they were visual sensors. Checking its own auditory receivers, the central computer realized that the predators were sending out sound waves, possibly using them as sonar to measure *Faraday*'s size and distance.

Suddenly one of the beasts darted in toward *Faraday* on a collision course. It pulled up at the last instant and merely brushed against the vessel's metal hull. *Faraday*'s sensors measured the force of the impact; internal monitors reported that no damage had been inflicted.

Another of the creatures bolted in and banged harder against the hull. Then a third, harder still. Internal monitors registered the jolt. Central computer's decision tree showed that if the impacts increased in strength it would be necessary to initiate defensive maneuvers.

A human brain, awash with emotions, would have felt fear, and perhaps curiosity. Why were these predators banging into the vessel? What was their objective? It must be clear to them that the vessel is not edible: It can't be prey. Why were they attacking?

Faraday's central processor, though, merely recorded the attack so that the data capsule could send off the information once it was launched.

From several rungs down the priority directives came the conclusion that the other half of the predators, those that had continued on their original course, must still be tracking the leviathans. But that was of secondary interest now. Self-preservation was most important. That, and getting all this new data out on a capsule so that the human directors could benefit from it.

Another predator slammed into *Faraday*, hard enough to throw four internal pressure monitors off-line for 3.0025 seconds. Puzzling behavior. Checking the decision tree again, central computer found that it was time to test the theory that the predators were behaving territorially.

Faraday activated its secondary propulsion system, leaping upward on a jet of superheated steam. The predators bolted out of the vessel's way and *Faraday* left them far behind, milling about, emitting sound waves on at least four different frequencies. They avoided the plume of steam that the vessel spurted out, sensors reported.

Faraday checked the data capsule, making certain that all these observations were filed in its memory core, then released the capsule.

At the extreme range of its sensors, *Faraday* saw that the predators who had attacked it had now re-formed into a group and were heading in the same direction as they had been before they broke off to attack. Their speed was much higher than before. If a computer could be surprised, *Faraday*'s central processor would have whistled with astonishment.

CONTROL CENTER

inda Vishnevskaya twitched with surprise. She sat at her console in the control center, alone except for the forlorn figure of Max Yeager, dozing in one of the visitor's chairs up by the curving bulkhead. The rest of her crew were not needed; no data capsule from *Faraday* was expected for another twelve hours. She could have left the center completely unattended; if anything happened the comm system would automatically alert her.

But she sat stubbornly for hours at the console, knowing that nothing was going to happen, but unwilling to take the chance that an emergency might arise that would need her immediate attention.

Yeager hovered around the consoles endlessly, taking only brief breaks. He even brought trays of food in, littering the area where he sat with crumbs and emptied cartons. Vishnevskaya at least had the good sense to take an hour for each mealtime and go to the galley before she hurried back to her console.

She was half drowsing when the message light began flashing and the audio pinged. Startled, she saw the main screen automatically power itself aglow and a list of alphanumerics began scrolling across it.

A data capsule! Unscheduled. Vishnevskaya realized something unusual must have happened down in that deep, dark ocean of Jupiter.

She started to turn to shout the news to Yeager, but saw that the burly engineer was already standing at her shoulder, peering intently at the symbols flashing across the screen.

"What's gone wrong?" he demanded, his voice hoarse, growling.

.   .   .

Andy Corvus was swimming with the dolphins again. The aquarium was big, filled with fish that everybody said were bright and colorful, but to Andy they were merely varying shades of gray. And the sleek, grinning dolphins chattering to each other. The translator built into Andy's face mask picked up only a few words:

"Squid below . . . warmer . . . fast current . . ."

Baby was growing fast, he realized. He almost failed to recognize her as the young dolphin glided up toward him.

"Hello, Andy."

"Hello, Baby!" he said, happy that she was speaking to him.

"Race?"

Andy shook his head, not an easy thing to do in the water with the breathing mask. "You always win. You're too fast for me."

Something like mirth seemed to emanate from Baby's whistling reply. The translator told him, "You're slow, Andy."

"I do the best I can."

"Two legs not good."

Andy thought for a moment, then replied, "My two legs work fine on land."

Now Baby fell silent. Andy watched her circle around him, then go up to the surface for a gulp of air. When she came back she said, "Water better. No fish on land."

Deirdre watched the display screen as the enlarged image of a *Volvox aureus* colony swam busily through a drop of simulated pond water. She had worked very hard to alter the purified water of station *Gold*'s drinking supply into the rich brew of pond scum that tiny *Volvox* thrived in.

The microscopically small green sphere was in the process of reproducing. Deirdre watched, fascinated as always, while the creature's cells began to fission, splitting into specialized gonadal cells, male and female.

No privacy for you, she thought. It seemed silly to be studying these microscopic algae in hopes of learning more about the gigantic leviathans. Then she remembered that Dr. Archer had also asked her to look at the images that the leviathans displayed on their mammoth flanks. Pictures, Deirdre thought. He believes the leviathans communicate through pictures. And he wants me to interpret them for him.

With a resolute shake of her head she told herself, It's crazy. He's grasping at straws, just like he said. Looking back at the screen's display of the reproducing *Volvox*, she thought, We're all grasping at straws. Like the blind men and the elephant, we don't really have the faintest idea of what we're dealing with. But I promised him I'd look into the imagery and see if I can make any sense of it. I'll have to fit that in, somehow. When I'm not talking with Andy's dolphins or studying these little buggers.

The new cells were faithfully arranging themselves into a another colony, but—as usual—the cilia that propelled the colony through the water were on the inside of the newly created sphere. Deirdre leaned forward intently, watching as the spherical creature dutifully turned itself inside out, and the cilia began chugging away, moving the newcomer out of the microscope's field of view.

Turning to the smaller readout screen beneath the main display, Deirdre saw that the sensors had acquired the data she needed: a detailed list of the chemicals that flooded the interior of the colony's tiny sphere. Those chemicals were what triggered the reproductive phase, she knew. They guided the tiny creature's creation of a new version of itself: the microbial analog of the pheromones that trigger human reproduction.

"Gotcha," she murmured, with a satisfied smile.

The galley was crowded when Deirdre arrived, but none of her usual friends were in sight. She picked up a tray and took a salad and a mug of fruit juice, then found a table for herself. Before she could sit down, though, she saw Andy Corvus enter the galley, looking glum despite the garish orange slacks and emerald green pullover he was wearing.

She waved to him and waited while he packed his tray with a vegetarian lunch and sauntered over to her.

"How's it going?" Deirdre asked as Andy sat down.

He made a loose-jointed shrug. "Baby talks to me, but I'm not getting any new information, really. Not adding to the vocabulary."

"Maybe there's nothing more to get," she said. "Maybe you've got their entire language down."

"I'd hate to think that. They're smart, Dee. They must have more in their minds than just fish and water temperatures."

She said nothing, stuck a fork into her salad.

Corvus's phone jangled. Frowning, he pulled it from his shirt pocket. "This is Corvus. . . . Yes . . . yes, I did. Uh-huh . . ." Suddenly his eyes lit up. "You did? And the record shows it? No doubt about it? Wow!" He positively beamed at Deirdre. "Okay, thanks! Thanks a lot!"

"Good news," Deirdre guessed.

"The report from Scripps, in California, just came in. Baby's mother was culled from the Pacific Ocean by a research team when she was practically a newborn. Younger than Baby is now."

"And?" Deirdre prodded.

"They pulled her out of the ocean because sharks were attacking her pod. One of the other young females had already been killed."

"Her sister," Deirdre said.

"Just like she told you!" Corvus was almost bouncing up and down on the chair in his enthusiasm. "Just like she told you! That's the confirmation that we need! You made real contact with Baby and the rest of the dolphins!"

Corvus jumped to his feet. "You know what this means?"

Before Deirdre could reply he went on, "This means you really did make meaningful contact, Dee! We can prove it now!"

Deirdre had never seen a grown man look so excited. People at other tables were turning toward Corvus, staring. She half expected Andy to jump up on their table and dance a jig.

In the control center, Max Yeager was eagerly leaning over Vishnevskaya's shoulder, staring at the multiple screens on her console.

"The bastards're slamming into her!" he growled.

"No damage," Vishnevskaya muttered.

The display screens showed *Faraday*'s sensor views of the predators and the reading of the internal monitors as, one by one, the big sharklike creatures banged into the vessel.

"No damage," Vishnevskaya repeated each time one of the beasts attacked.

Yeager felt each lurch as a punch in his gut. Anger seethed inside him. Why are they assaulting her? What in the name of hell do they expect to get out of such a stupid, pointless attack?

Vishnevskaya tapped an enameled fingernail against the central computer display screen. "It's making a decision to get away from them," she said.

"About time," said Yeager. "I didn't design her to be a punching bag."

"Propulsion activated . . ." Vishnevskaya leaned back in her chair and exhaled a relieved sigh. "Ah, she made it. She got away."

"Stupid goddamned sharks," Yeager grumbled. "Maybe I should've designed some defense weapons for the ship. Electric fields. A few megavolts would show those damned fish to back off."

Vishnevskaya smiled up at him. "Not to worry, little father. Your baby took good care of herself. The danger is past."

Yeager nodded. "Yeah, maybe. But if the sharks keep putting themselves between our baby and the leviathans, how's she going to fulfill her primary directive? How's she going to study the leviathans if the sharks stay so aggressive?"

CONFERENCE ROOM

G rant Archer took careful note of how the quartet of people arranged themselves around the conference table: Corvus sat on his right, with an unhappy crooked pout on his face. Deirdre Ambrose sat beside him, looking radiantly beautiful even in a casual white pullover and dark slacks. Corvus is color blind, Archer recalled. Is she wearing black and white because of that?

Max Yeager looked tired as he pulled out a chair on the opposite side of the table, dark bags under his eyes and a two-day beard darkening his chin. His tan coveralls were wrinkled, as if he'd been sleeping in them. Archer's nostrils twitched as he caught a whiff of stale, musky body odor. Yeager's sour scent didn't seem to bother Linda Vishnevskaya, though: The petite, intense chief of mission control sat beside the beefy engineer with a contented smile on her heart-shaped face.

"We're all here," Archer said, by way of starting the meeting. "Good."

"Is this all of us?" Vishnevskaya asked, looking surprised. "Shouldn't Dr. Johansen be here?"

Clasping his hands on the tabletop, Archer replied, "He'll join us later. At the moment he's showing Mrs. Westfall through the fluid dynamics lab down in wheel three."

The four of them looked puzzled.

With a slightly guilty smile, Archer said, "I want to get the latest information you have directly from you, without Mrs. Westfall in the way. Johansen is serving as a decoy, for the moment."

Deirdre said, "She'll see through that soon enough."

"I know." Archer sighed. "But I do want to hear what you've accomplished without all the politics that Mrs. Westfall and the IAA carry with them."

"Okay," Yeager said crisply. "*Faraday* popped a data capsule earlier today. Those shark-things attacked her, banged into her repeatedly."

"Any damage?"

"Nothing that her internal repair systems couldn't handle."

Vishnevskaya added, "The sharks positioned themselves between the vessel and the stream of organics that we believe would have led us to a herd of leviathans."

Archer stared at her. "You're sure of that?"

"You can review the data transmissions and see for yourself," Vishnevskaya replied.

"We've never seen that kind of behavior before."

Yeager suggested, "Maybe it's because *Faraday*'s so much bigger than any other probe you've sent into the ocean. Maybe the earlier probes were too small for them to worry about."

Nodding, Archer murmured, "That's something to consider."

"Unfortunately," Vishnevskaya said, "*Faraday* has not found any leviathans yet. The creatures are not in their usual feeding territory."

"Scared off by the sharks, do you think?" Archer mused.

Yeager shrugged. "Ask your behavioral specialists. We're just engineers."

"We don't have any behavioral specialists," Archer confessed. "Until now neither the leviathans nor the sharks have shown enough different kinds of behavior to call for specialists."

Andy Corvus gave a humphing little grunt and said, "Exopsychologists. A new field of study."

His brows rising, Archer said, "You might be right, Dr. Corvus."

"Andy," he said automatically.

Archer replied, "Well, if you expect me to call you Andy, I suppose you'll have to call me Grant."

"Deal," said Corvus. "Grant."

"I wonder who we could get to work as an exopsychologist?"

Corvus lifted his arm and jabbed a forefinger down at the crown of Deirdre's auburn hair. "Here she is."

"Me?" Deirdre blurted.

Archer asked, "What do you mean, Andy?"

Leaning forward slightly, his lopsided face totally serious, Corvus said, "Deirdre's made really meaningful contact with the dolphins. She's a natural. She's found out more about them in a couple of swims than I've been able to get in weeks and weeks. I think, if anybody would be able to make contact with the leviathans, Deirdre's the one who can do it."

For a long silent moment they all looked at Deirdre, who was too surprised to say anything. She remembered that Dr. Archer had asked her to study the images that the leviathans displayed on their flanks and she hadn't even started looking at them yet. She saw the unspoken question in Archer's eyes and had to look away from him, feeling guilty about not doing what he'd asked.

It's too much, Deirdre said to herself, apologizing silently to the station director. There's just been too much happening all at once. I'm sorry . . .

Finally Archer turned toward Corvus and asked, "Andy, do you truly believe that any human being can make meaningful mental contact with the leviathans?"

"To be completely honest," Corvus said, "I don't know. There's a lot of unknowns involved in this. But if I can get a probe into one of them, I think Deirdre's more likely to establish contact with them than anyone else."

"Ms. Ambrose, that means that you'll have to go down into the ocean when we send *Faraday* out with a crew," Archer said, staring into Deirdre's troubled eyes. "Are you willing to do that?"

"I . . ." Deirdre hesitated, glanced at Corvus, then looked back at Archer. "I don't know. This is all . . . kind of a surprise to me."

"To us all," Archer said. "But if Andy is right, you hold the key to making contact with an intelligent alien species."

FLUID DYNAMICS LABORATORY

Katherine Westfall felt certain that they were trying to hypnotize her. She sat in a comfortably padded chair, her entire field of vision filled by wall screens that displayed swirling, shifting patterns of soft colors. Dr. Johansen's calm, flat, slightly nasal voice droned:

"These are the currents flowing through the Jovian ocean. As you can see, the organic particles produced in the clouds above drift down into the sea and ride along on the currents, which are generated by Jupiter's very high rate of spin. Coriolis forces predominate in this mechanism, especially since gravitational effects from Jupiter's moons are almost completely negligible. The ocean is heated from below, of course, by the gravitational energy released by the planet's ongoing contraction."

Katherine watched the drifting, eddying patterns, thinking how pleasant it would be to close her eyes and sink off to sleep.

Johansen continued, "The currents are quite regular, considering all the possibilities for anomalies that arise in turbulent flow. In fact, the only major aberrations we've observed in the patterns of the organics' flow have occurred when a sizeable impactor hits the Jovian atmosphere, such as the comet Shoemaker-Levy 9, almost exactly a century ago. A major cometary impact occurred just a few weeks ago, in the northern hemisphere, and this has disrupted some of the currents of the infalling organics."

It's like being in church when I was a kid, Katherine was thinking. You have to sit there and listen and not squirm and try to stay awake.

"In actuality," Johansen's voice droned on, "we use the organic

particles as handy markers to map out the currents, and the distur-
bances in them. Unless disturbed by a major impact, they generally
tend to drift downward until thermal currents rising from deep
below . . ."

Go to sleep, Katherine said to herself. Just close your eyes and
take a little nap. But then a knife-sharp voice in her mind rang out,
That's just what they want! They *want* to bore you to sleep! They're
doing this to you on purpose, to get you out of the way while they're
busy doing god knows what behind your back!

Snapping her cold gray eyes wide open, she said brusquely,
"Thank you very much, Dr. Johnson."

Johansen flinched with surprise. "Er, it's Johansen, Mrs. Westfall. My name is Johansen."

"Of course it is." Westfall got up from the chair. The screens
still swirled their softly colored displays. "Excuse my error."

"We're not finished with the presentation, Mrs. Westfall. The
work we're showing you here represents two generations of observations and detailed fluid mechanics calculations. It goes all the way
back to—"

"I'm certain it's very important," Westfall said, putting on a placating smile. "But the time is rushing by and I have so much to do. I'm
sure you understand." She made a show of checking her wristwatch.

"Of course," Johansen said, looking defeated. He glanced at his
wrist, too. "You're a very busy woman."

Westfall caught the hint of sullen resentment in his tone. And
ignored it.

Johansen clicked the remote controller in his bony hand and
the screens went dead gray. Westfall blinked as the overhead lights
glowed to life.

"I appreciate your taking the time to show me all this work your
people have been doing," Westfall said as Johansen slid back the
partition that had screened this corner of the fluid dynamics laboratory from the rest of the lab. He was so tall that she had to crane her
neck when he was standing beside her.

"I hope it's been helpful to you," he said, pouting like a little
boy who was disappointed with his birthday present.

Westfall allowed the scientist to lead her through the laboratory, past workbenches where younger men and women stood bent over their instruments, past apparatuses that were entirely meaningless to her, and out into the wheel's circumferential passageway, where two of her aides were waiting for her.

"No need to escort me," she said to Johansen. "I know you're very busy and I can find my way. Thank you very much for such an interesting presentation."

"You're entirely welcome," Johansen said, weakly.

With her two dark-suited young men dutifully trailing after her, Westfall headed briskly for the elevator that would take her back to the first wheel, where Archer's offices were housed. She glanced back over her shoulder and saw Johansen ducking back inside the laboratory.

He's going to call Archer, she thought, and warn him that I'm on the loose.

In the conference room, Archer's pocketphone buzzed softly. Deirdre was glad of the interruption. They want me to go down into the ocean, she was thinking. They want me to ride in Max's vehicle, to live in that high-pressure liquid for days on end.

Looking across the table to the weary-eyed, unshaven Yeager, Deirdre asked, "Max, if you can't find the leviathans, do you still intend to send a human crew down into the ocean?"

Yeager shrugged his husky shoulders. "That's up to him," he said, tilting his shaggy head toward Archer. "I'm just the guy who designed the ship."

Archer snapped his phone shut and tucked it back into his tunic pocket. "Mrs. Westfall's left the third wheel. She'll probably burst in here in a few minutes."

"Goodie," said Andy, mirthlessly.

"All right," Archer said, "we'd better wrap this up. What are our conclusions?"

"The whales have moved away from their usual feeding grounds," Yeager said.

"And the sharks have gotten together in a bigger gang than we've ever seen before," Vishnevskaya added.

"Could those two things be related?" Deirdre asked.

"Got to be," Corvus said.

"There's something else," said Archer. "Maybe it's just a coincidence, but two and a half weeks ago a sizeable comet smacked into Jupiter."

"In the leviathans' feeding grounds?" Corvus asked.

Shaking his head, Archer replied, "No, it was several thousand kilometers north of that area. And it never reached the ocean, it exploded in the clouds."

"So?" Yeager asked.

"It disrupted the flow of organic particles out of the clouds at that latitude," Archer said. "We sent a pair of small probes to map the changes in the flow pattern, but they didn't get very much data before they were crushed by the pressure."

Deirdre saw where he was heading. "You think that the flow of organics was disturbed so much that it forced the leviathans to leave their normal feeding grounds?"

"It's a possibility," Archer said.

"Then where the hell are they?" Yeager demanded.

Archer merely shook his head.

"How do we find them again?" Corvus wondered.

"Follow the sharks," said Deirdre. "Let the sharks find them for us."

Yeager shot a disapproving frown across the table. "The sharks don't like having *Faraday* around them. They butted her until she left their area, remember?"

"Trail them at a distance," Corvus said. "Keep *Faraday* as far away from the sharks as her sensors will allow."

"Will that be far enough away so that the sharks won't turn back and attack her?" Vishnevskaya asked.

Archer puffed out a sigh. "We'll have to try it and see."

Yeager's chin sank down into his chest. He obviously did not like the idea of risking his vessel against the Jovian sharks.

At that moment the conference room door slid open and Katherine Westfall stepped in, smiling sweetly.

"Ah, this is where you are, Dr. Archer," she said. "None of your aides seemed to know your whereabouts. You really should be more careful about keeping them informed."

Archer shot to his feet. "Mrs. Westfall! Finished with your tour of the fluid dynamics lab already?"

She stood by the doorway, eying the four others seated around the conference table.

"Yes. It was very interesting, but much more than I could digest in one sitting."

Archer walked around the table toward her. "Sensory overload. I'm afraid Dr. Johansen sometimes pours it on too heavily."

"Indeed," Westfall agreed thinly.

Extending his arm to her, Archer said, "We've just finished up here. Let me take you up to my office and we can discuss what you'd like to see next."

Westfall took his offered arm. As she turned to allow Archer to lead her out of the conference room she said sweetly to Deirdre, "Oh, Ms. Ambrose. I'm looking forward to seeing you later this afternoon. Why don't you pop over to my suite and have tea with me. Around fourish?"

Deirdre nodded dumbly, knowing it was not an invitation but a command.

Dorn, meanwhile, was sitting on the bottom of the immersion center's tank, breathing high-pressure perfluorocarbon liquid while he attempted to pilot a simulated spacecraft. The technicians had set up a simplified control console for him to operate. It was more like playing a child's game than a really demanding simulation, Dorn thought, but he went through the motions without complaint.

"Rendezvous and docking maneuver," the console's speaker called out, its synthesized voice ominously deep in the thick liquid environment.

"Rendezvous and docking," Dorn acknowledged.

A different voice said, "Notching up the pressure ten percent."

"Ten percent," Dorn said. Not that there's anything I can do about it, he thought. Unless I want to stop this exercise altogether.

The pressure was bearable, so far. And Dorn was pleased that his skills as a spacecraft pilot returned to the forefront of his mind so easily.

"You're doing fine, Dorn." That was Dahlia's voice. Even through the distortion caused by the high-pressure liquid Dorn recognized her easily. "All your readouts are well within normal range: respiration, heart rate, everything."

All to the good, he thought. I'm showing them that I can pilot Max's submersible when they're ready to send in a crewed mission.

"Upping the pressure another five percent," said the technician's distorted voice.

"Five percent," Dorn acknowledged, wondering how far they would go—how far he could take it.

Sitting in a comfortably upholstered chair in Archer's office, Katherine Westfall watched the wall screen display with sheer fascination written clearly on her modeled features. The cyborg was sitting at some sort of console, manipulating keypads with his human hand and his artificial one. He appeared to be in a swimming tank of some sort: The watery light glimmered off the metal side of his face.

"He's actually breathing that liquid?" she asked, in a voice filled with wonder.

"He is indeed," said Archer, sitting next to her. "The liquid is loaded with oxygen, and he can breathe it just as normally as we breathe air . . . almost."

Westfall shuddered inwardly at the thought of it. But she kept her voice even as she asked, "And all the crew members will have to breathe it?"

Archer nodded. "It's because of the pressure down at the depths where the submersible will be operating. Immersing the crew in the perfluorocarbon allows them to withstand much greater pressures than if they were in air, even pressurized air. With the perfluorocarbon every cell in their bodies becomes pressurized. In air, their body cells would be crushed."

With an effort, Westfall took her eyes from the screen and turned to Archer. "That's rather inhuman, don't you think?"

The scientist spread his hands in a gesture of helplessness. "It's the only way we can get people down that deep. Lord knows we've searched for other possibilities. Prayed for them, even."

Arching a pencil-thin brow, Westfall said, "The Lord hasn't seen fit to answer your prayers."

"He works in mysterious ways," Archer replied softly.

"And you're determined to send people down there again, after all these years."

"We've learned as much as we can with robotic probes. If we're going to make meaningful contact with the leviathans—"

"Why is that so important?" she demanded.

Archer clearly looked surprised. "Why? Because they're an intelligent species."

"You can't honestly believe that those beasts are intelligent."

"Why not? Do you think God isn't big enough to create more than one intelligent species?"

"But . . . you don't know it for certain. You're assuming it. There's no real evidence that they're intelligent."

A slow smile spread across Archer's bearded face. "You're perfectly right, Mrs. Westfall. I'm following a hunch. I have some reasons for my hunch, but they're mostly subjective."

"So?"

Still smiling, Archer said, "Mrs. Westfall, most people think that science is a strictly rational, unemotional business. All data and numbers, no human feelings at all. Well, that's dead wrong. Do you want to know how science really works?"

Westfall smiled back at him, thinly. "Do tell."

"A scientist gets a hunch. An insight. An idea that he knows how something works. He might spend the rest of his life trying to prove that he's right. His best friends might spend the rest of their lives trying to prove that he's wrong! It doesn't matter, in the long run. In the long run, what they uncover—the guy with the hunch and the others who disbelieve him—what they uncover is new facts, new observations, new measurements. Everybody learns. In the long run it doesn't matter if the fellow's hunch was right or wrong. What matters is trying to prove it, or disprove it. That's where the new understandings come from."

Westfall stared at him for a long, silent moment, then said in a voice as sharp-edged as a stiletto, "And it doesn't matter how many people you kill along the way."

"It is uncomfortable at first," Dorn admitted. "But you adapt to it quickly enough."

Deirdre shook her head. She had met Dorn for dinner, after spending more than an hour in Westfall's suite, telling her everything that had transpired in their meeting with Dr. Archer, answering her pointed questions as well as she could.

"They want me to go on the mission," Deirdre said.

Dorn looked up from his cup of chilled soup. "You?"

"Andy thinks I could make contact with the leviathans," she said.

Dorn said nothing. She couldn't tell from his utterly blank expression what he was thinking, but she thought he might be trying to control a sudden anger.

Then she saw Corvus carrying a dinner tray toward them. "Here he comes now," she told Dorn.

Corvus slid into the chair between the two of them and plunked his tray on the table. "Hi!"

Dorn rumbled, "Deirdre tells me that you want her to go with us in the submersible."

"Right." Corvus nodded happily. "Dee's got the knack. She's the best one to try to make contact—"

"No," said Dorn. It sounded like a funeral bell tolling.

Corvus's brows hiked up. "No?"

"You will not risk Deirdre's life on this mission into the ocean."

"Who made you mission commander?" Corvus replied, his face going serious. "You're going, aren't you? I'm certainly going. Why can't Dee go along with us?"

"It's too dangerous."

"Wait a minute," Deirdre interrupted. "I have something to say about this, you know."

Dorn looked implacable. "It's too dangerous for you."

"But not for you?"

"What happens to me doesn't matter. But you have your whole life ahead of you."

"Dorn, you're very sweet," Deirdre said, placing a hand on his human arm, "but this is my decision to make, not yours."

"Besides," Corvus added, "it's not all that dangerous. Uncomfortable, yeah, breathing that liquid gunk. But Max says the mission shouldn't be really dangerous. His ship is perfectly safe . . . as long as we stay within its limits."

Dorn looked from Corvus's slightly unbalanced face to Deirdre's calm beauty and then back to Corvus again.

"Then please explain to me," he said, very firmly, "why Max is not here having dinner with us."

MISSION CONTROL CENTER

Linda Vishnevskaya had allowed Max Yeager to sit at one of the consoles. It was better than having him hover over her, breathing down her neck.

The control center was deserted except for the two of them. Nothing had been heard from *Faraday* since the unexpected data capsule had popped out of the clouds the day before. Another capsule was expected at noon today.

Yeager sat impatiently at the console, reviewing all over again the data that the last capsule had carried. The sharks' attacks had ended when *Faraday* backed away. The vessel was safe as long as it kept away from the predators.

How far away? Yeager asked himself. How close can she get before those damned monsters attack her again? They didn't do any damage, but she's not designed to be a punching bag for those monsters. She can take the g forces of flying through the atmosphere and dropping into the ocean, but that bludgeoning from the sharks is different. If they keep battering at her like that something's going to shake loose sooner or later.

The sharks are looking for the leviathans, Yeager understood. Those big whales are the sharks' food. So if we can just trail the sharks for a while, we ought to come upon the leviathans. Sooner or later. Better be sooner. She's due to leave the ocean and fly back here in another thirty-two hours.

Yeager realized that Vishnevskaya was standing over him. He almost chuckled at the incongruity of their sizes. Standing, she was just about eye level with him while he was seated.

"When is the last time you had a decent meal?" she asked him.

Shrugging, "I dunno. I grabbed a sandwich a little bit ago."

"That was this morning. It's now almost dinner time."

"I'm not hungry."

She wrinkled her nose. "When's the last time you took a shower?"

He frowned.

"Max," she said, resting a hip on a corner of the console's desktop, "it's no use sitting here hour after hour. You can't help your baby. She's doing fine down there."

"She might pop another capsule."

Vishnevskaya leaned across the console's keyboard and clicked its power switch. The screens went dark.

"Whattaya—"

"Max, little father, I am pulling rank on you. As director of flight operations I order you to get the hell out of here."

Yeager blinked at her. This tiny golden-haired pixie, standing with her fists planted on her slim hips, her violet eyes steady, unwavering . . .

"You're *ordering* me?"

"That's right. Leave the control center. Get yourself a decent meal. If anything happens I will call you immediately."

"You're ordering me." Max didn't know whether to laugh or scream at her.

"Out. Now." She pointed toward the doors. As Yeager pushed himself up from the console's chair she added, "And take a shower!"

Faraday glided through the dark, turbulent sea, keeping as far from the pack of predators as it could while still observing their position with its longest-ranged sensors.

The predators were moving purposefully, steadily, in one direction, massed into a column. Central computer's human analog program pulled up an image of an army of human soldiers marching along a barren, war-ravaged plain.

They could go faster, central computer concluded. In their attacks on *Faraday* itself they had certainly showed much more speed. But now they were coasting along almost leisurely as they moved ever deeper into the hotter depths. The safety program showed that the vessel was approaching the design limit on depth, but so far the increasing pressure and external temperature had not caused any problems. So far.

Suddenly the sharks veered off to the left. Sensors showed that a huge formation of leviathans was moving slowly out there, so far distant that it was difficult to discriminate individual bodies among the mass.

Why were the predators moving away from their prey? Central computer pondered this question for more than a full second, while simultaneously questioning the decision tree program about firing off another data capsule to report this unexpected behavior.

The decision tree concluded that the predators' behavior did not in itself warrant launching a fresh data capsule. But the priority directive flared in central computer's list of objectives: Observe the leviathans. With the predators distracted, even temporarily, *Faraday* obeyed its programming and sped toward the massive assemblage of leviathans. This was an opportunity that it could not resist.

Katherine Westfall tapped her foot impatiently on the plush carpeting of her sitting room. Those fools! She said to herself. Those doddering old fools!

The latest message from IAA headquarters on Earth had her seething with frustrated anger. The council was divided on the question of forbidding Dr. Archer to send a crewed mission into Jupiter's ocean. Split almost evenly down the middle, nine in favor of banning the mission, seven against the motion. Westfall's own vote would make it ten to seven, but the chairman of the council—a geriatric case who should have been put out to pasture long ago, in Westfall's view—ruled that the vote fell one short of the two-thirds majority needed for such a critical decision.

Two-thirds majority! Westfall wanted to throw something, she was so angry. She actually picked up a small decorative vase from the end table by the couch and raised her hand, but stopped herself.

The chairman was a scientist, she knew. Undoubtedly a friend of Archer's, or at least he's in sympathy with a fellow scientist's aim.

Westfall shook her head. They don't care about who has to risk her life. Who might get killed. They're blind to the risks: All they want is to learn new knowledge, regardless of the costs.

She carefully replaced the vase on the end table and sat herself on the couch, trying to relax the tension that was knotting her like a rope.

And what do you want? she asked herself. Retribution for your sister's death? Don't kid yourself. You never really knew her. She's an excuse, not a reason. Why do you want to stop Archer? The answer flashed in her mind immediately: Because Grant Archer is in line for membership on the governing council. And once he's on the council he could swiftly rise to the chairmanship. He's that kind of person: quiet, unassuming, friendly—and single-minded in his determination to put science ahead of everything else. He won't seem to want the chairmanship, Westfall knew. He'll act surprised when they offer it to him. But he'll take it. Oh yes, he'll take it and run the council his way and I'll be just another member out in the cold, without any real power.

Westfall felt a pang of fear clutching at her innards. She remembered her mother telling her over and over, You're not really safe unless you're on top. You've got to be in command, otherwise they can walk all over you. Clenching her tiny fists, she told herself, I've got to stop Archer, one way or another.

She stared at the empty armchair across the coffee table. Only a few hours ago Deirdre Ambrose had sat in that chair and dutifully reported that Archer was encouraging her to become part of the crew that was going down into the ocean.

Westfall could see that Deirdre was clearly afraid of the idea. But they'll cajole her into going, she knew. They'll make it clear that if she wants any kind of a career in scientific research she'll have to do what they tell her. They'll kill her, just like they killed Elaine.

Suddenly Westfall broke into a smile. Of course! What a fool I've been, she said to herself. I've been battering at them to no avail. Archer is determined to send a crew into the ocean. He has his friends on the IAA council and elsewhere in the scientific community; they'll let him get away with it.

And when the mission fails, when those people in the crew are maimed or killed, Archer will be blamed for it. Of course! Westfall almost laughed aloud at the simplicity of it. Let him send them! He'll be writing his own resignation. They'll be killed and it will be easy to see that I've been right all along. Then they'll cancel all this nonsense of human missions into Jupiter's ocean. Then Archer will resign in disgrace—or be fired by the IAA council. Then I can cut their research budget down to where it should be and stop all this nonsense of trying to talk with those alien monsters.

Then I can be elected chairman of the council, as I should be.

She actually did laugh out loud. "And then I can purge the obstructionists off the IAA council! I'll fill the board with my own people and make those scientists dance to my tune!"

LEVIATHAN

Leviathan's sensor parts saw the lights flashing back and forth among the Elders, deep in the core of the Kin's spherical formation. None of its nearby companions lit up; whatever the Elders were discussing was not being transmitted to the others of the Kin.

The darters were still out there, trailing the Kin at a long distance, just barely within sensor range. They wouldn't attack the entire family of us, Leviathan thought. We could crush them if they tried to.

But hunger is a powerful force. Leviathan felt it gnawing at its own parts. If the Elders don't lead us to a new stream of food soon, Leviathan knew, members of the Kin will begin to dissociate, unable to control their starving parts. And once that begins the darters will swoop in and feast.

A message was flashing from one member of the Kin to another, making its way outward from the Elders toward the edge of their formation. When at last Leviathan saw the message glaring from the flank of its nearest fellow, it felt stunned.

The Eldest had decided to leave the group and go off alone to dissociate. Suicide, Leviathan knew. The darters would swarm all over it as soon as it separated itself from the Kin. But the Eldest was firm in its decision. It was willing to sacrifice itself so that the Kin could get away from the darters; willing to allow the predators to devour its parts while the rest of the Kin fled to safety.

Nothing like this had ever happened within Leviathan's memory. Leviathan protested, flashing a message urging the Elders to turn on the darters and drive them away. We are much stronger than they! Leviathan signaled. We can fight them without sacrificing any of our members.

But the Eldest signaled back, No. Better that one dies and the rest of the Kin survive. There must be new currents of food nearby. Find them while the darters are busy feasting. Grow strong and have many buddings.

Leviathan felt helpless in the face of the Eldest's decision. Suddenly its sensor parts shrilled an alarm. An alien! Leviathan's brain recognized what the sensors had detected. One of the strange, cold alien creatures was approaching the Kin. But this one was much larger than any of the previous aliens. Almost as big as a full-grown darter.

Leviathan flashed the information inward toward the Elders. Quickly their reply came back: Ignore the alien. It cannot help us or change what must be.

But Leviathan wondered, Is the alien helping the darters? Is the alien the reason why the food stream disappeared and the darters have grown so bold?

III
PREPARATIONS

If everything is under control, you are going too slow.

—Mario Andretti

IMMERSION CENTER

Deirdre had never swum before. Living in the *Chrysalis II* habitat, the nearest thing to a swimming pool had been an ancient bathtub that her father had imported at tremendous cost from London. The nearest lake or seashore was some three hundred million kilometers away, on Earth.

Even when she made contact with the dolphins she stayed out of the water, under Andy Corvus's encouraging direction. She experienced what Baby felt like swimming effortlessly through the big aquarium tank, but she had never gotten herself wet.

So she felt more than a little trepidation as she approached the immersion center, Andy at her side. Deirdre had searched station *Gold*'s storerooms for something to wear in the immersion tank and found a black maillot which, the logistics clerk assured her, was considered very fashionable swimwear back Earthside. It had been left at the station by a planetary physicist who had gotten herself pregnant and transferred back to Selene.

Wearing a white terry cloth robe over the one-piece swimsuit, Deirdre had gone with Andy down to the immersion center.

"Nervous?" he had asked her as they walked along the passageway.

"A little," she admitted, shaving the truth considerably.

"I'll have to go through this, too, you know."

"I know."

"But not today," Corvus said. For once, Andy looked dead serious. As they walked down the passageway leading to the immersion center, his slightly uneven face was set in a tight expression of concern.

Deirdre said, "I watched some videos last night of people scuba diving back on Earth. It looked like fun."

"It's fun swimming with the dolphins," he said, trying to sound brighter.

They reached the double-door entrance to the immersion center. Corvus reached for both handles and slid the doors open.

"Well, after you're finished they want me to go in," he said.

Deirdre smiled gently at him. I'll be the test subject for you, she said to herself. After you see me get through it, then you'll have the courage to do it yourself. But then she thought, If everything goes right. If there aren't any problems.

Half a dozen people were waiting for them by the immersion tank. Deirdre saw what looked like a modest-sized swimming pool, glowing with light from below its surface that cast strange rippling shadows on the overhead.

But Dorn was nowhere in sight. The cyborg had promised Deirdre that he'd be present to lend her moral support. But he wasn't there. Deirdre felt disappointed, almost betrayed.

A short, stocky, dark-skinned man in a crisp white laboratory coat came up to her and brusquely extended his hand to Deirdre.

"I am Dr. Vavuniva," he said. "I am in charge here."

"Deirdre Ambrose."

"Yes. Of course." Vavuniva looked cranky, impatient frown lines creasing his forehead. His dark eyes shifted toward Corvus. "And you?"

"Andy Corvus. I'm scheduled for a dunking this afternoon."

"Dunking?" Vavuniva snapped. "This is not a frivolous matter, Dr. Corvus."

"No," Andy quickly agreed. "Of course not."

A pretty young woman with a digital clipboard stepped between Deirdre and Dr. Vavuniva. Deirdre saw that she was wearing a colorful flowered dress beneath her white lab coat. She was no taller than Deirdre's own shoulder, and there was a delicate little flower tattooed on her golden cheek.

"You have viewed the orientation video?" she asked, proffering the clipboard.

"Yes," Deirdre said, nodding as she signed the form with the attached stylus.

The other technicians were all men, mostly young: Deirdre's own age, she thought. One of them, a gangling blond youngster, seemed hardly out of his teens. He was staring openly at her. Deirdre smiled at him, and the youngster actually blushed.

Corvus stepped up and put himself between Deirdre and the technician, frowning at the kid. Oh Andy, Deirdre thought, none of the guys can get within ten meters of me without you or Dorn or Max shooing them away. She sighed inwardly. It's good to have protectors, but still . . .

The young technician opened the gate in the railing that circled the pool. "This way, Ms. Ambrose," he said.

The Polynesian woman handed her a belt of weights. "You'll need this," she said softly. "We've adjusted it for your weight."

Deirdre thanked her and, opening her robe slightly, slipped the belt around her waist and clicked its catch. She stepped up to the gate, then pulled off her robe. The young technician gaped at her. She heard one of the other men whistle softly. Out of the corner of her eye she saw Andy bristling.

Vavuniva seemed angered by it all. "Into the tank," he said brusquely.

As she pulled her snug-fitting hood over her hair, Deirdre smiled at the men's reaction. Her swimsuit covered her from neck to crotch, although her arms and legs were bare. The suit was dead black but fit her snugly. She could feel her nipples straining against the fabric. Stepping over the rim of the pool and putting a foot into the water, she felt disappointed that nobody in the whole station had been able to make a pass at her since she'd arrived. Except for Max, of course, but he didn't really count: Max was all talk.

She glanced over her shoulder at Andy, who was now himself staring goggle-eyed at her. Good! Deirdre thought. He's got normal male reactions.

The water felt cold. As Deirdre started to climb down the ladder she remembered that this wasn't really water, it was liquid perfluorocarbon. She was going to have to breathe in it.

The pretty Polynesian woman leaned over the railing and reminded her, "You'll gag at first. Everybody does. It's a normal reflex. Don't panic. Just try to relax and breathe as normally as you can."

Deirdre nodded, thinking that it's easy to give advice. I wonder if she's ever gone into this soup. I wonder if any of them have. I'll bet that officious little Dr. Vavuniva's never even put a toe in this stuff.

The liquid was chilling, and somehow cloying, slimy. Deirdre forced herself to slowly descend the ladder, rung by rung. The liquid came up to her hips, her waist, her breasts, her shoulders. Another step and it'll be over my head, she realized.

Glancing up, she saw Vavuniva's dark face looking nettled, annoyed. And Andy beside him, watching her with his soft blue eyes, looking as if he'd lean over and pull her out if he thought that's what she wanted.

She smiled at Andy, then ducked her head into the liquid. The hood kept her hair dry. She blinked her eyes and found that she could see perfectly well. She held her breath, though. All well and good to claim that you could breathe this liquid, but Deirdre's body didn't really believe that.

Don't panic, she told herself. Plenty of other people have done this. Dr. Archer did, lots of others. Dorn, too. Why isn't he here, as he said he'd be?

Her lungs were burning. She had to breathe! Don't panic. Don't panic, she screamed silently. Take a breath, a deep breath. But her body refused to obey her mind's command. Deirdre squeezed her eyes shut, suddenly wishing that she were with her father back home, safe, warm, breathing normal air . . .

Involuntarily, she sucked in a breath. And gagged. Coughing, sputtering, her body arched painfully. And she realized that she was breathing! Her mouth open and gasping, Deirdre was breathing the liquid perfluorocarbon. It felt cold and oily and completely awful, but she could breathe it.

Her hands let go of the ladder rung and she sank gently down toward the bottom of the tank. Looking down, she saw there was a console of some sort set up down there. And someone sitting at it, looking up at her.

"Welcome," said Dorn, his voice magisterially deep in the perfluorocarbon liquid.

S ure enough, the predators had led *Faraday* to the leviathans. One sensor set after another confirmed that a huge agglomeration of the gigantic creatures was moving steadily through the dark sea in a massive spherical formation. The predators themselves had slowed their own advance and remained at a considerable distance from the leviathans.

Faraday's human analog program projected an image of lions hunting on a wide, grassy plain on Earth. Their prey was a herd of spiral-horned antelope, off in the distance, loitering by a sluggishly moving stream. The tawny beasts hunkered down in the long, waving yellow grass, crawling slowly on their bellies to get close enough to the herd to attack and kill. As some of the antelope stooped to drink, other members of the herd stood alert, ears twitching, sniffing the wind for a scent of danger.

An analogy, *Faraday's* central computer understood, programmed into the memory core to help the computer to recognize what its sensors showed of the alien undersea world.

The sharklike predators swam off to one side of the huge spherical formation of leviathans. They stayed the same distance from the outermost periphery of the herd, content to wait. For how long? Central computer's forecasting subprogram did not have enough data to make a meaningful prediction. But the time line showed that *Faraday's* mission was almost at its conclusion. Already the countdown for returning to the orbiting research station had started ticking.

A human observer would have found the situation maddeningly strange. The predators were following the leviathans' spherical formation, neither coming closer to their prey nor abandoning their long chase. The leviathans showed no indication that they recognized the danger lurking nearby.

One minute left in the mission, the time line showed. Main propulsion drive activated: intake valves open, fusion powerplant ramping up to heat the intake water into plasma. Propulsion jets ready and on standby.

Suddenly the spherical formation of leviathans shifted, split apart into two separate halves. From the core of the formation a mammoth leviathan glided purposefully outward, its flanks flashing colors that shimmered through the water.

Like a school of fish, the predators immediately turned as one unit toward the creature that was emerging from the leviathans' formation.

Faraday's priority hierarchy demanded that a fresh data capsule be prepared. This kind of behavior had never been observed before. The major priority, second only to self-survival, was to send this data back to mission control.

The time line showed forty-seven seconds left in the mission. Central computer concluded it could carry the data to mission control without risking a data capsule launch. But the priority hierarchy insisted that a capsule be launched. Redundancy, central computer recognized. Better to have the data relayed to mission control twice than not at all. If *Faraday* became incapacitated, unable to get out of the ocean, the data capsule would still deliver the information to mission control.

That decision took fourteen nanoseconds. *Faraday* ran a final diagnostic check on its main propulsion system even while its sensors showed that a huge leviathan was leaving the protective formation of its group and heading away from them, alone.

The predators slowly, warily approached the lone leviathan as it glided majestically away from its kin.

Twenty-five seconds to propulsion ignition, central computer's time line showed. Data capsule programmed and ready for launch.

The lone leviathan began to shudder as it swam away from its fellows. Part of the huge beast separated from its main body and floated aimlessly away. Not for long, though. One of the predators broke from its formation and slashed at the separated piece with scimitar-sized teeth.

The predators swarmed over the lone leviathan, tearing at it, while the rest of the leviathans swam slowly away, as if nothing were happening.

Launch capsule, central computer commanded. Ignite main propulsion drive.

Faraday launched the data capsule and milliseconds later lit up its main drive. Superheated steam drove the spherical submersible upward like a pellet fired from a rifle while the predators tore at the lone leviathan and the rest of the herd of gigantic creatures moved steadily away from the scene of the carnage.

rant Archer stood at the head of the conference table and looked at the various department heads arrayed along its length, chatting in muted tones with one another. Down at the foot of the table sat Max Yeager, looking wary, almost suspiciously, at the scientists flanking him on either side. At least Yeager looked presentable; he had shaved and put on some fresh clothes.

Katherine Westfall sat at Archer's right; she seemed mildly bored. Three of her aides were seated along the wall behind her.

"Let's come to order, please," Archer said, tapping the tabletop with a fingernail. The various conversations stopped; all heads turned toward him.

"We're here to review the results of *Faraday*'s mission," Archer said. Making a slight bow toward Westfall, he added, "And we're honored by the presence of a member of the International Astronautical Authority's governing council."

One of the scientists clapped her hands lightly and immediately the rest of them joined in. Westfall smiled demurely and raised her hands in a modest signal to silence them.

"*Faraday* returned three days ago," Archer resumed, "apparently undamaged. We'll review the significance of the data it carried back with it, but first I want to ask Dr. Yeager how his examination of the vessel's systems has gone."

Yeager had indeed shaved and scrubbed for this meeting. His long hair glistened as if he'd just stepped out of a shower. He was wearing a spanking new tunic and slacks of a golden brown sandy hue, yet they somehow looked wrinkled and baggy on him as he got up from his chair.

Pointing a palm-sized remote at the wall screen to his right, Yeager said, "I could spend a few hours going over all the details." The screen showed schematics of *Faraday*'s layout. "But the long and the short of it is that the ship performed well within specifications. All systems worked as designed; even though she took a bit of a battering from the sharks, there was no significant damage."

"*Significant* damage?" Westfall picked up on the word.

Yeager forced a smile for her. "By that I mean there wasn't any damage at all. All systems worked fine. She went down to her design limit depth—"

"How deep is that?" Westfall asked.

"One thousand kilometers below the surface," Yeager replied. A little sheepishly, he added, "Actually, she bottomed out at nine hundred and fourteen klicks."

"The vessel worked as designed," Archer said, cutting off any further dialogue. "Thank you, Dr. Yeager. Your ship performed beautifully."

Max grinned even more widely and sat down.

"However," Archer went on, his expression turning more serious, "we have less than satisfactory results from the mission."

Before Yeager could react Archer explained, "I mean that *Faraday* spent most of its time in the ocean searching for the leviathans, and almost as soon as it found them, the ship left and returned here."

"It followed mission protocol!" Yeager objected. "She was programmed to return at a specific time and that's just what she did."

"Precisely," said Archer.

Michael Johansen raised a long-fingered hand and said, "It's no reflection on you, Max. The bird left just as things were getting interesting."

Yeager muttered something too low for the rest of them to hear.

Westfall asked, in her soft little-girl voice, "What do you mean, just as things were getting interesting?"

Johansen turned to her. "Let me show you." He clicked his own remote and the wall screen darkened.

"More contrast," Johansen murmured. The screen brightened somewhat, showing the shadowy figures of leviathans gliding easily through the depths.

"The leviathans weren't in their usual feeding location," said the lanky Johansen, getting up from his chair like a giraffe climbing to its feet. "Most of the time *Faraday* was down there was spent searching for the creatures."

"And being attacked by the sharks," Yeager added.

With a nod toward the engineer, Johansen said, "Yes, but the primary objective of the mission was to observe the leviathans. By the time *Faraday* found them it had to leave the scene and return here."

"As it was programmed to do," Yeager insisted.

Archer stepped in. "As it was indeed programmed to do. No one's faulting the vehicle or its performance, Dr. Yeager."

"Yeah, but I see a lot of unhappy faces along this table," Max grumbled.

"That's not your fault," Archer soothed. "The problem is that the vessel was following the program we wrote for it, without the capability to change that programming in the face of unexpected events."

Yeager nodded, but still looked unhappy.

"We did learn quite a bit," Archer continued. "The leviathans have left the feeding area where we've always found them before."

Johansen interjected, "The stream of organics flowing in from the clouds above the ocean has been interrupted, probably by the impact of Comet McDaniel-Lloyd last month."

One of the biologists, a blocky-sized woman with a military buzz cut, said, "So they went searching for another stream to feed on."

"Exactly," said Johansen.

Archer pointed out, "*Faraday* found a larger grouping of sharks than we've ever seen before."

"And they attacked the vessel," said Johansen.

"No damage," Yeager said.

The buzz-cut biologist pointed out, "The sharks seemed to be exhibiting territorial behavior. Once the ship moved away from them they stopped attacking it."

"So what have we got here?" Archer mused aloud. "The comet impact disturbs the stream of organics falling into the ocean. The leviathan herd moves off to find a new feeding area. And the sharks come together in the biggest grouping we've ever observed."

"And drive away our vessel," the biologist added. "Territorial behavior, pure and simple."

"I don't know if it's pure or simple," Archer countered, with a placating smile, "but it's definitely behavior we've never observed before."

"The leviathans also exhibited new behavior," Johansen pointed out. The screen showed one of the gigantic creatures swimming away from the rest of the herd, going off alone. The sharks immediately darted after it.

Then the screen went blank.

"What happened?" Westfall asked. "What did they do?"

"We don't know," said Archer. "That's the point where *Faraday* left the area and returned here."

"As programmed," Yeager said.

"It's too bad the ship was programmed to leave when it did," Johansen said, looking at Archer rather than Max. "Just when things were getting interesting."

Archer nodded. Glancing at Westfall, he said, "This clearly shows the limit of robotic missions. If there had been a crew aboard the ship they would have stayed to observe these new behaviors. They wouldn't have left because of a preprogrammed schedule."

"If they had enough supplies on board to remain," Westfall countered.

"Yes, of course," Archer agreed. "But the point is, there's a limit to what we can accomplish with robotic missions. We need to get people down into that ocean again. We need crewed missions."

Everyone around the table looked toward Westfall. She sat in silence for several long moments, apparently deep in thought. Archer saw the tip of her tongue peek out from between her barely parted lips.

Calmly, deliberately, Archer said to her, "If we're going to learn more about the leviathans, if we're ever going to find out if they're intelligent and perhaps make meaningful contact with them, we've got to send crewed missions down there."

"In spite of the dangers," Westfall murmured.

"In spite of the dangers," Archer confirmed. "The crews will be volunteers, of course. They'll all know the risks they're running."

Yeager spoke up again. "I think this mission proved that *Faraday* is a tough bird. A crew will be safe with her."

"As safe as possible," one of the scientists muttered.

"Safe," Yeager said flatly.

Westfall heaved an almost theatrical sigh. "I see," she said. "I understand."

"Then you won't oppose a crewed mission?" Archer asked, his face alight with hope.

With some reluctance, Westfall said softly, "No, I won't oppose a crewed mission. I still think it's terribly risky, but I suppose I'll have to stand aside and let you try it."

A burst of grateful relief gusted from the scientists around the table. Westfall smiled at them, thinking, Give them enough rope and they'll hang themselves.

GRANT ARCHER'S OFFICE

eirdre felt a jumble of emotions as she entered Dr. Archer's office. She had deliberately come ten minutes early for the meeting, hoping to have some time to speak with the station director alone, but Archer was already deep in earnest conversation with a dark-skinned, very serious-looking man whose image was displayed on one of the office's wall screens. The data bar beneath his image read: DR. ZAREB MUZOREWA, UNIVERSITY OF SELENE.

Muzorewa had been director of the station before Dr. Archer, Deirdre knew.

Archer noticed her as Deirdre slid his office door back and waved her to a chair while the man on the wall screen was saying:

"It's true, Grant, she told the chairman of the council that she's withdrawing her objection to a crewed mission."

As she silently took a seat next to Archer, Deirdre could see that the station director was practically glowing with satisfaction. "That's great, Zeb," he said to the screen. "It's a big load off my mind. We can go ahead now without any worries."

Muzorewa's expression remained stony. "Don't get too happy about it, my friend. She repeated her concerns about the safety risks of the mission, but said you assured her the vehicle was safe and the crew would be volunteers."

"That's right," said Archer. "It's true."

"And the way she worded her message, she's withdrawing her objection—reluctantly—only for this one mission."

Archer waved a hand in the air. "That's good enough, Zeb.

Once we get a crewed mission in and back safely we'll have proved that crews can go down again."

"On the other hand," Muzorewa said slowly, choosing his words with obvious care, "if anything goes wrong with your crewed mission, it could spell the end of everything."

"Then we'll have to make certain that nothing goes wrong," Archer said.

Muzorewa's flinty expression eased slightly into a tentative smile. "If you can do that, you should be running the universe. Something will go wrong, Grant. It always does. You know that."

Archer admitted it with a nod. "I meant that we'll have to make sure that nothing major goes wrong."

Muzorewa nodded back. "Perhaps you should try the power of prayer."

"Prayer never hurts."

"Put your trust in the Lord. And keep your powder dry."

Deirdre recognized the quote: Oliver Cromwell, from seventeenth-century England.

Archer laughed. "Good advice."

"Good luck, then," said Muzorewa.

"Thanks, Zeb."

The wall screen went blank.

Turning to Deirdre, Archer explained, "Zeb was my mentor when I first came to this station. He's been a good and firm friend all these years."

"I see," Deirdre said. Suddenly she realized, "But how can you talk with him in real time if he's in Selene? The Moon's at least half an hour away, in light time."

"He's not in Selene," Archer explained. "Zeb's right here at the station, down in the third wheel. He just arrived less than an hour ago. He's carrying your nanomachines."

Still bewildered, she asked, "He got here from Selene in a week?"

"High-g boost. We know you need the nanotherapy as quickly as possible, so Zeb volunteered to zip out here with your nanos."

"You asked him to?"

"I didn't have to," Archer replied. "I simply explained the problem to him and he volunteered. Brought a couple of nanotechs with him. They developed your therapeutic nanos on the way here."

Deirdre felt overwhelmed. "They did this for me?"

His smile widening, Archer said, "Frankly, I think Zeb was happy to have an excuse to get back here. He's as curious about the leviathans as I am. He's the one who turned Dr. Corvus on to the problem of communicating with them."

"I'd like to thank him," Deirdre said.

"Tomorrow. Right now Zeb and his two technicians are in the infirmary in the third wheel, being checked out after their high-g trip: hernias, heart arrhythmias, that sort of thing. Also, I'm not sure that I want Mrs. Westfall to know that they're here."

"My goodness," said Deirdre. But she wondered if Grant Archer or anyone else could prevent Katherine Westfall from learning about Muzorewa's arrival.

"I know that you're supposed to report everything you learn to her, but I hope we can keep this from her, at least for a little while."

Deirdre saw the earnestness in his expression, heard the unvoiced question he was asking her.

"I . . ." She hesitated, wondering what she should do, then heard herself say, "I won't volunteer any information about Dr. Muzorewa and the nanotech specialists."

"Thank you," Archer said. "That could be very helpful." Then, leaning back slightly in his recliner, Archer said, "I notice that you're early for our little conference."

Feeling almost embarrassed, Deirdre said in a lowered voice, "I wanted to ask you . . ."

"Yes?"

"Andy—Dr. Corvus—he wants me to go on the mission with him."

"I know. He's very pleased with the ease with which you make contact with the dolphins."

Deirdre realized she was wringing her hands and purposely pressed them flat on the thighs of her creased slacks. "I . . . I'm not sure that I want to go down there."

Archer sat up a little straighter. "You did fine in the immersion tank."

"I suppose so," Deirdre said, suppressing a shudder, "but I really didn't like it. I don't know if I could stand being in that slimy stuff for days on end."

"I know how you feel. I understand. I didn't like it much myself when I was in the soup."

"What will happen if I don't go?"

With a shrug, Archer said, "It just makes Corvus's job that much more difficult. Not that establishing communications with the leviathans will be easy, under any circumstances." He hesitated a heartbeat, then added, "And, of course, I was hoping that you might be able to make some sense out of the visual imagery the leviathans use to communicate."

"I just . . ." Deirdre faltered, then admitted, "I'm afraid!"

Strangely, Archer smiled at her. "You have every right to be. I'd wonder about your sanity if you weren't."

CLINIC

Katherine Westfall found Dr. Mandrill in the middle of his morning rounds, accompanied by two women in white while moving slowly through the clinic's sole ward. Only three of the ten beds were occupied.

With a polite little cough she caught the portly doctor's attention as she stood by the ward's main door. He frowned at first, but immediately smoothed his expression into a forced smile. After whispering a few words to his aides he waddled up the aisle between the rows of beds to her.

"This is a surprise," said the doctor, in a low tone. "I didn't expect you—"

Westfall cut him off. "My time is important, Doctor. I need some information from you. Quickly."

"As soon as I finish—"

"Now," she snapped.

Barely suppressing his anger, Dr. Mandrill dipped his double chin and acceded, "Now."

He led her out of the ward and down the short passageway to his office. Once the door was closed, Mrs. Westfall said, "My informants tell me that a Dr. Muzorewa has arrived here from Selene."

"Muzorewa? Himself?" The doctor's brows hiked up. "He was director of this station, before Dr. Archer."

"He came with two nanotechnicians."

"Indeed?"

"That's what I've been told."

"What would bring the respected Zareb Muzorewa back to station *Gold*?" Dr. Mandrill mused. "And with a pair of nanotechs?"

"That's what I'm asking you."

Mandrill went to his desk and slid heavily into its swivel chair. "Selene is a center for nanotechnology research and development," he said. "But Muzorewa was a fluid dynamicist, not a nanotech man."

Still standing, Westfall asked, "Could nanotechnology be used to kill the rabies virus?"

The doctor blinked his red-rimmed eyes once, twice.

"Well?" she demanded.

"I suppose it's possible . . . if one engineers nanomachine disassemblers specifically to attack that particular virus."

"They'd need samples of the virus, wouldn't they?"

With a heavy-shouldered shrug Dr. Mandrill replied, "Perhaps not actual samples. Three-dimensional imagery would do, most likely."

Westfall leaned both hands on the back of the chair in front of the doctor's desk. "So they could produce therapeutic nanomachines and use them to kill her virus."

"Her?" Understanding dawned on Mandrill's dark face. "Ah! You're talking about Ms. Ambrose."

"Nanomachines could wipe out her specific type of rabies virus?"

Mandrill nodded warily. "If the nanos were specially designed to attack that variety of virus. It all works by shapes, you know. Like keys and locks."

"They could cure her," Westfall muttered.

"But nanomachines can be dangerous," the doctor pointed out. "The type of nano you're talking about might be able to disassemble other types of organic molecules, as well."

Westfall's eyes brightened.

"In street slang they're called gobblers. The great fear has always been that gobblers would get loose and tear apart everything they come into contact with. It's been called 'the gray goo problem.' That's why nanotechnology is forbidden on Earth. They could reduce everything they touch into a slime of broken molecules."

"Gray goo. Yes, I've heard of that."

"But of course in Selene the nanomachines are handled with great care. Tremendous care. The same would apply here, naturally. Dr. Archer wouldn't allow—"

"He already has," Westfall snapped, with a hint of triumph in her voice.

As Deirdre opened the door to Grant Archer's office, she saw he was deep in conversation with a tall, handsome black man. He looked like a statue carved in ebony: very grave, very powerful. Then he turned toward her and smiled, and his face became delightfully human. She recognized him as Zareb Muzorewa.

"You must be Ms. Ambrose," he said in a deeply resonant voice as he rose to his feet.

"Deirdre Ambrose," said Archer, waving Deirdre to a chair beside the black man. "Meet Dr. Muzorewa."

Archer was smiling broadly. He seemed wonderfully pleased to have Muzorewa in the room with him. "This is the first time Dr. Muzorewa's been out here in . . . what is it, Zeb, ten years?"

Muzorewa's brows knit in thought. "Closer to twelve. I must say that you've enlarged the station far more than I ever could, Grant."

Archer shrugged modestly as Deirdre took the chair beside Muzorewa.

"I'd like to thank you," she said as she sat down, "for coming all this way to help me."

Quite seriously, Muzorewa replied, "I must confess that it wasn't only to help you. I want to disabuse my idealistic friend here of his notion that the leviathans are intelligent."

"You're wrong, Zeb," Archer said gently. "They are intelligent."

"Without tools?" Muzorewa scoffed. "How could a species develop a high order of intelligence without tools? Tool-making is a hallmark of intelligence."

Archer countered, "A hallmark of *our* intelligence. Other species follow different paths. The dolphins, for instance."

"Now you're saying that dolphins are intelligent?"

"They pass knowledge on from one generation to another," Archer said. "Deirdre made that discovery just recently."

Muzorewa looked unconvinced. "Tool-making was a key to our developing intelligence. My anthropologist friends tell me that making tools made us intelligent. Dolphins, whales, the leviathans—they live in an environment where tool-making is impossible. They'll never utilize fire. They have no energy source available to them outside of their own bodies."

"But they tell stories to each other, Zeb. The dolphins do that. And the leviathans flash pictures to one another. They're conversing, exchanging information. That takes intelligence."

As Deirdre wondered how long this argument would go on, the office door slid open and two people—a man and a woman—stepped in.

"Dr. Archer," said the man. "Are we interrupting? You did ask us to come to your office."

Muzorewa got to his feet again. "Grant, Ms. Ambrose, I'd like you to meet Franklin and Janet Torre, nanotechnicians from Selene."

Deirdre nodded toward them. Siblings? she wondered. Maybe twins. Both of the Torres were short, delicately built, with round faces that had a sprinkling of freckles across their snub noses. Both wore identical pale blue one-piece coveralls.

As they pulled up chairs, Muzorewa said, "Back at Selene they're called the Terrific Torre Twins. They're the best nanotechs in the solar system."

Janet Torre started to object, but her brother grinned jovially and said, "I've got to admit that they're right, since I'm not afflicted with false modesty."

"Or true modesty, either," his sister wisecracked.

Everyone laughed, and Deirdre felt at ease.

"Now then," said Muzorewa, getting serious, "we are here to get this modified rabies virus out of your body."

"Are you a nanotech specialist, too?" Deirdre asked.

Muzorewa shook his head slightly. "No, no. I'm here strictly as an observer." He turned back toward Archer. "To tell the truth, I welcomed this opportunity to see what Grant has accomplished with this old station."

Archer looked pleased.

Leaning forward, his childlike face utterly serious, Franklin Torre said to Deirdre, "We've 'ginned up a nanomachine that disassembles the virus analogs we built in our lab back at Selene."

His sister took up, "But we've only worked on analogs, based on the three-dimensional imagery that Dr. Archer sent to us."

"So we need to get a sample of the real virus from you," Franklin resumed, "and see if our nanobugs will chew it up."

"And if they don't?" Deirdre asked.

He looked surprised at the question. "We'll modify the nanos so that they work right. No sweat."

His sister nodded her agreement.

"You'll be working down in the third wheel," Archer said. "My people are setting up an isolation area for the nanotech lab."

Janet Torre said, "Can you rig the passageways leading in and out of the area with high-frequency ultraviolet lamps? We engineer our nanomachines to be deactivated by hard UV."

Archer said, "I meant to ask you about that. Wouldn't it be dangerous for people?"

"Not really," said Janet. "You just need a few meters to be exposed to the UV. People can get through it without harm, as long as they don't linger in the area."

"I wouldn't want to go sunbathing out there," Franklin quipped.

"It's just insurance that no active nanomachines will get out of the lab," Janet added.

"People worry about nanos," Franklin Torre said lightly. "It's pretty silly, really. A machine that's specifically engineered to destroy one certain type of molecule isn't going to develop a taste for other molecules."

"Tell that to the crazies back on Earth," Archer muttered. "Nanoluddites."

Muzorewa held up a finger. "Be fair, Grant. With twenty billion people on Earth there are plenty of fanatics and madmen who would happily develop nanomachines into terror weapons."

"I suppose," Archer admitted.

"A disassembler developed to take apart one kind of molecule," said Janet Torre, "could be modified to attack a wider range of molecules."

"Only by somebody who knows what he's doing," said her brother. "And is nuts."

"That's what they call gobblers," Muzorewa said, his red-rimmed eyes looking sad, wary.

Deirdre asked, "Can the nanomachines actually cure me of rabies? How fast will they work?"

"I'll explain all that over dinner," said Franklin Torre.

The room fell silent. Deirdre heard in her mind her father's warning about smooth-talking blokes. But Franklin Torre didn't look like a smooth-talking bloke to her. He seemed more like a smiling little leprechaun.

"Dinner?" she replied, pleased and a little alarmed at the same time. "With both of you?"

Franklin glanced at his sister and said, "Oh, Jan-Jan's going to be too busy. It'll be just you and me, Deirdre."

D eirdre looked over the galley but could not see Franklin Torre. She had agreed to meet him at the galley's entrance at 1900 hours. She had purposely arrived ten minutes late, to make certain he'd be there waiting for her. But he was nowhere in sight.

She had put on a modest pair of forest green slacks with an overblouse of lace-decorated pale lemon. As she stood at the galley's entrance she saw several people, mostly men, turning to stare at her.

"Don't tell me a beauty like you is all alone."

Startled, she turned to see Rodney Devlin grinning at her. He was in his usual white chef's jacket, spotless for a change. His brick red hair was shaved close, as usual, while his mustache was thickly luxuriant.

"I'm waiting for someone, Mr. Devlin."

"Red. Call me Red. Everybody does."

Deirdre nodded and made a smile for him.

"Well," said Devlin, pointing, "you won't have to wait long."

Andy Corvus came ambling through the galley doors.

"Hi, Dee," he said, with a lopsided grin. "Going in to dinner?"

"I . . . um, I'm waiting for somebody, Andy," Deirdre said, feeling uneasy that Devlin was still close enough to hear everything they said.

"Not Max, I hope."

"No, not Max. And not Dorn, either. Somebody you haven't met yet."

Corvus looked puzzled. Deirdre thought he was about to scratch his head as he stood there frowning slightly.

"Hello, there!"

Franklin Torre came striding up to them, a happy wide smile on his round, snub-nosed face. Deirdre realized for the first time that Torre barely reached her chin.

Feeling slightly awkward, she introduced the two men to each other. Torre shook hands with Corvus, who looked as suspicious as a policeman.

"Franklin's one of the nanotech specialists," Deirdre tried to explain. "From Selene."

"Oh," said Corvus.

Torre's expression suddenly went solemn. Almost whispering, he said to Corvus, "You're infected with nanomachines, aren't you?"

"Me?" Andy yelped. "No!"

"Yes, you are," Torre insisted. "Don't try to hide it."

"What are you talking about? I'm not—"

Torre suddenly broke into a wide grin. "Viruses, man. Viruses. They're natural nanomachines and you're full of 'em!"

"Huh?"

Laughing, Torre tapped Corvus on the shoulder and said gleefully, "Gotcha! You should see the expression on your face!"

With that, he took Deirdre by the arm and led her grandly into the galley, leaving Andy standing at the entrance, looking befuddled. Deirdre looked back at him over her shoulder, trying to apologize with her eyes. Andy just stood there, obviously hurt.

Deirdre said to Torre, "That wasn't nice, Franklin."

Torre shrugged. "I couldn't help it. Nobody realizes that our bodies are filled with natural nanomachines."

"It still wasn't nice to trick him like that," she insisted.

With a sigh, Torre said, "He'll get over it."

Glancing back at Andy again, Deirdre saw that Devlin had disappeared. Back into the kitchen, she surmised. Andy was standing at the galley's entrance alone now.

Torre showed her to a table for two. As they sat, Max Yeager and Dorn joined Corvus, who was still staring in her direction. The expression on Andy's face worried Deirdre. He seemed . . . she groped for a word. Hurt. That's how Andy looks: wounded, as if I've hurt him.

Torre paid no attention to Deirdre's distress; he talked all through dinner about his nanotech work and how the disassemblers he and his sister had designed would destroy any rabies virus in her body.

"You ought to come out to Selene one of these days," Torre said cheerfully, "and see our lab. Finest in the solar system. It was started by Professor Zimmerman himself, one of the real pioneers in the field."

Deirdre listened with only half an ear. She couldn't help watching Andy, across the room, picking listlessly at his dinner.

"Selene's a terrific place," Torre was going on, oblivious to her inattention. "You'd love it there. I could get you a reservation in the best suite in the Hotel Luna."

"That would be nice," Deirdre said absently.

Once they finished dinner they had to walk past the table where Corvus, Yeager, and Dorn were still sitting over coffee and dessert. Andy followed Deirdre with his eyes. She could feel him staring at her back as she left, her arm firmly in Torre's grip.

As they neared Deirdre's door, Torre said, "They've got Jan and me quartered down in the third wheel."

"Not up here, with everybody else?" Deidre asked, stopping in front of her door.

"No," he said, with a theatrical sigh. "I've got to go all the way down there." Then his face brightened impishly. "Unless you let me stay in your place!"

Deirdre shook her head. "I don't think so, Franklin."

"Frankie," he said softly, reaching for her.

Deirdre fended off his grasping hands. "Frankie, I think you ought to go back to your own place now."

He raised both hands in mock surrender. "You don't know what you're missing, Dee."

Thinking that she knew exactly what she was rejecting, Deirdre said, "You're rushing too fast, Frank."

He took the rebuff easily enough. "Okay. I'll see you tomorrow down in the lab we've rigged in the third wheel, then."

"That's fine, Frankie," said Deirdre. "I've got to go down there anyway to work with the dolphins."

Grinning at her, he said, "See you tomorrow, then."

Deirdre felt grateful that he wasn't more aggressive. He could use his nanotech work to pressure me, she thought. But he didn't. Maybe he will later, but for now he's being pretty reasonable. For now.

That night she dreamed of dolphins. And Andy Corvus watching her swimming with a sad, betrayed expression on his slightly misshapen face.

The day was long and difficult. After giving a blood sample to Janet Torre, Deirdre spent the morning in the dolphin tank, swimming with Baby and learning more of her vocabulary. Baby chattered and clicked away, usually faster than the translator built into Deirdre's swim mask could follow. But one thing came through clearly: Baby's parents had told the young dolphin the tales that they had heard about the open sea, the endless water that was too deep to reach the bottom, where tasty squid darted in numbers too big to count and the upper layers were warm with sunlight and wave-tossed.

"They're not happy here, Andy," she told Corvus once she had climbed out of the tank. "They want to be in the ocean, free."

Corvus shook his head. "Baby's never been in the open ocean, Dee. Her parents were scooped out of the sea when they were practically newborns, younger than Baby is now."

"But they remember the ocean," Deirdre said as she toweled off. "At least, they remember tales they've been told about it."

She thought that this sign of intelligence would please Andy. But he merely shook his head and replied, "I suppose we ought to write a paper about it."

"We certainly should," said Deirdre.

Corvus chewed his lip for a moment, then said, "Looked like you and that new guy had a good time at dinner last night."

"Frankie?" Deirdre blurted. "He's one of the nanotechnicians from Selene."

"I know."

"They're going to get rid of the viruses in my body."

Corvus said forlornly, "That's more than I can do for you."

NANOTECH LABORATORY

For three days Deirdre spent her time mostly in the third wheel, giving blood samples to the Torres and then swimming with the dolphins while Corvus watched her, glum and sad-eyed. Each evening she had dinner with Franklin Torre, fearing that it would be terribly ungrateful of her to refuse him. After all, Deirdre told herself, he's come all the way from Selene to help me. The least I can do is be sociable.

Torre always made halfhearted passes at her after dinner and always took her rebuffs with rueful good grace. "You don't know what you're missing," he said each time. Deirdre simply smiled and said good night.

Once alone in her quarters, she began to study the files of the leviathans' imagery. Sitting at her little desk, staring intently at the display screen on the wall, Deirdre tried her best to make some sense of the aliens' images. But the images were incomprehensible to her. They didn't seem to represent anything visually. They're abstracts, she thought, nothing but splashes of color that flash on and off so fast I can barely make out their shapes. I haven't a clue to what they could possibly mean.

When she entered the makeshift nanotech lab on the fourth morning Franklin Torre announced, "Our little bugs are starting to work."

"They are?"

Pointing elatedly to a graph on the rollup display screen taped to the bulkhead, Torre said, "Look at the red curve. It's definitely taken a downward trend."

Janet, smiling just like her brother, said, "By the time you go down to the ocean your system will be rid of the virus completely."

"That's wonderful!" Deirdre said.

"I think we ought to celebrate," said Franklin. "How about dinner tonight?"

"Again? We've had dinner together every night since you arrived here," Deirdre said.

"Yeah, but tonight should be special," Torre countered. "Tonight we can toast to victory over the rabies virus."

Deirdre nodded, but in her mind's eye she saw Andy's disconsolate face. "Dinner," she murmured, feeling that she was doing the wrong thing.

"Are you all right?" Janet asked.

"Yes," said Deirdre. "Fine."

"No puncturing today," Franklin said happily. "We won't need any more blood samples."

"That's good."

Janet handed her a plastic cup of orange juice. "Your morning cocktail," she said. "Chock-full of nanobugs."

Deirdre accepted the cup from her and sipped at it.

Glancing at her brother, who was intently peering at a laptop display, Janet asked softly, "Are you really okay? You look a little . . . unsettled."

"I'm worried about Andy . . . Dr. Corvus."

"Oh?" Her hazel eyes widened.

"It's . . . personal," said Deirdre.

With a nod, Janet called to her brother, "Frankie, I'm going to walk Deirdre over to the dolphin tank. You don't need me for anything important this morning, do you?"

Without taking his eyes from the screen, Franklin answered absently, "Everything's under control here. Take the day off if you want to."

Janet grinned at her brother's back, then said to Deirdre, "Come on, let's talk."

.   .   .

Katherine Westfall was far from happy as she sat in her comfortable lounge watching the report from the head of the IAA's legal department. The man's image filled her wall screen. He was wearing a somber dark jacket, the expression on his once-handsome face set in a grim scowl, as if he knew the news he was bringing would not be welcomed.

"The long and the short of it," he said, in a bleak, droning voice, "is that while nanotechnology has been banned in all its aspects everywhere on Earth by the Nanotech Treaty of 2039, human communities off Earth are not bound by the treaty's provisions. In fact, the nation of Selene fought its war of independence mainly to be free from restrictions on nanotechnology."

The lawyer's office was in the IAA headquarters complex in Amsterdam, on Earth. Westfall could see palm trees outside his window, and the sea glittering beneath a bright sun. Much of Amsterdam and the rest of the Netherlands had been flooded by the greenhouse warming and then painfully regained from the encroaching waters by a generation of hard, ceaseless labor.

She started to interrupt the man's sermon, then realized that the distance between Earth and Jupiter meant that he wouldn't hear her words for a quarter of an hour, at least. So she bit her tongue and continued to listen to his dreary monologue.

"The upshot is," the lawyer continued, "that the scientists on station *Gold* are free to engage in nanotechnology research and use nanomachines as they see fit." His dark brows rose slightly as he added, "So long as they follow standard operating procedures and take all the necessary safety precautions. These include—"

Westfall angrily snapped her fingers and the lawyer's image winked out.

I'll get no help from the lawyers, she told herself. Archer and his minions can play with their nanomachines and cure the Ambrose girl of her rabies. That will break my control over her completely.

Closing her eyes briefly, Westfall wondered what her next move should be. It's obvious, she told herself. You've got to make those nanobugs into a dangerous threat, something that will attack the station and the people in it.

Then she smiled. No, she realized. Not attack the station. I need nanobugs that will attack that ship Archer's sending into the ocean. Destroy the ship and the people in it.

I need a nanotech specialist, she realized. And quickly.

SACRIFICE

So what about Dr. Corvus?" Janet asked as she walked with Deirdre down the third wheel's main passageway toward the dolphin tank.

Deirdre glanced down at Janet, hesitating. She looked so much like her brother: short, slightly built, her light brown hair in bangs that framed her round face. Her eyes were light, too, a bluish brown hazel color. They looked bright, honest, trustworthy.

"I think I've hurt him," Deirdre said at last.

"Hurt him? How?"

"I've been going to dinner with your brother every night since you two arrived here. I think Andy feels hurt over that. He sure acts unhappy."

"Has Frankie come on to you? Is he making a pest of himself?"

Deirdre said, "Nothing I can't handle. He's actually a lot of fun to be with."

"My brother?"

"Yes," Deirdre said. "Of course, he can be . . . very attentive."

"He can be an insensitive jerk about women," Janet grumbled.

"Not just about women," Deirdre said. "He made something of a fool of Andy that first night. Made him look kind of stupid."

With a sigh, Janet said, "Frankie's a jokester. He likes to think he's a comedian."

When Deirdre didn't respond, Janet asked, "Were you and this Corvus guy involved before we came here?"

"No, not really. We were just friends. Along with Max Yeager and Dorn."

"Dorn?"

"The cyborg," Deirdre explained. "The four of us rode out here on the same torch ship and we sort of became buddies."

"And now Corvus feels hurt because you're having dinners with my brother."

"There's nothing going on between us," Deirdre said.

For several paces neither woman said anything. Deirdre saw the doors to the dolphin tank area up the passageway ahead of them.

"There's something more," she admitted. "Andy—Dr. Corvus— he wants me to go with him on the mission into the ocean. He says I'd be better able to make contact with the leviathans than he would."

"And you don't want to go?"

"I'm scared! Living in that perfluorocarbon liquid for days and days. Hundreds of kilometers deep in the ocean. People have been killed on missions like that!"

They reached the double doors and stopped.

Very businesslike, Janet summed up, "So you think that Corvus is jealous of my brother and he'll be hurt even more if you refuse to go on the mission with him."

Deirdre nodded. "That's about it."

"Okay." Janet grinned as she slid the doors open. "Let's have dinner together, all four of us."

"All four of us?"

"You, me, my brother, and Dr. Corvus."

"Dinner," Deirdre murmured.

"Let's see how much of this we can thrash out over a decent meal," Janet said cheerfully.

Deirdre didn't know how Janet arranged it, but when she came down to the galley for dinner that evening, Andy was already sitting at a table with the Torre twins. Both men jumped to their feet when they spotted Deirdre and waved her over to the table.

Feeling tense, Deirdre sat between Corvus and Franklin, opposite Janet. Automatically she scanned the busy, noisy galley for Dorn and Max, but neither of them was in sight.

"Dee and I have been talking," Janet said, without preamble, "about this mission into the ocean that you're planning, Andy."

Deirdre blinked with surprise. Janet was already on a first-name basis with Andy, and calling her Dee. She doesn't waste any time, Deirdre thought.

"That's the reason we're here," Corvus said, his eyes focused on Deirdre. "To get down there and make contact with the leviathans."

"I don't know if I can do it, Andy," Deirdre blurted.

He looked surprised. "But you're working fine with Baby and the other dolphins. You went through the perfluorocarbon immersion with no trouble."

"Andy," said Janet, in an almost motherly tone, "what Dee's trying to tell you is that she's frightened of the prospect. She didn't come here to take a cruise in the Jovian ocean."

Corvus's brows shot up. "You don't want to go?" he asked, in a little boy's disappointed whimper.

Forcing herself to keep her hands in her lap, Deirdre replied, "It's not that I don't want to, Andy. I'm afraid to. I'm scared."

He blinked, digesting the information. Then Corvus shook his head as if he were arguing with himself. At last he said, "Dee, I don't blame you for being scared. This is all new to you."

Franklin Torre muttered, "I'd sure be scared."

Ignoring him, Corvus went on, "If you're scared, Dee, you shouldn't go. I want you to be safe. I want you to be happy."

"Even if it means your mission might not succeed?"

"Don't worry about that," Corvus said softly. "That's not your problem."

"But it means so much to you," Deirdre blurted.

"Not as much as you mean to me, Dee. You mean a lot more."

NANOTECH LABORATORY

Katherine Westfall rode down the elevator to the third wheel, escorted by two of her personal assistants, both tall, well-built young men in dark tunics and slacks, hired for their physical strength and agility rather than their intelligence. They thought of themselves as hired muscle, she knew; she thought of them as boy toys.

Archer thinks he can keep this nanotech business secret from me, she was telling herself. The fool. I know everything that happens in this station. Everything, thanks to that lowly cook.

She had heard about Rodney Devlin before she ever left Earth: the so-called Red Devil was a major source of information about the goings-on of the station. Nothing happened, it seemed, without Devlin knowing about it. And Westfall was making sure that Devlin reported everything he knew to her. Not in person, of course; she didn't want to be seen in the presence of this menial. But her staff stayed in contact with Devlin and kept her informed daily. What the Red Devil knew, Katherine Westfall soon learned.

One of her female aides had called ahead to inform the chief nanotechnician that the IAA councilwoman was coming to visit his lab. "Don't ask permission," Westfall had told her aide. "Simply tell him I'll be there."

Following the directions displayed on her pocketphone, Westfall strode two paces ahead of her strapping assistants until she reached the section of the third wheel's main passageway where the makeshift nanotech laboratory was housed. Flashing displays on screens on both sides of the passageway's bulkheads warned: DANGER—HIGH INTENSITY ULTRAVIOLET RADIATION. She ignored the displays and strode up to the door that bore NANOTECHNOLOGY LABORATORY on its identification screen.

As she reached for the door's handle it slid back before she could touch it, revealing a slightly built young man with a round, freckled face and sparkling hazel eyes.

He smiled broadly and made a courtly little bow. "Mrs. Westfall, I presume."

Katherine Westfall nodded graciously and stepped into the lab area. Turning, she told her assistants, "Wait outside, please."

Franklin Torre's grin morphed into open-mouthed alarm. "Uh, Mrs. Westfall, you don't want them to stay out there. The UV isn't good for them, not for long exposures."

Feeling nettled, Westfall gestured abruptly to her assistants. "Come inside, then. Stay here by the door."

She looked around. The laboratory area was small, scarcely as large as her own sitting room, up in the top wheel.

"You don't seem to need much space, do you?" she said to Torre.

With a good-natured shrug, Torre replied, "Nanomachines are teeny little things. About the size of viruses. We don't need that much room."

"I see. And you are . . . ?"

"My name's Franklin Torre. I'm the director of the Zimmerman Nanotechnology Lab, at Selene."

"Ah. Dr. Torre."

"Mr. Torre," Franklin corrected. "I never finished my doctorate. Got too busy doing real work."

"I understand your sister is here with you," Westfall said.

With a bouncy nod, Torre replied, "Yes, she is. You have good sources of information."

Westfall looked around the smallish room again and saw that no one else was present.

Torre said, "Jan-Jan's not here at the moment."

"So I see."

Smiling pleasantly, Torre asked, "So what would you like to know about nanomachines?"

"Everything."

"Okay. Here's the fifty-dollar tour."

Torre walked her along the workbench that ran the length of the room and began to explain each and every piece of equipment on it: the electron microscope and its display screen, the stainless steel vat in which the nanomachines were built, the double-sealed domed chamber in which the devices were tested.

"Isn't all this dangerous?" she asked.

"Not really," Torre replied easily. "We take all the necessary precautions." Pointing to the gleaming vat in the middle of the workbench, "That's the only really hazardous area. When the disassemblers are first built they're nonspecific; they could attack a fairly wide variety of molecules. Over here in the dome we fine-tune them exclusively for particular molecules. They won't touch anything but those molecules once we've specialized them."

"I understand that you're producing nanomachines that will destroy a particular type of virus," she said.

"Rabies virus," Torre answered, looking impressed at her depth of information. "We're using blood samples from one of the scientists on the staff here. The virus seems to be different from the standard forms in the medical files. It must've been genetically engineered."

"Who would deliberately alter a rabies virus?" Westfall asked rhetorically.

Torre shrugged. "Not my end of the game. It doesn't make any difference to me who tinkered with the virus or how she got it into her bloodstream. My job is to wipe it out."

They were at the end of the workbench, on the far side of the room. Westfall leaned a narrow hip against the edge of the bench. Her two assistants still stood by the door like statues or well-drilled soldiers, arms folded across their chests.

"I must say that your laboratory isn't very imposing."

Torre chuckled. "Like I told you, nanos don't need much room. But they can accomplish tremendous things. Back at Selene we use nanomachines to build spacecraft of pure diamond. The nanobugs manufacture the diamond out of piles of soot, ordinary carbon. They turn individual atoms of carbon into sheets of structural diamond."

"That type of nano is called an assembler, isn't it?"

"Right!" Torre seemed delighted that she knew the term.

"But what you're producing here is a different type of thing altogether, isn't it?"

Nodding again, Torre said, "Yep. We're making disassemblers. Their job isn't to build up new molecules out of individual atoms. Their job is to take apart certain specific molecules, break 'em up into individual atoms."

"And the molecules they attack are the rabies viruses."

"Right again."

"Once you've programmed them."

"Programming isn't the right term to use, really," Torre admitted. "It's not like programming a computer. It's more like reshaping a machine tool. Mechanical, not electronic."

Just then the door to the laboratory slid open and Grant Archer stepped in, nearly bumping into Westfall's two guards.

"It's all right," she called to her men. "Let him through."

Archer clearly looked flustered as he approached Westfall and Torre. But he managed to put a smile on his bearded face and said, "I hope Mr. Torre here is showing you everything you want to see, Mrs. Westfall."

"He certainly is," Westfall replied, making her tone sound languid, almost bored.

"We're very lucky to have him here," Archer said. "He's helping Deirdre Ambrose recover from her viral infection."

Westfall straightened up and started walking slowly along the workbench, back toward the front of the room and the two dark-suited men waiting by the door. She lingered by the chamber where the unprogrammed nanomachines were created.

Her brows knit slightly and she asked, "But aren't nanomachines dangerous? Couldn't these things you're putting into Ms. Ambrose's blood destroy more than just her rabies virus?"

"No," Torre and Archer said in unison.

"But you told me—"

"Maybe I gave you the wrong impression," Torre said. "Nanomachines are machines. They're designed to do a specific job and that's all they can do. Once they're specialized they don't change or mutate on their own. They're not dangerous."

Tapping a lacquered fingernail on the stainless steel vat, Westfall insisted, "But you said the ones in here aren't specialized. They could eat up a large variety of materials."

"They never get out of this laboratory," Torre explained, with some impatience showing in his reddening face. "Not until they're fine-tuned for a specific type of molecule."

"Aren't they called gobblers?" Westfall asked in her hushed, little-girl voice. "Haven't they been used to kill people?"

Torre's face was flushed. But before he could reply, Archer said, "Yes, nanos have been used to murder people. They were deliberately designed to attack any carbon-based molecules they encountered. They were designed and used by madmen."

"That's why they're banned on Earth," Torre said, controlling himself with obvious effort. "Plenty of madmen back there."

"Yes, of course," Westfall murmured. Then, "So the gobblers you're building here can only attack rabies viruses."

"The specific type of virus that's infecting Deirdre Ambrose," Torre said.

"And it couldn't get loose and attack anything else?"

"No, it couldn't," Torre said firmly.

"Besides," Archer put in, "the nanobugs couldn't survive outside this laboratory environment. The passageway outside is drenched in high-intensity ultraviolet light that will deactivate the nanos on contact."

"Ultraviolet light," Westfall murmured.

"We design the nanos to be deactivated by UV," Torre said. "It's a standard safety precaution."

Westfall nodded, apparently satisfied. "Thank you for a very enlightening tour, Mr. Torre," she said.

His composure recovered, Torre extended his hand as he said, "If there's anything else you want to know, just give me a holler."

"Yes. I'll do that." As she approached the door, one of her guards opened it for her and she swept regally out of the lab.

Archer puffed out a breath of air. "I wonder how she found out that you were here," he muttered.

Torre waggled a hand in the air. "Well, she seems satisfied that we're not going to destroy everything in sight."

Archer looked at the still-open door. "I hope so."

But as she stepped into the elevator with her two assistants, Katherine Westfall was thinking, There's no security at that lab at all! Anyone could walk right in and take a sample of their nano-machines. They must lock the door at night, but we could get through without any real trouble.

Then she asked herself, How can I get a sample of the gobblers that haven't been specifically programmed yet? I'll need some nanos that can attack a wide variety of things.

Max Yeager was surprised to see Linda Vishnevskaya sitting at the central console in the otherwise empty control center. All the other consoles were dead and quiet, the big wall screens also blank, except for the one at the front of the chamber that showed *Faraday* hanging in orbit outside the station.

"What're you doing here?" he asked, almost in a growl.

She turned, her violet eyes wide with surprise.

"What are *you* doing here, Max?" she countered.

He sagged into the chair of the console closest to her. Jabbing a thumb toward the image on the wall screen, he explained, "Big meeting tomorrow morning to decide the date for launching her back into the ocean."

Vishnevskaya's face relaxed into a warm smile. "So the little father has come to check out his baby one more time."

Yeager made a sour face. "I'm an engineer, not a sentimental old fart."

"No, not sentimental," she said, straining to keep her face serious. "Not at all."

"I'm trying to work out a defense system for her. Something that'll keep those damned sharks off her."

"You want to protect your baby," said Vishnevskaya, with an impish gleam in her eye.

"She's a machine, a ship," Yeager protested. "I've got a couple of daughters, you know. I can tell the difference between a machine and a human being."

"You are married," Vishnevskaya said.

"Divorced. Almost twenty years ago." Yeager looked uncomfortable, but he added in a near-whisper, "Who could put up with an engineer for a husband?"

Vishnevskaya lapsed into silence.

"I was figuring," Yeager said, getting back to business, "that we could rig the outer shell with a high-potential electric field. Shock anything that comes within a dozen meters of her skin."

"A dozen meters?" Vishnevskaya shook her head slightly. "Electric fields dissipate rapidly in water, don't they?"

"The water's slightly conducting. It's laced with ammonia and other ions. Acidic."

Arching her brows, Vishnevskaya admitted, "It might work, then."

"I think I can make it work. Just enough to keep those damned sharks off her."

"Could you use the light panels on the outer hull?" she suggested.

"The light panels?" Yeager thought about it for all of a second. "Nah. Archer and the science guys wanted them so they could flash pictures at the leviathans. Try to communicate with them visually."

"Yes, but—"

"No, I need something more than a bunch of blinking lights to defend her," Yeager said.

"You're going with her, aren't you?"

Yeager flinched with surprise. "Going with her? What do you mean?"

Smiling almost sadly, Vishnevskaya said, "You're going to insist that you be one of the crew. You can't let her go down there without you."

He tried to frown, but instead his expression melted into an admission of defeat. "Yeah, I want to go with her. I don't know if Archer and the other paper pushers will let me, though."

Vishnevskaya gave a little sigh, then said, "It would help if you volunteered to be immersed in the perfluorocarbon. You could show Archer and the others that you can stand the physical pressure."

Yeager brightened slightly. "You're right. I ought to get some time in at the immersion center."

He got to his feet and headed for the door, leaving Vishnevskaya sitting in the emptied control center, wishing she had kept her mouth shut.

Red Devlin was startled when Katherine Westfall suddenly showed up in his kitchen.

It was well after midnight. The rest of the kitchen crew had gone to their beds, but not Devlin. This was his domain and he worked his own hours. He had been tinkering with one of the serving robots, replacing the LED display screen that covered its flat top.

"Mr. Devlin?"

He jerked erect, dropping the pliers he'd been holding; they clattered onto the tiled floor. The kitchen was in its off-hours lighting, pools of brightness separated by swaths of dark shadow. The woman stood in shadow, silhouetted against a cone of light.

"What're you doing here?" he snapped, annoyed at this intrusion into his domain.

"I'm Katherine Westfall," she said, stepping closer to him. "I need to talk with you."

Devlin wiped his hands on his grimy apron. "Mrs. Westfall?"

It was her, all right. He recognized her from the images he'd seen on the nets. Small, slightly built, her face sculpted in planes and hollows like a statue out of ancient Egypt. She wore a one-piece coverall of coral pink that fitted her like a second skin. Jewelry glittered at her wrists, her throat, her earlobes.

"You are Rodney Devlin, aren't you?" she asked, in a voice that was almost a whisper.

"Yes'm," he replied, wiping his hands again before extending his right toward her.

Westfall barely touched his hand. "I understand that you are quite good at getting things done."

For one of the few times in his long life, Devlin felt embarrassed. Here was this elegant lady and he was in his grease monkey's apron, his wiry red hair uncombed, his bushy mustache straggling. She was inspecting him, eying him up and down, as if he were a horse or a pet that she was considering buying.

"I do my best, Mrs. Westfall," he said.

"How long have you been here at station *Gold?*" she asked.

"Long as the station's been open, ma'am. More'n twenty years."

Westfall nodded. "You're older than you look," she said absently. "You ought to get the gray streaks out of your hair, though."

He didn't know what to say.

"You've been getting away with a lot of illegal activities over all those years, haven't you?"

Devlin's mouth dropped open.

"Drug manufacturing, smuggling equipment, brewing liquor, VR sex simulations . . . it's quite a list."

"Uh, ma'am, I may have done a few things in my time that're outside the rules, but nothing that was illegal."

"Extralegal," Westfall said, the hint of a smile at the corners of her lips.

Devlin shrugged. "Can't run an operation like this station by staying inside the rule book every step o' the way. People need things that the rules don't cover, y'know."

"Perhaps," Westfall conceded.

Sensing that she was after something, Devlin asked, "So what is it I can do for you, ma'am?"

She hesitated. After a couple of heartbeats she said, "You understand that my people have uncovered enough evidence against you to put you away for the rest of your natural life."

"Now wait—"

"Don't bother to deny it. I can produce witnesses that will swear to your illegal activities."

"Extralegal," Devlin amended. But his palms were starting to sweat.

"Whatever," said Westfall. "As a member of the IAA's governing council, it's my duty to see that the laws are obeyed and the regulations enforced."

Devlin's tension eased. She's after something, he realized.

"Mrs. Westfall," he said, lowering his head slightly to indicate some contrition, "whatever I've done, I've never harmed anybody. I've helped this place to function better, more smoothly."

"Have you?"

"I have, ma'am. And I'm ready to help you, if you need something that's, ah . . . stretching the rules."

"Do you know those two nanotech people who came here from Selene?" she asked, her tone suddenly sharp, brittle.

Devlin nodded. "I run meals down to 'em every day."

"Then you know their nanotechnology laboratory."

"I know where it is."

"Good," Westfall said. "I need a sample of nanomachines. And I need it without anyone knowing about it, except the two of us."

Devlin ran a hand over his close-cropped brush of red hair.

"Can you do it?" she demanded.

He tugged at his mustache momentarily, then replied, "Sure." To himself he added silently, I'd rather steal nanobugs than go to jail.

DORN'S QUARTERS

'm sorry to intrude on your privacy like this," Deirdre said as she stood in the doorway of Dorn's compartment.

"It's not a problem," the cyborg said, gesturing her into the room with his human hand.

"I should have called first," she said, stepping past him.

"It's not that late," he said as he slid the door shut. "I just got back from dinner."

"Yes, I know. I saw you leave the galley."

Looking around, Deirdre saw that Dorn's quarters were the same sized room as she had, a few dozen meters down the passageway. But somehow it looked austere, barren. The bed was made with military precision. The display screen above the desk was blank. The desk itself was completely bare. No decorations of any kind. It's as if no one really lives in here, she thought.

"I saw you in the galley, as well," said Dorn. "With the Torre woman. I thought about asking to join you . . ." He left the thought unfinished.

Deirdre said, "We would have welcomed your company."

For an awkward moment neither of them said a word. Then Dorn broke the silence. "Won't you sit down? Would you like something to drink? I can make coffee for us."

Moving to the armchair in the corner of the room, Deirdre replied, "Coffee would be fine."

Dorn stepped to the minuscule kitchenette on the other side of the room. Deirdre noticed all over again how lightly he moved, how lithe he was despite half of his body being metal.

"May I ask why you've come to visit me?" he asked, his back to her as he poured ground coffee into the machine.

"Maybe I shouldn't have."

"No, no, it's all right. I'm simply curious. Something's bothering you, that much is clear."

"Dorn, are you really a priest?"

He half turned to look at her over his shoulder. Deirdre could see only the metal half of his face, unreadable.

"I thought of myself as a priest for many years. Not of any organized religion. I was on a mission to find the dead who'd been abandoned to drift in space after the Asteroid Wars. I considered it my sacred duty to find them and give them proper funeral rites."

"That . . . that was a very holy thing to do. More than any other priest did."

The coffeemaker chugged and spewed steam. Dorn turned to face her. "Like many priests," he said gravely, "I am celibate. I have no option."

"Oh!" Deirdre felt awful, as if she were prying where she had no right to.

"The surgery," Dorn explained.

"That must be . . . difficult for you," she limped.

The human half of his face tried to smile. "It's not that bad. I have no physical urges. Only memories."

How terrible, Dierdre thought. But she couldn't find any words to speak aloud.

The coffee machine pinged and Dorn turned back to it. He poured two cups of steaming black brew and brought them to the tiny round table beside Deirdre's chair. Then he pulled up the desk chair and sat facing her.

"So," he said. "I am not really a priest. But you need someone to talk to and I am willing to listen." Before Deirdre could say anything, Dorn added, "And, like a priest, I will treat your words as private and entirely confidential."

"It's about Andy." Deirdre surprised herself by blurting it out.

"The mission into the ocean."

With a slight shake of her head, Deirdre said, "It's more than just the mission. It's about Andy and me . . . our relationship."

Dorn asked, "Do you have a relationship?"

"We're friends. I like Andy a lot. And I know he likes me."

"Enough to be jealous of Franklin Torre."

"You know about that?"

Dorn half smiled. "I'd have to be totally blind not to recognize it. While you've been having dinner with Torre these past few nights, I've been eating with Andy. Not that he's done much eating."

"Oh dear."

Noticing that she hadn't touched her coffee, Dorn asked, "Would you like a sweetener? Some cold soymilk, perhaps?"

Deirdre glanced down at the steaming cups. "No, black is fine." She picked up her cup and sipped at it. The coffee was strong and hot.

Dorn took a swallow from his cup, then told Deirdre, "For what it's worth, I think Andy likes you very much. I don't know much about love, but he might very well be in love with you."

"When I told him I was frightened of the ocean mission he said I shouldn't go. He said I meant more to him than making contact with the leviathans."

Dorn said nothing.

"I mean, he's willing to throw away the whole reason why he came here to Jupiter, his chance for a breakthrough, his chance for success as a scientist. For me!"

Carefully putting his cup back on the little table, Dorn said, "You are a very beautiful woman. Andy is obviously smitten with you."

"But don't you see where this puts me?" Deirdre pleaded. "I like Andy, I think he's very sweet. But if I don't go down into the ocean with him I could be ruining his career. He'll hate me!"

"That's not what he's said. He told you that you mean more to him than the mission, didn't he?"

Impatiently, Deirdre replied, "Of course he did. And I'm sure he means it. Now. But what about after the mission? What about when he comes back without making contact with the leviathans?

He'll blame me, sooner or later. Instead of loving me he'll start to hate me!"

Dorn leaned back in the wheeled desk chair, making it roll slightly away from Deirdre. He clasped his hands together, one flesh and one metal, and held them prayerfully before his lips.

At last he asked, "If he actually did blame you for his failure, would that bother you?"

"Of course it would!"

"Why? Because you want him to like you, or because his failure would hurt his career, his life?"

Deirdre started to answer, but clicked her teeth shut. Her thoughts were swirling too much for a quick reply. How do I feel about Andy? Am I miserable because of my own ego or because I'll be hurting him?

Dorn sat watching her, silent as a graven image.

At last Deirdre heard herself say, "I don't want to hurt Andy."

"Do you love him?"

"I don't know," she answered. "I only know that I don't want to hurt him."

"Then you'll have to go on the mission with him," said Dorn.

Deirdre looked into his eyes: one gray as a stormy sea, the other a red-glowing optronic vidcam.

"Yes," she said, in an accepting sigh. "I suppose I will."

RODNEY DEVLIN

n his own mind, Red Devlin believed that he was the one who actually ran research station *Gold*. Oh, Archer and the other scientists thought that they were in charge, and on paper they were, but the old Red Devil was the bloke who really made the place hum.

He had come out to *Gold* when the station had first been built, more than twenty years earlier, when his youthful attempt to open a restaurant in Melbourne had ended in bankruptcy. His official job at *Gold* was chief cook for the station. That meant that he spent most of his time in the kitchen and galley, supervising the small staff of humans and larger contingent of robots that prepared and served food and drink for the station's personnel.

It also meant that he was responsible for obtaining the foodstuffs and drinkables that supplied the kitchen. And other things, as well.

Very quickly, Devlin became the station's unofficial procurer. He was able to acquire things, find things, bring people together, in a manner that was little short of Machiavellian. When a staff scientist needed a new set of sensors in too much of a hurry to go through the red tape of the station's regular procurement department, Red got the sensors for him and let him fill out the paperwork later. When someone needed some recreational drugs for a party she was throwing, it was the Red Devil that she turned to. When a lonely administrator needed diversion, Devlin smuggled in virtual reality sex simulations. He brewed "rocket juice" in a still that was tucked away among the scoopship operators' repair facilities. He hacked into the station's personnel files to speed transfers and promotions.

He called himself a facilitator. Many times, over the years he had been at station *Gold*, he'd heard people say admiringly that the station couldn't operate without him. Devlin knew he was the lubricating oil that made the machinery run smoothly.

Or so he thought of himself.

Now and then he considered leaving *Gold* and returning to Australia. He had enough money tucked away to retire in comfort. But his memories of Earth were not all that pleasant: orphaned at the age of six, a ward of the state, compulsory schooling and then training for the restaurant business that was so poor he went bankrupt right off. No, he told himself, here at *Gold* he was known and respected, even admired by many of the brainiest people around. It was a small, almost claustrophobic world, but Red regarded himself as a pretty big fish in this little pond, and that was the way he liked it.

But as he sat up in his narrow bed, he mulled over this latest twist in the station's sometimes Byzantine politics. Westfall wants a sample of nanomachines. Dangerous stuff, that. But she's powerful enough to chuck me in jail. Or at least get me thrown off *Gold*. What then? Where would I go, even if she doesn't railroad me into the cooler?

His room was small, little more than a nook near the kitchen. Devlin had never been one for creature comforts. His tastes for physical well-being were little short of Spartan. What he enjoyed most was the smiling admiration of the people around him. Scientists, engineers, administrators—men and women of good families and high education. They came to him for help. They *needed* the old Red Devil to solve their problems for them.

Now I'm the one who needs help, he thought as he stared sleeplessly at the blank display screen on the bulkhead at the end of his bunk. Westfall can ruin my life if I don't do what she wants. But what she wants might be dangerous, terribly dangerous.

Should I tell Archer about it? Devlin shook his head. Nah. He's too straight-arrow. He always shied away from me when he was a punk kid, just arrived here. Devlin remembered the first time he had offered to get some VR sex sims for the young Grant Archer. The kid had looked like he'd just been offered a deal to sell his soul.

Archer was a religious Believer back then. Still is, as far as Devlin knew. Married to the same woman all these years; no hint of him straying.

So what if I tell Archer about it? That'd set up a real head-to-head battle between him and Westfall. She'd wipe the floor with him. Grant could never fight the way she would. She'd have him tossed off *Gold* before he knew what hit him.

No, Devlin told himself, I can't bring Archer into this. I've got to find a way to satisfy Westfall without running the danger of setting nanomachine gobblers loose all over the place.

But how? How can I do that?

He decided the answer was more than he could hope to achieve at the moment. But as he wriggled down into his bunk and closed his eyes for sleep, he realized he was wrong.

He knew the answer. It came from a story he'd been told at the orphanage, all those years ago. A story by somebody with three names: Hans Christian Andersen.

With some misgivings, Deirdre made her way along the main passageway toward the observation deck, where Max Yeager was waiting for her.

She hadn't seen Yeager for several days, not even in the galley at dinnertime. The station's phone system tracked him down almost instantaneously in the mission control center. From her own compartment's wall screen, Deirdre could see that Max looked haggard, unshaven, his thick mane disheveled, his coveralls wrinkled and baggy. Over his shoulder she could see a bright-looking golden-haired woman with violet eyes sitting at the main console.

"Dee?" Yeager said, easing into a grin as soon as he recognized who had called him. "What can I do for you, gorgeous?"

Deirdre suppressed an annoyed frown. "Max, I need to talk to you."

"Sure." His grin became leering. "Your place or mine?"

"Be serious!"

"What's the trouble, Dee?"

"I need your advice. It . . . it's personal. Can we meet somewhere, in private, someplace where we won't be disturbed?"

His face totally serious now, Yeager said, "Okay, sure." He thought a moment, then suggested, "How about the observation deck?"

Deirdre nodded. "All right."

"I can be there in ten minutes."

"The observation deck," she said. "Ten minutes."

Now, though, as she neared the doors, Deirdre recalled that the observation deck was sometimes used for lovers' trysts. Max! she railed silently. Did I give him the impression that I'm interested in him sexually? No, she told herself. But what I said and what he heard could be two entirely different things.

So she felt distinctly nervous as she slid back the door to the observation deck and stepped inside. The door slid shut automatically and the lights inside dimmed. It was like standing out in space. Deirdre could see myriads of stars spread across the infinite black, the beauty of the universe stretching before her eyes.

But she had no time for the glory of the heavens.

"Max?" she called. "Max, are you here?"

Silence. Then the door slid open again, spilling light from the passageway into the compartment. Max Yeager's burly form was silhouetted briefly as he stepped through and the door shut once more, automatically dimming the lights.

"Sorry I'm late," he said, his tone apologetic. "I had to get loose from Linda; she wanted to come here with me."

Deirdre assumed Linda was the woman she had glimpsed in the phone screen.

"It's all right," she said. "I just got here myself."

"So here we are, beautiful, in this romantic spot, just you and me and a few zillion stars."

Deirdre said, "Behave yourself, Max."

"Do I hafta?" he said, in an imitation of a little boy's whine.

"Max, I need your advice."

"About what?"

Deirdre bit her lip, trying to frame her words. Max loomed before her in the shadows, a big shaggy presence.

"How dangerous will the mission be?" she asked.

In the dim light it was difficult to see his face, but his voice sounded surprised. "Dangerous? Like any flight mission, Dee. There's always the element of risk."

"But . . . going down into the ocean. Living in that liquid, breathing it."

"You're not going, are you?"

"Andy wants me to. He needs me to."

For a couple of heartbeats Yeager said nothing. Then, "You're scared, eh?"

"Terrified," she admitted.

"Then don't go."

"But Andy . . . he wants to make contact with the leviathans and he thinks I can be a big help to him."

"Then go."

"You're not helping me!"

Yeager stepped closer to her, so close she could smell the acrid tang of his unwashed coveralls. "Dee, honey, what do you want from me? I can't make up your mind for you."

"I need to know if your ship is safe," she replied. "I need to know if we can get through the mission without harm."

Yeager fell silent again.

"Will I be safe?" she asked, pleadingly.

"*Faraday* is as safe as I can make her. She's gone down into that ocean and come back again in tip-top condition. All systems performed as designed. She even took a battering from the sharks and survived virtually unscathed."

"Virtually?"

Yeager shrugged and gave out a low chuckle. "A couple of minor subsystems went off-line from the shock for a few seconds. They came back on-line, just as they were designed to do."

"So the ship is safe."

She sensed him nodding. "As safe as I know how to make her, Dee."

"Would you ride in it?"

"Sure. In a hot second."

It was Deirdre's turn to fall silent.

"I don't mean that there aren't risks involved," Yeager amended. "There're risks with any mission. But *Faraday*'s a hundred times safer than the tin cans they sent out on crewed missions twenty years ago. A thousand times safer."

"Really?"

Placing his hand over his heart, Yeager said, "On my honor as an engineer and a gentleman."

Deirdre smiled at him. "You are a gentleman, Max."

"Yeah, dammit."

The glassteel-walled deck suddenly began to flood with light. Deirdre could see Max clearly: He looked solemn, pensive.

"Jupiter's rising," she said.

The giant planet climbed into view, a huge overwhelming curve of glowing clouds, swirling and churning in multihued splendor.

"I'll be going into that world," Deirdre said, still more than a little frightened, but totally determined now.

"And I'm going with you," said Max Yeager.

"You? But—"

"I won't let you go without me, Dee. If anything happened to you I'd never forgive myself. But if I'm on board with you, if anything unforeseen happens, maybe I'll be able to fix it."

"But Max, you're not a scientist. Dr. Archer won't allow you to go."

"Yes he will," Yeager said, his tone as flat and final as a judge pronouncing sentence. "I'll make him allow me."

Andy Corvus sat glumly on his equipment box and watched the dolphins gliding sleekly through the water all around him.

That's the life, he thought. Just swim around and eat fish. No worries. No dangers. No fears about the future or regrets about the past. Nothing but the here and now.

The dolphins were talking to each other, ignoring his presence. Andy understood part of their chatter through the translator and the DBS probe in the circlet he had placed on his head. They were talking about food, which fish were the tastiest, how the squid tried to hide among the rocks on the bottom of the tank.

Baby was growing bigger by the day. Sleek and strong, she slid past Andy's watching eyes, propelled by thrusts of her powerful tail flukes.

"Hello, Andy," his translator crackled.

Surprised and pleased, Corvus replied, "Hello, Baby."

"Where's Dee?" Baby asked.

Andy's breath caught in his throat. Deirdre hadn't been down to the tank for days, yet Baby missed her.

"Dee's not here," Corvus said morosely. And, he thought, she probably never will come down here again.

"I'm right here, Andy."

He whirled, almost falling off the equipment box. And there she was, in a knee-length robe that covered her swimsuit, looking as beautiful as a woman could possibly look.

"Hi!" he said, bouncing to his feet.

"I'm sorry I've been neglecting you and Baby," Deirdre said.

"What with the nanomachine therapy and working on the *Volvox* and then Dr. Archer wants me to study the leviathans' pictures . . ."

"I understand," Corvus said, his spirits sinking again. "After all, if you're not going on the mission there's not much sense working with the dolphins."

"But I am going on the mission, Andy."

For a heartbeat or two Corvus couldn't believe what he'd heard. "You're going?"

"I talked it over with Dorn and Max. We're all going, the four of us together."

Corvus shook his head. "No, Dee, you're not going."

"Yes I am."

"But I thought . . . I mean, you told me you were scared."

"I still am."

"So why would you change your mind if you're still frightened?" Before Deirdre could reply Corvus thought he knew the answer. "You're doing this for me?"

"Partly," she said, with a bright smile. "And partly to help Dr. Archer. I mean, he's set up a scholarship for me at the Sorbonne. I owe him something, don't you think?"

Feeling confused, Corvus stuttered, "But . . . the risks . . . the danger."

"I'm scared, for sure," Deirdre admitted, "but I'm not going to let that stop me."

"No! I won't let you."

"Andy, it's not your decision to make."

He stared at her: so beautiful, so sweet. She's willing to do what she's scared of, Corvus told himself, because she knows it will help me.

"I can't let you do it, Dee," he said. "It really is dangerous. If anything happened to you—"

"It would happen to you, too, wouldn't it? I mean, we'll be in the ship together, you, me, Max, and Dorn."

He sagged down onto the equipment box again, his thoughts whirling. "What made you change your mind?" he asked.

Sitting beside him, Deirdre replied very seriously, "I decided that it was very selfish of me to refuse. This mission is important. Not just to you, Andy. It's important to Dr. Archer. It's important to our understanding of the leviathans. If we can make contact with an intelligent alien species . . . that's mind-blowing!"

"We might get killed," he said in a whisper.

"Max says the ship is safe. He's willing to go along with us, just in case anything goes wrong, but he says it's as safe as any ship can be."

"Down in that ocean," Corvus muttered. "Living in that perfluorocarbon gunk. With those sharks and the leviathans, totally cut off from the rest of the human race, cut off from any possibility of help."

"It's like the old-time explorers," Deirdre said gently. "Columbus was on his own once he sailed into the Atlantic. Peary and those other Arctic explorers were on their own, totally cut off from any possibility of help."

"A lot of those guys died."

"Yes, that's true."

"I don't want you to die," Corvus said. He grasped both Deirdre's hands. "I don't want you to die!"

She smiled again and leaned her forehead against his. "Andy, I don't want to die. But I couldn't stand staying here and watching you leave to go down into the ocean. I couldn't stand it if I stayed safe here and you got killed."

"But that doesn't mean you should get killed, too!"

"None of us are going to get killed," she insisted. "Max gave me his word. But if anything bad happens, it'll happen to all four of us."

He shook his head. "That's a weird way to make a decision."

"Remember what you said to Mrs. Westfall, the first night we were here on the station?"

"At Archer's dinner."

"You said that if you were prevented from trying to contact the leviathans it would be like chopping off your hands."

He grunted. "Your memory's too good. Besides, if you don't go with me, I'll still go down there. You won't be chopping off my hands." Then he grinned. "Maybe it'd be like chopping off a finger or two."

Deirdre looked down at their hands. "Not a finger. Not a little pinkie, even. I'm going with you."

Suddenly it hit him and he felt overwhelmed. *She means it! She's going to risk her life because of me.*

"Dee . . . I . . . I don't know what to say."

"You don't have to say a word, Andy. It's all settled."

"But it's so damned risky!"

"Max says it isn't," she repeated. "Besides, there's an old adage: 'Behold the lowly turtle. He only makes progress when he sticks his neck out.'"

Deeper than normal in the all-encompassing sea, the Elders found a new flow of food and the Kin sated their hunger. Leviathan's mouth parts took in the particles greedily as the giant Jovian creature glided along the down-welling current.

Messages of joy and relief were flashing from one member of the Kin to another, bright yellows and greens. Still stationed on the Kin's outer perimeter, Leviathan's sensor parts searched the dark water for signs of the darters. None down at this depth, not within detection range, at least.

But that didn't mean that darters were not out there, farther off. They had feasted on the Eldest when it had sacrificed itself for the good of the Kin. Soon enough they would grow hungry again and seek more prey.

Leviathan remembered its own encounter with a pack of darters back when it had gone off alone, away from the Kin. The ravening beasts had torn at Leviathan's hide, ripping and slashing to get at the inner organs. If that strange alien creature hadn't helped Leviathan, the darters would have won the struggle.

The aliens puzzled Leviathan. Who were they? Why had they intruded into the Symmetry? The Elders chose to ignore them, insisting that since they were not truly a part of the Symmetry they had no part to play in the life of the Kin. Leviathan thought otherwise.

Perhaps the aliens have come to destroy the Symmetry. Or perhaps—Leviathan goggled at the thought—perhaps they have come to *enlarge* the Symmetry. Are the aliens a sign that not even the Elders understand the Symmetry in all its fullness?

These were the thoughts that occupied Leviathan's mind as it grazed placidly on the food sifting down from the cold abyss above.

But then a new sensation shuddered through Leviathan's immense bulk. It felt different, strangely insistent. For some time Leviathan pondered over this odd, demanding, prickly feeling surging through its members. At last it realized what the sensation was: Leviathan was about to undergo a budding. It was time to swim away from the Kin and dissociate into its member parts, so that they could bud and then rejoin to form two leviathans where there had been only one before.

Leviathan realized that its budding would replace the number lost when the Eldest sacrificed itself. And it also realized that the darters would be out there waiting, when Leviathan was alone and terribly vulnerable.

GRANT ARCHER'S OFFICE

ll four of you?" Archer looked at them wide-eyed, startled.

Deirdre, Corvus, Yeager, and Dorn were sitting in a rough semicircle facing the station director, who was in his favorite recliner. But Archer snapped the chair straight up, suddenly intent with surprise.

"All four of us," Max Yeager replied.

Shaking his head, Archer pointed at Corvus. "You, Andy, yes, of course. This whole mission is aimed at your trying to make meaningful contact with the leviathans. And Dorn, to pilot the ship. But Ms. Ambrose? And you, Max?"

Corvus spoke up. "Deirdre is much better at linking with the dolphins than I am, Dr. Archer. She's a natural. Very empathic. If any of us has a chance at making a meaningful contact with the leviathans, it's Dee."

Archer turned his gaze toward Deirdre. "Are you willing to go on the mission?"

She lifted her chin a notch as she replied, "Yes, sir, I am. I've been in the immersion tank, so I know what that's like. I don't enjoy it, but I can put up with it."

"And the surgery?" Archer asked.

"Surgery?" Deirdre and Yeager yelped in unison.

"They'll have to implant a feeding port into your neck," Archer explained. "You can't eat normally in the perfluorocarbon, so you feed yourself through the port. It's implanted in your neck, connected to one of your carotid arteries. Like an intravenous drip."

"It's removable," Corvus added. "After the mission they can take it out."

"Unless you'll be going back in the near future," Archer said.

"I didn't know about that," Deirdre said, glancing at Corvus.

"It's minor surgery, really," Archer reassured her. "I didn't mean to alarm you."

Deirdre nodded, a little uncertainly, but said, "It's all right. I'll go through with it."

Archer smiled at her, then turned to Yeager. "Max, I don't think we'll have room for you in the ship. You know better than anyone how precious space is aboard *Faraday*."

"I have to go," Yeager said flatly.

"But to take you aboard I'd have to bump one of the scientists who's been training for this mission for months. It's bad enough to bounce a scooter to accommodate Ms. Ambrose: At least she has Dr. Corvus's approval. But you . . ." Archer put up his hands, palms outward, in a *what can I do* gesture.

Yeager looked the station director squarely in the eye. "I know. I'm just an engineer. I'm just the man who designed that bird and made it work. Well, if anything goes wrong with any of her systems, who do you think would be better able to take care of it than I?"

"All the systems worked fine when *Faraday* went into the ocean by herself," Archer said.

"But suppose something goes wrong?" Yeager challenged. "Down there in that ocean, cut off from communication with the station, what good would I be up here when the ship's out of contact?"

"But the ship worked fine," Archer repeated.

"Ever hear of Murphy's Law?"

Archer bowed his head slightly as he muttered, "If anything can go wrong, it will."

"So you'll need somebody who can fix it, whatever it is," said Yeager.

Archer puffed out a heartfelt sigh. "This is going to raise merry hell with the science staff. Johansen has his teams picked and ready to go."

Corvus said, "Look, sir, if this mission goes well there'll be others. The science staff will have plenty of opportunities."

"And if it doesn't go well?" Archer riposted.

"Then the scooters who had to stay behind will still be alive," Corvus said, with a sidelong glance at Deirdre.

When handed a lemon, make lemonade. Grant Archer remembered his father telling him that time and again when he'd been a child, living in genteel poverty back in Oregon. His father, a softspoken Methodist minister who was liked but not respected by their neighbors, had offered that bit of advice to young Grant on many bitter occasions.

"When handed a lemon, make lemonade," he repeated aloud to his wife. They were getting undressed, preparing for bed after a long day.

Marjorie gave him a puzzled look. "What brought that up?"

Sitting on the edge of the bed as he took off his softboots, Archer said, "Corvus and his Gang of Four. They all want to go on the mission."

"Deirdre, too?"

"Yes. Even Max Yeager."

Sitting beside him, Marjorie said, "But if you let them go, you'll have to bump a couple of the scooters, won't you?"

Archer nodded. "Yep."

"How are you going to deal with that?"

With a grin that was almost sly, Archer tapped the tip of his wife's nose and replied, "Make lemonade."

She said, "You look positively happy about it."

"I'm happy about my solution. I'm going to tell Johansen and the scientific staff that this mission is a full-system test. We're sending four volunteers into the ocean as a final test of the ship."

"They'll see through that," Marjorie objected. "They all know that Corvus is here to try his DBS system."

Nodding, Archer said, "That's right. The DBS experiment will be piggybacked on this test mission. That will be my official position." His grin widened. "I might even get Westfall to bless the idea of proceeding so cautiously."

Understanding blossomed on Marjorie's face. "Then the scientists who don't go on this mission can go on the next one."

Archer said, "Right. Nobody gets bumped. We're just adding a test mission to the schedule, for the sake of safety. Everybody gets what they want . . . more or less."

"You're getting to be a devious manipulator."

He put on a haughty expression. "No, I am utilizing my twenty years of experience as a capable administrator to make a fair, efficient, and productive decision."

Marjorie laughed.

He reached out and clasped her to him. "But I can be a devious manipulator when I—"

The phone buzzed.

"Drat!" Archer snapped.

"Let it go," Marjorie said, still in his arms.

But he turned enough to see the data bar on the bottom of the phone screen: Rodney Devlin was calling.

"Red?" Archer muttered. "What's he want at this time of night?"

Marjorie pulled back slightly and murmured, "There's only one way to find out."

KITCHEN

Sorry to drag you down here at this time o' night," Rodney Devlin said.

Looking at the man, Archer realized that the old Red Devil was aging. Gray streaks in his hair. His luxuriant mustache was turning thin and gray, too. Time for rejuvenation therapy, Archer thought. Maybe he doesn't realize it yet. Or doesn't want to admit it to himself.

"I imagine it's something important, Red," Archer said.

Devlin was standing behind a long table, a row of ovens behind him. Archer thought of the table as Red's version of a desk, a piece of furniture that established his status. A wooden block on Red's left held an array of knives. A heavy cleaver lay on the tabletop at his left.

The kitchen was eerily quiet. Archer rarely saw the galley when it wasn't filled with people, buzzing and reverberating with a hundred conversations, plates and silverware clattering, squat little serving robots trundling everywhere. Now it was dark and quiet, everything at a standstill, a few pools of light scattered through the shadows like lonely islands in a wide, engulfing sea.

"It's important, all right," Devlin said. His usual lighthearted toothy grin was gone: He looked deadly serious.

"You've decided to leave the station?" Archer guessed.

Devlin's eyes went wide with surprise. "Leave? Why would I leave?"

Archer shrugged. "Why not? You must have tucked away a considerable nest egg after all these years. Don't you want to go back Earthside and retire in ease?"

Devlin's lean face twisted into a scowl. "Earthside? Back to that zoo?"

"It's home, isn't it?"

"Do you think of it as *your* home?" Devlin asked, some of his old smirk returning.

That stopped Archer. He hadn't been back to Earth for nearly ten years, he realized, and that was just for a brief scientific conference. Both his children lived in Selene; when he and Marjorie visited them they never even thought about hopping across to Earth.

"This is home," Devlin said, tapping a fingertip on the stainless steel–topped table. "Crikey, the last I saw of Melbourne, the city was half underwater from the bloody greenhouse flooding."

"But . . ."

"Grant, I don't remember much of what they pushed down my throat in school, but I remember one line from some long poem they made me read: 'Better to reign in hell than serve in heaven.' This ain't hell, o'course. But Earth ain't heaven, either."

He's right, Archer admitted to himself. This is home. Puzzled, he asked, "Then just what do you want to see me about?"

"You don't approve of me, do you? Never did."

Archer hesitated before replying, "If you mean the extracurricular things you do—"

Devlin laughed. "Extracurricular. Westfall calls it illegal."

"Mrs. Westfall?"

"She said she could chuck me in jail if she took a notion to."

"Katherine Westfall threatened you?"

All traces of a smile gone from his face, Devlin replied, "Why d'you think I asked you t'meet me here in the kitchen after midnight? Instead of in your office durin' regular hours?"

Archer immediately understood. "So she won't know that we've talked together."

Devlin gave him a sly grin. "Right. That lady's got spies all over this station. She knows just about everything that goes on around here."

Archer realized that he had suspected something like that, but apparently Westfall's tentacles were more deeply entwined in the station's operations than he had thought.

"And she's putting pressure on you?" he asked.

Devlin said, "She's squeezin' me, Grant. Squeezin' me hard."

"What does she want?"

"Nanomachines."

Archer felt as if an electric shock jolted through him. "What on Earth does she want nanomachines for? What type of nanos?"

With a shrug, Devlin said, "Gobblers, I think you call 'em."

"Good Lord!"

"Yeah, that's what I thought. They're dangerous, ain't they?"

"They could be. Extremely dangerous."

Very calmly, Devlin said, "If I don't give 'er what she wants she'll yank me outta here and send me back Earthside to face a judge and jury."

"I won't permit it," Archer said. "I'll protect you, Red."

His knowing smirk returned. "Protect me? How? I'm guilty. You know that, Grant. I'm a smuggler. A drug dealer. A sex procurer."

"VR sims," Archer said, weakly.

"She could pile up enough evidence to land me in jail for lots o' years."

"But—"

"No buts," Devlin said flatly. "She's got me by the short hairs."

"Then . . . what do you want to do?"

"That's my business, Grant. You don't want t'know and I don't aim to tell you. I've got it figured out, but I don't want you gettin' in my way."

Archer felt his brows knitting in perplexity. "I don't understand, Red."

"I'll do what I've got to do," Devlin said. "I'm tellin' you now, man to man, that I won't do anything to put this station in danger. This is my home, y'know. I'm not goin' to let gobblers loose and turn the whole place into a gray goo."

"Then what are you going to do?"

"Like I said, you don't want t'know. I just want you to rest easy that I don't aim to hurt this station or anybody in it."

Archer couldn't think of anything to say. Devlin's been on station *Gold* longer than I have, for the Lord's sake. He knows the ins and outs better than anybody, knows the people here. But can I trust him? Can I let him deal with nanomachines? Gobblers?

Looking at Devlin's taut, rebellious expression, Archer asked himself, Can I stop him? Short of locking him up and tipping off Westfall that I know she's trying to use him, can I prevent the Red Devil from doing what he thinks he has to do?

Archer knew the answer. No, I can't.

Devlin saw the fear and distrust in Archer's face.

Okay, he said to himself, I know you don't trust me, Grant. I know you never approved of the things I do. For more'n twenty years you've looked down your snoot at me. Now you're goin' to learn different. Now the shoe's on the other bloody foot.

NANOTECHNOLOGY LABORATORY

Franklin Torre's normally genial expression was lost in a puzzled, almost suspicious stare.

"And just what is it you want down here?" he asked Rodney Devlin.

Devlin was wearing his usual white cook's T-shirt and baggy pants, immaculately clean this early in the morning. He grinned as he looked from Torre to his sister, standing next to him, and then took a quick scan of the nanotech lab. Small, he thought. More like a kid's playroom than a proper laboratory. The two people facing him were both in white lab smocks. They looked enough alike to be twins. Or clones.

Janet Torre mistook Red's silence. "You *do* realize this is a nanotechnology lab, don't you?"

Devlin nodded briskly. "That's what they told me."

"So why are you here?" Franklin asked again.

With a careless shrug, Devlin said, "Well, you're new here. I'm sort of like the station's unofficial meeter and greeter. I'm sorry I haven't come down to say hello earlier. Been kinda busy, dontcha know."

"I don't understand," said Franklin.

"Have the folks here been takin' good care of you? Is there anything you need?"

"Such as?" Janet demanded.

Devlin kept his sunny smile in place, although he was thinking that this would be much easier with the guy by himself instead of the two of them together.

Shrugging again, Devlin replied, "Oh, stuff the paper pushers can't supply for ya. Entertainment vids, maybe. Or certain foods—"

"Lobster," Franklin Torre exclaimed.

Devlin blinked. "Lobster?"

"At Selene we can have a lobster dinner anytime we want," Torre said.

"Aquaculture," Janet explained. "They have big fish farms at Selene. Shellfish, too. More protein per watt of energy input than meat animals."

Scratching his head, Devlin said, "Well, I can requisition some from Selene. Might take a while, though."

"I like lobster," Torre said.

"Anything else?" asked Devlin. "Technical supplies, personal items . . ." He hesitated, then in a slightly lower voice went on, "You're a long way from all your friends. Maybe you need some VR simulations."

Janet arched a brow at him. "You mean sex?"

Trying to look innocent, Devlin said, "Well, yeah, if that's what you have in mind."

Torre glanced at his sister. The two of them were grinning slyly. "No," he said to Devlin. "We don't need sex sims."

For once in his life Devlin felt embarrassed. "Well . . . if there's anything you do need, anything at all, you just call on ol' Red. I can cut through all the regulations the paper shufflers put on ya."

"Thank you, Red," said Janet.

Changing the subject to what he really came for, Devlin said, "So this is a nanotech lab, eh?"

"It's sort of rough and ready," said Torre, "but, yes, this is our nanotechnology laboratory."

"We never had one here before," Devlin said, taking in every detail of the room. "You must be here for something special."

"That's right," Janet said. And nothing more.

"Aren't nanomachines dangerous?" Devlin asked, all innocent curiosity. "I mean, I've heard stories . . ."

"Everything's perfectly secure here," Torre assured him. "We have all the necessary safeguards in place."

Devlin said, "Sign out in the hall said something about UV lights."

"That's to protect against any nanos that might get out of the lab," Torre explained. "Ultraviolet light kills them."

"Deactivates them," Janet corrected. "They're machines, not organisms."

Torre nodded at his sister.

"So there's nothing at all dangerous in here?"

Torre stepped over to a domed stainless steel chamber sitting on the lab bench. "The only dangerous thing is in here," he said. "When we first construct the nanomachines they're undifferentiated, not yet specialized for a specific task."

"If they got loose at that stage there could be trouble," Janet added. "We'd have to flood this area with high-intensity UV." She pointed to the lights hanging from the ceiling.

Gobblers, Devlin thought. They're talking about gobblers. But he didn't mention the word to them, didn't want them to get the slightest bit suspicious.

"So what happens to 'em?"

Tracing a finger along the pipe leading from the domed chamber to a smaller, square container, Torre said, "The undifferentiated nanos are fed in here, where we reshape them and program them for the specific task they're designed to perform."

Janet pointed to the display screen at the end of the workbench. "You can see them here."

Devlin followed the pair of them to the screen. It showed a half-dozen shapes that looked to Devlin like little mechanical toys, each with two grasping arms attached to its main body.

"That's them, huh?"

"That's them," said Torre, with some pride in his voice. "They'll seek out molecules of a specific shape and take them apart into their constituent atoms."

"Atoms! They must be pretty small."

"The size of viruses. A couple of nanometers across."

"Wow!"

Janet Torre looked at her wristwatch, then said, "Actually, we do have a lot of work to do. . . ."

"Oh! Sure!" Devlin backed away from the display screen. "I'm sorry for gettin' in your way."

Torre walked him toward the door; his sister sat on a stool by the display screen and turned it on.

"I appreciate your takin' the time to show me around," Devlin said.

"That's okay." Then, glancing back at his sister and lowering his voice, he said, "Can you show me some of those VR sims you mentioned?"

Acting surprised, Devlin said, "The sex sims? Sure. Any time. Just come and see me in the galley. Any time."

"Uh, can you tailor them? Put specific people into them?"

"Who'd you have in mind?"

"Well, there's this girl from the Belt . . . her name's Deirdre Ambrose . . ."

Devlin's surprise was genuine now. "You know Dee?"

"We've dated a couple of times."

"So you want simulations of her, do ya?"

"If you can do it."

With a nonchalant shrug, Devlin said, "I'll see what I can do, Frankie old boy."

Torre grinned and ushered Devlin through the door. Once outside in the passageway, the Red Devil grinned also. I've got the layout now, he told himself, and there's no real security in there. Scientists. They think everybody's honest.

LAUNCH PARTY

The largest conference room in the station's first wheel had been cleared of its furniture by Katherine Westfall's assistants, except for the long conference table, which had been pushed against one wall and loaded with drinks and trays of finger foods.

Red Devlin stood at one end of the table in a spanking clean white outfit, smiling benignly at the crowd of scientists, engineers, technicians, and administrators who crowded the room. The wall screens displayed views of Jupiter as seen from the station, and scenes of the leviathans recorded by the robotic probes that had been sent into the ocean.

Katherine Westfall, the party's hostess, stood by the door, graciously greeting each new arrival. She wore a splendid gown of shimmering blues and indigos that shifted and sparkled with each move she made. Grant Archer and his wife stood beside her, smiling and chatting amiably.

Deirdre was off in a corner, feeling self-conscious from the feeding port that had been implanted in her neck. She knew that her high-collared dress covered the site, but still felt that it bulged noticeably. She glanced at Dorn and Max Yeager, standing beside her; their shirts covered their ports completely. Andy Corvus, standing halfway across the room deep in conversation with one of the launch controllers, scratched unconsciously at his port.

Andy and Max had both been shaved bald. The mission protocol required it: Living for days on end in the perfluorocarbon meant that all excess hair had to be removed from their bodies. Andy looked like a scrawny newborn chick without his thick mop of red hair. Max somehow looked nobler, wiser, more serious, almost like a bust of some august Roman emperor. Dorn, of course, had no body hair to shave off.

Deirdre had put off her own shearing to the last possible moment. She dreaded losing her thick shoulder-length auburn locks. At least she wouldn't have to go completely bald, Isaac Lowenstien had told her.

"You can go with a buzz cut," the head of the station's safety department had allowed. "That'll be good enough."

When he saw the unhappy expression on Deirdre's face, he tried to console her. "Hey, you're lucky. In the old days they depilated you completely, head to toe. Took months to grow your hair back."

Deirdre thought that it was scant consolation.

A petite woman in a form-hugging jade green jumpsuit stepped up to Yeager, smiling brightly at him. Deirdre noticed that she had a splendid crown of radiant golden curls.

Tipping her fluted glass toward Max, she said, "To you, little father."

Yeager looked embarrassed, but touched his glass to hers. Turning to Deirdre and Dorn he introduced, "Linda Vishnevskaya, mission control chief."

Vishnevskaya said, "You are going on the mission with Max. Take good care of him, please."

Deirdre thought that the woman was slightly drunk. She herself was drinking only fruit juice; she didn't want alcohol in her bloodstream, not with the mission launch less than forty-eight hours away.

"We will take good care of each other," Dorn replied, very seriously.

"Of course, of course," said Vishnevskaya. Patting Max's shoulder, she went on, "But Max is very special. He cares about his ship like a loving father."

Yeager's face reddened noticeably.

Standing at the end of the laden conference table, Red Devlin watched the partygoers with professional interest. Food's holding out all right, he said to himself. Archer unbent enough to let me rustle up some faux champagne and rocket juice, but nobody seems to be getting sloshed too badly. Of course, the night is young.

He saw that Grant Archer had moved slightly away from Mrs. Westfall and was deep in conversation with Dr. Johansen, the scientist who headed the group studying Jupiter. Mrs. Archer and Westfall were yakking away at each other like old friends. Funny, Devlin thought, how two women can both talk at the same time and keep the conversation going without missing a beat.

Michael Johansen was still less than happy with Archer's decision to send Corvus and the other three on the mission.

"That ship was built for scientists to go into the ocean," he was telling Archer, raising his voice just enough to be heard over the chatter of the crowd.

"We've been through all this, Mike," Archer said gently. "The decision has been made. And implemented."

Shaking his head, Johansen said, "You can still add a man to the crew. One scientist. There's room—"

"I'm sorry, Mike, but the answer is no," said Archer. "This mission is strictly to see if Corvus can make any meaningful contact with the leviathans." He hesitated, then added in a lowered voice, "And to see if the ship works without killing anybody."

Johansen frowned. "You're wasting an opportunity to acquire more scientific data, Grant. Corvus isn't going to get bubkes, you know that."

Archer grinned at him. "You've been hanging around Ike Lowenstien too long, you're starting to speak Yiddish."

"This isn't a joke, Grant."

More seriously, "Only God knows what Corvus will accomplish, Mike. I don't know and neither do you. That's what research is all about. If you already know the answer, you're not doing research."

Johansen's long, angular face settled into a gloomy pout. Even Katherine Westfall, halfway across the crowded room, could see that the scientist was displeased.

Westfall turned back to Marjorie Archer, who was still going on about some biochemical studies she was undertaking. "Would you excuse me, Marjorie? Now that everyone is here I ought to offer a toast to the mission's success."

Marjorie looked more relieved than displeased. "Oh. Of course. I've been bending your ear long enough."

"Not at all," said Westfall. "Not at all." But she stepped away gladly and headed toward Rodney Devlin, who was still standing at the far end of the table, like a sentry in a white apron.

Devlin saw her coming and recognized the little nod that Westfall gave him. He quickly poured two champagne flutes. Handing them to her one by one, he said, "This one's for you, ma'am, and this one's for Ms. Ambrose."

Smiling knowingly, Westfall took the glasses and made her precarious way through the crowd toward Dierdre, Dorn, and the others. Devlin was right behind her, clutching three more of the long-stemmed glasses. Westfall handed one of the flutes to Deirdre as Devlin passed out the other three to Yeager, Dorn, and Corvus.

Then Devlin emitted an ear-piercing whistle that stopped every conversation dead in its tracks.

Into the sudden silence, Westfall said in her little-girl voice, "I want to propose a toast to the crew of the good ship *Faraday*: May you find what you're looking for."

Everyone in the crowded room raised their glasses and repeated the toast. Deirdre, Max, Andy, and Dorn smiled appreciatively and sipped.

That's a good girl, Westfall said silently as she watched Deirdre down her faux champagne. Drink it down. The nanomachines will do the rest.

IV
THE MISSION

Did He who made the lamb make thee?

—"The Tiger"
William Blake

IMMERSION CAPSULE

This is it, Deirdre said to herself as she ducked through the small round hatch and sat herself on the padded bench that ran around the interior of the circular chamber.

She waited for one of the men to make a comment about her skinned scalp. The buzz cut was hardly a centimeter long; Deirdre felt almost naked. She had nearly cried when she saw her beautiful auburn curls piling up on the floor as they cut her hair away.

Andy Corvus, already seated, extended a hand to help her. Dorn had gone in first; he was sitting by the control panel of blinking lights and keypads set into the capsule's curving bulkhead. If Andy noticed her haircut he said nothing about it.

Max Yeager came through the hatch behind Deirdre, looking serious, almost grim. She thought that he must be reconsidering his decision to come on the mission. Not even Max said anything about her hair. Maybe being bald has made him more thoughtful, Deirdre surmised.

"Hope none of us are prone to claustrophobia," Corvus said. It was an attempt at humor, but it fell flat.

"Helluva time to think of that," Yeager grumbled.

All four of them wore nothing more than black elastane tights that hugged their bodies like second skins, lined inside with medical sensors that reported their heart and breathing rates, body temperatures, and blood pressures. Arms and legs bare except for a few more sensors plastered to the skin. Necklines low enough to allow easy access to the feeding ports in their necks. Deirdre was surprised at how buff Andy looked: lean but sinewy. She tried not to stare at

Dorn's half-metal body. She realized how uptight they all were when no one commented on how she looked in her revealing maillot, not even Max.

Dorn said gravely, "If anyone has second thoughts, now is the time to act on them."

Deirdre felt a sudden impulse to get up and squeeze back through the hatch. But one look at Andy's expectant face froze her in place. He's depending on me, she thought. I can't leave, not now.

Nodding, Dorn said, "Very well. We begin the mission."

He touched a keypad and the hatch swung noiselessly shut.

"Here we go," Deirdre heard herself say.

"Initiating immersion," Dorn said into the tiny microphone built into the control panel.

"Initiating immersion," a voice crackled from the grillwork of the speaker. Deirdre thought it sounded like that little blond woman who was the chief of the mission control team.

Thick oily perfluorocarbon liquid began to flow across the capsule's deck, quickly covering their bare feet and rising toward their knees.

"Why do they have to keep it so cold?" Yeager groused. "They ought to warm it up a little."

"Like soup," Corvus said.

"Yeah. Gazpacho."

Deirdre said, "I prefer lobster bisque."

"Where'd you ever get lobster bisque?" Yeager demanded.

"We imported it from Selene," Deirdre explained as the chilly liquid reached her hips. "It's expensive, but we bring it in at least once a year, for the holidays."

"Lobster bisque," Yeager muttered, with a shake of his head.

The perfluorocarbon had climbed to their waists. Deirdre realized she was biting her lip. Andy was smiling nervously, Max staring down at the rising liquid. Dorn was turned slightly away from her, focusing on the control panel; she could only see the etched metal side of his face.

Deirdre tried to steady her breathing as the liquid rose to her breasts, then her shoulders, and up to her chin. Relax! she commanded herself. You've been through this before, several times. Just relax and try to breathe normally.

She couldn't, of course. None of them could. Deirdre closed her eyes as her body spasmed and her lungs began to burn from holding her breath. She could sense the others struggling also, but kept her eyes shut tight. She didn't want to see them, it would only make things worse.

At last she sucked in a breath and gagged on the cold, slimy liquid. Her body told her she was drowning even while the rational part of her brain insisted that it was all right, she'd be perfectly fine, just try to relax and breathe normally.

Breathe normally, she repeated to herself. As if this is normal.

After a few year-long seconds of coughing and nearly retching she began to breathe almost naturally. Opening her eyes, she saw that the three men were also gasping, shuddering, looking terribly afraid, as if each breath would be their last. Their breathing slowly steadied, though, and soon enough they were all breathing the perfluorocarbon. Just as she was herself.

Her lungs felt raw, and there was a cold knot in the pit of her stomach, but she was breathing.

"Immersion complete," Dorn said, his voice strangely low, reverberating like a moan from hell.

"Copy immersion complete," came the voice of the mission controller, also low now, distorted.

Looking squarely at Deirdre, Dorn asked, "Is everyone all right? Any pains? Any problems?"

"I'm . . . all right," Deirdre said, her own voice sounding like a bassoon in her ears.

"Okay," said Corvus.

"No problems," Yeager said. Deirdre thought it sounded grudging.

"Very well," said Dorn. "Now we ratchet up the pressure."

Deirdre knew it would take precisely three hours to increase the perfluorocarbon pressure to the point where it was designed to be.

Three hours of sitting in this cramped little metal womb and doing nothing except waiting for your body to break down, your internal cells to implode, your brain to go berserk.

None of that happened. They talked to one another, meaningless chatter to pass the time. Corvus made a few pathetically weak jokes. Yeager kept telling them that "all things considered, I'd rather be in Philadelphia." No one laughed.

Deirdre thought she felt a dull pain in her abdomen, but it was so slight she didn't mention it. Psychosomatic, she told herself.

Then she remembered her conversation with Katherine Westfall, at the party Dr. Archer had given them a few nights earlier.

After her toast with the faux champagne, Westfall had pulled Deirdre to one side of the crowded conference room and smiled coldly at her.

"I understand that your case of rabies has been cured," she said.

Deirdre nodded happily, the champagne tickling her nose. "Yes. Dr. Mandrill says there's no trace of the virus in my blood now."

"Thanks to nanotherapy," Westfall said.

Deirdre nodded again, uncertainly this time. She didn't know how much she should admit to.

"You're a very fortunate young woman. Dr. Archer went to great lengths to help you," Westfall said. It wasn't a question.

"I'm very grateful."

"I'm sure you are."

"Now I can go on the mission without any worries . . . about my health, that is."

Westfall said nothing, merely maintaining her sphinxlike smile.

A little hesitantly, Deirdre asked, "Do you still want me to keep you informed? Once we come back, I mean."

With the slightest shake of her head Westfall replied, "That won't be necessary. Not at all. I'm fully satisfied with my other sources of help."

Deirdre's blood had run cold at the sight of Westfall's eyes. Although her lips were smiling, Katherine Westfall's eyes were like a pair of razors, like the eyes of a poisonous snake.

"Full pressure," Dorn announced.

Deirdre snapped out of her memory. The capsule was fully pressurized. Time for the next step of the mission.

"Now we separate from the station and rendezvous with *Faraday*," said Yeager, needlessly. They all knew the procedure. Max is talking because he's nervous, she thought.

Indeed, Yeager chattered every step of the way, his voice basso deep in the perfluorocarbon, as the capsule left station *Gold* and glided the short distance to *Faraday*, co-orbiting with the station. While Yeager told them all how cleverly he had designed the system, the capsule locked onto *Faraday*'s main hatch. Led by Dorn, the four of them swam down the long metal-walled tunnel that penetrated through the twelve pressure spheres of the ship and ended at the ship's bridge, in the vessel's core.

Deirdre floated into the spherical chamber and looked around at the consoles and display screens studding the bulkheads. It was just like the simulators that they had trained on, back in the immersion center aboard *Gold*'s third wheel.

"Well," said Yeager, "here we are."

"Home sweet home," Corvus said, with a lopsided grin. Even his voice sounded weirdly deep, distorted.

Then Yeager leaned toward her and said, in a near whisper, "By the way, you look sexier than ever in that buzz cut."

Deirdre smiled with relief.

S tanding in *Faraday*'s cramped bridge with little to do while the ship swung in orbit around massive Jupiter, Deirdre felt a dull ache in her stomach, as if she had eaten something that disagreed with her. It's the pressure, she thought. We'll all have aches and pains from the pressure. They warned us about it, about how the diaphragm will feel sore from working in high pressure. But in the back of her mind she saw Katherine Westfall's reptilian eyes glittering at her.

Deirdre's assignment was to monitor the ship's sensor displays—unless or until Corvus made contact with the leviathans. Her station was to the right of Dorn, who stood at the bridge's central console and handled the ship's controls. Dorn also stayed in contact with the mission controller. Sure enough, Deirdre saw on the display screen built into Dorn's main console that the controller was the little blond Russian woman who had seemed so friendly with Max.

There were no chairs in the ship's bridge: none were needed as they floated weightlessly in the perfluorocarbon liquid. Yeager had slid his feet into the restraining loops beside Dorn, and was busily tapping out commands on the auxiliary keyboard of the central control console, at the cyborg's elbow. If Dorn was annoyed by the engineer's behavior, he gave no sign of it.

Corvus's job was devoted exclusively to the deep brain stimulation equipment. He had run his console, on Dorn's left, through a perfunctory systems check as soon as they had departed from station *Gold*. Now, with nothing to do while *Faraday* orbited Jupiter, Andy had floated over to stand beside Deirdre.

"What's Max doing?" Deirdre asked Corvus as he hovered beside her. She tried to whisper but her voice still sounded like a moaning foghorn.

"Checking out the ship's systems, I guess," Corvus answered. "He wants to make sure everything's working right before we go diving into the clouds."

Deirdre remembered that the mission control chief had teasingly called Max "little father" at the party. Now she saw how apt the label was. She watched as Yeager methodically called up every one of the ship's systems and subsystems, ticking off the green lights with a tap of his finger against the console display's touchscreen.

At last Yeager turned toward her with a half smile and said, "Everything's in the green."

"Isn't that what you expected, Max?" she asked.

"Yeah. Sure." His smile widened. "But it's good to see my baby's working the way she should."

Dorn turned slightly from his post at the control console and announced, "Time line indicates we should take a meal."

"Already?" Deirdre asked.

"We've been aboard for nearly eight hours," said Dorn.

"That long?"

"Twelve hours since breakfast," Corvus said.

"I don't feel hungry," said Yeager.

"That's because your stomach is filled with perfluorocarbon," Dorn said. "We won't feel normal hunger pangs."

Corvus said, "Yeah, the medics told us about that, didn't they?"

"We must take meals on schedule," Dorn said, very seriously. "Otherwise our performances will deteriorate."

"Wouldn't want to deteriorate," Yeager said, heading for the food dispenser. Then he added, "Could be dangerous."

Deirdre watched Max as he floated over to the dispenser. It looked like a tall, oblong vending machine, except that its face was blank metal with a single square display screen built into it, and it had a slim hose hooked to one side.

"I think I'll have a filet mignon, medium rare, smothered with onions," Yeager joked as he unlimbered the hose.

"And ketchup," Corvus added.

Yeager shot him a disapproving glare.

Deirdre watched, half fascinated, half in dread, as Max clamped the end of the hose to the feeding port in the base of his neck. His expression was strange: He seemed to be trying to smile, but the revulsion he felt was clearly etched on his face.

The dispenser's screen lit up briefly, showing what looked like a pie chart, all cherry red except for a tiny sliver of gray. That must represent Max's meal, she thought.

Within a minute the dispenser gave out a tone that would have been a bell's ding in normal air. In the perfluorocarbon it sounded more like a metallic clunk. Max disconnected the hose and held it out for Corvus.

"Delicious!" he announced. "The steak was a little underdone, though."

Corvus took the hose from his hand. "What's for dessert?" he wisecracked.

One by one the men went to the dispenser and hooked the feeding hose to their ports. Yeager took over at the control board when Dorn went for his meal. Deirdre hung back, wondering what it felt like.

Dorn held out the hose to her. "It's your turn, Dee," he said, almost solemnly.

Taking a deep breath, Deirdre accepted the hose from Dorn's prosthetic hand.

"You need any help with that?" Yeager asked, with his old leer.

Deirdre felt grateful for it. Max breaks the tension, she thought.

Aloud, she replied, "Keep your distance, Max. I can do this for myself, thank you."

She pushed the end of the hose against her feeding port and felt a sharp, brief sting as its hyperfine needle penetrated the port's protruding shell. Her teeth clenched, Deirdre watched the dispenser's display until it dinged and the screen said FEEDING COMPLETE.

She felt no different, but was glad when she disconnected the hose and hung it up in its slot on the dispenser's side. What an awful way to have a meal, she thought.

Dorn, back at his control post, said into the built-in microphone, "Atmospheric entry retroburn in one minute."

The blond woman's image in his display screen nodded. "Retroburn in sixty seconds, on my mark. . . . Mark!"

Deirdre slid her feet into a pair of restraining loops set into the deck. We're going into the clouds, she said to herself. We're going into Jupiter.

eviathan signaled to the nearest member that it must soon leave the Kin for budding. The message flashed inward, toward the Elders, glimmers of blue and green flickering through the vast formation.

Once again Leviathan pondered why the Elders insisted that members go off alone to bud. That makes us vulnerable to the darters, Leviathan reasoned. It would be better to stay within the formation, protected against their slashing insatiable teeth.

Many members of the Kin never returned from their buddings, Leviathan knew. Why do the Elders insist on risking our members so? They say the Symmetry demands it. They say that it has always been so, thus it must always remain so.

Leviathan wondered why. Could it be that those members who budded successfully, who fought off the darters and returned to the Kin, made the Kin stronger? The weak fed the darters, the strong returned to the Kin.

But of what good is that? Leviathan asked itself. Once a member returns to the Kin it is safe from the darters. The predators never attack the Kin in all its strength. They would be destroyed if they tried.

The Symmetry. Everything we do is intended to maintain the Symmetry. That must mean that the darters are part of the Symmetry. A new realization shocked Leviathan's consciousness. Does the Symmetry require that we offer ourselves to feed the darters? Does the Symmetry demand that we sacrifice members of the Kin to keep the darters among us?

How could this be? Leviathan wondered. Why don't we protect

our own members against the darters? Why do we allow them to kill our own kind?

Is it to make the Kin stronger? To get rid of the weak ones? Sacrifice individuals for the good of the group?

Leviathan considered that possibility with loathing. Why don't we attack the darters? Why do we allow them to feed on us? We could kill them all and then the world would be safe for the Kin. We could bud in peace and safety, once the darters are eliminated.

That would alter the Symmetry, it is true. But what's wrong with that? We could make the Symmetry better, safer, stronger.

Leviathan wished it were close enough to the Elders to show them this idea. At its present station, out on the periphery of the Kin's formation, messages had to be relayed inward from one member to another before they reached the Elders. And then the Elders' answer had to be relayed back.

If we could show them my thoughts directly, display my ideas to their eyes without others in between, perhaps we could convince them. Perhaps we could make them see the rightness of our concept. A world without darters! A world without fear, where we could bud in safety and grow in numbers without limit.

Leviathan wanted to break free of its station on the Kin's periphery and swim deep into the formation and confront the Elders directly. But such insolence was unthinkable. The Elders would have nothing to do with such an upstart.

And besides, the urge to bud was building within Leviathan's member parts. Soon it would be irresistible, a blind unreasoning urge that would blot out all other thoughts, all other needs. Instead of swimming inward toward the Elders, Leviathan knew that very soon it would have to leave the Kin and face the ravening darters. Alone.

KATHERINE WESTFALL'S QUARTERS

Rodney Devlin looked properly humble as he was ushered into Westfall's sitting room by the cadaverous, dark-suited aide who served as her personal secretary. His shaved scalp gleamed as if it were polished with oil, while Devlin's lean, lantern-jawed face seemed somehow to be almost mocking behind his red mustache, despite his lowered eyes.

Westfall nodded to the aide and he silently left the sitting room, sliding the door shut without a sound. She was wearing simple lounging pajamas as she sat on the room's comfortably upholstered sofa. Devlin was in his usual white working clothes, rumpled and stained, looking altogether scruffy.

"They're off on their journey into the ocean," she said as the erstwhile cook crossed the carpeted floor toward her.

"You fed her the nanos?" he asked, his voice low and respectful, his chef's floppy hat clutched in his hands.

"At the party, when you gave them to me," Westfall said. "They should start to work on her within a few hours, from what you told me."

Devlin nodded mutely.

"And then they'll go to work on the others," Westfall added. "Which will be the end of their mission and the destruction of Dr. Grant Archer and his scientific minions."

A puzzled expression on his mustachioed face, Devlin asked, "Why're you doin' this? What've you got against Archer and those people in the submersible?"

"That's my business," Westfall said coldly. "You can be glad that you're not going to jail. That's enough for you to know."

"Yes'm."

For several heartbeats the room was silent, Westfall eyeing Devlin like a cat watching a mouse, Devlin standing there waiting for her next words.

At last she said, "Tell me about this man Muzorewa."

"Zeb?" Devlin's face showed surprise. "He useta be director of this station."

"I know that. He's been something of a mentor to Archer, over the years, hasn't he?"

Shrugging, Devlin replied, "I s'pose so. Kinda like a father figure to him, almost. Grant was just a young pup when he first came here, y'know. Zeb took him under 'is wing, so to speak."

"If Archer is relieved of his position as director of this station, would Muzorewa take the job again?"

Devlin puzzled over that question for a moment. Tricky one, that, he said to himself. Why's she asking? What's she after?

"Well?" Westfall demanded.

"I don't think so," Devlin answered. "Zeb's got an endowed chair at the university in Cairo. And he's a high mucky-muck at Selene University. I don't see him comin' back here."

Westfall nodded, satisfied. Devlin got the feeling he had just saved Zeb Muzorewa's career. Or maybe his life.

Linda Vishnevskaya checked the mission profile displayed on the leftmost screen of her console against the actual performance of *Faraday*. The two curves overlapped almost perfectly.

To the image of Dorn in her central screen she said, "You should be breaking through the clouds in six minutes."

The cyborg nodded solemnly. "Six minutes," he repeated. "All systems are performing within nominal limits."

Vishnevskaya glanced at the color-coded lights running along the right side of her console. All green.

"The ship is running smoothly," she agreed. "Please congratulate Dr. Yeager for me."

Dorn asked, "Would you like to speak with him?"

Fighting down the impulse to smile happily, Vishnevskaya said tautly, "Yes. For a moment."

Dorn turned away from the screen and called to Yeager, who slid into view on the display.

"Everything is going well, little father," she said, dimpling into a smile despite herself.

Yeager looked slightly embarrassed. "So far, so good," he muttered.

"How do you feel?" she asked, quickly adding, "The medical team is monitoring your physical conditions, of course."

"I feel okay," Yeager said. "Kind of chilly in this soup, but I guess we'll get warmer as we dive deeper into the ocean."

"Yes." Vishnevskaya studied Yeager's face. He seemed normal, despite the perfluorocarbon he was immersed in. Perhaps his face was a little puffy, but the medics claimed that was to be expected.

"Well," she said, "I just wanted to wish you good luck before communications cut off."

He nodded. A little warily, she thought. As if he were afraid of saying something he didn't want the others to hear.

"Thanks. We'll be okay."

"Of course. You designed the vessel well."

"See you when we get back."

"Of course," she repeated.

"So long, kid."

"Good luck," she said again, feeling inane, frustrated.

Yeager slid out of the display screen's field of view and Dorn came back. "We're on trajectory," he said. "Time line is on the tick."

Vishnevskaya nodded at the cyborg. But she was thinking, Max, don't get hurt. Make your ship perform as it should and come back safe. Come back to me.

Grant Archer sat alone in the gallery that circled the mission control center. As he looked down at the handful of men and women working the consoles he thought, I should have gone on this mission. I should have gone with them.

A cold, almost sneering voice in his head ridiculed the thought. Gone with them? At your age? What would you do down there in that cold blackness? You'd be useless.

Archer nodded to himself, his eyes fastened on the big wall screens that displayed data from *Faraday*'s systems.

I'd be a burden to them, he admitted silently. But I'd be with them. I'd be facing the same risks that I've asked them to face. I'd share their fate.

Totally alone in his melancholy, Archer bowed his head and prayed silently, Yea, though I walk through the valley of the shadow of death . . .

To his alarm, he found that he could not speak the next line, not even to himself. He did fear evil. He feared for the people he had sent into Jupiter's dark, alien sea.

He feared the malice of Katherine Westfall.

We'll break through the clouds in two minutes," Dorn said, his eyes focused on the mission profile curve.

Yeager was standing behind him, his feet anchored in floor loops as he swayed slightly in their liquid world. Deirdre thought of the undersea plants she had seen in vids of Earth.

"Shouldn't you power up the sensor screens?" Corvus asked. He was at his station, to the left of Dorn in the cramped compartment.

The cyborg nodded toward Deirdre. "Powering the sensor screens," he said as he touched an icon on the control panel's master screen.

All the screens on Deirdre's console lit up, but Deirdre saw nothing except swirling waves of color racing past.

"Wow!" Corvus blurted. "We're really moving!"

"Diving like a falcon," Yeager agreed.

"It doesn't feel as if we're diving," Deirdre said.

"That's because we're inside," Yeager explained. "We share the same relative motion as the ship."

Dorn intoned, "Breakout in one minute."

"The flight engineers call this a hypersonic descent," Yeager went on, perfectly serious. "We're gliding through the atmosphere at Mach 12."

"Gliding?" Deirdre asked. "At Mach 12?"

Yeager nodded tightly. "Gliding. Saves on the propellants we'll need to launch ourselves back out of here when the mission's finished."

"That's why we have those aerodynamic fins attached to the ship's exterior," Dorn said.

"Right," Yeager agreed. "And once we're in the ocean they'll serve as steering vanes."

The ship was definitely shaking now, buffeting seriously.

"And the atmosphere's ten thousand kilometers deep?" Deirdre asked, remembering the figure from their briefings.

Without turning from his control panel displays, Dorn nodded. "Ten thousand kilometers, roughly. Just about as deep as the Earth's diameter. It's—"

"Look!" Deirdre shouted.

The display screens suddenly cleared and showed a vast panorama of steel gray ocean stretching far below them. The horizon was far, far away, much more distant than the horizon on Earth. Enormous, Deirdre realized. This is an enormous world. The sky was blanketed with soft pastel clouds, bulbous and billowing as far as the eye could see.

"We're below the clouds," Deirdre breathed. It sounded silly, even to herself. The buffeting was getting worse, but no one seemed to take any notice of it. Am I the only one who's frightened? she asked herself.

"Look over there," Corvus said, pointing.

Little puffs of greenish clouds floated low across the ocean's rippled surface, and other, darker smudges dotted the view.

"I'll focus the telescopes on them," Deirdre said, glad to have something to occupy her hands. The smudges grew into an armada of iridescent balloons sailing majestically across the boundless ocean, glittering in the pale light that filtered through the clouds.

"Look at them," Deirdre gasped, pointing. "They're beautiful!"

"Clarke's Medusas," Corvus murmured. "Completely adapted to living airborne. They never land anywhere."

"There isn't any land to land on," Yeager said. "Nothing down there but a seven-thousand-klick-deep ocean."

"They spend their whole lives aloft," Deirdre said.

"They're just sailing along," Yeager said, a hint of awe creeping into his voice, "on winds that must be at least four hundred knots."

"It's home to them," Corvus said.

Deirdre watched the medusas, fascinated. Long tendrils trailed from their colorful main bodies. Sensors, she recalled from her briefings.

"What's that?" Yeager asked, pointing a trembling finger at a thin, flat ghostly figure that glided past the medusas.

"Spider-kite," said Corvus. "They eat the organic particles raining out of the clouds."

"So do the medusas," said Deirdre. "No predators have been found among the organisms living in the atmosphere," she quoted from memory. "They all feed on the particles coming down from the clouds. Like manna from heaven."

"That doesn't mean there aren't any predators," Corvus said.

Yeager countered, "Been popping probes into this atmosphere for almost half a century. No predators have been identified."

Corvus remained unconvinced. "Still . . ."

"A world without predators," Deirdre said. "Like heaven. Every creature is safe, content."

Without looking up from his screens, Dorn said dryly, "Let's hope there aren't any predators that like to eat little round metal ships."

If he had meant it to be lighthearted, the humor fell flat. Nobody laughed.

INTO THE OCEAN

We'd better strap down now," said Dorn. "We'll be entering the ocean in five minutes."

Deirdre was still watching the panorama of medusas and spider-kites and long-winged birds that glided effortlessly through Jupiter's clear hydrogen atmosphere. Endlessly fascinating, she thought. A whole extraterrestrial ecology adapted to living in this wild, airborne environment. She had expected the medusas to be big, and they were, dwarfing the puny *Faraday*. But the spider-kites were almost as big, wide expanses of gossamer floating out there on winds that were shaking this ship like a leaf in a hurricane.

Faraday was buffeting heavily now. The four of them swayed and lurched in their liquid surroundings. Deirdre thought that if they hadn't secured themselves to the deck with the foot loops they would all be bouncing off the bridge's spherical bulkhead.

Corvus touched her shoulder. "Come on, Dee, time to strap in."

Andy looks tense, she thought. I suppose I do, too. But she gazed once again at the shimmering, coruscating medusas gliding placidly through the hurricane winds, their long slender tendrils swaying gently, almost hypnotically. They're so beautiful, Deirdre thought.

She pulled her bare feet free of the deck loops and floated to the bulkhead. It took an effort; the ship was shaking so hard that she missed the safety harness attached to the bulkhead and bumped painfully against the curving metal instead.

"Are you okay?" Corvus asked.

Nodding, Deirdre muttered, "Clumsy." She clutched the safety harness and pulled it over her shoulders, then reached down for the straps that secured her thighs.

Looking up, she saw that Andy and Max were doing the same. For once Max was strictly business: no leering innuendos, no offer to help her with her straps. Deirdre smiled inwardly. Max is just as uptight as the rest of us, she realized.

Dorn's harness was different, looser, dangling from the overhead so that he could remain facing the control panel. He turned his head and checked the rest of them.

"Ocean entry in three minutes," he announced.

Deirdre was still watching the medusas on the display screens that circled the bridge.

"The cameras are saving this imagery, aren't they?" she asked, knowing that it was so but wanting Dorn or Max to confirm it.

"Everything's being recorded," Yeager said.

"Good," Deirdre murmured. Those medusas are works of art, she thought. When we get back I'm going to beam this imagery to every art museum in the Earth/Moon system. They're too beautiful for only the scientists to look at.

"Two minutes to entry," said Dorn.

The ship's buffeting was getting worse. Deirdre felt the harness straps cutting into her as *Faraday* shuddered and jittered down through the lowest levels of the atmosphere.

"What's that?" Corvus yelped, pointing a shaking finger at the display screens on Deirdre's console.

She turned and saw one of those huge birdlike creatures, its wings outstretched, its long sword-thin beak dipping into the frothing surface of the ocean.

"Skimmer," Yeager hollered. "Like on Earth."

"Look at the numbers on the data bar!" Corvus cried. "It's big enough to wrap us up in its wings."

"They grow 'em big on this planet," Yeager said, with grudging admiration.

As if it could hear them, the skimmer lifted its beak out of the water and seemed to look straight into the camera. Then, with a single flap of its enormous wings, it soared up and out of the camera's view.

"Had its fill of fish," Yeager muttered.

"It doesn't eat the manna," Dorn said. "There are predators in this world after all."

"I'm glad it doesn't eat round metal objects," said Corvus, remembering Dorn's earlier attempt at humor.

"Didn't show any curiosity about us."

Deirdre said, "Maybe we frightened it."

Corvus grinned and replied, "Well, it sure as hell frightened me."

"There are bugs that eat metal in the clouds of Venus," Yeager said.

"Not here, though," Corvus said.

"Thank goodness," said Deirdre.

"One minute," Dorn announced.

The view outside grew misty as they neared the surface of the ocean. Spray from the waves, Deirdre realized. The boundary between atmosphere and ocean isn't as distinct as it is on Earth. She wondered if Jupiter's incredible spin rate had something to do with that. The planet's more than ten times bigger than Earth, yet its day is less than ten hours long. That must whip up tremendous currents in the ocean.

"Retroburn in ten seconds," Dorn called out.

Deirdre felt her body surge against the restraining harness, but it was a gentle push, more like being pressed forward by a partner on a dance floor than being slammed by a hard blast of retrorockets.

The display screens went blank, then turned dark. She felt another jolt, harder this time, and then the ship's buffeting eased into a soft rocking motion, like a baby's cradle. It was soothing, almost, after the hard bumps through the atmosphere.

"We are in the ocean," Dorn told them. "Thirty meters deep and heading deeper."

"Great entry," Yeager congratulated. "Smooth as a baby's butt."

"Thank you," said Dorn. "Your control systems did most of the work."

"Can we unstrap now?" Corvus asked.

"What happened to the screens?" Deirdre asked.

"Not much visible light penetrates the water," Yeager replied before Dorn could. "It gets a lot darker as we go deeper."

"Switching to infrared," Dorn said.

It wasn't much better. Deirdre couldn't make out much of anything on the screens. Just darkness, with the vague hint of wavering forms that might have been simply her imagination. But then she saw something drifting by.

"Snow?" she called out.

"Manna," said Yeager.

Corvus explained needlessly, "It's a stream of organic particles. They form in the clouds and fall down into the ocean. The leviathans feed on them."

We know that, Deirdre thought. Andy's just reciting facts to hide his nervousness.

"We have entered the ocean approximately twelve kilometers from the spot that the mission plan called for," said Dorn. "Now we follow this stream of organic particles down to the level where the leviathans feed."

For once, the cyborg's deep voice sounded satisfied, almost pleased.

We're where we ought to be, Deirdre said to herself. Close enough, anyway. Now all we've got to do is find those giant creatures.

Deirdre began to feel bored. The display screens remained dark. There was nothing for her to see, nothing for her to do. They had unstrapped from their restraining harnesses: *Faraday* swayed gently in the ocean's surging current.

Corvus had gone to his console to check the status of his DBS equipment. He seemed quite content to run his tests, checking and rechecking the gadgetry. Yeager stood beside him, swaying easily with his feet in the deck loops, running equally incomprehensible diagnostic checks on the ship's systems.

Deirdre looked over Dorn's shoulder at the screens of his control panel, trying to make out what the blinking lights and colored curves meant.

As if he sensed her behind him, Dorn said softly, "All systems are performing well."

"We're going deeper?" she asked.

"Yes. Following the stream of organics. We've passed the three-hundred-kilometer mark."

"And there's still nothing out there."

Dorn made a noise that might have been a chuckle. "I'll put the sonar returns on-screen."

The display screens lit up with ghostly images, strange, alien shapes.

"Activating the visual subprogram," Dorn said, touching a key on his control panel.

The vague grayish shapes suddenly sharpened into clear imagery, brightly colored creatures, some sleek and swift, others that looked misshapen and horribly ugly to Deirdre's eyes.

"Fish!" she exclaimed.

"The Jovian equivalent," said Dorn. "The ocean is teeming with them at this level."

Deirdre watched them, fascinated.

"The colors are added by the visual subprogram," Dorn explained. "The actual creatures probably don't look this way."

That didn't matter to Deirdre. She watched the Jovian fish flicking across the sensor screens. In the distance she saw an undulating, flattened thing that trailed a set of wavering tentacles. The data bar running across the screen's bottom said it was nearly three kilometers across.

"It's like a big, floating bedsheet," Deirdre said, awestruck.

"With tentacles," Dorn added.

As they watched, the flat undulating creature moved closer. It seemed to slither through the water, its tentacles wavering as it moved. Deirdre thought it looked monstrous, horrible. It made her blood run cold.

Suddenly one of its tentacles shot out and seized one of the fat, slow-moving fish. Before Deirdre could even gasp it pulled the fish in and shoved it, still wriggling and struggling, into a round mouth on its underside. Deirdre saw that the mouth was ringed with flashing teeth. The fish disappeared into that maw.

"It's a predator!" Corvus said, sounding surprised. "We didn't know there were predators at this level. Nobody ever saw one of those before."

"A discovery," Dorn said evenly.

Yeager glided up beside Corvus. "The bio guys thought all the critters at this level lived off the manna."

"That's what they told us at the briefings," Deirdre recalled.

"Well, they were wrong, weren't they," said Corvus.

"That's what science is all about," Yeager said, a little pompously. "Busting up somebody's pet theory."

Dorn tapped the time line display with a prosthetic finger. "Time for Dee and Andy to take their rest period."

Deirdre felt surprised. Six hours already? We've been in the ocean six hours?

Yeager turned to her with his old leering smile. "You need some-body to tuck you in, honey?"

"No thank you, Max," Deirdre replied sweetly. "I can do it my-self. I'm a big girl."

"In all the right places," Yeager retorted.

With Corvus trailing behind her, Deirdre swam to the narrow hatch that led to the bunks. She pulled out a fresh set of tights from the storage drawer beneath her coffin-sized bunk, then ducked into the lavatory briefly. The toilet had been adapted from zero-gravity systems developed for spacecraft: It clamped Deirdre's bottom firmly. She wondered what would happen if she couldn't pull free of it once she was finished.

But the collar unclamped easily enough. Deirdre stood up and changed into the fresh tights, then pushed through the doorway to the cramped space where the bunks were stacked, three on one side, two on the other. They were little more than long narrow shelves. While Corvus ducked into the lavatory Deirdre grasped the hand-bar atop the opening to her bunk and slid her body in.

She thought she'd be too tense to sleep, but her eyes closed as soon as she lay her head down. She dreamed of that slithering, de-vouring monster seizing her in its tentacles and pulling her toward its slashing teeth. But at the last moment of her dream the monster suddenly was Andy Corvus, and he was holding her tenderly in his arms.

RESEARCH STATION *GOLD*

rant Archer came back to the control center and walked down its central aisle to stand behind the mission control chief as the screens on her console suddenly went blank, every one of them. Looking around, he saw that all the other consoles had gone dark, as well, together with the big wall screens.

Linda Vishnevskaya half turned in her chair and looked up at Archer. "That's it," she said. "They're out of contact now. They're into the sea."

Archer nodded. "They're on their own."

Vishnevskaya got slowly, tiredly to her feet. Her tousled blond curls barely reached Archer's shoulder. "On their own," she murmured.

The other controllers were getting up from their consoles, stretching, working out the kinks in their bodies after sitting at their posts for so long. The whole mission control center seemed quiet, subdued, as if something had gone wrong.

"You'll maintain a skeleton crew here, just in case?" Archer asked the chief controller.

She nodded. "One person. That's enough to notify me and get everyone back here if something unexpected happens."

"And if all goes as planned?" he prompted.

"Then we'll hear from them in exactly one hundred and fourteen hours," Vishnevskaya said, with a weary smile. "Of course, they will be sending up data capsules on schedule."

"Good," said Archer. He slowly climbed the stairs to the top level of the control center, where Katherine Westfall sat in one of the spectator's seats, flanked on either side by a pair of blank-faced young men in dark tunics and slacks.

Trying to sound cheerful, Archer said to her, "They're in the ocean, right on schedule. For the next five days they'll be out of contact with us."

Westfall stood up, and her two aides rose like automatons beside her. In her deceptively soft voice she said, "If something should happen while they're in the ocean . . ." She left the rest unsaid.

Archer thought she looked almost . . . expectant. As if she *wants* something to go wrong. But he told himself he was being paranoid. Why would she want them to have trouble down there?

Linda Vishnevskaya left the control center reluctantly. She couldn't overcome the feeling that nothing bad would happen to the mission as long as she stayed at her post. She knew it was stupid. Sheer emotion. Still she lingered, climbing the steps toward the exit as slowly as a child heading for a dentist's chair.

Max, she thought. I know you have children my age and you don't even know I exist except as a fellow technician. But I love you, Max. Come back to me. Don't get yourself killed down there.

LEVIATHAN

The urge to dissociate was growing stronger. Leviathan swam upward toward the cooler waters above, hoping that the darters would be less likely to seek their prey there. Its sensor parts could not detect darters within their range of observation, but Leviathan knew how swiftly the predators could swarm in and overwhelm a lone member of the Kin, especially when it was in the process of dissociating.

Already some of the flagella members were shuddering with the desire to split away and begin budding.

Not yet, Leviathan insisted. Not yet. Be faithful. The time is coming but it's not yet here.

Leviathan had purposely steered away from the current of downfalling food, reasoning that the darters would lurk near it in hopes of trapping a solitary member of the Kin. There is safety in doing the unexpected, Leviathan thought.

Hunger gnawed dully in Leviathan's inner organ parts. Even the sensor parts and faithful dull-witted flagella began to send hunger signals to Leviathan's central brain.

Wait, Leviathan told its members. Better to be hungry than to be eaten by darters.

The water was cooler at this level, which made the hunger pangs all the more insistent. No darters in range, the sensor parts reported. Leviathan could feel the trembling urge to dissociate growing stronger, stronger, rising toward an irresistible convulsion. In a few more moments the craving would be unstoppable and Leviathan would begin to disconnect into its separate components.

One of the flagella members detached from Leviathan's body,

shuddering uncontrollably as it drifted away. Still no darters within sight, the sensor parts reported.

But wait! Something was moving out in the cold darkness, coming closer. Leviathan desperately commanded its member parts to resist the craving to dissociate. Its brain studied the image the sensor parts were observing.

Not darters. Something strange. Almost as large as a full-grown darter, but misshapen, round, spherical, cold, and hard-shelled.

Something alien.

S omething's out there," Dorn muttered as he stared at the central display on his console.

Corvus floated to his side and peered at the screen. "I don't see anything."

Deirdre and Yeager came up, too, floating high enough in the perfluorocarbon liquid so they could look over the shoulders of the two men.

Dorn said, "Pressure sensors are showing that something is moving out there, sending an irregular pattern of waves through the ocean."

"Fish?" Yeager suggested.

"Switching to active sonar," said Dorn.

Faraday's sonar system used sound waves at too low a register for human ears to detect. But almost immediately Deirdre saw a shape appear on Dorn's central screen. Glancing at her own console, she saw the same image.

"Seventy-three kilometers away," Dorn muttered.

Corvus nodded. "At that distance the thing must be at least ten klicks across."

"We got one!" Yeager hooted.

A leviathan, Deirdre realized, peering more intently at the screen. The image was gray and grainy but she could make out the beast's streamlined shape, studded with what looked to her like little pods. No, she remembered from her earlier briefings, those are fins, hundreds of fins that propel the animal through the water.

Yeager asked, "Any of those shark things around?"

"None in sight," Dorn replied.

"So far, so good," the engineer muttered.

"We've got to get closer," Corvus said. "Closer."

Without glancing away from the screens, Dorn said, "Slowly. We'll approach slowly. We don't want to alarm the creature."

Alarm it? Deirdre asked silently. How could we frighten something that big? That powerful. We're like a little child's toy compared to it.

Then Corvus said, "Hey! It's coming apart!"

Katherine Westfall stood alone in the observation deck staring out at the hard, unblinking myriads of stars blazing their light against the infinite blackness of the universe. Like people, she thought. We each shine with our own light, struggling against the darkness of inevitable death.

But is death truly inevitable? With rejuvenation therapies one can live for hundreds of years, she told herself. And in another century or two we'll know even more and be able to extend our lifespans even further. Death needn't be inevitable, not if you have access to the latest medical techniques.

And to have access to the latest medical techniques you need money, Westfall reminded herself. Money and power. She thought back to her childhood, when she had neither. To her mother drudging away in restaurant kitchens night after night, year after year, coming home exhausted, throwing herself on her bed only to get up again the next day and go back to work.

For what? For me, Mother always said. So that I could have a better life. Yes, I found a better life. I married it. I saw my chance and I took it. I'll never be poor again, never be powerless, never have to worry that if I don't please this one or that one I'll be thrown out into the street.

She remembered her mother's death, wretched and shriveled from the tumors that fed on her body. The best medical care in the world couldn't save Mother. All they could do was to ease her pain at the end. And Elaine, the sister she never knew, the scientists couldn't save her. They killed her, really. If it wasn't for men like Grant Archer and that Muzorewa person, my sister would still be alive today.

The stars were slowly moving across the glassteel window of the observation deck. Westfall smiled inwardly as she imagined herself the center of the universe, with all the stars of heaven revolving around her. A pleasant thought, she felt. That's the kind of power that could keep you safe forever.

And then the stars began to dim as Jupiter's mighty radiance flooded the observation deck. Even before the body of the massive planet swung into view, its powerful glow dimmed the stars themselves. Westfall felt the warmth of that glow touching her cheek, making her suddenly nervous, frightened.

Stand your ground, she told herself. Face your fears.

Jupiter rose from beneath her feet, a mammoth overwhelming presence, a true god, streaked with whirling, racing clouds, dotted with storms, powerful and all-engulfing.

Katherine felt the terror she'd known when strange men would come home with her mother, laughing powerful men who patted her on the head and shooed her off to her own corner of the room.

She hated those men. And she hated her mother for needing them. I don't need anyone, she told herself. I destroy anyone who stands between me and safety. I'll destroy Archer. He'll never become chairman of the IAA. I will.

Face your fears, she said to herself as she squared her shoulders and stared into Jupiter's swirling, seething clouds. You think you can conquer me? Giant planet, king of the gods, you're nothing but a tool for me to use. I'm not frightened of you. I'm not. I'm not.

She laughed aloud at the sight of mighty Jupiter. Archer's destruction will begin down there, Katherine Westfall told herself, with the destruction of that ship he sent into those clouds, with the death of the people he sent into that ocean.

The ache in her midsection had grown into a knot that throbbed in her chest, but Deirdre tried to ignore it as she stood by her sensor console watching the leviathan. Andy swayed in the perfluorocarbon liquid beside her. Dorn was watching the sensor display on a screen of his control console, Yeager beside him, bending forward eagerly.

"It's coming apart, all right!" Corvus said. "Look!" He was excited, but in the perfluorocarbon his voice still sounded deep, almost sonorous.

"We've caught it in the act of reproducing," said Dorn.

"Jovian pornography," Yeager cracked. Deirdre shook her head at him.

"Get closer," Corvus urged.

"No," Deirdre said, surprising herself. "Stay back."

Dorn half turned, a questioning expression on the human side of his face.

"If it's reproducing we should give it as much privacy as we can," Deirdre said.

"It's just an animal," Yeager argued. "It doesn't have any feelings of modesty."

"How do you know?" Corvus asked.

"Animals have feelings," said Deirdre. "They can get very annoyed when you bother them at the wrong time."

"You wouldn't want to annoy something that big," Corvus added.

Dorn said, "I think discretion is the better part of valor in this case."

Deirdre smiled to herself, thinking, *Henry IV*, Part I, act five, scene three.

She asked Dorn, "Can the spectrograph laser work at this range?"

"It should pick up something," Dorn replied.

"Could you activate it for me, please?"

"On console two."

Deirdre floated over to the console built into the compartment's curved bulkhead and slipped into the foot loops there. On its screen she saw the spectrograph's deep green laser beam lancing through the dark water. She touched the electronic keyboard and the visual display was immediately replaced by a string of alphanumerics. Plenty of chemical species in the water around the creature, Deirdre saw. The water's saturated with the Jovian equivalent of pheromones and sex hormones.

She heard Yeager sneer, "Exoporn." Max was still watching Dorn's main screen and the leviathan shaking itself apart. "We could sell this footage to some of the freaks back Earthside."

"Oh Max," Deirdre chided.

Dorn said, "We can stay at this distance and observe without—" Suddenly he stiffened. "Sharks approaching."

Leviathan saw the alien clearly, hovering in the distance. Stay together, it commanded its member parts. We can't dissociate while a stranger is near.

But several of the mindless flagella had already broken free and were floating off. Leviathan tried to resist the mounting urge to dissociate. It would be too dangerous with the alien so close. We must stay together.

Sensor parts were drifting away. Deep within its armored hide, Leviathan's vital organs were pulsing with the need to disassemble, to end their unity and begin the ancient passion of dissociation and recombination.

With stunning swiftness the need overpowered Leviathan. Everything else dwindled into nothingness. Nothing else mattered. The gigantic creature surrendered to the impulse, to the shuddering ecstasy of dissociating. The presence of the alien was overwhelmed in the driving compulsion to reproduce, the insistent orgasmic irresistible joy of release.

But as it at last surrendered to its primitive need, Leviathan's brain registered a sudden terrified warning from the last of its functioning sensor parts. Darters!

That was the last thing Leviathan recognized. Its mind went blank. Its final thought was that death and rebirth are forever intertwined.

"Sharks?" Yeager barked. "Where?"

Dorn ran his fingers across the console's electronic keyboard and the main display screen shifted to show a half-dozen sleek, dangerous shapes hurtling toward the cloud of pieces that had been a single leviathan only moments earlier.

"They'll attack while the leviathan's helpless," Deirdre said.

"Predators," Yeager muttered scornfully.

"We've got to do something to help!" said Corvus.

"Do what?" Yeager snapped.

"Drive them away," said Deirdre.

Dorn shook his head solemnly. "Should we try to interfere in the natural processes of their world?"

Impatiently, Corvus insisted, "I came down here to try to make contact with the leviathans. I don't want to stand here and watch it served up for lunch!"

"It's helpless," Deirdre said.

"It'll be a massacre," Corvus added.

Dorn looked up at Yeager. "Do you think we could discourage the sharks?"

Yeager made a sound that might have been a grunt. In the perfluorocarbon it sounded more like a moan.

"I attached a couple of electron guns to the outer hull. We could shock 'em if we can get close enough."

"How close?" Dorn asked. But he was already activating the ship's propulsion system, steering toward the approaching sharks.

"Fifty meters," Yeager said, clearly unhappy. "Closer."

Dorn nodded. Deirdre could hear the hissing rumble of the propulsion jets and felt the surge of acceleration. In the display screen the charging sharks' images began to grow larger.

"The charge of the light brigade," Yeager murmured.

Deirdre remembered a line from the poem: "All in the valley of death rode the six hundred." Then she thought, We don't have six hundred. There's only the four of us.

"So how's the sim?" Devlin asked.

Franklin Torre glanced over his shoulder before whispering, "Terrific. It's like being with her."

Devlin nodded. It had been simple enough to take a standard VR simulation and dub Deirdre Ambrose's face in place of the porn star. It was a pretty ragged job of dubbing, but apparently Torre didn't mind.

The two men were standing in a corner of the busy galley, slightly away from the lines of chattering people who were filling their dinner trays. Torre seemed to be worried that his sister would see him, Devlin thought.

"So you're happy, then?" he asked, with his impish grin. "No complaints?"

"Uh . . . can you get one that's a sort of Arabian Nights setting?" Torre asked, his cheeks reddening slightly.

"Harem scene? Sure. How many girls do you want?"

His face flaming hotter, Torre said, "Doesn't matter, as long as one of them's Dee."

"Can do, Frankie old chum. No problem."

As Devlin began to move back toward the kitchen, Torre clutched at the sleeve of his stained chef's jacket.

"Those nanos I gave you . . . what did you do with them?"

Putting on an innocent expression, Devlin said, "Oh, them? I took 'em myself."

"Yourself?"

"Yeah. They're harmless, aren't they?"

"Well, not altogether . . ."

"You mean they're *not* harmless?"

Torre whispered harshly, "I told you they can act on the gastric juices in the stomach."

"Yeah, yeah, but it'd take them forty-eight hours to show any symptoms."

"They're not symptoms!" Torre snapped. "Not unless something goes wrong."

Devlin patted him on the shoulder. "Now what could possibly go wrong, chum? Huh?"

THE CHARGE OF THE LIGHT BRIGADE

Deirdre watched, wide eyed, as the sharks seemed to leap closer in her console's central screen. She tapped at the keypad symbols and slaved her sensor display to one of the screens on Dorn's console so he could watch what she was viewing without turning to look at her console.

Andy was frozen in place behind Yeager, who was bending slightly forward, just to Dorn's left.

"Hold on," Dorn said calmly. "This might get violent."

Deirdre wormed her bare feet more firmly into the deck loops and grasped the handgrips on her console.

Faraday was hurtling toward the band of sharks. Deirdre counted six of them on her console screen, bulleting single-mindedly toward the remnants of what had been a huge leviathan.

That's their food, she thought. We're trying to stop them from eating. We're interfering in the natural order of this world. But then she looked again at Andy's face, his soft blue eyes wide, his cute lopsided grin replaced by open-mouthed anxiety. Andy's here to study the leviathans, Deirdre told herself. If we let the sharks eat this one we'll have to go deeper and try to find another.

Max growled, "Get 'em, Dorn. Blast right into them."

Instead of being wary of attacking the sharks, Max was suddenly belligerent, aggressive.

"Bang into my baby, will you?" Yeager snarled, his voice deepening into an oath of vengeance. "We'll show you!"

Dorn glanced over his shoulder at Yeager and shook his head.

The sharks suddenly seemed to become aware of *Faraday* charging at them. They veered from their course and split up, heading in all directions. Several of them raced out of the screen's view. *Faraday* zoomed past them, then Dorn swerved the ship into a tight turn. Deirdre swayed so hard one of her hands slipped free of the grip on the console's face.

They were heading back toward the sharks, which appeared to be milling about confusedly. Then a pair of them turned toward *Faraday*.

"They're going to ram us!" Corvus yelped.

"The hell they are," Yeager growled, leaning over Dorn's shoulder, his finger extended, ready to press one of the console's keypads.

Dorn slapped his hand away. "I'll handle it," he said, without looking up from his screen.

The sharks were on a collision course, so close their streamlined bodies filled the screen. Deirdre braced for a crash.

"Now!" Yeager bellowed, and Dorn mashed his prosthetic hand on the keypad that fired the electron guns.

Deirdre's screen filled with a blue-white flash that almost blinded her. Blinking tears away, she saw both sharks thrashing, convulsing.

"That got 'em," Yeager exulted.

But not for long. The sharks writhed and flailed erratically for a few minutes, then straightened out and began to swim normally again.

"Where are the others?" Corvus asked.

The screen's view widened to show the other sharks gobbling at the dismembered pieces of the leviathan. Deirdre noticed that several of the pieces had come together; the creature was already rebuilding itself.

Without a word Dorn arrowed the ship toward the greedily feeding sharks. They sensed the danger and broke off, splitting up into separate pairs. They run in pairs, Deirdre thought. They never move alone.

Again *Faraday* charged at the confused sharks. This time all four of them converged on the ship, hurtling toward it at frightening speed.

Dorn waited until Deirdre was certain they would collide with the sharks, then hit the electron gun button again. Again the blue-white flash and again the sharks twisted away, dazed.

But only temporarily. Within minutes the six of them had reorganized and were swimming normally once more. Dorn maneuvered *Faraday* between their formation and the reassembling pieces of the leviathan.

Consciousness returned to Leviathan slowly. At first it could sense nothing but the unutterable pleasure of fissioning. No organized thoughts, no memories, no fears: nothing but the sensual delight of creating two from one.

Then recombination. The ancient rhythm of joining, of coming together, of connecting. Brain and gills. Mouth parts and inner organs. Sensor members and strong, steadfast flagella.

Almost complete. Leviathan remembered who it was, remembered the Symmetry and the Kin and—the darters.

Another member of the Kin swam nearby. It was Leviathan also. They flashed recognition images to each other, orange and pale yellow. The Symmetry had been preserved. The budding was complete. Now there were two where only one had existed before.

But what of the darters?

Like awakening from a dream, Leviathan began to search about itself. The darters were moving in when the dissociation began. We were in danger. How . . . ?

Leviathan and its replicate sensed the darters out there, close enough to stir the water with their thrashing. And something else.

The alien. That strange spherical hard-shelled alien was charging at the darters. At them! It was between the pack of darters and the Leviathan and its replicate, attacking the predators. Or were the darters attacking the alien? Leviathan saw harsh blue-white sparks flash in the water and the darters raced away from the alien, one of them convulsing wildly as the others backed off.

The alien is protecting us! Leviathan realized. But now the darters were attacking it. The alien needed protection now.

Without needing to communicate with its replicate, Leviathan drove straight at the darters, its replicate at its side. Simultaneously they bawled the undulating note that rose and fell in perfect unison, the bellowing overpowering profoundly deep bass note that reverberated through the water like the voice of doom.

CONTACT

"What the hell is that?" Yeager bellowed as the deep thrumming sound reverberated through *Faraday*'s cramped bridge.

Deirdre clapped her hands over her ears. The sound was painful.

Dorn ran his fingers across the electronic keyboard of his main console. "Turning off the sonar and the exterior microphones," he muttered.

Deirdre could barely hear him through the overwhelming blare. The sound undulated through the bridge, rising and falling, an impossibly deep bass pulsation that rattled the bones and shook the insides of the four humans. Deirdre felt as if her lungs were about to burst.

Corvus pointed a quavering finger at Dorn's central screen. Deirdre saw his lips moving but she couldn't make out his words. Looking at the screen, she saw that the sharks were swimming away as fast as they could, fleeing the overpowering sound.

"It's coming from the leviathans," Deirdre said, barely able to hear her own voice. She felt as if her head was stuffed with thick goo, as if she were going deaf.

Max was wincing with pain, Andy had clamped his hands over his ears and was shaking his head in misery. Dorn remained stolidly at his post before the main control console. The noise didn't seem to be affecting him as much as the others, Deirdre thought.

Abruptly the sound shut off. Deirdre felt it rather than heard it. The pressure inside her head suddenly disappeared, although her ears were throbbing with the pain of it.

"They're gone," Dorn said. She heard his perfluorocarbon-deepened voice as if through a pair of pillows stuffed against her ears.

The sharks had left the area. Dorn's central screen showed no sign of them, only the two massive leviathans. Deirdre read the numbers from the ranging laser displayed across the bottom of the screen: The creatures were twelve kilometers away, but still so huge that they loomed like a pair of giant monsters.

"They drove the sharks away," Corvus said, with awe in his voice.

Max Yeager rubbed at the bridge of his nose with both index fingers. "Damned near split my skull," he muttered.

Their voices were still muffled in Deirdre's ears, but she could hear them well enough now.

Dorn said, "They're coming closer."

Leviathan and its replicate edged closer to the alien. Strange, thought Leviathan, the replicate does exactly what we do. Then it thought, Of course. It is us. A duplicate of us. Or are we a duplicate of it? Which of us is the original, which the replicate?

It didn't matter. In time the two leviathans would change as they faced different life experiences. It is all part of the Symmetry, Leviathan told itself. We begin as a unity but diverge as we learn and grow.

The alien seemed quiescent now. It floated before them, inert and seeming almost dead except for the narrow beam of light that lanced from its skin and splashed against the hides of the two leviathans, first one and then the other.

It's not dead, Leviathan realized. But it is strangely dark.

It was perfectly spherical, although studded with finlike appendages, Leviathan's sensor parts reported. Its skin was hard, unyielding; it echoed back the sound waves the sensors beamed at it with no absorption at all.

It must be intelligent, Leviathan thought. It attacked the darters when we were dissociated and vulnerable. It protected us. Why?

Leviathan flashed questions to the alien. Who are you? Why are you here?

The alien remained dark, except for that one narrow beam of light.

"I wish we had bigger screens," Deirdre said.

Yeager nodded, his eyes fastened on Dorn's central display as the leviathans swam closer. "I should have plastered the whole interior bulkhead with screens," he said.

The gigantic creatures were coming so close that the screens could no longer show all of their enormous bulk. Deirdre saw that their massive bodies were studded with oarlike appendages. And eyes! Those must be eyes, she realized. Hundreds of them running the length of their bodies. And all of them looking at us. It made her blood run cold.

Suddenly the flanks of both leviathans lit up with a display of bright colors: red, yellow, green, bright periwinkle blue.

"Wow!" Corvus goggled at their display.

"That's not false color from the visual subprogram," Yeager shouted. "That's real!"

"Activating the visual cameras," Dorn said. Even his voice trembled a little.

The images shifted, changed, colors coming and going, shapes altering, transforming before their staring eyes.

"They're showing off for us," Corvus said.

Deirdre suddenly understood what was happening. "No," she said, feeling a trembling excitement. "They're trying to talk to us!"

COMMUNICATION

Talk to us?" Yeager asked, incredulous.

"That's the way they communicate with each other," Deirdre said. "Visually. Through images."

"That's why we have the display panels on the outer hull, isn't it?" Corvus said.

"Yeah," Yeager admitted. Somewhat grudgingly, Deirdre thought. "But are those images supposed to mean something? They look like gibberish to me."

"You don't speak Jovian, Max," said Corvus.

"Should I light up the panels?" Dorn asked.

"Yes," said Deirdre. "And could you give me control of them on my console? Please?"

"Done."

Deirdre had to enlarge the view from the outside cameras to see the entire display flashing from the leviathans' flanks. With trembling fingers she traced an outline of the huge creatures and displayed it on the ship's light panels.

Both leviathans immediately changed the images they were displaying. The colored shapes flickering across their flanks turned to a mixture of various shades of yellow and pale lavender.

"Look!" Deirdre shouted. "We've made contact with them!"

Max Yeager, leaning over her shoulder, said sourly, "Contact my hairy butt. They're just flashing colors, that's all."

"But it must mean something!" Deirdre insisted.

"Yes," said Dorn. "But what?"

Leviathan could see that the alien was flashing images, but they made no sense. Mere gibberish. Its replicate swam around the strange spherical creature, asking it where it came from, why had it come to their domain. Leviathan was trying to thank it for keeping the darters at bay while it was budding.

The alien obviously was trying to picture something for them, but its images made no sense. Splashes of color without form, without inner structure, without meaning.

Bring it to the Elders, the replicate suggested just as Leviathan itself thought of that possibility. But how can we make it understand that it should follow us back to the Kin? Leviathan wondered.

"It's nothing but gibberish," Yeager said, still standing so close behind Deirdre that she could feel the ripples in the perfluorocarbon when he moved. Andy had come up at her other side, staring intently at her screen.

"I've displayed an image of the two of them," Deirdre said, feeling frustrated. Her chest was beginning to knot again.

"Maybe the color has something to do with it," Max suggested. "Maybe they can't see that shade of blue."

"But that's the color of their hides," Deirdre said.

Yeager shrugged. "Maybe they're into abstracts. Like Picasso or some of those other painters. Try changing the color."

Deirdre shifted from blue to green, and when that got no response from the leviathans, she went to bright red, then a softer pink.

"Nothing," Yeager mumbled.

"Not exactly nothing," said Dorn, from his console. "Their images are changing."

"It's all gibberish," Yeager said. "They're just making dumb displays, like octopi do back Earthside. They change colors all the time; it doesn't mean diddly-squat."

Deirdre asked, "Dorn, are we recording all this?"

"Yes," he replied. "And copying it for the data capsule we're scheduled to launch in . . . two hours and seventeen minutes."

"Maybe the scientists at the station can make some sense out of this," she murmured.

It's all so frustrating, Deirdre thought. They're trying to communicate with us, I *know* they are. But what do those splotches of colors mean? How can we speak to them? How can we understand them? The knot in her chest twisted tighter. She grimaced from the pain.

CATS AND MOUSE

should've seen this coming, Rodney Devlin said to himself as he hurried along the dimly lit passageway. I should've known she'd want to shut me up for good.

Devlin knew every nook and cranny of station *Gold*. Seldom seen outside the galley and its kitchen, the Red Devil still managed to roam through the whole station, every level, every passageway, every office and laboratory and workshop—usually late at night when almost everyone else was asleep.

No virtual reality tours of the station for him. Devlin walked the passageways, poked into compartments, tapped out security codes to unlock doors, and examined everything from Grant Archer's office to the immersion tank down in the third wheel. In person, in real time. More than once, over the years, he had slipped into someone's compartment, like a sneak thief. More than once he had stayed when the sleeper was a desirable and willing woman.

This night he knew he needed every scrap of knowledge he possessed about the station's layout. Three of Katherine Westfall's bully boys were looking for him. Devlin felt like a frightened little mouse being chased by three very large and determined cats.

He had been finishing up his menus for the coming day, shortly after midnight, when he saw them come into the kitchen from the galley, three muscular young men in dark suits with faces made of granite. They're not here to invite you to a party, Devlin told himself. As the three hunters searched along the kitchen's counters, stoves, ovens, Devlin slipped behind the silent row of oversized food processors and out the back door.

Once in the passageway that ran behind the kitchen, he hesitated briefly. *Where to go? It'll take them a few minutes to search the kitchen and figure out that I'm not there. Then they'll try my quarters. In the meantime I've got to find a safe hideout.*

Where? And for how long? Till morning, at least, he realized as he started jogging down the passageway, his softboots making practically no sound on the tiles of the deck.

Once they see I'm not in the kitchen, they'll probably go to the comm center and check the surveillance screens. Crikey! Maybe they've already got somebody at the comm center who can see me right now!

He hurried along the passageway, glancing at the tiny red lights of the surveillance cameras set up near the overhead every fifty meters or so. *It's no good,* he said to himself. *They can run the surveillance chips and see wherever I go. There's no place to hide. Unless . . .*

Nikki Gregorian sat tensely at her desk in the station's communications center. Chewing on her lip, she stared at the digital clock on the wall. It seemed to be stopped. Time was standing still. All the surveillance screens were dark. None of the station's cameras was functioning, and they would not come on-line again for another two hours. She was alone in the center, halfway through her duty shift, and all the screens were as dark and dead as corpses.

It was a risk, deliberately turning off the cameras, but the money was worth it. A breathtaking amount of money. *Keep the cameras off for three hours,* the handsome young man had told her. *No one will know. And even if they figure it out and fire you, you'll have enough money to return to Earth and retire.*

She didn't ask why he wanted the cameras off. She knew he worked for Katherine Westfall and the money he was willing to transfer to her account back Earthside was enough to allow her to retire comfortably before the year was out. Good-bye to station *Gold* and its cramped, sterile confines. Back to Earth to live in style.

Still, she wondered what they were up to. What were they doing, that they wanted all the station's surveillance cameras turned off?

Katherine Westfall could not sleep. She lay on the king-sized water-bed of her suite, dressed in lounging pajamas of emerald green, trimmed with gold, wide awake, waiting for her security team to report.

They should have found him by now. This station isn't that large that he can hide from them. They've shut down the surveillance cameras, of course; there will be no record of what happened to Rodney Devlin. But even without the cameras, they should be able to find the man. Why haven't they reported to me?

It seemed simple enough to her. Find Devlin and toss him out an airlock. Neat and clean. In the morning he'll have disappeared. Archer and his people can search the station from top to bottom and they won't find him. Devlin won't be able to tell anyone about the nanomachines.

Then when the *Faraday* doesn't come back from its mission, Archer will be disgraced, and Devlin's disappearance forgotten. Four people killed, and it will be all his fault. Devlin, too. That will end Archer's career. He'll never be able to challenge me for the IAA chairmanship. He'll be finished.

But why haven't they reported? she asked herself for the hundredth time. They should have found Devlin by now and gotten rid of him.

She realized that she was perspiring slightly. And her stomach hurt. Nerves, she said to herself. You've got to get rid of Devlin. You can't have him here, knowing about the nanomachines. He'll hold that over your head. He's the type who'd blackmail you, threaten you, bring you down. Once they don't come back from the ocean, once he realizes what I've done, he'll have that over me for the rest of my life.

I can't let him do that. It's either him or me. And it's not going to be me!

Still, her stomach ached. A dull, sullen pain, as if she'd eaten too many sweets. Nerves, Westfall told herself. Steady on. They'll find Devlin and deal with him. Then you'll be safe. Then there will be no one who can threaten you.

But the pain in her gut was getting worse.

D eirdre stared in open-mouthed awe at the two leviathans. The enormous creatures were swimming on either side of *Faraday*, flashing messages—she *knew* they had to be messages—along the lengths of their flanks.

Those hundreds of eyes looking at us, she said to herself. Those hundreds of fins paddling along. And the colors! Spectacular splashes of reds and greens, yellows, blues, and phosphorescent white. They *mean* something. They've got to mean something. They can't just be simple displays. They're trying to speak to us.

Dorn's deep voice reverberated through the perfluorocarbon. "I have programmed the computer to repeat the shapes and colors that the leviathans are displaying."

"Monkey see, monkey do," Yeager muttered.

Corvus said, "Good. They'll see that we've received their messages and we're acknowledging them."

"But what do they mean?" Deirdre wondered aloud.

With a wistful smile, Andy said, "You're the artist, Dee. You tell us."

She shook her head. "I wish I could."

"We're scheduled to send out a data capsule in fifty-three minutes," said Dorn. "All of these images will be included."

"But what do they mean?" Deirdre repeated.

Leviathan saw that the alien was repeating the images it was flashing. For more than a hundred beats of the flagella Leviathan and its replicate had been picturing to the alien the beauties of the Symmetry, explaining to this strange, cold, uncommunicative creature how the Kin dwelled in harmony with the world, feeding on the streams of food that came from the cold abyss above, staying well away from the hot abyss below, avoiding the darters that preyed on individual leviathans when they separated from the Kin to duplicate.

Nothing. The alien simply glided along, dark and silent, its hard round shape as uncommunicative as the tiny swimmers that also followed the food streams. To its replicate Leviathan flashed an image of the alien, a blank spherical shape. The replicate replied with the same.

Why doesn't it answer us? Leviathan wondered. The replicate drew an image of one of the tiny swimmers. Its meaning was clear: The alien may be a living creature, but it is clearly not intelligent. It doesn't picture images to us because it can't. It is dumb, mindless.

But if that is so, Leviathan thought, then how did the alien suddenly appear here, in the world of the Kin? How did it get here? Why is it—

Wait! The alien's spherical flank suddenly lit up with colors! It can communicate! Or at least it's trying to.

Nothing but gibberish, flashed the replicate. There is no structure in its images, no meaning.

But it's trying to say *something*, Leviathan pointed out. It's displaying the same colors that we have used.

Imitation, pictured the replicate. That's not intelligence, it's merely mimicry. The lowliest swimmers can mimic images better than this hard-shell.

But it's trying, Leviathan insisted. It's trying.

"We're scheduled to release a data capsule in ten minutes," Dorn announced.

"Well, it'll have something to show them," Yeager said.

Deirdre noticed that Andy hadn't spoken a word in nearly an hour. He merely stood beside her, his feet anchored in deck loops, swaying slightly in their all-encompassing liquid like a strand of kelp on the floor of the sea on Earth, staring raptly at Deirdre's display screen. But every few minutes he kneaded the bridge of his freckled nose.

"Are you all right?" she asked him softly.

"Huh?"

"Do you feel okay?"

He squeezed his eyes shut, then blinked, as if coming out of a trance. "Okay? Yeah, sure."

"No aches or pains?" Deirdre pressed.

He shrugged crookedly. "Got a helluva headache, that's all."

She nodded. "It's the pressure. I've got an ache in my chest. It started in my gut but it's settled in my chest."

"Yeah," he said absently, his attention back on the screen.

Deirdre looked at the display again. The leviathans were flashing colors so quickly she could hardly follow them. It was like watching a fireworks display speeded up to a wildly supersonic pace.

She turned slightly and saw that Max was checking out the data capsule on the console beside Dorn. The cyborg had both hands on his control keyboard. Keeping up with the leviathans wasn't easy: Dorn had to keep the main propulsion system running at nearly full power merely to stay even with them, and the currents generated by their flippers bounced their vessel like a cork in a typhoon.

"The data capsule's ready," Max said.

Dorn nodded, then tapped a prosthetic finger on the screen to his left. "Ejection in three minutes."

Deirdre murmured to Andy, "If only we could make some sense of their messages."

Corvus said nothing, still riveted to the display screen.

"Nothing but splotches of color," Deirdre said.

"I don't see colors," Andy said, his voice low, his eyes not moving from the screen.

"I forgot," said Deirdre. "This must be more pointless to you than to the rest of us."

"Pointless?" Corvus seemed genuinely surprised. "You mean you can't see the pictures they're showing us?"

IMAGES

ictures?" Deirdre asked.

Corvus nodded and pointed at the screen. "In those gray splotches. Can't you see the pictures?"

"No . . ."

"They're showing images of themselves again. Now it's changed to an image of us. Round little circle next to the two leviathan shapes."

"You can see images?" Deirdre strained her eyes, staring at the rapidly shifting contours of color splashed along the sides of the two leviathans.

"Yep," Andy replied.

"Capsule launch in one minute," Dorn intoned.

"Wait!" Deirdre shouted. "Don't send the capsule!"

Yeager turned toward her. "We've gotta send the capsule, Dee. It's on the mission assignment list."

"Wait," she insisted. "Andy says he sees images in the leviathans' displays. They're sending messages to us!"

Dorn turned halfway from his post to look at her and then focused both his eyes on Corvus. "You see images?"

Andy nodded vigorously. "Don't you?"

Linda Vishnevskaya stared at the screen in the center of her control console. Blank. She glanced at the digital clock display to the right of the screen: 0600 hours.

They're launching the first data capsule, she said to herself. We should pick up its radio beacon in half an hour, as soon as it breaks out of the ocean.

She waited impatiently, fingers fidgeting in her lap. This early in the morning, the mission control center was manned only by Vishnevskaya herself. She didn't need any of her team simply to monitor the emergence of a data capsule. The capsule was programmed to climb out of Jupiter's atmosphere and establish itself in a circular equatorial orbit. From there it would beam the contents of its memory core to the communications satellites in stationary orbit around Jupiter, which would relay the data to the receivers aboard station *Gold*. In less than two minutes after the capsule popped out of the ocean they would begin receiving its signal.

Vishnevskaya sensed someone entering the visitors' gallery up along the top of the control center's circular chamber. She didn't bother to turn around, but instead moved her head slightly so she could see the newcomer's reflection in the dark screen on her console.

It looked like Katherine Westfall. Vishnevskaya felt surprised. Why would Mrs. Westfall show up this early in the morning for something as routine as a data capsule?

"The mission time line calls for launching the capsule now," said Dorn. "If we don't—"

"You can delay the launch for a few minutes, can't you?" Deirdre pleaded.

"Why?" Yeager demanded.

"Take out the color from the images the leviathans are showing," she said.

"Take out—"

"I'm seeing images," Corvus explained, his voice high with excitement even in the sound-deepening liquid perfluorocarbon.

Yeager frowned at him.

"I can't see colors, but I'm seeing pictures," Corvus insisted. "Drawings. Like stick figures, almost."

Dorn's face was impassive, but he muttered, "Canceling capsule launch." His human hand reached for an orange-glowing button on his console.

Deirdre stared at her display screen while Dorn and Yeager leaned toward the central screen on the cyborg's control console.

Pointing over Deirdre's shoulder, Corvus said, "See? Can't you see the images?"

The swaths of color along the leviathans' flanks were now gray on the display screen. And Deirdre saw . . . pictures! Shapes. They were crude, almost like stick figures. But definitely shapes.

"That's the two of them!" she yelped.

"With us in between," Dorn said. "That round figure must be us."

"God *damn*," Yeager breathed.

"And there," Corvus said, "that must be a stream of organics coming down from up above."

Now the displays on both leviathans' flanks showed many more creatures, a whole herd of them.

"They're telling us that they eat the organics," Deirdre said.

"And there's lots of them!" Corvus added. "Dozens."

"A hundred or so," said Dorn.

As they watched, the leviathans' displays changed so rapidly they couldn't follow them. It was like watching a speeded-up video.

"The computer can slow it down," Yeager said.

"Not yet," Corvus snapped. "Let's get it in real time first."

"Is all this being recorded in the data capsule?" Deirdre asked.

"Yes," Dorn replied. "Automatically."

Deirdre felt her whole body quivering with excitement. The pain in her chest was still there, she could still feel it, but it was nothing but a minor annoyance now. The leviathans are speaking to us! She could see the meaning in their imagery!

"That looks like those sharks," Andy said.

"And that's us, rushing toward them," Deirdre added.

Yeager muttered, "The charge of the frigging light brigade."

"They're replaying our little battle," Dorn said.

"But they don't show themselves splitting up, reproducing," said Corvus.

"They don't do leviathan porn," Yeager said, with the barest hint of a chuckle.

It was difficult to make sense of the images, they flickered on and off so rapidly. It looked like the two leviathans charging at the sharks, but it was too swift for Deirdre to be certain, the images of the sharks flicked off so quickly. Then at last she saw the circular image of their own ship and the two leviathans on either side of it. The sharks were gone.

"They've replayed our battle, all right," Corvus said.

The leviathans' displays went blank. The enormous creatures swam on either side of *Faraday* in silence.

"What now?" Yeager asked.

"Maybe they're waiting for us to reply," Corvus suggested.

"So what do we say?" Yeager demanded, " 'Greetings from planet Earth?' "

"Replay what they just showed us," Deirdre said.

"Replay their imagery?" asked Dorn.

Nodding, Deirdre said, "Show them that we received their message and we understand it."

"We *think* we understand it," Yeager corrected.

"At least show them that we received it," said Deirdre.

"Very well," Dorn agreed, turning back to his keyboard panel.

Andy's lopsided grin went from ear to ear. "Well, they're intelligent, all right. We've established that much."

Dorn glanced at the mission time line displayed on the auxiliary screen on the left side of his console.

"We should have launched the data capsule ten minutes ago," he said.

"Pop it now," Yeager urged. "It oughtta make Archer and the rest of the scooters pretty damned happy."

Linda Vishnevskaya stared at the digital clock display. Ten minutes, she realized. They should have launched the data capsule ten minutes ago. She felt a cold hollow in the pit of her stomach. Something's gone wrong, she knew. Something's gone terribly wrong.

Behind her, up in the otherwise empty visitors' gallery, Katherine Westfall got to her feet and quietly stole out of the mission control center. She couldn't suppress the victorious grin that curled her lips, despite the ache in her gut that still gnawed at her.

GRANT ARCHER'S OFFICE

Archer was shocked when he slid back the door to his office and saw Rodney Devlin sound asleep in one of his recliners. The Red Devil was snoring lightly; he was in his usual white chef's uniform, stained and wrinkled from use. Even in sleep his face looked lined with worry, his mustache bedraggled. In his right hand he tightly clutched his pocketphone. Glancing at his wristwatch, Archer confirmed that information from the first data capsule should be coming in within a few minutes. But what's Red doing in my office? he wondered. And how did he get in here?

Archer almost smiled at that last question. Red can go anywhere he wants to, the station director realized. He's got the combination to every lock in the station. Probably memorized every last one of them.

He made a polite little cough and Devlin snapped awake, sitting up so abruptly Archer feared he'd pop some vertebrae.

"Grant!" Devlin said, his voice slightly hoarse.

"What are you doing here, Red?"

With a slightly hangdog look, Devlin answered, "Hidin' out."

"Hiding out? From whom?"

"Westfall's goons. They came after me last night. I think they were out t' kill me."

Archer sank into the faux-leather armchair next to the recliner. "You'd better explain all this to me, Red. Slowly."

His expression turning rueful, Devlin said, "Westfall wanted me t' provide her with some gobblers so's—"

"Gobblers? Nanomachines?"

"Right. She wanted—"

"And you got them for her? Gobblers?" Archer felt his insides begin to shake with fear. And anger.

"Relax, mate," Devlin said, holding up both hands as if to shield himself from attack. "I told you I wouldn't do anything to harm the station. Remember?"

"But you provided her with gobblers!"

His old sly grin spreading slowly over his face, Devlin said, "I provided her with nanos, I did. But not what she wanted."

"Then just what in blazes *did* you do?"

Linda Vishnevskaya drummed her fingers on the edge of the console. Nothing. No data capsule. They should have launched it fifteen minutes ago. We should be getting its beacon signal by now.

But there was nothing. No beacon from a data capsule. Nothing but silence in the nearly empty mission control center.

Vishnevskaya stared at the blank display screen as if she could make the capsule appear by sheer willpower. Nothing. Silence.

She waited another ten minutes. Then ten more, each second of the time stretching her nerves agonizingly.

Max, she thought. What's happened to you? Why haven't you sent out the capsule? What's going on down there in that damned ocean?

At last she could stand it no longer. With the reluctance of a woman facing a firing squad, standing on a gallows, staring death in the face, she clicked the intercom switch on her console and said in a low, choked voice, "Mission report: The first data capsule scheduled to be released from *Faraday* has failed to appear. Reason unknown."

She heard her own words: *Faraday* has failed. Oh Max, Max, she thought, fighting down the sobs that rose in her throat. Max, has Jupiter killed you?

Devlin was still explaining himself when the phone on the serving table next Archer's recliner chimed. Glancing at the screen's data bar he saw that it was Katherine Westfall calling.

Archer leaned close to the phone's camera eye so that his image filled its field of view and commanded, "Answer."

Mrs. Westfall's face looked positively haughty. Without a greeting or a preamble of any kind she said in an almost sneering voice, "I suppose you know that they've failed to send their data capsule."

Archer stiffened. "No, I didn't know."

"You realize what this means, don't you?" Westfall demanded. "Something's gone wrong down there."

"Possibly," Archer replied.

Westfall's face hardened. "Not merely *possibly*. They were scheduled to release a data capsule and they haven't done it. Something's gone wrong. They could be dead. If they are, it's your responsibility."

Grant Archer pulled in a deep breath before replying. Then, "Perhaps you should come to my office. We can discuss this more fully here."

"Yes," Westfall agreed. "We need to discuss this disaster more fully, don't we?"

The phone screen went blank. Archer turned back toward Devlin, who was still sitting upright on the recliner.

"I'd better get outta here," Devlin said.

"No, Red. You stay right where you are. I want you here when she comes in."

Devlin's russet eyebrows rose toward his scalp. "I'd rather not, y'know."

"I'm not asking you, Red," Archer said, with steel in his voice. "I'm ordering you."

Katherine Westfall didn't bother to summon any of her aides or security guards as she strode down the passageway toward Grant Archer's office. No need, she told herself. I'll have this moment all to myself. I want to savor the look on his face when he realizes that his career has been shattered.

Should I tell him that Elaine O'Hara was my half sister? No, she said to herself. That's none of his business. Keep the family connection out of it. But maybe I'll hint that the IAA will launch an investigation into his criminally negligent leadership that led to the death of four people. Once I'm chairperson of the governing council that's just what I'll do. I'll pay him back for my sister and make certain he'll never hold a scientific post anywhere in the solar system.

She looked forward to reaching Archer's office. Westfall felt strong, confident. If it weren't for the nervous twinge in her stomach, she thought, she'd feel absolutely perfect.

Red Devlin was fidgeting nervously as they waited for Westfall's arrival.

"You're certain that they were out to murder you?" Archer asked, still sitting on the little desk chair.

Devlin gave him a sour look. "They pop into my kitchen after midnight. Three of 'em. They weren't lookin' for my recipe for lemon meringue pie."

"And why did you hide out here, in my office?"

Devlin brushed at his bristly hair. "Couldn't think of anyplace better. Figured they'd be watchin' the security cameras so they'd know where I went. I was hopin' that they wouldn't bust into your office. If they did, I was gonna phone you, send you a panic SOS."

Archer nodded. "According to the security log, all the passageway cameras were turned off for a couple of hours, starting at midnight."

Whistling between his teeth, Devlin said, "So there wouldn't be any evidence of them shovin' me out an airlock."

"She got to the technician on the midnight shift," Archer said, clear distaste on his bearded face.

"She can get to just about anybody, one way or th' other."

"It looks that way, doesn't it?" said Grant Archer.

He tapped his phone console's miniature keyboard and saw Katherine Westfall marching along the passageway like a conquering empress. At least the surveillance cameras are back on, he thought.

Turning back to Devlin, Archer pointed as he said, "Red, get into the lavatory there. I'll call you when I want you."

The Red Devil looked positively grateful as he hurried to the little room. He's frightened of confronting Westfall, Archer thought. Can't blame him; I'm not looking forward to this myself.

DEEPER

ndy Corvus glided over to Dorn's side. "Can you send them a picture about my DBS probe?"

The cyborg looked up from his console screens. "If you draw the picture for me I'm sure that I can run it on the outer hull's display lights."

Nodding somewhat nervously, Corvus slid through the perfluorocarbon liquid to the console built into the curving bulkhead on Dorn's left. Deirdre disengaged her feet from the floor loops at her console and made her way past Max Yeager to stand at Andy's side.

"Can I help you?" she asked softly.

Corvus nodded without taking his eyes from his console's central screen. His attempt to draw a picture looked ragged to Deirdre, childish and uncertain.

"Here," she said. "Let me." She leaned across his lanky frame and poised her fingers above the arrow keys on his board. "What do you want to show?"

"I want them to understand that we're going to fire a probe into the hide of one of them."

"A harpoon." Yeager snickered. "They'll love that."

"That's what we're here for," Corvus said, with some heat. "That's what this mission is all about. Remember?"

"We've already made contact with them," Yeager countered. "We don't need your brain probe."

"We sure do! If it works we can get inside their minds and *really* start to understand them."

"If it works."

Dorn said mildly, "If the leviathans accept being harpooned."

And if the DBS actually records their brain functions, Deirdre added silently. She didn't say it aloud because Andy had enough opposition to deal with from Max.

"There," she said, nodding toward Andy's screen. "Does that show what you want them to see?"

Leviathan saw that the alien was repeating the message it had flashed. Deep in its central brain Leviathan pondered the meaning of this. Could this alien be intelligent? It signaled the replicant, asking its opinion.

The replicant signed the same sort of puzzlement that Leviathan itself felt. Of course, Leviathan reasoned. The replicant has not had enough experiences to deviate much from our own thoughts.

Leviathan reviewed what it knew about the alien. It was larger than any of the other aliens that had invaded their domain. It gave no sign of feeding on the particles drifting down from the cold abyss above. It had attacked the darters when Leviathan was replicating and helpless. That is a sign of intelligence, the willingness to help another.

Leviathan remembered another alien it had encountered, long ago. It too had fought a pack of darters and been hurt in the battle. When it was sinking into the hot abyss below, Leviathan had tried to help it, actually carried it on its own back upward, away from the cruel heat and crushing pressure of the depths. The alien had repaid this kindness by scalding Leviathan's wounded hide with searing heat. Then it fled up into the cold abyss, never to be seen again.

Now this new alien had appeared. It was much larger than the earlier one, but like it, this alien was hard-shelled, cold, unlike any of the Kin or the darters or any other creature Leviathan had seen in the ocean.

And it is trying to communicate, Leviathan saw. At least it is repeating the message I showed to it. Mimicry? Not true intelligence but dumb mimicry?

The alien had gone dark. It glided through the waters between Leviathan and its replicant, silent, cold, and dark.

Suddenly its flank lit up. Brilliant red, shifting to orange and then green. The colors must mean something to it, but they were nothing but empty displays to Leviathan.

Then pictures began to form. Leviathan saw itself and its replicant displayed, with the alien between them.

Now the imagery showed an arm growing out of the alien's curving hide. Thin and undulating, like the tentacles of the filmy beast Leviathan once encountered in the chill waters high above.

It's trying to speak to us, the replicant signaled.

Leviathan flashed a swatch of yellow to show it agreed.

In the alien's imagery the thin, flexible arm reached out from its own hide and touched Leviathan's. There it remained, while pulses of color raced along the arm, running from Leviathan to the alien.

It wants to feed on us! the replicant signed, in agitated hot white.

Leviathan watched, fascinated and horrified, as the alien clearly showed that it wanted to attach a feeding arm to its hide and devour some of Leviathan's flesh.

No! blazed the replicant.

Leviathan, too, felt the instinctive fear and revulsion. A part of its mind wondered why the alien seemed to be asking permission to feed off its flesh. Because it is so small and weak? Leviathan asked itself. The alien showed no teeth, no mouth parts at all. Its hide was smooth and hard.

And then a small mouthlike opening appeared in that hard smooth hide and a feeding arm began to emerge from it, snaking toward Leviathan.

Without another thought, Leviathan and its replicant both dived down toward the warmer, safer waters where the Kin dwelled in all their numbers.

"They're going away!" Corvus yelped.

"Diving deeper," said Dorn.

"Your probe scared them, Andy," Deirdre said, feeling almost heartbroken with disappointment. "We were so close . . ."

Yeager simply shook his head and asked, "So what do we do now?"

Dorn replied, "Release the data capsule. And then go down after them."

"Deeper?"

"Deeper."

"How far down can we go?" Corvus asked.

"The ship's designed for a thousand klicks," Yeager replied. "Deeper than that and the pressure could become a problem."

"A problem?" asked Deirdre.

"He means it could crush us," Corvus said.

Deirdre looked at Yeager and saw that that was exactly what he meant.

Dorn's hands were already playing across his controls. "Data capsule released," he announced. "Following those leviathans now."

Deirdre glanced at Andy, who was muttering unhappily as he reeled his DBS probe back into the hull. Her chest ached and she wondered how deep they could go before the pressure began to really hurt.

Katherine Westfall swept into the office without even a tap on the door. Red Devlin was hiding in the lavatory and Archer was on his feet, standing between his favorite armchair and the little serving table that held the phone console. He put down the handset and made a tight little bow to Mrs. Westfall.

"What have you to say for yourself?" she demanded.

Instead of the apprehension he'd felt only moments earlier, Archer barely suppressed a smile as he replied, "About what?"

Westfall blazed, "About the failure of the vessel you sent into the ocean! About the death of four volunteers aboard that vessel! About your criminal indifference to the danger you exposed them to!"

He let the smile show as he gestured to one of the armchairs. "Let's talk this over calmly, shall we?"

"Four deaths," Westfall said as she sat down on the edge of the chair. "Four murders."

Sitting on the chair facing her, Archer said, "I just received a call from the mission control chief. The data capsule has shown up. It was a half hour late, but it's in orbit around Jupiter now."

Westfall's mouth opened, but no words came out. She clamped it shut so tight that Archer heard the click of her teeth.

"Four murders," Archer said coldly. "The question is, who tried to murder whom?"

"The capsule arrived in orbit?" she asked. "That means that . . ."

Archer said, "That means that they're not dead. Something delayed their launch of the capsule, that's all."

"They could still be in trouble. Does the capsule say what's happening down there?"

"Dr. Johansen and his people are looking at the data," Archer said. "He'll phone me with their preliminary findings in a few minutes."

"I see."

"If anything's gone wrong with the mission . . . if the crew is in any kind of difficulty, Johansen will call me immediately, of course."

"Of course," Westfall said, in her little-girl whisper.

Almost casually, Archer asked, "Why did you assume they had died? Why did you assume the worst?"

Westfall blinked several times before replying, "When they failed to launch their data capsule on time, naturally I thought—"

"You thought they were dead."

Her chin went up a notch. "Dead. Yes. That's right."

"Sorry to disappoint you."

"What do you mean by that?" Westfall snapped.

Archer turned toward the closed door of the lavatory. "Red," he called. "Come on out here."

For a moment nothing happened. Archer said to himself, He couldn't have gotten out of the lav. There's only the one door to the room.

Slowly the door slid back and Rodney Devlin stepped hesitantly into the office. Archer noticed that Red had cleaned himself up a bit. His spiky hair was brushed relatively smooth, his white outfit looked neater, if not cleaner. But the expression on his face was clearly uneasy, apprehensive.

Westfall stiffened for a moment, but she recovered enough to ask, "What's he got to do with anything?"

"He's the one who got the nanomachines for you," said Archer.

With some of her old haughtiness, Westfall replied, "I don't know what you're talking about."

"Nanomachines," Archer repeated. "Gobblers. Murder weapons."

Fixing Devlin with a steely gaze, Westfall said, "I don't know what this criminal may have told you, but he's a born liar. Everyone knows that."

Devlin pointed a finger at her as he said, "You told me you'd chuck me in jail if I didn't get a sample of gobblers for you."

"Which you wanted to feed to Deirdre Ambrose at the launch party, just before she left with the others on the mission," Archer said to Westfall.

"I did no such thing!"

"I can get Franklin Torre to testify that he gave Devlin a sample of nanomachines."

"What of it? That doesn't prove that I asked him to do it," Westfall countered. "This man is a known procurer, a smuggler, a thief, and a liar. No one in his right mind would take his word over mine."

"That's right," Devlin said, clenching his hands in front of himself. "Nobody would take my word against yours. I knew that. That's why I did what I did."

"You obtained gobblers and fed them to Ms. Ambrose at the party," Westfall said to Devlin.

"I got nanos, all right," Devlin said. "But I fed 'em to you, not her."

Westfall's face went white.

"You've got those nanos in you right now, lady. You drank 'em down at the party."

She stared at him, wide-eyed. "You . . ." Suddenly Westfall launched herself at Devlin, screeching wildly, her clawed fingers seeking his face, his eyes. The Red Devil threw his arms up to defend himself, and Archer, startled by her fury, jumped out of his chair and wrapped his arms around her middle and dragged her away from Red.

"I'll kill you!" she screamed. "I'll kill you!"

Archer pushed her down onto one of the recliners. Westfall fell back onto it, her chest heaving, her face contorting wildly. Suddenly she burst into racking sobs.

"You've killed me," she blubbered in her high, thin voice. "You've murdered me."

Your medical readouts are all within acceptable limits," Dorn said, without taking his eyes from the data screens of his console. "How do you feel? Any problems?"

The cyborg was still standing at his post before the ship's controls, his feet locked into the deck loops that kept him from drifting in the perfluorocarbon liquid. Yeager stood behind him, Corvus was at the console on his left. Deirdre looked up from the empty sensor screens toward Dorn's control console.

She could see from the screen at Dorn's right that they were diving deeper. The curve that showed the ocean's pressure against the outer hull was rising steeply.

"How do you feel?" Dorn repeated.

Andy Corvus pinched the bridge of his nose. "I've got a headache."

"My back hurts," said Yeager, clamping both hands just above his hips and arching his spine slightly.

Dorn said, "There's nothing indicating physical problems on your data readouts."

"It's not serious," Yeager said. "Just tension, most likely."

Corvus turned toward Deirdre. "Dee, what about you?"

"I have a sort of tightness in my chest," she answered.

"Maybe a massage would help." Yeager leered.

"Oh, Max," said Deirdre. She tried to scowl at him but couldn't work up the mood.

"Internal pressure is rising as we descend deeper into the ocean," Dorn said coolly. "Please report any increased discomfort immediately."

"What about you, Dorn?" asked Deirdre. "How do you feel?"

The cyborg flexed his prosthetic arm. "A slight stiffness in my shoulder. I don't think it's related to the pressure increase."

"You need a lube job," Yeager joked.

Tapping the mission time line display with a finger of his human hand, Dorn said, "Feeding time for Deirdre and Max. Then sleep."

Yeager's usual leer reappeared on his beefy face. "I wonder if the two of us would fit in one of those sleeping slots."

Smiling sweetly back at him, Deirdre said, "You'll never know, Max."

He grumbled but disengaged his feet from the deck loops and drifted over to the food dispenser. "Let's see," he muttered as he picked up the feeding hose, "I think I'll have lamb chops, Caesar salad, and peach pie à la mode."

Despite herself Deirdre chuckled at Max's inanity. "Me, too," she said. But she shuddered inwardly when Yeager offered the feeding hose to her.

"Ladies first," he said, with a gallant little bow.

Trying to hide her revulsion, Deirdre plugged the hose into the feeding port at the base of her neck. Max turned his face away. *He's as grossed out by this as I am,* Deirdre realized, *but he's too macho to admit it.* Then she saw that Andy was staring at her, the expression on his strangely mismatched face a mixture of sadness and heart-melting compassion. *My goodness,* Deirdre thought, *Andy looks as if he's going to break down and cry.*

As it dove deeper alongside its replicant, Leviathan wondered if they had run away too soon. *Maybe we should go back,* it signaled to the replicant.

And let it feed on us? came the reply.

Maybe it's starving and needs to feed, Leviathan signed.

Not on us! the replicant signaled, in fierce blue.

Leviathan thought that the replicant was right. *And yet . . .*

You return to the Kin, it signaled. *We will go back and observe the alien.*

Observe it? What for?

To try to communicate with it. To try to tell it that we cannot allow it to feed on us.

It must know that already, signed the replicant.

Perhaps, Leviathan replied. We will see.

With that, Leviathan turned back toward the upper level where the alien was, its flagella members beating strenuously against the down-welling current.

Her feeding finished, Deirdre floated into the sleeping compartment. Once again the five shelves built into the bulkhead reminded her of the slots into which corpses are slid in a mortuary.

Pulling the hatch to the bridge firmly shut she quickly stripped off her maillot and pulled another from the slim storage locker beneath her bunk. Got to get this on before Max bursts in here, she told herself. If he sees me undressed he'd probably pop a blood vessel. She almost giggled at the thought of it. Max was all bluster, she thought. He'd be embarrassed if he saw me nude. She remembered Max's reaction when she had awakened in the station's infirmary after being frozen aboard the torch ship. Just the fleeting sight of her bare breasts had turned his face scarlet.

No sense embarrassing him again, Deirdre told herself. Then she added, No sense taking the risk that he'd be more aroused than embarrassed, either.

She slid into her coffinlike bunk just as Yeager tapped on the hatch and pulled it back.

"Are you decent?" he asked gruffly. "I hope not!"

"I'm already in bed, Max," she said, staring at the metal overhead a few centimeters above her nose.

"Want some company?"

"No, thank you."

"Um . . . I'm gonna peel off this swimsuit and get a fresh one," Yeager said. "No peeking."

Deirdre smiled to herself and echoed, "No peeking."

After a few moments she heard Yeager slither into his narrow bunk and mutter, "Cripes, there's not even room to turn around in here."

Deirdre said nothing. The pain in her chest was still there, throbbing dully, and she felt unusually tired. Weary. As if the weight of the world were pressing in on her.

Of course, she said to herself. It's the pressure. The pressure's going up as we dive lower. It's going to get worse. A lot worse.

She closed her eyes and commanded herself to sleep. You've got to rest, she thought. Relax. Think of something pleasant and just drift off to sleep.

She found herself thinking of what it would be like to have Andy in this tight narrow space with her. What it would be like to feel his body pressing against her. She fell asleep smiling.

GRANT ARCHER'S OFFICE

rcher had never seen the Red Devil look so shaken. Devlin was staring at Katherine Westfall as she lay across the recliner, blubbering uncontrollably. A bloodred scratch streaked Devlin's left cheek, his hands were still raised to defend himself.

"You've killed me," Westfall was sobbing. "You've murdered me."

"It would be a primitive kind of justice," Archer said. "An eye for an eye, as it says in the Old Testament. You tried to murder the crew of *Faraday*."

She looked up at Archer in a cold fury, her eyes blazing, her tears turned off just as abruptly as they had started.

"You can't prove that," she said, her voice murderously low. "It's my word against his."

"It doesn't matter," said Archer. "This is never going to a court of law."

Westfall suddenly clutched at her midsection. "The gobblers! They're tearing me apart!"

Archer turned to Devlin. "Tell her the truth, Red."

Devlin was clearly nervous; when he looked down at Westfall he seemed positively frightened.

"W-well," he stammered, "the, uh . . . the truth is—"

The phone chimed. Archer glanced at the screen and saw Michael Johansen's name on the data bar.

"Hold it," he snapped. To the phone he called, "Answer."

Johansen's narrow, angular face was alight with a big toothy grin and eyes crinkled with joy.

"They did it!" he fairly shouted. "Grant, they've made contact with one of the beasts. That's why they delayed sending up the capsule. They've communicated with the leviathans! They *are* intelligent. Those gigantic creatures are intelligent!"

Archer felt his knees go weak. He sank down onto one of the armchairs, suddenly breathless, overpowered.

"You . . . you're sure?" he gasped.

"I'm piping the raw data to you," Johansen said, beaming. Archer had never seen the big Norwegian so riotously happy, his normal stiff self-control thrown to the winds. Behind Johansen other scientists were pounding each other's backs, hugging and kissing and almost dancing with excitement.

"It's true, then," Archer breathed. "The leviathans are intelligent."

"Intelligent enough to communicate with us!" Johansen exulted.

"And the crew? They're all right?"

"They're fine! They simply delayed sending the capsule because they were getting such terrific data."

Archer nodded weakly. "Thanks, Michael. I'll look at the data and then call you back."

The phone screen went blank, but the data download light beneath it flickered madly.

"What about me?" Westfall cried. "I'm dying!"

"Red, tell her the truth."

Devlin brushed nervously at his ragged mustache while Westfall stared at him with her whole life in her eyes.

"Red," Archer insisted.

"They're not gobblers," Devlin said, his voice low, almost apologetic. "Torre wouldn't give me gobblers and I wouldn't ask for 'em."

"Then what's eating me up?" Westfall demanded.

Looking even more flustered, Devlin said, "Torre gave me a batch of assemblers . . . the kind o' nanos that build new molecules outta atoms they find around 'em."

Westfall sat up in the recliner, her tear-streaked face going hard, angry. "New molecules?"

Devlin nodded. "They're buildin' up in your stomach and intestines right now. They'll keep on buildin' up for a hundred hours or so. Then the nanos are programmed to shut down."

"What are they building?" she demanded.

"Some carbon dioxide," Devlin answered, almost mumbling. "Mostly methane."

"Carbon dioxide? Methane?" She pronounced it *meethane*.

Archer said, "You're feeling pressure in your abdomen, aren't you?"

She nodded.

"It's gonna get worse before it gets better," Devlin said. "You're gonna be burpin' a lot, and . . . uh . . ."

"Flatulence," said Archer.

Westfall leaped to her feet. "Flatulence?" she screamed.

"You're not gonna be very good company for the next few days," Devlin said.

"It's harmless," Archer added quickly. "Embarrassing, but harmless. Apparently Franklin Torre has a juvenile sense of humor."

Some of the old deviltry returned to Devlin's face. "Gas attack," he muttered.

"You bastards!"

Archer raised his hands in a placating gesture. "I had nothing to do with it, Mrs. Westfall. *You* ordered Red here to provide you with gobblers. *You* intended to feed them to Deirdre Ambrose, to kill her, to kill the whole crew of the submersible. That's attempted murder, four counts."

She stared at the two men, open mouthed, eyes blazing. For a long moment the three of them stood in the center of Archer's office, facing each other. Then Westfall's expression changed, her eyes became wary, calculating.

"You can't prove a thing," she said, her voice coldly furious. "It's my word against his."

"And Dr. Torre's," Archer added.

"There's no proof."

Archer conceded the point with a curt nod. Then, "The IAA's governing council is very sensitive to scandal. Members of the council must be above reproach."

"So that's what your scheme is," Westfall said. "To kick me off the council. To get yourself elected chairman."

Archer shook his head. "God forbid. All I want is to continue our work here. You saw what Johansen said: They've made contact with the leviathans. The creatures are intelligent! Compared to that, your little power game is child's play."

"Then what *do* you want?"

"The freedom to continue our work here. To study the first intelligent alien species humankind has encountered."

"And what about me?"

"You can go back to the council and get yourself elected chairman—as long as you don't try to slash the research budget."

"Ahh." Westfall looked almost pleased. "I knew you were after something."

"I'm after knowledge," Archer said. "I want to study an alien intelligent species. Learn about them. Teach them about us."

"No matter who it kills."

"No one's gotten killed," he said, his voice steel-cold. "No thanks to you."

"Your crew hasn't returned yet. They could still die down there."

Archer started to reply, thought better of it, and said merely, "We're all in God's hands, Mrs. Westfall. Those who choose to seek out more knowledge about His universe might be risking their lives, but it's in the best cause of all."

Westfall nearly sneered. "Religious claptrap."

"Maybe," Archer conceded. "But seeking knowledge has always been to the benefit of the human race, no matter what the risks."

Drawing herself up to her full height, almost up to Archer's shoulder, Westfall said, "Very well. Continue your little games. I'll return to Earth and get myself elected chairman of the council."

Archer smiled. "That's *your* little game. And you're welcome to it."

She swept out of the office, almost as haughtily as she had entered it.

Devlin let out a low whistle. "You've made yourself a real enemy there, mate."

"She was an enemy before she ever came here, Red. But we've got some control over her now, thanks to you—and her own blind ambition."

Suddenly Devlin broke into a big grin. "Well, leastways, she's gonna be holed up in her quarters for the next few days, belchin' and fartin' to beat the band."

Archer grinned tightly at the Red Devil. "Get back to work, Red. I've got to see what that data capsule's told us."

LEVIATHAN

ts flagella working hard against the downward current, Leviathan's sensor members at last reported that the alien was close enough to observe.

It's a strange creature, Leviathan thought. Featureless, almost. Perfectly spherical. Its shell is hard, not like flesh. Even Leviathan's own armored hide members were not as stiff and inflexible as the alien's shell.

It's moving toward us, Leviathan realized. The alien was coming lower, following the downward current but slowly, agonizingly slowly. A trail of heated water emerged from its rear. Leviathan remembered the alien it had met so long ago, how it had sprayed scalding heat while Leviathan was carrying it on its back up toward the cold abyss from which it had appeared.

Studying the alien, Leviathan wondered, Can that hot jet be the way it propels itself? There were no flagella members on the alien. Perhaps it pushes itself through the water like the tiny squid do, squirting water through their nozzles.

The alien wasn't eating the food particles that drifted downward on the current. It doesn't graze, as we do, it realized. That arm that it wanted to connect to us must be for feeding. What else could it be?

Keeping its distance, Leviathan observed the alien as it slowly, painfully, pushed its way deeper into the realm of the Kin.

Deirdre awoke slowly. Blinking her gummy eyes, she heard Max humming to himself and realized he must be up and out of his bunk already. He's humming to let me know he's awake and I shouldn't slide out of my bed until he goes back to the bridge.

She lay there silently until she heard Max slide back the hatch to the bridge and then push it shut again. Then Deirdre slithered out of her bunk and floated to her feet. There was no need for washing, nor for a toilet. The liquid nourishment they took went directly into the bloodstream; the digestive system was inactive. They hardly had to use the complicated, sealed toilet, much to her relief. Running a hand over her scalp Deirdre remembered that there wasn't any point in brushing her hair; it had been cut too short to matter.

So, taking in a deep breath of perfluorocarbon, she went to the hatch that opened onto the bridge. Her chest still hurt, a dull sullen ache like a bruise inside her lungs.

The instant she slid the hatch back Yeager beamed at her and said loudly, "Ah, sleeping beauty is back among us."

Deirdre smiled and glided to her station, to the right of Dorn. The cyborg disengaged his feet from the deck loops and said, "Time for Andy and me to sleep."

"Eat first," Corvus said, grinning.

Yeager nodded and took up Dorn's usual station at the control console.

"One of the beasts has returned," Dorn told Yeager. "It's hovering out there, at the limit of our sensor range. It appears to be watching us."

"Maybe it's hungry," Yeager cracked.

Corvus shook his head. "It eats the organic particles. It's not interested in us."

"Not for food," Dorn said.

"I'll keep an eye on him," said Yeager.

"Call me if anything changes," Dorn said. "Anything at all."

"Aye-aye, skipper," Yeager replied, making a sloppy military salute.

Dorn grunted and turned toward the hatch to the sleeping area. Corvus trailed behind him. As he passed Deirdre, Andy asked in a near-whisper, "You okay, Dee?"

She nodded, despite the pain in her chest. "And you?"

"Can't seem to shake this headache."

"Is it getting worse?"

He shrugged. "I've had it so long now it's hard to tell."

"Maybe some sleep will make it better."

"Maybe," he said. Then he pushed away and swam through the hatch, leaving Deirdre alone with Yeager.

Why is the alien here? Leviathan asked itself for the hundredth time. What does it want?

The aliens that had appeared earlier were smaller, and shaped differently. They were silent, for the most part, and when they did try to communicate the signals they flashed were nothing but meaningless gibberish. But this alien is different: bigger, more intelligent. It can speak meaningfully.

Perhaps it is lost, Leviathan reasoned. This is not its usual domain. It doesn't live here, it comes from the cold abyss above. Why doesn't it return there? Why has it invaded the realm of the Kin? Why is it upsetting the Symmetry?

And it is moving deeper. Soon it will be at the level where the Kin are. Perhaps the Elders will know how to deal with it.

Leviathan pondered these questions as it accompanied the alien deeper, down to the warm and pleasant depth where the Kin thrived. Then a new thought occurred to it: The alien wanted to feed off us. Perhaps it is lost and starving.

Leviathan remembered when itself had been lost and hungry, high up on the edges of the cold abyss above. It had battled darters and been caught in the vicious swirling currents of a mammoth storm, thrown far from the realm of the Kin. Starving to the point where its members began spontaneously dissociating, Leviathan had been stalked by a filmy, tentacled monster. In a desperate fight, Leviathan had killed the beast and devoured it.

Perhaps this alien is in the same frantic need, far from its own kind, lost and starving. Perhaps it will dissociate and never be able to recombine again.

KATHERINE WESTFALL'S SUITE

A trick! Katherine Westfall fumed. He tricked me! The two of them, standing there so pompous and self-righteous.

She strode past the startled secretary in the anteroom, through the empty sitting room, and on into her bedroom, seething with fury. The pain in her abdomen was worse, sharper. She stopped before the full-length mirror. Her stomach looked bloated. Not much, not enough to notice, really. As if I'm pregnant, she thought. As if that smug-faced Archer's knocked me up.

Her fists clenched with helpless frustration, Westfall felt a lump in her stomach working its way up her chest. She belched, surprising herself with the violence of it, the disgusting sound, the crudity. Devlin's done this to me, she growled silently. Him and that psalm-quoting Archer.

She realized that she felt better. A little. Got rid of some gas, she told herself. How much more will there be? How much longer? A couple of days, from what Devlin said. I'll have to stay locked away from everyone else until the nanos disable themselves. I can't have anyone see me like this. Or smell me.

Sitting on the edge of her bed, Westfall thought, I'll kill them. I'll kill them both. They can't do this to me. Not without paying for it. I'll destroy them!

But then she realized, Archer's no fool. He'll have Devlin on video, telling the whole story. And that nanotech person, Torre, he'll back up Devlin's story. Archer will keep their testimony hanging over me. If anything happens to either one of them the whole story will come out. I'll be ruined.

Worse than that, I'll look stupid. Duped by a damned cook! The council will demand my resignation in a hot second.

She drew in a deep breath, trying to calm herself. And burped again. Damn them! she screamed silently. Damn them both.

Time. I'll have to bide my time. Give Archer what he wants, it's little enough. Get myself elected council chair. Then wait. Sooner or later an opportunity will come up. I'll get Archer and that rat-faced cook. Both of them.

Westfall nodded to herself, satisfied. Patience is a virtue, she remembered her mother telling her. Time heals all wounds. As long as Archer doesn't oppose me for the chairmanship I can afford to be patient.

Then she thought, Of course, if those creatures actually are intelligent, Archer will be the darling of the scientific world. He'll be unassailable. For years to come. Patience, she told herself. Patience. Revenge is a dish best served cold.

Suddenly her innards cramped painfully and she practically hobbled toward the lavatory.

eviathan saw that the alien was moving deeper, although it was painfully slow. It is a creature of the cold abyss above, Leviathan reasoned. The warmer regions are not its natural domain.

Then why is it pushing downward? it asked itself. What is it seeking?

It isn't feeding, Leviathan saw. The plentiful stream of food particles drifted down past the alien, who ignored them. It is pitifully small, it thought. It must be hungry. If we offered to let it feed off us, how much could it eat? Not enough to weaken us, surely.

But such a thought stirred revulsion in Leviathan's mind. To let another creature feed off our flesh! Even if it merely devours some of our hide, the inert armor members of our outermost layer, it would be . . . monstrous.

Leviathan pondered the situation while watching the alien slowly, slowly forcing its way down toward the realm of the Kin, trailing a stream of hot bubbles behind it.

What does it want? Leviathan asked itself again and again. Why is it here?

Dorn floated through the hatch from the sleeping area, flexing his prosthetic hand slowly.

"Max, you may be right," the cyborg said. "My arm needs lubrication. I think the perfluorocarbon is reacting with the joints."

Standing before the control console, Yeager shook his head. "Those joints are sealed, aren't they? The gunk can't get into them. Besides, perfluorocarbon is pretty much nonreactive, that's why we chose to use it."

"Then what is making my arm feel so stiff?"

"Pressure," Yeager said, tapping the data screen on the right side of the console. "Look at that pressure curve. We're getting damned near our design depth limit."

Dorn made a sound that might have been a grunt. "Eight hundred and thirty-eight kilometers deep. We still have a long way to go."

Corvus emerged from the sleep area, a dejected frown on his unbalanced face.

"Your headache?" Deirdre asked.

"Sleeping didn't help," he said. "If anything, it's worse now than before."

Taking up his place at the control console, Dorn said, "We are all suffering from the increased pressure. This will get worse as we go deeper."

"I'm all right," Corvus said, trying to grin.

"Dee?" the cyborg asked. "How do you feel?"

"I'm all right," she echoed. In truth, Deirdre's chest pain seemed worse than before. Not a lot worse, she told herself. It's bearable. I can stand it.

"Max," asked Dorn, "how is your back?"

Yeager grimaced slightly. "I wouldn't want to play handball right now, but it's okay . . . just kind of stiff."

"Like my arm," Dorn said.

"We could both use a lube job," Yeager muttered.

The four of them stood at their posts. Deirdre slipped her feet into the deck loops in front of the sensor display console, Corvus took his place on Dorn's other side at the DBS station. Yeager floated slightly behind Dorn, scanning the systems status board.

"All systems in the green," he said to no one in particular. "No, wait. One of the thruster jets just went yellow. Self-repair initiated automatically."

Anchoring his feet before the control console, Dorn scanned the displays. "Our medical readouts are all within acceptable limits," he announced.

Yeager quipped, "Acceptable to who?"

"Whom," Deirdre corrected.

Yeager shot her a mock scowl.

Looking back at her screens, Deirdre blurted, "One of the leviathans is approaching us!"

Corvus twisted around to look at the sensor screens. "Yeah! Look at it!"

Dorn had the same image on his center screen. "It's flashing signals at us."

"How do you know it's signaling at us?" Yeager demanded.

"Nobody else around," said Corvus. "The other critter isn't in sight."

"I think it's trying to tell us something," said Deirdre.

Leviathan felt maddeningly frustrated. It had swum back to the alien and clearly signed that it would allow the strange little creature to feed off it. But the alien made no response.

It was as if the alien were blind and senseless, as if it were as stupid as the fish that swam dumbly unaware of anything except feeding and reproducing.

No, wait. Leviathan's sensor members saw that the alien was signaling back. Perhaps it isn't stupid after all, Leviathan thought, merely unutterably slow.

But the alien's signals meant nothing. It seemed to be repeating Leviathan's own message, a dull-witted repetition that seemed to be mere mimicry, not true intelligence.

Or is this the way it communicates? Leviathan asked itself. Through mimicry? Could that be possible?

It wasn't mimicking anything we showed it when it displayed that it wanted to feed off us, Leviathan remembered. That wasn't mimicry. It was more like a request. Or perhaps a demand?

Play its game, Leviathan thought. Meet mimicry with mimicry. But go one step farther.

"It's coming awfully close," Deirdre said, trying to keep her voice calm, keep the fear out of it.

The huge creature was moving nearer, so close that the ship's cameras could no longer display the beast in its entirety. So close that she could feel their ship dipping and jouncing in the currents surging around them from the huge creature's motion. Her sensor screens showed its mountainous flank gliding closer and closer, row upon row of flippers working tirelessly, hundreds of unblinking eyes staring at her, bright splashes of color flickering along its hide.

"It's signaling again," Corvus called out, needlessly.

Deirdre adjusted the display to remove all color and once again the intricate line drawings appeared, like the blueprints of some vast alien building, huge and bewildering.

"What's it trying to say to us?" Dorn asked.

"Earthling go home," said Yeager.

"I've got the computer slowing down the imagery," Deirdre said. "It flashes its pictures so fast I can hardly tell one image from another."

Her central screen began to display the leviathan's pictures at a slowed pace.

"Earthling go home," Yeager repeated.

"No! Look!" Corvus wrenched himself free from his foot loops and surged over to Deirdre. Slipping one hand across her shoulders, he pointed with the other. "Look! That's the image we sent out before!"

Deirdre nodded. The leviathan was repeating the picture they had displayed, the image showing the DBS probe emerging from their vessel.

"That's when they took off," Yeager commented.

"But now one of them's come back," said Deirdre.

As they watched, the screen displaying the drawings along the leviathan's flank showed the DBS probe connecting with its hide.

"It's telling us it'll let us probe it!" Corvus yelped. In the sound-deepening perflourocarbon his yelp sounded more like the coughing grunt of a stalking lion.

Corvus launched himself back to the DBS console as he cried, "Dorn, reel out the probe! Do it now, before he changes his mind!"

It's not a *him*, Deirdre thought. Nor a her. The leviathans are asexual. No genders. They're all neuters. Or maybe they're like the *Volvox,* hermaphrodites.

She stayed silent as she watched her screens. The thin fiber-optic line of the DBS probe snaked out toward the huge, all-encompassing flank of the leviathan.

"This is it!" Corvus said.

Turning from her screens, Deirdre saw that Andy had already settled the optronic sensor circlet on his shaved head. It looked a little too loose for him, ridiculous, almost, pushing down on his ears. But the expression on his face was taut concentration, eyes wide, mouth a thin slash of a line, hands hovering over his keyboard.

"This is it," he repeated, in a grim murmur.

Deirdre realized that Andy's entire life was bound up in this moment. His reason for existence was about to come to fruition.

MISCOMMUNICATION

Leviathan watched in growing dread as the alien's feeding arm slowly, slowly snaked toward its flank. Several of the flagella members shuddered involuntarily, ready to dissociate. We must stay together, Leviathan commanded. If the alien's contact is painful, we will move away from it.

The sensor members on that side of Leviathan showed that the alien's feeding arm ended in a small circular mouth. But they could see no teeth in the mouth, only a set of minuscule flat squares arranged in orderly rows.

It took all of Leviathan's self-control to allow that alien mouth to touch its flesh. It made contact with the thick armor of Leviathan's hide, between two of the sensor members. The nearest flagellum froze for a moment, but Leviathan's central brain commanded it to resume stroking, and it did, obedient despite its naked fear.

Leviathan waited for some sensation: pain, discomfort at least. Nothing. The hide members were armored and deadened against sensation, that was their function, their part of the Symmetry, to protect the inner members against the slashing attacks of darters. The alien can't get through our hide, Leviathan realized. It can't feed on us.

Corvus floated in a half crouch, his arms bobbing buoyantly at chest level, his eyes closed. The optronic ring was slightly askew on his head.

"Is he conscious?" Yeager asked.

Deirdre shushed him, but in the perfluorocarbon it came out as a gargling stream of bubbles.

Corvus's soft blue eyes snapped open. "I'm conscious," he said tightly. "I'm not getting a thing. Not a damned thing."

"Nothing?" Deirdre asked.

"Nothing!" he cried. "To come all this way, to actually make physical contact with the beast, and then . . . nothing!" His face showed bitter disappointment, almost despair.

Deirdre suggested gently, "Maybe if I tried . . ."

Corvus shook his head. "It won't do any good. There's no contact at all."

"Perhaps your probe is placed in a poor spot," Dorn said.

"Yeah," Yeager added. "That critter's brain must be pretty deep inside its body someplace. Your probe doesn't penetrate deep enough, most likely."

Corvus's face went from anguish to anger to misery, all in a moment. He looked close to tears. Bleakly, he asked, "So what do you want me to do, burrow through the bastard, skewer him like Captain Ahab harpooning Moby Dick?"

Yeager started to reply, thought better of it, and simply shook his head. Dorn stared at Corvus wordlessly. Deirdre wondered what she could say, what she might do, to help Andy.

"It's a failure," Corvus moaned. "A complete flop. The creature's too big. We can't make contact with its brain."

Out of the corner of her eye Deirdre saw her screens flickering. Turning, she saw images flashing across the leviathan's enormous flank.

"It's signaling again!" she said.

The alien's arm is not for feeding, Leviathan decided. It isn't cutting at our hide member. It has no teeth to cut with.

Then what is the purpose of its arm? If not for feeding, then what?

A possible answer formed in Leviathan's brain. The alien is slow and weak, yet it was pushing its way deeper, trying to get closer to the domain of the Kin. But its progress is pitifully slow. Perhaps it is asking our help in going lower. Perhaps it wants us to tow it down to the Kin.

Leviathan remembered the other alien, long ago, who had helped it fight off a pack of darters and been grievously hurt in the battle. Leviathan had lifted that smaller alien on its back and helped it to return to the cold abyss above, from which it had come.

Of course! Leviathan felt that it understood the alien's request. It has come down from the cold abyss to meet with the Kin, to communicate in its limited way with the Elders. Why else would it be here? It doesn't feed on the particle streams. It doesn't feed on our flesh. It isn't seeking food, it's seeking contact, communication.

We can't understand it, Leviathan thought, but perhaps the Elders can.

With that revelation, Leviathan turned and headed deeper, down toward the realm of the Kin, with the strange, hard-shelled alien in tow behind it.

Faraday suddenly lurched like a tiny dog being tugged hard by a brutal master. The bridge tilted so suddenly that all four of the crew were jostled against one another. Deirdre's feet were wrenched out of their deck loops and she banged painfully against her console.

"What the hell was that?" Yeager shouted, steadying himself by grabbing Dorn's broad shoulders.

"It's dragging us deeper," the cyborg said, his normally impassive voice edged with surprise, even fear.

"Disengage," Yeager snapped.

"No!" said Corvus.

They all turned to Corvus, who was hanging on to the handgrips of his console as the vessel plunged steeply downward. Deirdre saw something close to panic in Max's wide eyes; even the human side of Dorn's face looked pasty, unsure. They're as frightened as I am, she realized. But Andy looked—indomitable, doggedly determined, like a man refusing to back down against impossible odds.

"We came here to communicate with them," Corvus said, grim as death. "That's what we're here to do. Ride it out."

"But it's dragging us deeper," Yeager said, his voice almost cracking.

"Good," said Corvus.

"How deep can we go?" Deirdre asked.

Regaining his self-control, Dorn said, "We're nearing our performance limits. Pressure is rising steeply."

"Can we disengage when we have to?" Yeager asked.

Corvus's pale blue eyes snapped at the engineer. "The problem is, Max, will the connection to the beast hold? He's putting a lot of strain on the connection."

"Where's it taking us?" Deirdre asked.

"To the rest of its kind, I hope," said Corvus.

Deirdre felt the pain in her chest burning. Don't take us too deep, Andy, she begged silently. Don't follow that beast down so far that we can't get back.

"Temperature rising," Dorn called.

"Pressure, too," added Yeager.

Corvus's lips curved slightly into a tight smile. "We're here to make contact with the leviathans. Well, that's what we're doing. Not the way we planned, but we'll have to settle for this."

"If it doesn't kill us," Yeager muttered.

Deirdre recalled a line from her classes in ancient history. Spartan mothers told their sons as they headed off to war, "Come back with your shield or on it." Victory or death.

Which will it be, she wondered.

Michael Johansen sat at the head of the long conference table, but he knew that wherever Grant Archer sat was the true power center of the meeting. Each of the younger scientists who had made presentations on the data returned from *Faraday*'s capsule had addressed his or her remarks to Archer, seated halfway down the table's length, not to him.

So be it, Johansen thought, sighing inwardly. Grant's a natural leader. He's the one who pushed for this crewed mission, he took all the heat from Westfall and the IAA council, he's facing all the risks if anything goes wrong with the mission. He's earned everyone's respect. Besides, Grant doesn't play power games, he doesn't need to boost his own ego at the expense of others.

More important, Johansen told himself, this mission has already succeeded. They've made contact with one of the leviathans. They've *communicated* with an alien creature, an extraterrestrial! Those gigantic animals actually are intelligent!

Despite his years Johansen felt a quiver of excitement racing through him. What a discovery! Contact with an intelligent extraterrestrial species. Of course, this first attempt at communicating with them was very limited, but it's just the beginning. They'll be giving out Nobels for this.

He barely listened to the presentation being made by one of the younger biologists as she earnestly plodded through the video imagery sent by the data capsule.

This is what science is all about, Johansen thought. The thrill of discovery. Opening new frontiers. The excitement of new knowledge. The prestige that comes from breaking through into a new world. My reputation is made. Even if those four amateurs in the submersible don't come back, this has been a successful mission. Groundbreaking. Historic.

Nobels, Johansen thought, seeing himself in Stockholm, mentally preparing his acceptance speech. If they die down there, he told himself, I'll throw in a few lines about how scientific exploration requires sacrifices. Martyrs, that's what they'll be. Martyrs to humankind's unending quest for knowledge.

We've already succeeded, he repeated to himself. Whatever happens down there doesn't really matter: We've made contact with an extraterrestrial species, proved that they're intelligent. The rest is just a footnote.

Faraday was shaking brutally as it plunged deeper, towed by the massive leviathan like a cork floater on a fishing line that had been seized by a sounding whale. Even in the thick liquid perfluorocarbon Deirdre could feel the shuddering that rattled every bone in her body.

"How deep are we gonna go?" Yeager asked. He was still standing behind Dorn, but he was pressing both his hands against the overhead to keep himself in place.

"We are still within design limits," said Dorn, his eyes on the control console's screens.

Yeager pointed out, "But we're approaching those limits pretty damned fast."

Deirdre had wormed her feet back into the deck loops, but she still hung on to one of the handgrips on her console as Faraday arrowed down, down, deeper into the dark and hotter depths. Beyond the shaking that rattled the bridge she could feel the vessel tossing up and down, like a raft in heavy surf, lurching and yawing. There's a rhythm to it, she realized as she tried to fight down the pain that burned inside her. It must be the rhythm of the leviathan's flippers, like the oars of an ancient galley.

"Only minor problems so far," Dorn said. "Structural integrity is still sound. Temperature within acceptable limits. Life-support systems performing nominally." Still, his voice sounded strained to Deirdre.

"My back pain is worse," said Yeager. "And I'm getting seasick."

Deirdre nodded in sympathy. She felt it, too. Nausea. And pain. The tightness in her chest was a hot burning knot that was growing worse each minute. It's the pressure, she told herself. How much can I stand?

She glanced across toward Andy. He was rubbing the bridge of his nose again. His headache must be getting worse, she thought. We're all suffering from the pressure buildup. But the expression on Andy's face was far from misery. He was smiling faintly, that absurd lopsided smile of his.

"How far down is this critter taking us?" Yeager demanded.

"As far as it wants to," Corvus snapped.

Dorn said, "We're approaching one thousand kilometers' depth. That's the vessel's nominal limit. If we exceed design limits we'll have to disengage and return to a safer depth."

Corvus shot him an annoyed look. To Yeager, he said, "Max, that design limit isn't absolute, is it? You built a safety factor into it, didn't you?"

"Yeah," Yeager said, halfheartedly.

"How deep can we really go?"

Yeager growled, "How high is up?"

"Fifteen hundred klicks?" Corvus demanded. "Can we go that deep?"

Yeager shook his head.

Deirdre thought, Andy's changed. He was crushed when his DBS equipment didn't work, but now he's taken charge. He's determined to communicate with the leviathans, one way or another.

The pounding was getting worse. The bridge was rattling so hard now that the displays on Deirdre's console screens were blurring. Are the electronics failing or is it just my eyesight? she wondered.

She called to Dorn, "Are your screens blurry?"

The cyborg turned his head toward her, its human side set in a grim rictus that almost matched the metal half. "You're having a problem with your vision?"

Squinting at the fuzzy screens, Deirdre said, "I . . . I don't know if it's me or the displays."

"The system monitors show no indications of failure," said Dorn.

"It must be my eyesight, then," Deirdre replied.

"Vibration's getting worse," Yeager said, pointing a shaking finger at the monitor screens.

"Everything is still within design limits," Dorn insisted. Then he added, "Barely."

"The equipment's within design limits," Yeager countered. "But we're not."

Leviathan swam deeper, seeking the Kin but being careful not to dive too swiftly. Leviathan thought that the alien was probably fragile, so it had to descend slowly, gently. After all, the alien is a creature of the cold abyss above, Leviathan reasoned. This region is foreign to it.

What if it can't live in the warm domain of the Symmetry? Leviathan wondered. It doesn't belong in our region. It isn't part of the Symmetry, it's an alien.

Then a new thought: Does the alien have a Symmetry of its own? It must have! It comes from the cold abyss above; there must be an alien Symmetry up there somewhere, a region where the alien lives with its own kind.

This was something to think about: another Symmetry. An alien Symmetry. Why would the alien leave its own place and invade ours?

Leviathan had no answer. It hoped that the Elders would know—or at least learn what the answer might be.

We must bring the alien to the Elders. Leviathan confirmed its earlier decision. The Elders must see this creature, signal with it, learn from it.

Fighting down its inner impatience, Leviathan swam still deeper, cautiously moving slowly, gently, so that the alien would not be harmed. Or frightened.

"Andy, are you all right?" Yeager asked.

"Yeah, yeah, I'm okay," Corvus replied as he swayed in the foot loops, his eyes closed, both hands massaging his forehead.

"You don't look so good," said Yeager.

"I've got the mother of all sinus headaches, that's all."

Yeager nodded, then clasped Dorn's metal shoulder. "The crew's going to hit failure mode before the equipment does, pal."

Dorn said nothing; the cyborg didn't take his eyes from the screens of his control console.

"Did you hear me, robot?" Yeager snapped. "We can't go much deeper. We're all gonna crack up!"

Deirdre saw the fear in Yeager's face and understood what he was trying to do. Max is scared, she realized. He wants to turn back but he's too timid to say it, so he's blaming it on our physical condition.

Corvus said tightly, "I can take it. I'm not going to crack."

"Not till your head explodes," Yeager growled. He turned toward Deirdre. "Dee, how are you?"

The pain in her chest was like a knife twisting inside her, but Deirdre said, "I'm okay." She was surprised at what an effort it took to gasp out the two words.

Corvus slid over to her. Bobbing in the liquid before her he asked in a near whisper, "Are you really okay, Dee?"

"Yes," she said tightly.

"If it's too much for you we can go back up."

"And leave the leviathan?" Deirdre asked. "Quit the mission?"

Andy's gentle blue eyes looked sad, but he said, "There'll be other missions, Dee. You're more important than anything else."

"But Andy," she said, panting from the pain, "we've come . . . all this way . . ."

Corvus turned toward Dorn. "Take us up."

The cyborg looked over his shoulder at Corvus.

"Up! Disengage and get us the hell out of here!"

"Are you certain—"

Hunched over from the pain in her chest, Deirdre caught a glimmer from her sensor screens.

"Look!" she gasped. "More of them!"

thought I'd find you here."

Grant Archer turned and saw Zareb Muzorewa stepping into the glassteel bubble of station *Gold*'s observation blister.

"Hello, Zeb," Archer said softly.

The transparent compartment was flooded with light from Jupiter. The planet was so large that it encompassed their view, a mammoth swath of gleaming colors spreading as far as their eyes could see, many-hued clouds racing along in turbulent ribbons, a wide circular storm system spiraling far off to their right.

"Come to see it for yourself, have you?" Muzorewa stood several centimeters taller than Archer, a broad-shouldered, muscular figure next to the compactly built station director.

"This is as close as I can get."

Muzorewa nodded. "We've been closer."

"And we've got the scars to prove it," Archer said, tapping his thigh.

Muzorewa took in a deep breath. "Well, you've done it. You've proved that they're intelligent. The data from the capsule shows that the leviathans can communicate."

"I haven't done it," Archer said. "I just helped to set things up so that *they* could do it."

"You'll get a Nobel out of this."

"Not me. Them."

That brought a smile to Muzorewa's deeply black face. Archer smiled back at the scientist, both men basking in the glow from the giant planet.

"Well," Muzorewa said, "at least you'll be named chairman of the IAA governing council."

"God forbid!" Archer blurted, shaking his head. "What would I want that for? Go back Earthside to sit at a desk and spend my life in conference rooms? No thanks. I'll stay right here."

"But everyone thinks—"

"Zeb, I was never interested in the IAA position, no matter what others may have said. Why would I leave here, just when things are getting really interesting?"

Muzorewa fell silent for several moments. Then, his eyes on the swirling splendor of the giant world, he murmured, "I wonder what they're seeing now, at this moment. What are they doing right this instant?"

THE KIN

More of them!" Deirdre repeated.

Andy Corvus gaped at the screens of her console. Wordlessly, Dorn put the sensor views on his control console's screens.

"Look . . . at . . . that," Yeager breathed, drawing out each word.

The screens were filled with leviathans; the huge, massive creatures were surrounding *Faraday*, gliding up on all sides. Deirdre stared at them, feeling like a little child in the midst of fairy-tale giants. They were truly enormous, their immense bodies decked with rows of eyes that all seemed to be looking straight at her. Bright splashes of color flashed across their flanks: vivid blues and greens, hot reds and oranges, brilliant whites.

"God almighty," Corvus whispered.

Unbidden, the words of an old poem rang in Deirdre's mind: "And we are here as on a darkling plain . . . where ignorant armies clash by night."

As they stared at the leviathans they barely noticed that the vessel's shaking, jarring ride had smoothed. *Faraday* was still riding up and down, still shuddering, but the vibrations were much gentler now, almost pleasant.

"There's dozens of 'em," Yeager said, his voice filled with awe.

"More like a hundred," said Corvus, staring at the screens. "Look at the size of them!"

Checking the data bars on her screens, Deirdre saw that even the smallest of the leviathans was more than ten times bigger than their vessel.

"They're talking to each other," she said as the gigantic creatures flashed multicolored signals to each other. The images changed so rapidly that she could make no sense of them.

"Maybe they're talking to us," said Corvus.

Yeager shook his head. "How can we make sense out of it?"

"The computer will slow down the imagery," said Dorn. "Perhaps enough for us to understand them."

"Should we signal back to them?" Deirdre asked.

"Replay their images," Corvus said. "Show them that we're receiving their messages, even though we don't understand them."

Leviathan signed that it had brought the alien for the Elders to see. And explain, if they could.

Its message flashed inward through the Kin to the core where the Elders dwelled. Leviathan saw that the alien was flashing, too, repeating its own message, but much slower. Mimicry again. Is that all it can do? It's so weak, Leviathan thought. Weak and slow.

Dozens of the Kin gathered closer to Leviathan, flashing a myriad of questions. Where did the alien come from? Why is it attached to you? Is it feeding on you? Does it hurt? What does it want? Why is it here?

Leviathan signaled back to them as much as it knew, but that merely raised the Kin's curiosity.

At last the Elders' response came flashing through the Kin to the periphery where Leviathan waited, with the alien still attached to it. The other members of the Kin saw the message and made way for Leviathan to take the alien inward, to the waiting Elders.

"We're a lot deeper than we ought to be," Yeager said, pointing to the graphs on Dorn's screens. It showed that *Faraday* was nearly fourteen hundred kilometers below the ocean's surface.

"Well, this is where the leviathans are," said Corvus, "and we came here to contact them."

"Should we detach the probe?" Deirdre asked, leaving unsaid "So we can get away quickly if we have to?"

Dorn flicked his eyes up and down the system status screens.

"We've trimmed out at neutral buoyancy for this depth. The compression support arms are handling the stresses and all systems are functioning close to normal."

"So far," Yeager muttered.

"So far," Dorn agreed.

"What about life support?" Deirdre asked.

"No apparent problems," Dorn said, his eyes on the screens. The curves on the life-support displays were near their redlines. Before anyone could respond, he asked, "How do you feel?"

"Rotten," Yeager snapped.

"I'm okay," Corvus said quickly. Then he turned to Deirdre, "Dee, what about you?"

In the excitement of being surrounded by the leviathans Deirdre had forgotten the pain in her chest. It was still there, worse than ever. But I can deal with it, she told herself.

With a brief little nod, she said, "I'll be all right."

"Very well, then," Dorn said. "The question remains, should we detach the probe or not?"

"Wait a sec," Yeager protested. "What about you, pal? How do you feel?"

The cyborg hesitated, as if thinking over the question. Then, "Stiff. Sluggish. This pressure is degrading the performance of my prosthetics."

"But not enough for us to leave," Corvus prompted.

Dorn made a weary smile with the human side of his face. "No, Andy. It's not bad enough to force us to leave."

Corvus said, "I've been thinking. If we detach from the beast, then we'll have to move on our own power."

Yeager said, "That's what the fusion propulsion system is for."

"Yeah, but if we activate the fusion drive we'll be squirting out hot steam. Our friends out there might not like that."

Dorn nodded slowly. "They would not understand that we eject the steam to propel ourselves."

"Would they think we're deliberately trying to hurt them?" Deirdre wondered aloud.

Suddenly the bridge seemed to wrench sideways. All four of them lurched and grabbed for supports.

"Doesn't matter now," Yeager said, wedging his hands against the overhead once more. "The big guy's towing us again."

THE ELDERS

Through the herd of leviathans they moved, towed by the one that had brought them down to this depth. Deirdre watched in silence as they glided through the massive formation of the majestic creatures. They seemed to move away from *Faraday*, making an avenue for their vessel and the enormous animal that was towing it. The ride was fairly smooth, nothing like the shaking, violent dive earlier.

Deirdre's chest still hurt, but the pain seemed no worse than before. I can stand it, she told herself as she stared at the screens' displays. I can put up with it.

"Where's he taking us?" Yeager asked.

"Deeper into the herd," said Corvus.

"Into the center of their formation," Dorn added.

"Why?" Yeager demanded. "What's he up to?"

With the fragile alien in tow, Leviathan moved slowly, carefully, through the Kin. Ahead, at the core of their formation, waited the Elders.

There were five of them. Always five. When the Eldest had left the Kin to sacrifice itself to the waiting darters, another member of the Kin became an Elder. There had to be five. Why, Leviathan did not know. But it had been so for longer than the memory of the eldest among them.

The Elders hovered around Leviathan and the strange hard-shelled creature in its tow.

Here is the alien, Leviathan signed to them.

In unison, all five of the Elders signaled, Your replicant told us that you had gone back to find it.

It appears to be intelligent, Leviathan flashed. It is slow, but it is capable of mimicry. Perhaps it can communicate with us, tell us of its world.

For long moments the Elders remained dark. Then the new Eldest asked, Why is it attached to you?

Leviathan replied, It is small and weak. We allowed it to attach itself so that we could bring it to you.

It could not find us on its own? asked another of the Elders.

Perhaps it could, but towing it seemed better, more certain.

Again the Elders went dark. Without waiting for them to ask, Leviathan showed them how the alien helped fight off the darters when it was budding.

Instead of showing gratitude, one of the Elders signaled hotly, It interfered with the Symmetry!

It saved our life, Leviathan flashed back. It allowed us and our replicant to add to the Kin.

Darters are a part of the Symmetry, signed the disgruntled Elder. For all of existence we of the Kin have lived with the darters.

And died with the darters, Leviathan shot back.

Thus it has always been. Thus it must always be. That is the Symmetry.

Why must it always be? Leviathan demanded. Perhaps the alien is showing us a better way.

Destroying the Symmetry is a better way? the Elder signaled in glaring blue.

The darters are changing their ways, Leviathan pointed out. They are coming against us in larger numbers than ever. They cut us off from a stream of food. We should change our ways to meet this new challenge.

The Eldest lit up in solemn green: It is the alien that poses a challenge to us. Why is it here? What does it want of us? How will it affect the Symmetry?

.   .   .

Andy Corvus pinched two fingers over the bridge of his nose as he studied the slowed-down replay of the leviathans' colorful displays.

"Even in slow motion I can't make much sense of it," he admitted. Pointing to his screen, he continued, "I mean, that circle there has got to represent us. See, it's attached to one of the beasts, just like we are."

Deirdre nodded. She too had put the computer's slowed imagery on the central screen of her console. "And those look like those shark things."

Nodding back at her, Corvus said, "I think he's telling those others about how we fought off the sharks when he was attacked."

"Could be," Deirdre said.

Dorn and Yeager were still watching the real-time displays.

"They're jabbering away at one another," Yeager said. "Looks like a fireworks display."

"Perhaps we should try to get their attention," Dorn suggested. "Show them that we can communicate."

"How?" Yeager demanded.

"Show them where we come from," said Dorn. "Draw pictures of the planet, then the solar system. Point out that we come from Earth—"

"That wouldn't make any sense to them," Corvus objected. "They have no idea that they exist in a planet, I betcha. All they know is this enormous ocean."

Deirdre said, "We could at least show them that we come from outside the ocean."

Still looking doubtful, Corvus replied, "And how are you going to do that, Dee?"

She smiled tightly at him. "Let me draw something. Maybe I can get a visual image across to them."

Yeager tapped a finger against the mission time line display on Dorn's console. "We're due to pop another data capsule in half an hour. How do you think they'll react to that?"

She was in misery, her stomach bloated, gas expelling itself in loud, obscene outbursts.

Her comfortably furnished bedroom had become a prison cell. I can't let anyone see me like this, Katherine Westfall told herself for the hundredth time that hour. I'm a prisoner, an exile, until this horror passes—if it ever does.

She had ripped off her clothes and now wore nothing but a floor-length dressing gown of pure silk, pale dawn pink, decorated with muted oriental scenes of graceful gardens and languid women in kimonos.

She broke wind again, and ground her teeth at the shamefulness of it. The stench. If I ever get the chance to destroy Archer . . .

The phone chimed.

"Who's calling?" she asked. The data bar at the bottom of the screen spelled out DR. GRANT ARCHER.

Westfall went to the desk and sat primly on its cushioned little chair. "Answer," she said, huddling close to the screen so that the phone's camera could see little more than her face and shoulders.

Archer's dead-serious face filled the screen, strangely boyish despite the fringe of iron-gray beard.

"I've reviewed the data from their capsule," he said without preamble. "They've definitely established meaningful contact. The leviathans communicate visually; they produce pictures on their flanks."

"Congratulations," Westfall said acidly.

"I thought you'd like to know."

"Thank you."

For a moment Archer fell silent. Then, "Actually, I called to ask you a question."

"Did you?"

"Why?" Archer's expression became almost pleading. "Why did you want to stop the mission so badly that you were willing to kill those four people?"

"You scientists have killed lots of people," she said, all the old anger and hatred simmering anew inside her.

"People have died in the pursuit of knowledge, that's true," Archer admitted. "But we've never set out to deliberately murder anyone."

"Those missions into the ocean. How many have been killed on them?"

Archer's expression hardened. "I was on one of those missions. We stopped sending people down there for more than twenty years."

"But you've started again."

"On a much safer vessel. There are risks, of course, but now we—"

"You murdered my sister!" Westfall blurted.

"Your sister?"

"Elaine O'Hara. She was my sister."

"Lane is dead?" He looked shocked by the news.

"She's dead. She never recovered from that death ride you sent her on."

"But I didn't send her," Archer said. "I was one of the crew, I wasn't in command."

"You would have sent her if you were in charge. You would have killed her."

Archer seemed confused, unsure. "I . . . I had no idea she was your sister. I thought the world of Lane . . . we . . . she and I . . . she was a truly lovely woman."

"And now she's dead. Thanks to your pursuit of knowledge." Westfall put a venomous accent on her last three words.

For long moments Archer was silent. At last he lifted his chin a notch and said, "I think you need help, Mrs. Westfall. I hope you seek psychiatric therapy."

She allowed herself a cold, thin smile. "The last refuge of a scoundrel," she said. Then she clicked off the connection.

THE SYMMETRY

The new Eldest showed how troubled it was about the invading alien with a display of pulsating greens and yellows. Since time immemorial we have lived with the Symmetry, it signaled. This alien creature is outside the Symmetry. It cannot be anything but a threat to our way of life.

Leviathan flashed back, It has not harmed us in any way. It saved our replicant and us from the darters—

That in itself is a violation of the Symmetry, two of the Elders glared simultaneously.

But why must we allow the darters to feed on us? Leviathan demanded. Why must we always follow the old ways?

That is the Symmetry, all five Elders replied in unison. We must all accept the Symmetry. Without the Symmetry we will be lost.

Leviathan began to reply, but then saw that the alien was trying to speak to them. Look! Leviathan flashed. The alien is signaling!

The Elders went dark. Leviathan realized that all five of them edged slightly closer to the alien, which was flashing pictures slowly, painfully slowly.

Leviathan had plenty of time to inspect the alien's images and think about what they meant. It showed itself, an unmistakable small round object, attached to Leviathan, surrounded by the Elders. Then a confused series of images flickered from its rounded hide, changing so slowly that Leviathan wondered if the alien thought the Elders were unintelligent, dim-witted.

The alien pictured its encounter with Leviathan during its budding, and the fight with the darters. This could be mere mimicry, Leviathan thought, repeating what I showed to the Elders earlier.

But then the alien's pictures showed it rising above Leviathan and the darters, upwards into the cold abyss from which it had come. The pictures became strange, unintelligible. The alien seemed to be showing other creatures, weird slim-snouted things with long thin flagella members that flapped slowly. And bulbous, many-colored things that seemed to hang motionless, hardly alive, with long sinuous tentacles dangling from their globular bodies.

Slowly, slowly, the pictures continued to change. The little round image of the alien rose above the strange creatures, through a smear of blurry colors, and then out into a darkness that was speckled with tiny points of white. As it rose, the blurred colors below it bent into a curve and the curve became another round thing, streaked with colors, while the alien itself became little more than a dot.

The alien went dark.

What does it mean? Leviathan asked.

It's nonsense, replied one of the Elders. Senseless jibbering, the product of an unintelligent mind.

Perhaps not, signed the Eldest. Perhaps it is a different kind of mind, not unintelligent, but different.

But what does it mean? Leviathan repeated.

It is not of the Symmetry, signed the newest Elder, therefore it has no meaning. It has nothing to tell us. We should ignore it.

We can't ignore it! Leviathan insisted. It is here. It exists.

It has no meaning, the Elder insisted.

It is not part of the Symmetry, signaled another. It will destroy the Symmetry if we pay any heed to it.

All the Elders went dark, fearful of the threat to the Symmetry. The alien bobbed on its tether, dark also.

Then Leviathan thought, What if the alien has come not to destroy the Symmetry, but to enlarge it?

"That's the best I could do," Deirdre said.

"Looked good to me," Corvus replied. "You showed them where we come from, showed them they live in a planet. Showed them that we come from outside their world."

His eyes still fixed on the control console's screens, Dorn said slowly, "I wonder if they can grasp that idea. It must be entirely foreign to them."

Yeager said, "Well, they're going to see something else that's entirely new to them when we pop the next data capsule."

Dorn nodded thoughtfully. "Perhaps it would be best if we disconnected the DBS probe before we fire the capsule."

"Yeah," Corvus agreed. "I wouldn't want to be tethered to that beast if it gets scared and decides to dive deeper."

Deirdre nodded, but she said, "I'd like to show them what we look like."

"You can show me what you look like anytime," Yeager said, breaking into his old leering grin.

"Time line calls for data capsule launch in eight minutes," Dorn said.

"Disconnect us first," said Corvus.

"Disconnecting."

The alien has removed its arm from you, the Eldest pictured.

Leviathan flashed a soft orange sign of agreement. It had hardly felt the alien's attachment to its hide. The disengagement was even less noticeable. Leviathan saw that the alien remained in the midst of the Elders as its arm slowly withdrew into its spherical body. It is not trying to flee from us, it thought.

New pictures began to glow on the alien's hide. Leviathan's sensor parts focused on them while its brain tried to understand what the alien was showing.

First it showed the circle that Leviathan thought represented the alien itself. Then the circle grew larger and shapes took form inside it. Four strange shapes, elongated, with things like tentacles extending from their bodies. But they looked too thick and short to be tentacles. And there was a rounded knob at one end of each body.

What are they depicting? the Eldest asked.

None of the Elders replied; they were all studying the strange images.

Leviathan guessed, Those could be members of the alien's body, like our own inner organ members.

But they seem to move about inside its body, one of the Elders pointed out.

Strange.

It is alien, Leviathan pictured. Of course it is strange.

The images inside the picture of the alien faded away. For maddeningly long moments the alien showed nothing but the circle representing its own body.

Has it nothing more to tell us? the Eldest asked.

The newest Elder signed, It's not intelligent enough to show us anything meaningful.

Suddenly the alien's imagery showed a tubular object leaving its body and speeding upward, toward the cold abyss above.

Leviathan immediately understood. It is telling us that it will dissociate!

The Eldest flared in blue distaste, Dissociate? Here, amongst us?

Revolting, flashed another of the Elders.

Obviously, signaled the Elder next to it, the alien is of a low mentality. Its ways are crude and disgusting.

It is *alien*, Leviathan insisted. Its ways are different from ours.

It is feeble-minded, signed the newest Elder. Slow and feeble-minded.

Leviathan countered, Then how is it that the alien has come into our realm? How could it be feeble-minded if it left its own region in the cold abyss above and came down here to find us?

DECISIONS

Capsule launch in one minute," Dorn called out.

Yeager said, "Better hang on tight. If those beasties out there start thrashing around we're gonna get battered but good."

"We've told them we're going to launch the capsule," Corvus said. "They won't be frightened."

"You hope," Yeager snapped, as he wormed his feet firmly into the deck loops and wedged both hands against the overhead.

Deirdre reached for the handholds on her console, noting that Andy and Dorn were doing the same. Her arms felt heavy, weary; every movement she made caused the pain in her chest to flare hotly.

Dorn flexed his prosthetic hand slowly as he said, "Our life-support readouts are nearly touching the redlines. We'll have to cut our mission short."

"No," Corvus snapped immediately. Even in the sound-deepening perfluorocarbon his voice was a high-pitched yelp. "We're communicating with the leviathans! We're *talking* with intelligent aliens!"

"Do we want to die down here?" Yeager growled.

"We haven't hit any redlines yet, have we?" Deirdre asked. "Can't we stay until we actually reach the limits?"

Dorn seemed to take a deep breath, then replied, "Capsule launch in thirty seconds."

Leviathan watched the alien begin dissociating, but it was unlike any dissociation it had ever known or heard of. A solid chunk of the alien shot out of its body like a miniature darter, heading straight up toward the cold abyss above. Then—nothing. Leviathan waited with the Elders, but the alien did not detach any more of its members.

After a seeming eternity of waiting, the Eldest signaled, It merely separated one member.

And the member did not bud, pictured another of the Elders.

Does it understand that the Symmetry demands that we bud alone, away from the Kin?

And feed the darters, Leviathan thought; but it remained dark.

The alien apparently has some sense of decency, said the newest Elder. At least, the member it detached does. It goes off to bud alone, as is proper.

It fled away from us, flashed the Eldest.

Perhaps, Leviathan signed, it is frightened of us. Perhaps it is not budding. Perhaps it has merely sent one of its members back to its own realm.

For what purpose? asked the Eldest.

Leviathan hesitated before answering, knowing that the Elders would not be pleased at its thought. To tell them about the Kin, it answered at last. To tell its fellow aliens that we exist.

All five of the Elders glared hot white. Yes, Leviathan realized, that frightens them.

"Rest period for Dee and Max," said Dorn.

Deirdre grimaced inwardly at the thought of feeding herself again through the port in her throat.

Yeager said, "Why don't we just get the hell out of here? What can we accomplish by stooging around with these critters?"

"We're talking with them!" Corvus fairly shouted. "We're learning about them."

"And getting sicker every minute," Yeager countered. "I don't know about you, pal, but my back is killing me. I feel like I'm two hundred years old and I'm carrying a six-hundred-kilo gorilla on my back."

Hotly, Corvus said, "We came down here to communicate with the leviathans—"

"Which we've done. Now let's haul ass and get back where we belong."

"We belong here!"

"Even if it kills us?"

"We're not dead yet, Max. Far from it."

Dorn interjected, "Our physical condition is deteriorating. At the present rate we will not be able to stay at this depth for the scheduled length of the mission."

Corvus glared at the cyborg. Deirdre could see anger smoldering in his normally placid eyes. And Yeager was staring defiantly at Corvus. Andy wants to communicate with them so badly, she thought. He's willing to risk his own life for this. He's willing to fight Max and even Dorn. I can't let him carry this to the point where they'll be enemies.

She reached out and touched Yeager's shoulder. "Come on, Max. It's dinnertime."

Yeager blinked at her, then made a forced little grin. "Yeah. Let's have the blue plate special."

Deirdre saw some of the angry tension ease out of Andy's body. Dorn looked slowly from Corvus to Yeager and then to Deirdre. He dipped his chin a bare centimeter at her and Deirdre understood that Dorn recognized what she had just defused.

The alien is dark, signed the Eldest.

Leviathan signed, It told us that it would dissociate one member only, and that is what it has done.

Now it says nothing.

The newest Elder maintained, If it is intelligent, its intelligence must be of a low order. It has nothing to tell us; we should ignore it.

The Eldest disagreed: Its presence among us is a change in the Symmetry. We must protect ourselves against any disruption.

It seems peaceful enough, Leviathan signed. Even helpful, when it protected us against the darters.

But that is not part of the Symmetry! another of the Elders flashed in urgent blue. We have always faced the darters alone. The alien disrupts the Symmetry.

The alien *enlarges* the Symmetry, Leviathan countered. The alien shows us that our understanding of the Symmetry has been limited.

All of the Elders went dark, pondering this new thought. Leviathan waited, hoping that the alien would light up again and prove that it was intelligent—and beneficial.

At last the Eldest decided. It signed to Leviathan, You will take the alien to the edge of the Kin and remain there with it. Whatever it tells you, you will report through the Kin to us. Try to learn from it, but do not allow it to interfere with the Kin in any way.

Leviathan realized that the Eldest was choosing the wisest path, and flashed its agreement in muted tones of orange and yellow.

Then Leviathan wondered, How do I tell the alien what it must do?

TROUBLE

Deirdre awoke from her sleep period feeling far from rested. Her entire body felt sluggish, weary. The pain in her chest seemed worse than before, she thought, a hot throbbing that sent waves of agony through her whole body. It's the pressure, she knew. We're down deeper than we ever planned to be.

She saw that Max was still asleep, tucked into his cramped shelf like a corpse on a slab. His breathing was a labored gurgle, as if he were half strangling. Should I tell Dorn? Deirdre wondered. Max's physical condition is displayed on the life-support readouts, she told herself. If he's in any trouble Dorn would know it right away.

She felt too tired to change into a fresh maillot. We'll be leaving soon anyway, she thought. She hoped.

The alarm buzzer that signaled the end of their sleep period stirred Max. He banged his head as he forgot where he was and tried to sit up. Muttering curses, he slid out of the bunk, rubbing his forehead.

"Whoever designed this bucket ought to have his head examined," Yeager said, grinning sheepishly.

"Yes, Max," said Deirdre. "And you should allow more room for crew comforts on the next model."

"I'll make a note of that."

Deirdre slid back the door to the bridge and gasped. Dorn was floating a meter or so above the deck, Andy fluttering helplessly over him.

"He just passed out," Corvus said, his voice shaking. "Half a minute ago he was fine, then he just slumped over, unconscious."

Yeager pushed past Deirdre and rushed to the cyborg's inert body. Deirdre went to her console, but glanced at the life-support readouts on Dorn's screens. A row of glaring red lights. Flicking to the readouts for the rest of them, Deirdre saw that several of the curves had crossed their redline limits. We're dying! she realized. The pressure is killing us.

Yeager glanced at the displays, too. "He's in trouble."

Corvus said, "I can see that!"

"We've got to figure out what's wrong with him, and fast."

Stating the obvious, Corvus said, "We're just down too damned deep."

"Helluva time for you to admit that," Yeager growled.

Deirdre saw in her central screen, "The leviathan is lighting up again."

She was certain it was the one they had met and attached themselves to. It was hard to tell any differences among the mountain-sized creatures, but Deirdre thought the one they had attached to was slightly smaller and sleeker than the others that had gathered around their vessel.

It was lighting up, flashing a set of images against a background of red and yellow. What does it mean? she wondered. What is it trying to tell us?

Patiently, Leviathan showed the alien that it was going to take its usual place at the outer rim of the Kin, and the alien must come along with it.

The alien remained dark, mute.

How can I make it understand? Leviathan wondered.

"He's got a pulse," Corvus said, gripping the unconscious cyborg's human wrist.

Yeager squinted at the medical readouts. "Pulse steady but weak. Breathing rate going down. What the hell's wrong with him?"

Deirdre was feeding the leviathan's signals through the computer program that slowed them, trying to ignore the pain that was radiating through her body. Maybe I can figure out what it's trying to tell us if I can look at the images at a slower rate. But she couldn't help turning away from her screens to glance at Dorn's unconscious body.

The Eldest flashed to Leviathan, The alien does not respond.

It's gone dark, Leviathan agreed.

It doesn't understand what you are trying to tell it, signaled one of the Elders.

Or it doesn't *want* to understand, signed another.

No, it's too stupid to understand. It's not truly intelligent, it merely mimics what we tell it.

Leviathan thought otherwise, but kept its opinion to itself. Remembering its encounter with the other alien, long ago, Leviathan decided that there was one way to get the alien to move, whether it acknowledged its message or not.

"We have to get back up to the station," Corvus said. "Get medical attention for Dorn."

For all of us, Deirdre added silently.

Still scanning the medical readouts, Yeager muttered, "Or at least up to a higher level, where the pressure isn't so bad."

"Back to the station!" Corvus snapped.

Deirdre saw that Dorn was floating gently in the perfluorocarbon, unconscious, his arms bobbing in the liquid. His breathing seemed deep and slow; his human eye was closed, the prosthetic camera dark instead of its usual red gleam.

"His artificial eye," she blurted. "It's off."

"So what?" Yeager said.

"It never goes off," she said. "Not even when he sleeps."

Corvus grasped her meaning. "Maybe it's the mechanical side of him that's failed?"

Yeager looked from Corvus to Deirdre and then down at the unconscious Dorn. "Sounds nutty."

"The medical readouts don't cover his robotic systems," Deirdre said. Then she added, "Do they?"

"No, you're right," said Yeager. "I'll pull up the diagnostic program for his prosthetics. Andy, we'll have to plug him into the main computer. Find the connector cable."

But as Corvus launched himself toward the hatch of their sleeping area the vessel suddenly lurched and tilted wildly.

"What the hell?" Yeager shouted as he slammed painfully against the main console. Dorn's inert body glided across the bridge's narrow confines and buckled against the food dispenser. Deirdre's feet were wedged into the deck loops but still she swayed so hard that she banged her shoulder against her console. Corvus missed the hatch and rammed into the bulkhead alongside it.

"What's happening?" Deirdre whimpered.

As gently as it could Leviathan slid beneath the alien and pushed against it with its back. Once before it had lifted an alien up to safety as it sank down into the hot abyss below. That had been easier, because that alien's body was flat. Circular, hard-shelled, but flat. It could ride easily enough on Leviathan's back.

But this alien was round, spherical. It bounced off Leviathan's back instead of riding smoothly.

Doggedly, Leviathan nudged the alien outward toward the edge of the Kin's formation, in obedience to the Elders' decision. The alien bounced along as Leviathan's flagella members patiently propelled it onward.

Leviathan remembered that the earlier alien had repaid its piggyback rescue by spraying scalding heat against its hide. Then it had shot upward, into the cold abyss above, never to return.

What will this alien do? How will it react to being pushed back to the edge of the Kin?

Holding on for dear life to her console's handgrips, Deirdre tried to make sense of the leviathan's slowed-down message while Yeager and Corvus analyzed Dorn's cybernetic systems. Yeager was muttering a continuous string of swearing as *Faraday* lurched and bounced madly.

"Sonofabitch is battering us to death," Yeager growled, in between choice curses and words Deirdre had never heard before.

"It's pushing us," Deirdre said, trying to focus on the display in her central screen.

Corvus had connected the cable that linked Dorn's mechanical side with the vessel's main computer. Yeager was trying to trace the cyborg's systems, but the constant banging and jarring made it almost impossibly difficult.

Between lurches, Deirdre saw that the leviathan had signaled to them that it was going to move away from the core of the creatures' massive spherical formation, out toward the edge, and they should follow along with it.

"It's pushing us outward," Deirdre said. "It wants us to move out to the rim of their formation."

"Helluva way to make us move," Yeager rumbled.

"Maybe if we light up our propulsion system we could go more smoothly," Corvus suggested.

"Maybe," Yeager agreed.

The alien suddenly moved off on its own, squirting a spray of heated water behind it. Leviathan was glad that the alien was not resting on its back, remembering the other alien that had scalded its hide.

Swimming alongside the alien, Leviathan again flashed its message that they were heading out to the edge of the Kin. Other leviathans in the formation swung wide of the alien, allowing them to pass through without hindrance.

It does understand, Leviathan realized. It's just so excruciatingly slow. Leviathan flashed that message to be passed inward to the Elders.

QUESTIONS

Their ride smoothed out and Yeager stopped his cursing. Corvus hovered over Dorn's unconscious body while Deirdre reluctantly turned back to her console to examine the messages from the leviathan in the computer's slowed playback.

Nodding, she reaffirmed, "It wants us to stay here with it."

Without taking his eyes from the screen showing Dorn's diagnostics, Yeager asked, "Where's 'here'?"

"We're on the periphery of the leviathans' formation. They travel in a sort of ragged spherical grouping, it looks like."

Corvus muttered, "They took us in to the center and now they've put us out on the edge. That's weird."

"Maybe they're willing to allow us to stay with them," Deirdre suggested.

"Not for long," said Yeager, grimly. "Dorn's dying."

Leviathan had a thousand questions that it wanted to ask the alien. Where did you come from? Why are you here? Do you eat the food that drifts down to us, or something else? Why do you spew out scalding hot water when you move? What is your hard shell made of?

Knowing that the alien's mind worked very slowly, Leviathan decided to ask one question at a time and repeat it as often as necessary until the alien finally understood and pictured an answer. Then it would go on to the next question.

First question: Where do you come from?

"He's dying?" Deirdre was shocked. "But you said his medical readouts . . ."

"They're sinking," Yeager said. "It's slow, but he's going downhill."

"Why? What's wrong with him?"

"The pressure. It's got to be something connected to the pressure."

Corvus said, "We've got to get him back to the station. Quick."

"Too bad we can't send him back in one of the data capsules," said Deirdre.

Yeager gave her an odd look. "That's something I should've thought of," he muttered. "Have to add it to the next version of this bucket."

"But what's wrong with him?" Deirdre repeated.

Corvus waved a hand at the diagnostic screen. "His mechanical systems have shut down for some reason. Without them functioning, his human side can't function either, not for long."

"It must be something in his central computer system," Yeager said, eyeing the screens as if he could force them to tell their secrets by staring at them hard enough.

"Can you access his computer?" Corvus asked.

With a shrug, Yeager said, "I can try."

Deirdre turned back to her console and saw that the leviathan was flashing signals again.

Where do you come from? Leviathan asked patiently, over and over again.

As it asked, it realized that the alien proved that the world was much larger than even the Eldest had realized. Larger and more complex, with strange hard-shelled alien creatures in it. Who knew what else might be in the farther reaches of the world?

Leviathan felt a thrill of curiosity. How big is the world? What other strange creatures might be in it?

Deirdre frowned with puzzlement as she studied the computer's playback of the leviathan's message. The same line drawings, repeated endlessly. The computer display automatically washed out the colorful splashes of pale yellow and brighter orange that made the line drawings difficult to distinguish.

It showed a small circle next to a sketch of a many-flippered leviathan. The circle must be us, Deirdre thought, and the leviathan figure must be him. Then the circle rose above the image of the leviathan, slowly heading away until the leviathan's image dwindled and dropped out of the picture.

It knows we come from higher up in the ocean, Deirdre reasoned. But then the image of the circle faded gradually until it disappeared altogether. What's that supposed to mean? she wondered.

"I'll be damned!" Yeager snapped. "Look at that!"

Turning from her screens, Deirdre saw Max pointing at one of the diagnostic displays on Dorn's control console.

"Sleep mode?" Andy said, peering at the printout. "What's that mean?"

"His central computer's shut down," said Max.

"Shut down?"

"It's an old computer programming trick. When the CPU inputs exceed the program's design limits, the damned computer shuts down its active functions. The geeks used to call that 'sleep mode.' It's from a dozen programming generations ago."

"Why does it do that?" Corvus asked.

"To protect the core programs, keep them from getting infected or overstressed."

Deirdre said, "But it's harming Dorn."

With a bleak nod, Yeager said, "His human half needs the mechanical systems. He's got pumps inside him that run his endocrine system and servomotors that power his mechanical parts. His heart is mechanical; its function depends on those systems, too."

"His heart's shutting down?"

"It's slowing," Yeager replied. "The blood flow to his brain is too little to let him stay conscious."

"But why's the computer doing this?" Corvus demanded. "It's killing him."

Yeager shook his head. "Goddam bucket of chips is protecting itself and letting his human half die."

"You've got to do something, Max!" Deirdre insisted.

"Yeah, I know. We've got to get out of here. But how? Dorn's our pilot. I'm just his backup. You expect me to run this bucket while he's unconscious?"

Leviathan began to wonder if the Elders had been right. Perhaps the alien isn't really intelligent at all: It merely mimics the images we flash at it.

The vision Leviathan had idealized began to fade from his hopes for the future. The world might be much bigger than we had thought, it told itself, but there are no truly intelligent creatures in it, no one that we can communicate with, no one that we can learn from.

W e've got to get out of here," Corvus repeated.

"I know," Yeager agreed. His tone sounded tense, almost angry.

"Can't you pilot this ship?"

Yeager hesitated, then answered, "In theory."

"In theory?" Corvus yelped.

Grudgingly, Yeager explained, "I designed this bucket, all its systems. But that doesn't mean I have the reflexes, the skills to actually pilot her."

"You said it was highly automated," Corvus said, almost accusingly.

Deirdre piped up, "The ship ran completely automated, all by itself, didn't it?"

Looking miserable, Yeager said, "Yeah, but to set it up that way means reprogramming its central computer. That could take hours."

"We don't have hours," said Corvus. "We've got to get Dorn out of here *now*. At least up to a higher level, where the pressure isn't so bad."

Yeager seemed frozen with indecision. "I know," he muttered. "I know. But . . . piloting . . . suppose I screw it up? I could kill us all."

"We need Dorn?"

"We need Dorn."

Deirdre listened to the two men while still focusing her eyes on the figures that the leviathan drew, again and again.

"Andy," she called, "could you wake Dorn up with your DBS equipment?"

"He's in a coma, almost."

"But couldn't you make contact with his mind?" Deirdre asked. "Get him to wake up? Maybe if he were conscious he could override his computer."

Corvus bit his lip, glanced at Yeager, then said tightly, "It's worth a try."

Leviathan saw that a message was flashing toward it from the Elders, lighting up the waters in stern blue as it passed outward from one member of the Kin to the next.

Finally the member next to Leviathan transmitted the Elders' question: If the alien is truly intelligent it would communicate freely with you. Has it done so?

Fighting down its first instinct to admit that the alien's intelligence was limited to mimicry, Leviathan replied carefully, Its mind works very slowly. We have asked it where it comes from and are waiting for a reply to our question.

Leviathan could foresee the Elders' next response, their sneering disdain for this slow, dull alien creature. They are afraid of the alien, Leviathan thought. Behind their scornful belittling is the fear that the alien will upset the Symmetry.

Wondering how it could communicate meaningfully with the alien before the Elders decided to drive the stranger away, Leviathan saw with a flash of grateful joy that the alien was lighting up again.

It's trying to communicate! Leviathan thought hopefully.

Deirdre saw out of the corner of her eye that Andy was fitting one of his DBS circlets onto Dorn's head. Maybe that will work, she thought. Max looks terribly nervous, frightened. If they can't wake Dorn, Max is going to have to try to fly us back to the station.

It took an effort of will for her to concentrate on the message the leviathan was drawing. The same imagery again. A picture of the leviathan with us beside it. Then it shows us rising above the leviathan, going up farther and farther, until we fade out and dis—

Of course! Deirdre realized. It's asking where we come from! It

knows we came down to this level of the ocean from up above. It
wants to know where we originated!

Deirdre worked her keyboard swiftly, calling up the earlier imagery she had shown the leviathan. She patched it together with the
leviathan's question and transmitted it to the lights on the vessel's
hull.

Her imagery showed the leviathan's original picture of itself with
Faraday beside it, then the vessel rising until the leviathan figure
dwindled and disappeared. But now, instead of fading away—Deirdre
figured that was the leviathan's way of asking its question—the imagery of their vessel continued upward, out of the ocean, through the
clear atmosphere populated by spider-kites and Clarke's Medusas, on
through the wide smear of clouds and out into space. The tiny
sphere that represented *Faraday* moved on away from the planet until the imagery showed Jupiter as seen from space, a flattened sphere
streaked with many-colored clouds.

Smiling with satisfaction, Deirdre wondered if the leviathan
could possibly understand what she was trying to tell it.

The pictures made no sense to Leviathan. The alien seemed to rise
up into the cold abyss above, and then moved on to realms that became stranger and stranger.

Gibberish? Leviathan asked itself. No, it decided. The alien is
trying to tell us something, trying to explain where it comes from.
Of course it would all seem strange, even senseless, to us. It comes
from a different part of the Symmetry. Naturally its realm would
seem strange, totally unlike anything the Kin has experienced before.

We were right! Leviathan told itself. The alien is intelligent—
and the Symmetry is much larger and more complex than we had
ever thought.

It began to signal these new thoughts inward through the Kin,
toward the Elders.

"It's working!" Yeager said. Then he added, "I think."

Corvus was linked to Dorn: Both of them had DBS circlets on

their heads. Yeager was peering eagerly at the readouts on the diagnostic screens.

"I'm talking with the leviathan," Deirdre called to them, then added, "I think."

Dorn's prosthetic eye began to glow red, feebly, then his human eye slowly opened.

"Dorn!" Corvus said eagerly. "Can you hear me?"

"Yes."

"Your central computer's shutting down. Can you override it?"

"No."

"But it's killing you!"

Slowly, obviously in pain, Dorn replied, "It is following its programming."

"But it's killing you!" Corvus repeated.

Dorn said, "The prosthetics are protecting themselves. The fact that the flesh is dying is an unfortunate side effect."

Corvus looked up at Yeager. "Max, you'll have to pilot us out of here. It's up to you."

Yeager uttered a heartfelt "Shit."

ESCAPE

eirdre could see that Max was clearly frightened as he orally set up the command console's navigation program.

"It's up to you, Max," she whispered to herself. "Dorn's life depends on you." Then she realized that all their lives depended on Max's ability to pilot their vessel.

The leviathan was flashing signals at them again, the flickering of its glowing hide lighting up her communications screen.

Dorn seemed conscious, but barely so. Floating lethargically in the perfluorocarbon, the cyborg watched in silence as Yeager set up the navigation program.

Corvus unconsciously touched the optronic circlet crowning his head and said to Yeager, "Dorn's thinking that you've got to cancel the buoyancy program. You have to do something called 'blow negative' before the vessel can start to rise above this level."

"Right," said Yeager, and he resumed murmuring instructions to the central computer's voice-recognition system.

Deirdre shook her head, wondering if they were going to get out of this alive. Dorn's too weak to speak now, but Andy's picking up his conscious thoughts through the DBS link. Max is learning the difference between designing the ship and making it work.

"Dee," Andy called to her, "you'd better keep your eyes on your screens. Looks like the creature's signaling again."

Turning back to her console, Deirdre saw that the leviathan was flashing a different image. She hunched forward slightly, leaning against the deck loops her feet were wedged into. The leviathan was picturing several of its own kind, with a broad swath of tiny dots flowing down toward them. Then the picture abruptly changed to show *Faraday* in the middle of the little dots, all alone.

Even slowed by the computer, the imagery made little sense to Deirdre. The dots probably represent the organic particles that drift down out of the clouds, she thought. That's what they eat. But why does he put us into the stream? What's he trying to say?

"Better tell our friend that we're going to be heading up," Andy told her.

Deirdre nodded and began drawing a picture on her touch-sensitive screen with her outstretched finger.

Leviathan's sensor members studied the message the alien was drawing. It made no sense.

Leviathan was patiently asking the alien what it ate, but the alien seemed to be ignoring the question and instead showing that it came from higher in the Symmetry, from the cold abyss above.

We know that, Leviathan thought. The alien is stating the obvious. Why won't it answer our question about its food? Is it refusing to answer? Is it hiding something from us?

"I've got it set to fire up," Yeager announced, a shaky grin on his drawn face.

"Then go," Corvus said, without hesitation.

"Ten-second countdown," said Yeager. "Ten . . ."

"Wait," Corvus interrupted. "We ought to get Dorn strapped in before we start jouncing around."

Yeager nodded. "Yeah, right. Slide him into his sleep compartment."

"I'll help," Deirdre offered.

Together, she and Corvus pushed Dorn's barely conscious body into the sleep chamber and slid him into his coffinlike bunk.

"He'll be okay in there," Corvus said as he fastened the safety web at the foot of the enclosure. Deirdre heard the uncertainty quavering in his voice.

"It's the best we can do," she said.

With an abrupt gesture, Corvus waved Deirdre through the

hatch back onto the bridge, then followed her. They both slid their feet into the deck loops.

"Fire away, Max," said Corvus. Then he turned toward Deirdre and winked.

Surprised, she smiled back at him. Andy's trying to reassure me, she thought. In the middle of all this, he's trying to tell me not to be afraid. But she was afraid. And so was Andy, she knew. And Max.

"Ten seconds," Max said stiffly. "Nine . . . eight . . ."

The alien suddenly spurted up on a spray of heated water, heading for the cold abyss above. That's what it was trying to tell us! Leviathan realized. It's leaving us. It's heading home.

For several moments Leviathan considered what it should do. Follow the alien, or remain here with the Kin? Leviathan knew it should ask the Elders for their decision, but there was no time to wait for their deliberation. Without further thought, without asking the Elders for their guidance, Leviathan followed the alien, remaining far enough from it to avoid being scalded by the heat it was pouring out. Like a squid, Leviathan thought. It propels itself with jets of heated water. Of course. How else could it move? It has no flagella members.

The alien was ascending rapidly but Leviathan easily kept pace with it.

How high will it go? Leviathan wondered. How far can we accompany it? Will it have anything else to tell us?

Pointing to the diagnostics screen, Yeager sang out, "His readouts are picking up! His prosthetics are coming back on-line!"

Deirdre glanced at Max and saw the absolutely joyous look on his face. Andy was grinning, too. Then she turned back to her sensor screens. The leviathan was still alongside them, keeping pace with their ascent, staying off to one side to remain clear of their exhaust of superheated steam.

"All systems in the green," Max said, with pride in his voice.

"You're doing it," Andy said, his grin nearly splitting his face. "We'll have to start calling you Captain Max."

The leviathan was signaling to them again, Deirdre saw. She repeated the message she'd been sending: We're leaving. We're going home.

How far into the cold abyss will the alien go? Leviathan wondered, flashing that question as it swam alongside the ascending hard-shelled creature. Fish and squid and other creatures teemed through the chilly waters of this level. No darters in sight, Leviathan's sensor members reported. We're too high for darters, Leviathan thought. Still, it's good to be on the alert for them. They will attack a solitary leviathan if given the chance.

Still the alien rose.

The hatch to the sleeping area slid back and Dorn floated onto the bridge.

"Look who's here," Yeager announced.

Deirdre thought that Dorn looked weary, strained. Even the metal half of his face seemed somehow haggard, dulled.

"I apologize for my collapse," the cyborg said.

"No apology needed," said Corvus. "It wasn't your fault."

"My prosthetics are programmed to shut down when they are in danger of exceeding their design limits."

Yeager nodded. "Don't worry, pal. We're getting out of this pressure cooker as fast as we can."

"The mission?" Dorn asked.

"We've got enough data to keep the scooters happy for years," said Yeager. "Now's the time to go home."

Dorn glided to the command console. Bobbing alongside Yeager, he said, "I can take the con now, if you don't mind."

Yeager made an exaggerated bow. "You're welcome to it!"

Deirdre heard herself say, "Do we have to leave right away?"

All three men turned toward her.

Surprised at her own reaction, Deirdre asked, "Can't we stay at this level, at least for a little bit?"

"Why?" Yeager demanded.

Glancing at her sensor screens, Deirdre replied, "To say good-bye."

Several of Leviathan's flagella members were quivering with the anticipation of dissociating. We are too high, Leviathan realized, too close to the cold abyss above. If we go higher we will dissociate involuntarily.

But the alien was still rising, still climbing upward. How high will it go?

"It's sending another message," Deirdre said, staring at the flickering images on her central screen. The computer was washing out the colors and slowing down the rapidly blinking drawings.

"Leveling off," said Dorn, with something like the old strength in his voice.

"We can't stay here for long," Yeager warned.

"Why not?" Corvus snapped as he tucked the DBS circlets back into their container bin.

Yeager scowled at him. "We'll run out of supplies. We're only fitted out for four days—"

"And we've only been here for less than three," Corvus countered, pointing at the mission time line chart.

"And damned near killed ourselves," Yeager snapped.

Dorn raised his human hand. "I'm feeling much better now that we're up at a lower pressure."

"I'm not," Yeager growled. "I say we get the hell out of here as fast as we can. Take our data and go home!"

"So we take our winnings and leave the game?" Corvus challenged.

Yeager gave him a tight smile. "You gotta know when to hold 'em, and know when to fold 'em."

The human side of Dorn's face frowned. "What does that mean?"

Deirdre said, "The leviathan's trying to tell us something. Look."

The alien understands! Leviathan thought. The strange hard-shelled creature stopped its ascent and hovered in the chill waters, still far from the normal realm of the Kin but at least it wasn't heading farther into the cold abyss above.

It understands.

"What's it trying to tell us?" Corvus asked, hovering beside Deirdre in the perfluorocarbon liquid.

The computer-slowed imagery showed the leviathan rising. At least it seemed to be rising past the tiny shapes and dots sprinkled across the picture displayed on its flank.

"Those must be fish and other smaller creatures," Deirdre said, pointing. "And that stream of dots, maybe that represents the organic particles flowing downward."

"Maybe." Corvus nodded uncertainly.

"And there's the leviathan himself." Deirdre pointed. "And us, alongside him."

"Both rising."

"Yes."

Abruptly, the image of the leviathan began breaking apart. Deirdre and Corvus watched as the creature's image disassembled into hundreds of separate pieces.

"It's going to dissociate again?" she wondered.

Corvus shook his head. "It just did that a day and a half ago, when we first came down to this level."

"That was deeper than we are now."

"But now it's saying that it's going to break up again? Does that make sense?"

Deirdre thought she understood. "Maybe it's saying that it can't stay up at this level without breaking up! It's telling us that it's got to go back to its own level."

"And we've got to go back to ours," Yeager insisted.

Deirdre stared at the screen. The leviathan was still flashing the same imagery. It's so huge! she thought. Like a mountain floating loose in the ocean. But it's got to return to its own place. And Max is right, we've got to return to ours.

Reluctantly, she reached out to the touch screen and began drawing a farewell message.

Holding its members together with sheer willpower, Leviathan saw that the alien was signaling again.

It showed the image of Leviathan itself, diving downward until it disappeared past the lower edge of the image. And the alien, rising upward until it too disappeared from view.

The message was clear. The alien was leaving, returning to its own realm in the cold abyss above, leaving Leviathan to return to the Kin and the Symmetry.

But then the picture changed. It showed the alien returning, with more round little hard-shelled spheres just like itself, all of them swimming amid the Kin down where the Symmetry prevailed.

Leviathan understood the alien's message. It must leave now, but it will return—with more of its kind.

Leviathan duplicated the alien's message along its own flank, to show that it understood. You will return, Leviathan acknowledged. And we will be here waiting for you.

"It's repeating our message," Deirdre told the others. "It understands what we're trying to say."

"Maybe," Yeager said. "Maybe it's just mimicking what you drew."

Deirdre shook her head. "I don't think so, Max. It understands us."

Dorn called out, "Increasing buoyancy. Heading for the surface."

Corvus stood beside Deirdre and slipped his arm around her shoulders. "Heading for home," he murmured.

Deirdre nodded, her eyes on the sensor screens watching the enormous leviathan swim in a brief circle, then bend its broad back and plunge downward, deep into the depths of the globe-girdling ocean, heading back to its own domain.

"Good-bye," she whispered, surprised at how sad she was, how downcast she felt to be leaving the magnificent creature. "We'll come back," she said, knowing it was a promise she was making to herself as much as the leviathan. "We'll come back."

As *Faraday* rose smoothly through the ocean Deirdre felt the pain in her chest easing. Maybe it's psychosomatic, she thought. But no, the medical readouts had shown her heart laboring, her lungs straining down at the depths where they had been.

"Broaching surface in thirty seconds," Dorn announced.

The vessel jolted and shuddered as it bulled its way out of the ocean. Deirdre felt as if the sea was trying to keep them, hold them back, prevent them from getting away.

And then they were soaring through Jupiter's wide, clear atmosphere, the curve of the planet's vast bulk barely noticeable even when they were halfway to the clouds. Her eyes glued to the screens' displays, Deirdre saw a clutch of Clarke's Medusas drifting placidly off in the distance, colorful as old-fashioned hot-air balloons.

"Entering cloud deck," said Dorn. The displays showed a dizzying swirl of colors and the vessel buffeted and jittered in the typhoon winds of Jupiter's racing clouds. Andy gripped her tighter as Deirdre clung to him with one arm and reached for the console handgrips with the other. She saw that Max and Dorn were also grasping safety holds.

Suddenly the shaking and vibration stopped, as abruptly as a switch turning off, and the display screens showed the eternal black of space. Deirdre told the computer to increase its brightness gain and pinpoints of stars gleamed against the darkness.

"We're in orbit," Yeager said, his voice almost breathless with relief.

The curving bulk of Jupiter slid into view, huge, glowing with broad swaths of color. Just above its limb a single bright star glowed.

"That's the station," Andy said, relaxing his grip on her just a little. "We're almost home."

"But we'll go back to them, won't we?" said Deirdre, feeling as if she wanted to cry.

EPILOGUE

For it is a fact that to have knowledge of the truth and of sciences
and to study them is the highest thing with which a king can
adorn himself. And the most disgraceful thing for kings is to
disdain learning and be ashamed of exploring the sciences.
He who does not learn is not wise.

—Khosrow I Anushirvan
(Khosrow of the Immortal Soul)
Shah of the Sassanid Empire, Persia, 531–579

DECOMPRESSION

This is worse than being in the ocean, Deirdre thought. She lay in the narrow decompression capsule, unable to move. It was like being in a coffin, an elaborate high-tech sarcophagus, too tight to shift her arms from her sides, its ridged plastic lid too low for her to lift her head. Worse than the bunks in *Faraday*, she grumbled to herself.

"Stay still," the technicians had told her. "It's best if you just lay absolutely still while we bring the pressure down."

I have to stay still, she thought. There's no room to move in here. She was still breathing perfluorocarbon, still bathed in the cold, slimy liquid. Eight hours, the technicians had said. Eight hours minimum.

"You'll sleep through most of it," one of the technicians had said. "Just relax and sleep."

Wonderful advice, Deirdre thought. Just relax and sleep. Might as well, there's nothing else to do while I'm in here. Sleep. They're injecting a sedative into the perfluorocarbon, she knew. I wonder how they can determine the proper dosage? What if it's not enough? Or too much?

Her thoughts drifted to the leviathans. Those enormous animals. The one in particular that had tried to communicate with them. I wonder what he's doing now? I wonder if he's thinking about us.

Without consciously realizing it Deirdre slipped into sleep, dreaming of the leviathans, floating deep in the Jovian ocean and talking with the leviathan as normally and easily as she would speak to Andy or Max. The leviathan was telling her about himself, what it was like to live in that deep, dark sea, all the secrets of life in—

"Are you awake, Dee?"

Deirdre's eyes popped open and she saw Andy, Max, and Dorn leaning over the edge of her decompression capsule, beaming down at her. The capsule's top had been swung back. And she was breathing normal air!

"I was dreaming," she said.

"How do you feel?" Corvus asked.

Blinking, she replied, "Okay . . . I think."

Dr. Mandrill's dark, puffy face appeared between Yeager and Dorn. "Your life signs are quite good now, Ms. Ambrose," he said, with a bright toothy smile.

"Now?" Deirdre caught his unsaid meaning. "You mean they weren't before?"

Mandrill's smile narrowed a bit. "There was some damage to the myocardium, very minor—"

"That's the heart muscle," Yeager interjected.

"My heart?"

"Very minor damage," Mandrill emphasized. "Caused by the pressure, of course. Stem cell therapy is repairing the damage quite nicely."

Without asking, Deirdre began to push herself up to a sitting position. Corvus, Yeager, and Dorn all reached into the capsule to help her.

"Do you feel strong enough to stand?" Dr. Mandrill asked her.

"I . . . think so."

"How do you feel, Dee?" Corvus asked.

She thought a moment, then replied, "Hungry."

Mandrill's smile returned to full wattage. "That is a good sign! A very good sign!"

It took more than an hour of sensor scans and long lists of medical questionings, but at last Dr. Mandrill agreed that Deirdre could leave the clinic with her three friends.

"To the galley," Yeager commanded, pointing like a general ordering a charge. "I want a real steak!"

Her legs felt a little wobbly, but Deirdre went with them toward the elevator that led up to the first wheel and the station's galley.

Corvus wrapped his arm around her waist as they strode along the passageway.

"How are you guys?" Deirdre asked. "Dorn, are you okay?"

The cyborg nodded gravely. "My systems are functioning properly."

"Andy?"

"Fine. No more headache."

"And you, Max?"

Yeager frowned. "Lumbar stenosis. I've had it for years, from what the medics say. Didn't really bother me until we got squeezed by the pressure down there."

"Is it all right now?" Deirdre asked.

"It aches. Mandrill says they can work it out with microsurgery."

As they entered the elevator cab, Deirdre looked into each of their faces. "Then we're all okay?"

"Yep."

"Pretty much."

"I'll be fine," Yeager said, "once I tear into that steak."

DEBRIEFING

To Deirdre's surprise, Grant Archer was standing in the passageway when the elevator doors opened at the top wheel.

With an expectant grin on his neatly bearded face, he asked the four of them, "Are you ready for your debriefing?"

"Debriefing?" Corvus asked. "Now?"

"Yes, it has to be now," Archer said, starting along the passageway.

"Can't we eat first?" Deirdre pleaded.

"Yeah," said Yeager. "I'm hungry."

Dorn said calmly, "Debriefing is best immediately after the mission, of course, but we haven't had any solid food in days."

Archer said, "Well, I don't know . . ." But he was grinning even more widely than earlier, and Deirdre saw a twinkle in his eyes that she had never seen before.

Feeling confused, she walked with the men along the passageway and quickly realized that they were approaching the galley. Deirdre glanced at her wristwatch and saw that it was midafternoon; the galley would be closed. They'd have to settle for prepackaged snacks from the dispensers.

Andy Corvus said, "Let's have a quick bite and then we can go through the debriefing. Okay?"

Archer broke into a laugh. "Why not?" he said, as he trotted up to the galley's doors and slid them open.

Almost the entire station staff was jammed into the galley, all of them on their feet. They broke into applause as Archer led the four returning explorers into the galley. The assembled men and women roared and cheered, they clapped their hands together and pounded

Deirdre, Corvus, Yeager, and Dorn on their backs as they stepped into the galley. There were still more people on the wall screens' displays, all of them cheering ecstatically.

"I guess the debriefing will have to wait," Archer hollered over the noise of their reception, laughing like a boy at a surprise party.

Deirdre felt tears of joy filling her eyes as Red Devlin came up to them, wearing a dazzling fresh white chef's outfit, and led them to a table groaning with food and drink.

It was late. The party had simply gone on and on. Scientists from Michael Johansen down to the golden-skinned Dahlia came up to Deirdre and the others to express their happiness at the mission's success. News reporters from Earth and the Moon asked for interviews. Even Deirdre's father, gruff old George Ambrose, sent a message of congratulations from the rock rats' habitat at Ceres.

"You've made the biggest breakthrough since the invention of writing," Johansen told them, sloshing beer from the mug in his fist. "Meaningful contact with an intelligent extraterrestrial species. This is history!"

Archer seemed to be floating on air. With his lovely, dark-haired wife beside him, he raised his voice above the din of the party and announced, "We owe these four volunteers a debt of gratitude that can never be fully repaid. I don't know about the rest of you, but I'm willing to give them anything they want."

The crowd roared its approval.

"Ms. Ambrose—Deirdre—what can we do for you?"

Deirdre gulped and thought swiftly. "You've already offered me a scholarship at the Sorbonne . . ."

"Right," said Archer, smiling amiably.

"Could you keep a position open for me until I return? I'd like to work with the leviathans once I have my degree."

"Don't you think you'll want to stay on Earth?"

It was Deirdre's turn to smile. "I want to see Earth, of course. I want to experience it. But more than that I want to come back here and learn more about the leviathans."

Archer's face grew serious. "Fine. We'll be waiting for your return."

Then he turned to Andy. "Dr. Corvus? What about you?"

Without an instant's hesitation, Corvus answered, "I need to develop sensors that can scan the leviathans' bodies. We need to find out where their brains are, and how we can make contact with them with the DBS equipment."

Nodding, Archer said, "You want to learn how their brains work."

"More than that," Andy said, "I want *them* to learn how *our* minds work. I want to show them the world that they live in, the solar system, the universe."

With a puff of exhaled breath, Archer said, "That's a lifetime's work, Andy."

"I know."

Turning to Yeager, who had the petite blonde Linda Vishnevskaya clinging to his arm, Archer said, "I think I know what you'll be doing, Max."

"Building another compression shell for *Faraday*," Yeager replied. "Now that we know how deep we have to go to be with the leviathans, I can make my baby safer—and add a few comforts for the crew, while I'm at it."

"And get married, too," said Vishnevskaya, beaming up at Yeager.

The engineer blushed, broke into an embarrassed grin, and nodded vigorously.

"What about you, Dorn?" Archer asked.

The cyborg hesitated. Looking around at the sea of expectant faces, Dorn finally answered, "My wish is to remain here and pilot the missions into the ocean."

"Really? That's all?"

"It's quite enough," Dorn said. "I've found a purpose in my life. Helping to make meaningful contact with an alien intelligence is more than I had ever hoped to achieve."

Archer nodded slowly. "Me, too," he said softly. "Me, too."

FAREWELL

ndy Corvus walked alongside Deirdre down the passageway where their quarters stood a few doors apart. It was nearly midnight. They walked slowly, exhausted from the day's excitement, his arm around her waist, her head tilted against his.

"You're really going to Earth?" he asked, in a whisper.

"I'll come back, Andy."

He turned toward her and nuzzled her auburn hair. "I'm heading Earthside, too. Back to Dr. Carbo's lab at Rome."

They stopped at Deirdre's door. "We'll go on the same ship?"

With a nod, Corvus said, "No sense sending two separate ships out here."

"No, of course not."

Deirdre looked into Andy's soft blue eyes and saw her future in them. Without a word, she took him by the hand and began leading him back up the passageway, along the way they had come, away from their compartments.

Puzzlement showed clearly on his slightly awry face. "You're not going to . . . uh, sleep?"

"Not yet," Deirdre said.

"Then where . . . where are we going?"

"You'll see."

Katherine Westfall had not attended the party. She was in her suite, preparing to leave station *Gold* on the torch ship that the IAA had sent—at her demand.

Seething inwardly as she packed her toiletries in a hard-shelled travel bag, she tried to convince herself, All things considered, this trip has actually been rather successful. I can share the credit for sending the mission into the ocean. Archer has agreed not to compete against me for the IAA chairmanship. There's plenty of glory to go around.

She realized that the memory of Elaine O'Hara, the half sister she had never known, had been a self-deluding subterfuge, an excuse to justify her action against Grant Archer. Once Archer had made it clear he would not challenge her for the chairmanship, her anger over Elaine evaporated.

But now it was replaced by another fury. Archer and that rat-faced Red Devil. They had tricked her. Embarrassed her. Humiliated her. What's worse, Westfall realized, is that they had something over her that they could use any time they wished. That's a danger, she knew. A danger that must be eliminated, sooner or later.

Sooner or later. The time will come. The time *will* come. Archer and Devlin both. Revenge is a dish best served cold.

"The observation blister?" Corvus blurted.

Deirdre smiled at him as she slid back the door. "The observation blister," she said. "Just you and me, Andy. And the universe."

They stepped in and closed the door. In the dim lighting they could see thousands of stars hanging against the everlasting night.

Andy slipped his arms around her waist and pulled Deirdre to him. "Are you sure?" he whispered. "Really certain?"

"Yes," she breathed. "Aren't you?"

"Um . . . on the ship going back to Earth . . . I'm pretty sure the captain of a torch ship can perform a marriage."

"Marriage?"

"I mean, it'd be legal, just like we got married in a church."

Deirdre wrapped her arms around his neck and kissed him soundly. They made love slowly, languidly, as if they had all eternity to spend together, while mighty Jupiter rose and bathed their naked, glistening bodies in its majestic glowing splendor.

.   .   .

Leviathan swam with the Kin in the warm, rich waters of the Symmetry. The alien had gone, leaving in its place a thousand unanswered questions.

It will return, Leviathan told itself. It will come back. We have much to learn from it. We have much to look forward to.